CW01430689

The Devil's Garden

Delphine Rougier Investigations: Book 2

Sally Spedding

The right of Sally Spedding to be identified as the author of **The Devil's Garden** has been asserted by her under Copyright Amendment (Moral Rights) Act 2000.

All rights reserved.

Copyright © Sally Spedding 2019.

This book is a work of fiction. Names, characters, businesses, organisations, places, events and incidents are either the product of the author's imagination or used fictitiously. Any resemblance to actual persons living or dead, events or places is entirely coincidental.

No part of this publication may be reproduced, stored in or introduced into a retrieval system or transmitted by any other form or by any means without the prior written consent of the author. Also, this book may not be hired out whether for a fee or otherwise in any cover other than supplied by the author.

ISBN: 9781702529952

Published by DEATH WATCH BOOKS

Praise for Sally Spedding:

DOWNFALL
'I could almost taste the fear as Delphine and Captain Valon investigated. Twists and turns galore.' - *Graham Watkins. Successful Author of 'The Enemy Within' and historical non-fiction*

THE NIGHTHAWK
'True noir from Sally Spedding…like a cold breath on the back of the neck.' - *Adrian Magson. Bestselling Crime & Thriller author*

DEATH KNELL
'A visceral, chilling novel with twists and turns, which keep the reader gripped from start to finish.' - *Christoph Fischer. Best-selling author & Llandeilo LitFest organiser*

BLOODLINES
'A complex mystery which both chills and entertains.' - *Thomas Waugh. Crime/thriller author*

CUT TO THE BONE
'Sally Spedding has unquestionably got what it takes.' - *Crime Time*

BEHOLD A PALE HORSE
'Explores the fragility of love and humanity as mediaeval Europe's apocalyptic mindset gallops into the 20th century with brutal consequences. A thought-provoking journey into the macabre.' - *Dot Marshall-Gent. Former police officer, educator and 'Mystery People' reviewer*

THE YELLOWHAMMER'S CRADLE
'No-one does evil like Sally Spedding. Chilling. Seriously chilling. Fully 3D landscapes, full of menace in themselves, peopled by desperate characters…A very compelling read, hard to put down.' - *Thorne Moore. Author of best-selling chillers*

MALEDICTION
'An intense, intelligent, visceral thriller from the get-go. If you thought Dan Brown was the last word in clerical depravity, think again.' - *Peter Guttridge. Reviewer and crime/thriller writer*

COLD REMAINS

'This is a horror story and a mystery. If you like well-written, creepy thrillers, this is one to remember.' - *Geoff Jones. Eurocrime*

COME AND BE KILLED

'Sally Spedding is a font of creepy stories, the kind of tales which wheedle their way into your mind days and weeks later.' - *Western Mail*

PREY SILENCE

'Sally Spedding has written an excellent, creepy chiller of what can happen to ex-pats who fall foul of their new neighbours. The perfect gift for those who boast about their French idyll they're about to live.' - *Carla McKay. Daily Mail*

A NIGHT WITH NO STARS

An alarming story of surprises and shocks.' - *Gerald Kaufman. The Scotsman*

CLOVEN

'Sally Spedding has been credited with being a latter-day Du Maurier.'
- *Crime Squad*

WRINGLAND

'A tale of chilling menace and powerful atmosphere in haunted fen country. A ghost story handled with real assurance.' - *Barry Foreshaw*

Welsh-born, award-winning Sally Spedding's dark crime/thrillers, short stories and poetry are inspired by Wales and France where she lives.

www.sallyspedding.com

To Hannah and Katharine, with love, as always.

'I used to advertise my loyalty and I don't believe there is a single person I loved that I didn't eventually betray.'

Albert Camus

.

PROLOGUE

21st March 2004. 09:00 hrs.

Three thousand feet above sea level in the high lands of the Corrèze, the snow has begun to melt, creating strands of clear, icy water which caress bare granite and bone-hard soil alike, reflecting the vibrant blue sky. This is home to only the hardiest of creatures. The falcon, the hawk and other raptors. An occasional dog grown wild since escaping its lowland guarding pen, and, not since the start of the twentieth century, the polecat.

While this water, now a noticeable stream, gathers momentum towards the lower, more inhabited plateau, two men, dressed as if for the Arctic, lift out the first of two large, rectangular metal trunks from the back of their nondescript white van. The rancid smell of animal urine and ordure escapes from what could be bullet holes in its side, but both work without speaking, unlocking the large padlocks, which in turn triggers a collective howling until the double doors are at last flung open.

"They're so beautiful," says the taller man in a thick, northern patois. "So noble. Hegel would be proud."

"He would," agrees the other, drawing on his *Gauloises* then forcing double lines of smoke from his wide nostrils. They smile complicitly as the four adult male captives hungrily sniff the air and the ground under their paws, before racing each other up towards the nearest rocky brow of land to survey their new world for prey. Eight ears pricked; eight black and amber eyes on full alert.

Next, the second, identical trunk is lowered. Those same howls invade the silence, but higher, more excitable in tone. Their female scent has reached the males who wait and watch. Tongues slinky pink as they wail

1

their welcome, and before their deliverers can pull another celebratory cigarette from its packet, these new wolves have gone. Grey, brown, ochre, almost indistinguishable among the witch pits, the dolmens and *pierres levées* before that savage cull which the men's grandfathers and great-grandfathers remembered. Powerless to prevent.

The spent dimp is flung. The van doors slammed shut, and while the small pack laps at the nearest patch of melted snow, the vehicle which has brought them so far south clatters away out of sight.

LABRADELLE GENDARMERIE. AVENUE GÉNÉRAL DE GAULLE, 72300 LABRADELLE.

SARTHE.

13TH APRIL 2004

Mademoiselle Rougier,

I hope this finds you well and that your training at the École de la Gendarmerie Nationale in Saint-Arnoult is living up to your expectations. My own time spent there was memorable in so many ways. Not least because it was where I first met my wife.

This letter is to finally reassure you that rumours surrounding your late grandmother Emilie Rosheim's intervention at Oradour-sur-Glane with Private Franz Fleischer were unfounded. You and your father have nothing more to fear on that score. However, this means your beloved mother was needlessly killed, and for this, mere words of sorrow will never be enough.

Most of my spare time has been spent examining wartime archives in Limoges, Paris and Berlin, and speaking to the few, now elderly survivors of that terrible event in Oradour-sur-Glane in June 1944. Kommandant Diekmann and General Lammerding of the Das Reich Division already

2

had proof of the serious danger posed by that village. Their plans for a revenge attack on it after Tulle, well in place. Franz Fleischer and his sister's names already whispered as informants. Better to blame your grandmother and risk destroying her and her family than themselves.

I'm sure, that with the trials of former sous-Lieutenant Baudart and Patrick Gauffroi now over, and the latter's rightful sentence at Fresnes for your mother's murder, you and your father will welcome this news. The public prosecutor and former examining magistrate correctly quashed Gauffroi's rationale for this crime, focusing on his unstable psychological state and previous displays of violence when provoked. You both and the public are now better protected.

However, I must warn you, Jean-Marie Longeau still bears a grudge that you withheld his dead lover's whereabouts. So be wary, and don't hesitate to report any harassment on his part. As for Lucius Seghers, apparently ignorant of his father and aunt's wartime activities, he's been confirmed unfit to plead and will undergo further treatment at the Hôpital de la Sainte Vièrge in Tours for the foreseeable future. Meanwhile, Patrick Gauffroi will continue to be kept on suicide watch when transferred to La Santé in Paris in mid-October. This confidential information must be kept from your father. I'm sure you can appreciate why.

Sincerely yours,

Colonel Serge Valon

Ps. If you wish, I will send you those three letters your great-grandfather told your mother to keep hidden. You can then do with them as you think best.

1

"This one's for you, ignorant lunatic!" A hostile, female voice shouted behind him. "Hope you top yourself before I clap eyes on you again."

Then came the clank of his gaoler's keys, the squeal of old hinges before a rough shove into darkness. On his own after causing a small riot over the rotten horsemeat and curdled milk served up every day, Patrick Gauffroi stretched out both arms to touch the cell's cold, sweaty stone walls on either side of him. So much for the width. The length, he soon discovered, was little more. He still missed Fresnes and its 'vulnerable prisoner' unit, and worse, two of his recent 'back gate commutes' had failed. Unlike those of his violent father.

Having been sewn up after his post-mortem, Gauffroi's *père* had filled a box just like this, except his was veneered plywood. All that could be afforded at the time, but at least the farmer who'd been too ready with his fists had been properly dead. Job done.

Non...

Something was crawling upwards inside his prison jumpsuit still smelling of someone else's fear. Then another, nicking his flesh as they went. Cockroaches. The bastards were everywhere, as well as bluebottles big as bees, hovering in the stench of death. He slapped at the coarse, itchy fabric before squeezing each predator in turn. This sudden effort left him light-headed, and God only knew what time it was, for there was no watch or giveaway window. As for the sliding hatch on his door, that would only show the dyke's ugly face.

He pressed himself against the smooth, multi-locked barrier to freedom.

Revenge swelled inside him, replacing hunger. He couldn't help it. What he'd done to Irène Rougier seventeen months ago hadn't been a crime, despite what Colonel Valon, glorying in his promotion from captain, and the devious old examining magistrate, had decreed. He'd done France a favour. His homeland, grieving too long for Oradour-sur-Glane. So he'd argued in his own defence.

Today was the same date as when innocent blood had stained the summer sky red. Now look at his beloved country. Occupied by a different and growing enemy, pulsating silently in the shadows with entire *banlieues* under occupation and mosques on every corner. He felt sick with rage recalling how that decrepit Judge Georges Pertus summing up at his trial at Le Mans Assizes, had wiped the floor with him. A dangerous, lying '*marginal*' who, on seeing 'his target' Iréne Rougier dancing and singing to some Charles Trenet rubbish, had snapped. Pulled the trigger…

There is no justice…

François Rougier was the liar and Petrus, sniffing his generous pension, had believed him. But soon, very soon, everything would be changing.

*

His bruised fingers instinctively felt for his mother's rosary he'd worn after being collared on Christmas Day near Tours too long ago. They touched instead both red-raw channels on his throat. A legacy of two failed nooses. One fashioned from his plastic mattress cover. The other, his jump-suit's torn-off leg.

In hours of need in his previous cell, he'd clung to his childhood faith, only for that special circle of polished sycamore beads to be spirited away along with his other few possessions.

"Nothing so dangerous as the re-converted," both male 'pigs' had grunted three floors down, stripping him naked, tearing it from his neck, letting each supplication scatter across the sloping, tiles towards a drain.

*

Patrick Gauffroi waited, not daring to hope for anything in this last place God made. Like *Fin du Monde* farm all over again, reeking of Limousin milk, meat and dung, but with Karolina and young Roza Adamski gone. Fearful for their futures, they'd left the shelter he'd provided on his land, to return to Romania.

Then there was Delphine Rougier, who on the day they'd met, had lit a spark. Who'd never left his heart…

Listen.

Three taps on steel. Earlier than expected.

His own five taps replied.

Merci, Dieu…

The latest solitary confinement prisoner in the Boulevard Arago in Montparnasse, raised his bloodshot eyes to Heaven, little knowing that on the other side of his door, a death trap was set, ready to spring.

2

Friday 10th June 2005. Saint-Arnoult. 13:45 hrs.

'*...that rumours surrounding your late grandmother Amélie Rosheim and Private Franz Fleischer were unfounded...*'

Those three potentially explosive letters which the late Irène Rougier, née Rosheim, had secreted behind a stone in the barn wall at *Bellevue* farm in St. Eustache, duly arrived from Colonel Serge Valon to Delphine Rougier's temporary *poste restante* in Saint-Arnoult last September.

They'd promptly been burnt.

For this, she'd used one of her lit cigarettes and watched the small, symbolic fire devour those wrinkled pages; the life-destroying lies, leaving a few charred fragments blown away with one breath.

*

Seventeen months after her mother's murder, she stood in the town's Parc Voltaire listening to the delicate sounds of a summer afternoon. The sing-song chirrups of busy birds too small to see. The rustling of every kind of leaf overhead and around her, and above all, the scent of early geraniums clustered in the large flower bed nearby.

Such beauty was, just then, almost unbearable, but bear it she must, because there'd been no grave to visit. No bench or specially-planted shrub. Not even the kind of commemorative plaque provided by crematoria to stand in regimented lines like some soulless art installation. How could there have been, with that unlucky maiden name, and after what she, Delphine, had done? Sharing the deadly wartime secret with the outwardly likeable but unstable Patrick Gauffroi, product of a tough, violent home.

Yes, the elderly judge had dismissed his defiant defence, and despite Colonel Valon's well-meaning reassurance, Delphine knew the name 'Rougier' like 'Rosheim' could still carry the kiss of death in some quarters. But would being half way through her first year in Compagnie 1 at the *École de la Gendarmerie* in Saint-Arnoult be enough to protect her, should the killer ever re-surface?

How could she know?

Such a secret couldn't be airbrushed away, and the whispers surrounding that all-too public trial still flickered in her mind. Why she'd come to this park to remember those whom her feckless grandmother could still have betrayed sixty-one years ago. Yes, she'd perished too, but so had her kind, hard-working boyfriend. The fallout not ending there…

As for Patrick Gauffroi, he might well prove a model prisoner in his latest playpen - her fellow students' slang for gaol. Someone she should never have trusted, who might even be freed early, or seek a hefty media payout for peddling her mother's story. If so, what price a gagging order? She'd broach the question with her father who'd made a good profit after selling up their farm for a new two-bedroomed town house near Saint-Arnoult's elegant, eighteenth-century church. A man who'd borne his wife's family's past and proved himself a hero yet again at Gauffroi's trial, where he and Delphine, for their own safety, had testified for the Prosecution via video-link.

Despite the warm breeze, she pulled her camouflage jacket tighter around her body before gathering up her things, shifting her thoughts to the afternoon's surveillance programme, targeting and following potential suspects. Although she was enjoying it all, some unwelcome possibilities still tinged her new life.

These included fifty-two-year-old Lucius Seghers who could make a full recovery, and Jean-Marie Longeau an aggressively gay, part-time reporter, who'd barged his way in to the Le Mans court room only to find her absent.

"He'd better not spoil things here," she said out loud to herself. She, not him, had endured a rubbish job and survived *Bellevue*, her old dump of a home in the Sarthe for long enough.

At least both senior Seghers had done the decent thing by slitting their wrists and bleeding to death in their separate holding cells. But why, if he as Private Franz Fleischer really had been blameless all those years ago? Unless, despite wartime whispers, the cruel fate of so many newborns and some of their mothers found buried near *'Les Cigales'* had been reason enough.

*

Suddenly, too many shadows crowded in this otherwise welcoming part of France, and Delphine hurried towards the park gates to join the busy pavement beyond. However, as she stopped to cross the Boulevard Jean Moulin at the traffic lights, to short-cut back for her afternoon session, a half-familiar figure emerged from a Tabac opposite. Someone who turned to stare at her with obvious interest, before hastening down a nearby alleyway and out of sight.

Merde...

She'd either been hallucinating or that red-haired man in jeans and a black leather jacket had been a freaky double of Jean-Marie Longeau. Had he stalked her all the way from Le Mans? Whatever, there was no time to ask about him in that Tabac. She daren't be late back at the *École*. Besides, to some of the staff and other new recruits, she, a former hotel chambermaid, had arrived as something of a celebrity who'd helped solve three hideous crimes. Who'd stepped up to the mark when most would have run a mile.

But not all.

*

"We're not a holiday camp," snapped sous-Lieutenant Véronique Morel, a sharp-nosed woman with three unlucky kids, sitting behind a large desk marked RÉCEPTION. "You were given permission for an hour's outside visit only. Your group's already gone."

A moment of panic. Delphine's watch - an expensive gift from her father - showed 14:10 hours.

"Where exactly?"

"Wouldn't you like to know?" The smile short and sour, before the sous-Lieutenant swivelled towards her computer screen. No way would Delphine beg her of all people, for more information. Instead, she ran towards the main lecture hall, where a list had already been posted on the wall outside.

GROUP C. Compagnie 1. OBSERVATION & SURVEILLANCE. 14:30 HRS.

Lieutenant Colonel Mikhail Zanowski. Le Pont d'Argent.

Vite…

She unlocked her locker, grabbed her notebook and two-way radio, and then legged it past the cluster of new dormitories and the car park where her aged, turquoise 2CV glowed almost too vividly in the sunlight. Next, down the grassy slope to where her cohort of sixteen keen students had already gathered on a sightseeing spot, home to a vandal-proof telescope overlooking the Ruiseau d'Argent. A sizeable stream which would join the Corrèze River two kilometres away to the east. An attractive feature of an otherwise uneventful landscape.

Romain Vileneuf from Toulouse turned to watch her arrival. His gelled, dark hair and facial expressions similar to those of Martin Dobbs, whose gruesome death eighteen months ago at '*Les Cigales*' in the Causses de Quercy still kept her awake at night. She gave him a brief smile, then positioned herself within earshot of the Lieutenant Colonel, whose prematurely white hair just visible beneath his cap, and smooth, pink skin had everyone guessing his real age. With the tiniest of glances from his little brown eyes, he registered her lateness.

Not a good start.

*

Her camouflage gear suddenly felt like a boiling trap. Her boots too small, pinching her big toes, while perspiration had stuck her fringe to her forehead. There was no time to deal with it because individual record sheets were being handed out.

"Your operational zone is a radius of one kilometre," began Zanowski. "Including this bridge - the Pont d'Argent - which as you know, serves the two very different communes of Pierrefort and Moussac. The former is home to a working quarry, and the latter…"

"Lipizzaners," piped up one of the young women in a distinct Spanish accent.

"Indeed. And should you choose to observe your subject anywhere near *Les Chevaliers* stud farm, please show discretion and cause no disturbance. Understood?" He looked around. "Why might that be?"

"They'll be at it." That same female student obliged, triggering a collective titter. Following a disapproving look from Zanowski, everyone repeated their designated number and two-letter code. "Report back here at 17:00 hours," he added, checking both his identical watches gracing each hairless wrist. Patek Philippe, no less, noted Delphine without envy. "Coordinate now, at 14:28."

All did.

"In the event of an incident or emergency, radio me giving your precise location. You all know the protocol."

With that, he strode over to his immaculately valeted black Jeep Cherokee parked nearby and sat in it, waiting until everyone had dispersed. He'd promised pairings, but this was obviously his way of spoiling preconceptions, thought Delphine, aware of Romain Vileneuf and Aristide Abolego, a mixed-race twenty-one-year-old from the Paris suburb of Évry, hovering nearby in a haze of cheap after-shave.

"I'd still like to pair up," Romain admitted to her, before Zanowski yelled at him to get going.

"Me too," added Aristide, before getting the same treatment.

*

Delphine watched them go their separate ways, wishing she felt flattered, but she'd not come here to be side-tracked. Too much was at stake. She scanned her already familiar surroundings, trusting her instinct as to where might provide the best target. Yes, there was a dog walker ambling away towards the River Corrèze before it reached the significant and historic town of Saint-Arnoult. Even further away, an elderly man was picking blueberries, putting most of them in his mouth. But what made her stare for the longest was closer to home, not far beyond the bridge, slightly to her left. Under the revealing afternoon sun, two adult figures in dark clothes crouched between two granite rocks at the edge of the Ruiseau d'Argent. Were they relieving themselves? Or hiding, for some reason? Hard to tell…

NOTE 4.6. 'Surveillance is the keeping of someone under observation without their knowledge.'

So said her well-thumbed copy of the SPECIAL OPERATIONS HANDBOOK – SURVIVING AS AN AGENT IN OCCUPIED TERRITORY. A discreet, black hardback, which had formed the basis for her interview replies in May last year. Her Bible, in fact, having decided after her mother's murder, that the Virgin Mary and other religious characters had nothing comparable to offer.

Go.

She walked as casually as possible over the bridge's single carriageway edged by simple, steel barriers spanning the gurgling river water below. Her gaze occasionally strayed from a few tethered goats to her right, to a conveniently large plantation of chestnut trees further away to her left. These sprawled over the lush farmland towards the road to the two communes. So different to the barren wastes she'd encountered further south in the wintry Causses de Quercy.

Ideal, in fact.

Delphine kept this puzzling couple in her sight as she took the longest, most circuitous route towards the trees, concerned that her camouflage outfit and the beret which wouldn't be on her head for long, would prove too much of a giveaway.

Merde...

Midges. Huge ones cruising that shaded space around her, then darting towards her to target any exposed skin. She couldn't bat them away because that same couple - a grey-haired, middle-aged man and a woman, she was sure of that - were busy pulling two large, white plastic canisters from a bin liner. Delphine accessed her paternal grandfather's binoculars, still in perfect condition, and far superior to many newer models. She adjusted their focus, enabling her to watch the strange pair who seemed in a hurry, unscrew the red caps of each container, then emptying their yellowish contents into the river.

She took two photographs on her Samsung phone, hoping their definition would later prove good enough.

With her curiosity on full alert, she was tempted to creep closer, but where was any decent cover? Just a few dung-topped hummocks and the odd rock embedded in weeds. Besides, what on earth were they doing? And where, if any, was their vehicle? No time to wonder, as they both stood up, brushed themselves down before tossing the empty containers into the flow.

Charming, thought Delphine, seething at this casual vandalism. But hang on, they'd got two more heavy-looking bin liners and were heading upstream. The woman striding ahead of the man whose left heel dragged a little with each of his steps.

She was about to find another hiding place and hopefully jot down some notes, when there came a familiar smell of aftershave and the crackle of dead leaves behind her.

"Yo there!"

Aristide Abolego.

Delphine knew better than to execute a full body turn. Rather, she stepped sideways to glance at her follower, sweating more than her. Both armpits of his camouflage gear black with moisture. His Record Sheet already crumpled in his top pocket.

"I'm not sure about this," she said, trying to disguise her annoyance. It was bad enough with the midges returning to her neck, and the odd couple clearly up to something suspicious. "Lieutenant Colonel Zanowski made it clear…"

"He's a *con*," interrupted the one whose father had returned to Brazzaville just after his fifth birthday, and whose mother ran a cooked chicken stall in Les Halles. He swiped away the insect pests with his beret and they didn't come back. "I bet he came here straight from an *école supérieure* and played his cards right. Browned his nose where it mattered, then…"

"Ssh!"

"Why?"

"Look."

"Can't see anything."

Having arrived late at the Pont d'Argent, it was crucial to her that this afternoon proved a success. Was she being jinxed all over again, this time by someone with seemingly nothing to prove? Unlike herself.

"Over there," she pointed at the diminishing figures, like two dark sticks amid the heavy green landscape. "To me they're definitely *louche*."

"I don't know about doing all this stuff," said Aristide suddenly. "I mean, where we *should* be is on city streets where the lifters and sharks and pimps crawl out of the bloody brickwork 24/7. And terrorists. I mean, I sometimes wonder why I'm even here."

She crammed those old binoculars into her fatigues' pockets.

"To keep people safe."

"What would you do if your young bro had been stabbed through the heart in broad daylight and your Maman raped at gunpoint?"

Delphine stared at his open, clean-shaven face whose eyes told a different story. "I'm sorry."

"So am I, and when I'm done here, I'll ask to be posted back to Évry. To protect her and my little sister." He paused, then said, "It's your turn."

"For what?"

"Your story."

"It's too complicated. Besides, I'm trying to leave it behind. This is my big chance to break free…"

"I'm impressed." He offered her a cherry-flavoured chewing gum which she politely refused. "You did almost die over there on the Causses." He pointed south-east. "I picked up quite a bit about it on the internet."

Despite the cloying warmth beneath the trees, Delphine sensed a familiar unease sneak under her clothes.

"Have you been searching my name?"

"Course." His second laugh also seemed genuine. "When I saw it on the list for *Compagnie 1* here. I'd have been proud to help reel in those Seghers creeps. They should have been finished off before trying to be martyrs. Saddos."

"Look!" Delphine pointed after those two mysterious figures. "They're running, even though he's got quite a limp. Come on. Let's go!"

*

15:00 hrs.

Not one cloud interrupted the dense blue sky as she and Aristide crept towards the overgrown remains of an earlier stream-widening project blending with the surrounding land.

"Let's lie low here," she suggested, having memorised that exhaustive manual, as well as the Lieutenant Colonel's morale-boosting lecture yesterday afternoon.

"Just whisper, because what breeze there is, is blowing their way."

"Yes, boss." He smiled as he too, lay on his stomach to train his binoculars on the fleeing pair. His pungent after-shave still lingering.

In the brooding silence she detected the distant lowing of cattle. A plane somewhere, and from behind her, the faint noise of a vehicle crossing the bridge. She half-turned to observe it, and immediately her stomach tightened. Her fingers clutched at the thick grass as if for strength.

Everything about the silver Audi was familiar, but not its driver, who was too far away to identify.

"What's up?" Abolego hissed. "You've gone pale."

"Wouldn't you?"

She saw the car glide away beyond the chestnut trees until disappearing from view. Meanwhile, that man and woman - much smaller now - were zealously emptying two more cartons of that same yellow liquid into the water. Standing up this time, throwing the empties away, obviously confident they weren't being observed.

But *she* was. She could tell by the skin on the back of her neck beginning to prickle. Her breath stopped in her throat.

"Time to shift," she managed to say. "I'm in danger."

"How come?" Aristide raised himself, looking around. His movements like someone choosing sunbeds around a holiday pool. More irritating by the minute.

"I'm sure it's Jean-Marie Longeau who's turned up. A part-time reporter on *Le Maine Express*. He's found out where I am."

"Shit." Aristide frowned. "He's also been bad-mouthing you at every opportunity." He patted her arm. "But don't worry. You've got me, and if he starts any more tricks, he'll be lucky to see his next birthday."

But Delphine, who'd known Martin Dobbs' possessive lover, wasn't so sure.

3

Feeling oddly dizzy, all too aware that the vengeful Jean-Marie Longeau was probably exactly where she and Aristide had stood beneath those chestnut trees, both tracked the middle-aged couple further along the stream until reaching a significant bend. Here, a single-story stone-built farm and several outbuildings in good repair stood in several hectares of flat grazing land divided into two fields, surrounded by new electric fencing and a public warning notice.

DANGER DE MORT!

Strange, thought Delphine, forgetting that reporter for a moment. What was so special about the cattle she could see contained in these pastures? To her, they looked like ordinary, brown Limousins. Ten-a-penny in that region, but nevertheless providing valuable lean meat. Two bulls attached to thick ropes anchored to the ground, grazed in the nearest section, and at least thirty cows in the other. Both enclosures also contained two water troughs and another for supplements.

She shifted her gaze and realised the man and woman she'd just seen, had gone.

"Where the hell are they now?" She thought aloud, against all the rules. "They couldn't have just vanished."

"I wonder if it's their farm," said Aristide. His compact binoculars fixed on some activity by the bigger of the two barns. He handed over the binoculars. Like his phone, they were much lighter, sleeker than hers.

"Who knows? But I swear it's that same couple." She adjusted their focus to see even more. "They seem to be arguing. And why were they

18

messing with the stream? Unless deliberately polluting it. Poisoning it, even. What d'you think?"

As if flattered to have been asked, Aristide scratched his shorn curls, which emphasised a wide, square-shaped skull. So different from the typical Gallic variety. "But why? If it *is* their farm, surely their livestock drink from it where the bank gets lower…"

"Not these cattle. It's like they're in prison."

"I give up."

"No, think about it. Even our *École* and the local restos use crayfish from here. So, could they be rivals with another enterprise?" Delphine was back in her home village of St. Eustache. A cauldron of petty jealousies and mistrust for as long as she could remember. Where her father's enterprises had failed so miserably.

"We could ask at that farm."

"Not in our remit. We're only here to observe, remember? And anyhow," her voice softened. "I think, Aristide, it's best if you find your own target. There'll be a post-mortem on this before Study Time. Remember after the Forensic Procedures programme last month? Gruelling wasn't the word."

While waiting for a reply, she noticed a large, brown 4x4 suddenly appear beyond the farmyard which faced the stream. It skewed round on two wheels to ride the bumps and lumps of the ungrazed land until reaching the bridge. Definitely two people on board, and travelling too fast for her to catch its number plate.

"Someone's in a hurry," observed Aristide, obviously ignoring her suggestion to find his own target. "My God."

"I don't think they saw us. But you never know. Did you catch the number plate?"

"No."

"Shit."

Delphine glanced at her watch. There was still time for this likeable guy to find another focus. Besides, despite her rebuff to him, she really wanted to visit that farm, but on her own. Then she had an idea.

"Look," she pointed towards the edge of the chestnut trees; their crowns glowing nobly in the sunlight, but deadly dark beneath. "Why not try going that way towards Moussac and Pierrefort? See if you can find a silver Audi holed up anywhere, which may well be that prick Longeau's car."

That was the trigger he needed, and before she could remind him to try and neutralize his aftershave, he was off. Long, rhythmic strides raking over the grass. His head still defiantly bare. A free spirit. Something she could never be. She watched until he'd disappeared behind the trees, then began to run. All the while aware of how visible she was, and vulnerable.

*

What the hell was *that*?

Delphine stopped to shield her eyes and glance upwards. The cry of a predatory hawk or kestrel? But no. This had more resonance and depth. Besides, the sky was empty.

It came again, but this time she swivelled round to take in the slope of land the other side of the river, which soon became noticeably less green and scrubbier.

The 'wolves' word hovered in her mind.

Sshh…

She'd heard rumours of bears re-wilded in the Pyrenees, and closer to home, the wild boar. For the first time, she wished Aristide was alongside to confirm her fears. Supposing there were more than a couple of those ferocious black pigs? A whole pack? All on the lookout for easy pickings?

Get a grip, she told herself, resisting the urge to radio Lieutenant Colonel

Zanowski's emergency number. But the farm ahead had suddenly become an even more inviting prospect. She again clamped those old binoculars to her face and checked it out for more detail. Someone was closing the gate to the yard. A slim young woman, probably in her mid-twenties, with scraped-back hair like her own - except that she was blonde - and seemed, like the occupants of that large, brown 4X4, in a hurry. She wore jogging pants, a white tee-shirt with I ☺ NEW YORK on the back, and what looked like men's wellington boots, several sizes too big.

Hurry.

Within half a minute, she'd reached that very spot, with that departing figure heading for that same bigger barn. Her oversized boots slowing her progress.

*

A hand-made sign hanging from a wrought-iron pole set into the grass, announced the farm's name, *Air du Vent,* while the dark green mailbox by the gate showed its owners to be a M/MME. G. LAVROCHE. As Delphine jotted their name in her pad, she couldn't help sniffing the combined smells of grass and cattle dung. *Belle Vue Farm* all over again...

"Bonjour!" She called out after the young woman. "Please wait..."

Immediately, the stranger turned, shielding her eyes. Fear freezing her even-featured face.

"Who the hell are you?"

Delphine pulled out her ID card bearing a photograph that looked more like her mother back in the sixties. "I'm studying at the *École de Gendarmerie,"* she then gestured towards Saint-Arnoult. "I was just passing and noticed something odd going on."

The stranger barely looked at her details.

"Odd? What d'you mean? Here?"

By then, she'd come closer, and Delphine noticed a child's soft toy stuck in the top of her right Wellington boot. Inwardly, she told herself to be careful. No way could she risk a complaint of intrusion or of causing distress. She'd combine fact and fiction and show no sign of nerves.

"I'm on a footprint-detecting exercise," she lied. "Nothing very exciting, but I did happen to notice two people - a man and a woman back there - tipping a yellow liquid of some kind into the river."

The blonde nervously glanced round.

"When?"

"Just minutes ago. They did it twice."

"Come in."

"Are you sure?"

"I said, come in."

With practised movements, the stranger unlocked the new gate's padlock and led the way over an immaculate, stone-slabbed yard towards the farmhouse. Moments later, they passed a red Renault Twingo, a child's scooter propped against the smaller barn wall, and two spanking new, medium-sized livestock trailers.

*

The cool, kitchen-diner, complete with the latest fittings and state-of – the-art cooking range, took up much of the ground floor. An open-tread, wooden staircase to the side, led up to what seemed equally trendy and well-lit. No expense spared, thought Delphine. The Lavroches were doing very nicely, thank you. Even the large, aluminium-framed watercolours of local scenes tastefully hung along the walls added to the feeling of ease and comfort.

"Please sit," said the one who introduced herself as Natalie Lavroche. "And tell me exactly what you saw." She pulled off her borrowed

Wellingtons to reveal short, red socks decorated by silver hearts. She clasped the panda soft toy between both hands. "Were they oldies?"

"You could say that. Greyish hair? Dark clothing?"

"Yup. My parents."

Delphine kept to her story.

"Well, like I said, they repeated this procedure again, nearer here, and chucking the canisters into the stream. Four in all."

"Nutters," said their daughter scornfully. "Which is why me and Joel have got to go. It's getting worse."

"What is?"

"Their paranoia. No-one else is like it round here. And I don't want it rubbing off on my kid. He's a right to play outside if he wants to, and…"

"You mean Joel?"

The young woman nodded, glanced at her watch, then grabbed a denim jacket from the stairs' newel post and slid her socked feet into a pair of slip-ons. "He's six. I need to pick him up from school."

Edgy wasn't the word…

"So, this paranoia," Delphine persisted, while following her outside. "What's behind it?"

Suddenly the young mother spun round from her locking the front door. A wild, almost deranged look in her pale, blue eyes, perfect teeth bared as she let out a loud, high-pitched howl, making Delphine flinch.

"Got it?" she challenged, making for the Renault. A child's panda face glare-protector in place next to a rear seat. An unfamiliar number plate.

"Wild boar?"

"Get real."

Wolves?

"Do you mind unlocking that fucking gate?" Came the order.

"Not at all."

*

Delphine caught the house key that Natalie Lavroche threw out of her car window before revving up. "So, your parents were poisoning their own cattle's drinking water. Is that it?" She clicked the padlock shut once the car was on the other side and handed back the key.

"What do *you* think?"

"But why? Both enclosures have full water troughs."

"You'll have to ask them."

With that, Natalie Lavroche closed her window and within seconds, having reached the bridge, turned right for Saint-Arnoult. Her bright blonde hair still clearly visible. Delphine decided against having a proper snoop round the farm, and instead, called Aristide on her mobile.

No reply.

Damn.

She waited for his voicemail to kick in.

"Are you OK?" Aware that the cattle had stopped chewing to stare. "I'm on my way over to those chestnut trees… If you're still there, just stay put. Better still, call me back."

Afterwards, the silence around her seemed overpowering, too full of hidden possibilities. She pulled off her stifling berct and, having logged that Twingo's number plate on her Samsung, broke into a run.

4

Delphine gathered her breath beneath those full-blown chestnut trees whose shade seemed even darker, more oppressive than before. Harder for her to locate not only the spot where she and Aristide had observed the Lavroche pair, but also where he might have gone to check on that silver Audi.

If anything *had* happened to him, it would be her fault.

She then scoured the dry ground beneath her boots. The almost black soil formed from years of leaf decay yielded nothing. She sniffed, hoping to catch a trace of his aftershave, but it was the faintest whiff of diesel which lingered in that airless space. She shivered for the second time since leaving her excited fellow students by the bridge. Should she wait a bit longer or move to the far side of the plantation and a better view of the road to both villages?

Move.

*

A final look round, aware of her body tensing up, even though she needed to stay supple and co-ordinated in case of danger. That word made her stop again and listen hard for the tiniest sound, but only silence enveloped her. Like death, she thought.

Hello…

From the gloomy world of humous and history, something near her right boot glinted up at her, caught in a pinprick of sunlight. Pink chewing gum, indented with teeth marks, and glazed by saliva, but whose? Had Aristide met that reporter after all and given him the same gum she'd refused? Or was it his discarded in a hurry?

She gathered it up in one of her father's old handkerchiefs which he'd said would surely come in useful. He was right. Next, she focused on its surroundings, but again, not even a partial footprint was visible.

Mounting anxiety accompanied her out of the shade and over a dry gulley following the single lane road before the fork to both villages. There'd surely be no harm in calling Lieutenant Colonel Zanowski? At least to cover her back, in case of trouble. An ignoble thought for which she could almost hear her dead mother's disapproval. In reality, if anything *had* happened to Aristide Abolego, she'd take the rap.

BILLOUX QUARRY. 2KMS. DANGER!

The scruffy sign caught her unexpectedly, derailing her plan to notify the Lieutenant Colonel. Yet somehow, that stone-strewn road seemed to draw her along it, under a sun now partially covered by a strange-shaped cloud. Orange on top, almost black below, lowering the temperature.

"Aristide?" She shouted, although she shouldn't. "Where are you?"

She'd heard several students mention how the quarry's biggest granite mouth had been a suicide spot for one or two failures from the *École*, or farmers struggling with ever-decreasing EU subsidies. Yet surely Aristide, for all his *insouciance*, could never be considered at risk?

She quickened her pace until a huge logging lorry growled close by, making her veer into the drainage ditch and almost stumble. Then, a minibus, seemingly filled with casual labour from other countries. Sunburnt men and women, probably Roma, staring out at her as if she was an alien. What did she expect, in army gear, at a time when ethnic tensions were rising? Even Aristide had admitted his skin colour had caused him embarrassment during the few weekends' leave, away from the cosmopolitan capital.

So, where was he? And that silver saloon which had brought too many bad memories crowding back.

*

Suddenly, a five-barred gate festooned in razor wire, signing for the quarry itself, lay to her left, while a visitors' sign pointed to the right. Both weather-beaten, almost illegible, set amid overgrown weeds where silence held sway.

What a place to die, thought Delphine, pulling out her two-way radio, punching in Zanowski's number and waiting for the worst.

While that two-toned cloud left the sun clear again, she gave an update. Less complicated than a lie, and he listened without comment. When she'd finished, he suggested she return to base and copy up her notes while he and a colleague would take a look around.

"Best say nothing to anyone else at the moment," he added. "That just complicates things."

"Yes sir," she said, having omitted to mention her strange encounter with Natalie Lavroche and her even odder parents. "But I have found some of his chewing gum. Fresh too, by the look of it."

Pause.

"Let's hope we won't be needing it."

*

However, Delphine didn't leave immediately. Something about this eerily deserted lured her into negotiating the hazardous gate with cautious hope. The ideal spot for someone to take a rain check, as her sort-of-friend Cécile would say, or to hide if being pursued. Despite no obvious evidence this had happened, it was a possibility in that otherwise flat, exposing landscape.

She followed a tiny track almost hidden by huge nettles, glad not to be wearing shorts, yet careful to keep her bare hands out of their reach. The air soon became choking. Here buzzed a few bloated flies and yet more well-nourished midges. There, a pretty yellow butterfly or two. She was so busy observing where they travelled that she almost missed a sudden dip in the ground.

My God.

Having righted herself, she realised that barely a metre away was the edge to the widest, deepest scar she'd ever seen.

*

"Aristide?" She yelled. Panic straining her voice. "Where *are* you?"

Her question echoed in the ether like that of some alien, and when gone, she listened as if her very life depended on it.

Suddenly, the sound of an engine, belonging to what, she couldn't tell, drew closer. Was this a car? A truck? Something bigger? Delphine stepped back from the abyss. With her uncovered ears on full alert in the minimal breeze, that same sound became a silky purr that stopped altogether.

She crouched down behind a giant-sized group of nettles and rotted cow parsley. The stench of wild vegetation almost suffocating as she waited for what, she couldn't know.

"Delphine Rougier?"

Shit.

Someone was coming. The fetid air stirred by another's breath. But whose? Friend or foe?

"It's been a long time, hasn't it?" Came a voice she immediately recognised. A man she'd not seen since the video link of Patrick Gauffroi's trial. Jean-Marie Longeau, An angry witness who'd twice been forcibly restrained. "Too long for some, *hein*? Especially me." The words drew closer. Louder, accompanied by the rustle of weeds. The shift of more loose stones. "But you wouldn't understand that, would you? Greedy cow."

Delphine felt sick, biting her bottom lip until it hurt. She must say nothing. Do nothing, then this weirdo whom she'd spotted earlier coming out of the Tabac in Saint-Arnoult, might give up and go away.

"Well, are you enjoying your new life, here?" It was more a sneer than a question as he appeared from behind a dense clump of nettles and bramble. Still the same red hair, but not the Mohican spike. That same aggressive jaw line with an Adam's apple bobbing up and down in his throat. That same black leather jacket and extra-tight jeans.

"Funny how scum rises to the top…"

Shut up! Shut up…

"And don't think you'll ever shake me off. Why? Because in my hour of need, you let me stew. Me, the competition who got in the way of Martin Dobbs. Why you withheld information that might have saved the only person who…"

"Yo, bro! Back off or else…"

In shock, Delphine almost broke her vow of silence. The after-shave that wafted towards her was unmistakeable.

Aristide.

"Give her a break, you piece of chicken liver," he snarled, before the thwack of his fist, then another, connected with the other man's cheek. Jean-Marie Longeau groaned, then came silence in which she took a chance. Stood up and faced her tormentor being held in a headlock grip by her smug-looking fellow student.

"Perhaps it's time you realised you're flogging a dead horse," she said to her pursuer. "It's pathetic." She gave a half-smile which must have hurt as much as any fist.

"Never. And just you and this fucking ape remember that."

Ten minutes later, they met Lieutenant Colonel Zanowski next to Jean-Marie Longeau's somewhat scratched silver Audi. Its owner, having regained consciousness, was still bad-mouthing her, while the military man cuffed him then shoved him into the front passenger seat of his Jeep. Having made a brief call to the *École* on his two-way, he added, "Both of you stay with the Audi until Lieutenant Cassals and a colleague delivers you back to base. Don't touch anything. Understood?" He then turned to the sweating part-time reporter. "As for you, stalking and harassing one of our students, it's a criminal offence."

With that, he executed a nifty two-point turn in his Jeep and raced off towards the bridge.

Once he'd gone, Aristide grinned. "I'm glad I got that bastard's nuts. Serves him right."

"Thanks," said Delphine, digging out the remnant of his chewing gum that she'd found and handing it over. "It kills me to say this, but," she paused, "you're my hero. And I kept this in case…"

"Why?"

"Wondering if I'd see you again…"

The Parisian's large, brown eyes lit up.

"Don't get big-headed, mind. I *always* say things I regret later." She smiled properly, feeling the tension from the past hour seep away. But not quite.

"I need to tell you what happened after we'd split," she said. "It's beyond weird."

"Try me." Aristide helped her towards the car that still, to her, held an eradicable association with Jean-Marie's lover, Martin. Her former hotel's restaurant manager, for whom she'd carried a misplaced flame. Yet also someone she'd genuinely tried to rescue.

"Fire away," Aristide said, offering her a fresh piece of cerise-flavoured gum which this time, she took. "I'm listening."

But as Delphine began her account of the Lavroches and their uptight daughter, she could have sworn she heard that same primordial, almost plaintive howl coming from the direction of Saint-Arnoult itself.

5

18:00 hrs.

Even more unusual, orange-topped clouds had assembled overhead and by six o'clock, they not only obliterated the sun, but brought on the sense of an early dusk. She was thirsty and hungry. That flavoured gum still in her mouth making it worse.

"See you around," she said to Aristide, giving him an affectionate hug once they'd been brought back to the compound where everyone else had long vanished. She longed to peel off her sweaty gear and take a shower. Think about everything that had happened. "Thanks for what you did by the quarry," she added. "It could have been a disaster."

"No worries," he smiled. "And if that knobhead bugs you again, just tell me."

"I will."

"And as for what you saw earlier. That couple and their daughter, I'd leave well alone."

Delphine started.

"Why?"

He shrugged.

"These things can get nasty. I mean, where people have vested interests, whether it's religion or whatever. You just don't know where they're coming from."

"That's a bit of a cop out."

"And *I'd* say, how much do you value your life? You want to be a gendarme, yes?"

*

The afternoon's post-mortem would, unlike previous ones held in Study Time before dinner, be postponed until after breakfast tomorrow. Lieutenant Colonel Zanowski had taken a quivering, angry Jean-Marie Longeau to the gendarmerie in Saint-Arnoult to be held overnight. On returning, Zanowski tried to reassure her that because the stalker's statement showed no remorse for his actions or any sign of backing off, he'd be cautioned, closely monitored, and if necessary, tagged, with his mobile phone intercepted.

"He won't like that, sir," she said. "But I am grateful."

"You met his father apparently. At *Baccarès*, in Cousteaux."

How had he known that?

"Only briefly," she said, still puzzled.

"Nevertheless, he was quite taken with you. Liked your directness."

"Thank you."

"However, he's hardly his son's best friend. It's on record he wishes he'd been strangled at birth."

Delphine couldn't help flinching at that horrible phrase. But then why should this Lieutenant Colonel remember what she'd found in that hotel bathroom eighteen months ago? She also recalled her visit to Éric Longeau's fortress-like house. How his eyes had been full not of paternal love, but loathing.

"Nice," Aristide spoke for her, holding the cafeteria door open, releasing the sudden smell of spaghetti Bolognese which wasn't remotely appetising. She knew that as long as that part-time journo who'd inherited his lover's still-derelict Maison de Maître drew breath, she'd never be forgiven.

"Get yourselves something to eat." Zanowski suggested. "And remember, if you're asked any questions about the incident by the quarry, say nothing."

Once he'd strode away, Aristide whispered, "I told him my surveillance target was Longeau, after what you'd said about him. Is that OK?"

"Good move."

"Got to think on your feet here, haven't you?" He grinned, then went over to where the rest of his dormitory gang were waiting. Romain Vileneuf the only one, it seemed, not pleased to see him.

*

After dinner, during which she barely ate anything apart from nibbling at her crusty roll, she went to telephone her father from the payphone in the reception where Véronique Morel was still at her post. She glowered as Delphine approached. Perhaps her husband - half her size when last seen in September - was having to see to the kids and making a fuss about it. Delphine tried to be charitable. All those dependants and a full-time job with long hours must be a nightmare. But it was her choice...

"Oui?" François Rougier seemed on alert as he had been ever since the trial. "Who's this?"

"Chill, Papa," she said with forced cheerfulness, having given her name. She and her father had every reason to be on edge while Patrick Gauffroi was still alive. While she also had that reporter to worry about. Two men with black hearts...

"Are you in trouble?" he came straight to the point. "Please say *non.*"

"Course not."

"Good. Because I've some news. Have you heard it yet?"

"What?"

"About the *École Primaire St. Bernard.*"

"Never heard of it."

"Whatever. It's bad."

"Not Al Qaeda, then?" Given the continuing fallout from the Iraq invasion, with a soft-spoken fanatic never far away, it wasn't such a crazy question.

"No. Eight legs. Guess."

"I can't."

He could be so annoying.

Several of her fellow students were drifting by towards their rooms or the *séjour,* with its comfortable chairs and a decent coffee machine. One or two smiled at her before disappearing around a corner.

"Please," she urged him, suddenly wanting to follow them.

"Two adult grey wolves attacked some kids in the playground as they were leaving to go home. One's seriously injured with a throat wound. She's in intensive care at the hospital. Others were badly mauled…"

"My God."

Immediately Delphine thought of Natalie Lavroche and young Joel. Her undisguised contempt for her parents… "Any names?"

"Not yet."

She could have added more information but didn't, and when sous-Lieutenant Morel finally left her desk, added, "Look, Papa, I lied to you earlier. It's been a shit day here as well. Guess who's been sniffing after me."

"Gay boy?"

"You can't use that word," she hissed. "Just say Jean-Marie Longeau. OK?"

Silence, in which she sensed her father bristle. A man felled by the sudden, brutal killing of his wife, only recently beginning to eat properly and participate in any kind of social life he'd not had before. Notably with a pétanque team and supporting Saint-Arnoult's rugby club.

She then told him what she knew. "I've made a statement. And Aristide."

"Who's he?"

Delphine hesitated, acknowledging the straight-backed Parisian's salute as he walked by with a group of others.

"On the same course here. From Évry."

"And?"

Another sous-Lieutenant - this time, male - took over from Véronique Morel, who hastened out of the door.

"He's looked after me. He's alright."

"Aristide, you say? Is he a *noir*?"

Delphine wilted inside.

"Yes, but so what? Look, Papa, I'm twenty-two now, and I don't give a toss about the colour of people's skin. Some of our best cops aren't white. And when this course is finished, I'll be trying to get into the GIGN. Now there's a mixed bunch if ever there was."

"You'll be sent to some shit hole like Afghanistan. Mark my words."

"Don't be ridiculous. Anyway, about the wolves. If you do get any names, just ask reception to get hold of me."

"Damned stupid rules that you can't use your own mobiles except at weekends. I mean, what's that all about? Security's gone mad since my day."

Meaning he'd begun the same programme in Rochefort when he'd left his Catholic boys' school, but soon rebelled against the system. Proud to forego a well-paid career and sizeable pension. All big plusses for her, as never would she totally trust any man again. Not even good-looking Jules Charbon, a car salesman from Figeac, who'd occasionally kept in touch since generously lending her his new car for her mission of mercy to '*Les Cigales.*' Who also might be wanting her to repay her debt.

"So, make that call, OK?" She reminded her father.

Pause.

"I never knew when your mother was hiding anything, but I do with you," he said, out of the blue.

"What's that supposed to mean?" Summer rain suddenly hit the mesh-covered skylights overhead. Yet part of her was pulled towards his expectation like a nail to a magnet. He was all she had left, together with Irène Rougier's nice black coat she'd once adopted, now sharing his half-empty bed.

"Before Longeau made an appearance, I saw this strange, middle-aged couple," she said eventually, having made sure the guy at reception was busy. "While I was out on a surveillance exercise..." she stalled, hearing a mobile ringing in the background.

"Hang on," said her father, leaving her mid-sentence about the new electric fencing around their *Air du Vent* farm. "Just been told Lavroche is one of those school kids' surnames," he said, re-joining her. "And the girl in intensive care is five years-old. All I know. Touch and go, apparently."

Delphine's pulse seemed to have slowed.

"Lavroche?"

"I'll try and find out his first name and tell you tomorrow."

"His? You sure?"

"Yes."

"Does Joel ring a bell?"

"Damned, rabid devils," he went on as if deaf. "I'm telling you. They kill for the sake of it and keep on killing. Don't listen to the misguided lefties who are behind it all and say wolves are scared of humans. If that poor child dies - God forbid - there'll be big trouble. You'll see."

And as Delphine replaced the receiver in its cradle, recalling that mocking howl Natalie Lavroche had made, she realised that Aristide and

37

her father could be right.

6

"…how much do you value your life?"

Aristide's question re-surfaced in Delphine's mind, and once she was installed in her room in the dormitory block, its spare bed so-far unoccupied, she focused on two things. First, with the internet connection in place for the weekend, she'd discovered that the number plate of Natalie Lavroche's red Twingo originated in Haute-Saône. Nothing odd in that, she thought, clicking off her search of French departments. Many people buy cars wherever they can get a better deal, and the north-east was still considerably cheaper than the Corrèze. Or, that Renault could have been second-hand.

She then compiled her notes from memory for the next morning, plus a map of the farm and quarry. She decided to come clean about Aristide Abolego pairing up with her but emphasised how he'd promptly seen it as his mission to check out that threatening reporter.

When she'd drained the last drop of coffee from her styrofoam cup, she tidied her short hair, straightened her fringe, and set forth down the corridor and across the floodlit quadrangle to the staff restaurant and quarters.

In the half-full *Resto Bleu,* Lieutenant Colonel Zanowski was finishing a glass of red in the company of 'the brute' - the outsize and permanently florid Commander Alain de Soulibris who, as if to maximise his influential position, seemed to regard Compagnie 1 as a bunch of retards. Being ten years Zanowski's senior, retirement was probably on the cards. She certainly hoped so.

When Zanowski spotted her, he signalled for her to wait. His obvious annoyance at being interrupted made her hesitate, but not for long.

"Sir, it is important I see you," she said. "I'm sorry."

Having placed his napkin on the table, he came over and pulled the door shut behind him. A dark red semicircle arced over his top lip

"You know the rules about disturbing senior staff except in case of an emergency?"

"Of course, but my father's just told me about wolves attacking kids at the *École Primaire St. Bernard*..."

"And?" Giving nothing away.

"I have some background which might be crucial." She then wished she'd left her father out of it, but with no internet access or media access allowed during the week except by special dispensation, how else could she have known?

Zanowski glanced back at his companion whose glass was again at his fleshy lips.

"We are aware of the incident, Rougier, and the local police are dealing with it." Yet she could tell he was curious. "What background exactly?"

She hesitated. Perhaps she'd misjudged him and should keep both her and her father's information under wraps after all.

"I've made a mistake, sir. Confusing it with something else."

"It? What, exactly?"

But the moment had passed. Delphine stepped back, giving him that formal salute they'd all been trained to use, leaving him staring after her. As she ran over the glistening, wet quadrangle, she realised she must hide her notes and begin new ones which would, out of necessity, be all lies.

*

At exactly 20:00 hrs came a tap on her bedroom door. Although glad to be on her own, she flinched. Her ground floor accommodation opened on to a long corridor ending in a 'Service Only' door for cleaners and workmen, which in turn led to a row of jumbo-sized *poubelles*. Only the previous week had an intruder been caught on camera. A gipsy from a nearby encampment, looking for goods to sell on.

Perhaps the setting reminded her too much of that fateful *Hôtel les Palmiers*. Easy to enter, easier to leave.

"Who's there?" She moved to the spy hole to be met by a large, brown eye.

Aristide.

"Yo." A smile in his voice.

"Are you on your own?" She asked because unlike her, he'd made friends here. She wondered what he wanted.

"I am."

She'd just finished her notes, had a shower, and wore one of her mother's old jumpers and pyjama bottoms. Not a good look.

"You'll have to excuse my appearance."

"I love you just the way you are," he crooned, and she let him in but didn't lock the door as she usually did. In a grey sweat suit, he prowled around her space like a lion, missing nothing. Whatever he wanted surely wouldn't take long, and then she realised her notes were in full view on her table.

"Hey, you should write novels." He looked up at her admiringly. "That's really cool how you stalked that odd couple with their canisters. I like it…"

"Ssh!" Delphine eyed the door. "You never know who might be listening in." Meaning Véronique. Like a hawk overhead. Hovering. Waiting…

Talk of the devil…

"There's a call for you," came her unmistakeable voice from the corridor, followed by the slightest opening of the door.

Shit.

An eye and half a dry mouth suddenly retreated.

"Thank you," Delphine almost choked to say it. "Who from?"

"She wouldn't give her name." Next, came an exaggerated sigh. "This is most irregular."

She?

Delphine closed the door, keeping that same politeness in her voice. "I'll be along there now."

At this, Aristide, who'd ducked into the tiny *en suite* bathroom, emerged looking concerned. "I've got you into enough trouble today," he said, crossing the room towards her. "See you at the post-mortem tomorrow. Whatever you say, I'll back it up." They exchanged a high-five before he, having checked the coast was clear, slipped away,

*

Rain thudding on the skylight overhead followed Delphine towards reception where Véronique passed her the phone's receiver. No eye contact, just a bare-minimum civility which like thin ice, wouldn't take much to crack.

"It's me. Natalie Lavroche. We met earlier today, remember?" That voice taut as a newly-strung violin. Hysteria, too, barely disguised, and Delphine knew immediately what was coming next. "It's about my Joel. I had to tell you. He's in hospital, along with three other kids. Where I'm calling from. I'm so frightened, and what's more, my parents have vanished, when normally they'd have been in touch."

So, François Rougier had been right about the attack and that surname, after all. Unless…

"Is he in intensive care?"

"No, thank God."

"But OK?"

"Just."

"What happened, then?" Delphine angled herself away from Véronique's prying ears.

"He was the last to be attacked, apparently. The wolf that got him in the playground wouldn't leave him alone, but he put up a fight. His head and legs are badly scratched, and he's traumatised, but at least he's alive. Not like little Amélie Massenet. She didn't stand a chance…"

"Only five years' old, so I heard."

"Yes. And so adorable."

"This is awful news. I'm sorry."

"Not your fault. It's…" Natalie Lavroche stopped as if wary of saying any more.

"Look," said Delphine not wanting to lose her. "I'm holed up here during the week, however, I'll see what I can find out. Meanwhile…" she paused as the Lieutenant Colonel and the brute passed by the desk, mercifully deep in conversation until a loud burp issued from the older, more senior gendarme. "Which hospital? You've not said." Nor had her father.

"Never say I told you."

"It'll surely be on the news…"

"No. There's a media black-out. It's really weird."

A fleeting possibility came to mind that this mightn't be Natalie Lavroche after all.

"So is the fact you can't tell me."

"Marie Curie. OK?"

"Got it. Do your folks have a mobile?" She had to keep her on board.

"Yes. But the other weird thing is, it's dead. Maybe kaput. Something's wrong, I know it."

"What's their make of car and registration?"

Pause.

"Why?"

"I could get help looking out for it." Delphine saw Aristide pop his head round her room door, before quickly withdrawing. "Even go and check their farm…"

"No!" Her caller almost shouted. "Can't you see?"

"See what?" Véronique eyed her. "I don't understand."

"My partner… He's… Oh, Christ. I've been such a bloody fool."

"How?" Delphine tried to stay focused, as well as keep the young mother talking.

"I shouldn't be telling you this, but he belongs to something pretty weird. Ever since leaving school at sixteen."

"What exactly?"

"*La Vie Sauvage*. Have you heard of them? They're planning eventually to re-populate France with…"

Here, Natalie Lavroche seemed to run out of breath. Or had she said too much already?

"You were saying," Delphine reminded her.

"Wolves. I can barely bring myself to say that damned word."

The second hand on Delphine's watch was travelling round too fast. Her own father's comments still too clear.

"These people are fanatics. Mad, I'd say," her caller went on. "Especially since Amélie had her throat and chest torn out."

Delphine gripped the corner of the reception desk.

"But you wait, they're above the law. Nothing will be done."

"Looks like your parents were trying."

"What d'you mean?"

Be careful...

"Has this partner of yours been in touch?" She asked instead.

Silence.

"Look, why not give me your number?" her caller suggested.

"OK." But before Delphine could exchange hers, was immediately cut off.

Bitch Face was moving things around on her desk. The night shift about to begin. Dilemma. No way could she just bunk off. Yet she must get out of there. Natalie Lavroche had sounded scared. An innocent child had been killed in the most terrible way, and three others wounded.

Then came an idea and, as the sous-Lieutenant left her station with a scowl on her face, Delphine knew her plan might just be possible.

7

Although the *École*'s campus outside Saint-Arnoult was silent, its exterior bristled with imperceptibly moving security lights, leaving no area of its walkways and buildings untouched.

Delphine, therefore, had to be swift and agile to avoid exposure in one of the bright beams which could, after two minutes, trigger an alarm. She'd left Aristide behind in her room to impersonate her voice should anyone decide to pay a call. In turn, he had told both his room-mates, including Romain Vileneuf, that he'd wanted to chill out somewhere on his own. Whether or not they'd believed him wasn't something to dwell on now. She had to reach her father's house and scrounge a lift in his huge, new Mitsubishi Shogun.

She could have driven her 2CV from the parking area behind the sports hall, but that might have been too risky. And risk could deny her ambition its goal.

*

Her father was still up. Good, because sometimes he'd confessed to going to bed before nine just to let sleep numb his grief. But more and more, after Patrick Gauffroi's incarceration at Fresnes then La Santé, this need had lessened. Delphine was relieved, but nevertheless kept an eye on him because selfishly, he was all she'd got.

His face appeared, framed by a white PVC window nearest to his front door. A focal point to an open-plan lounge-diner, so different to its dark, fusty equivalent in *Bellevue,* where age and troubled histories had seeped through its old, damp stones.

For a moment, Delphine wondered if she was at the right house.

My God...

He seemed slimmer for a start; clean-shaven, in a yellow 'pull' and sharply-creased grey trousers. His shoes were the colour of glistening chestnuts. When her gaze rested on his once fine, black eyes that had drawn her then young mother into his bed, she wondered if their surrounding skin had been moisturised.

"You've been let out?" he said, before she could respond. Astonishment but also doubt in his voice. "I thought cage doors weren't open till tomorrow morning."

"Not quite, and you're right," she said, making her way past a small table and telephone, into the kind of room featured in advertisements for trendy furniture or properties defying their often centuries-old exteriors.

"I shouldn't be here."

"So, why are you?"

"Something's happened. It's serious. I need to take a closer look at a particular farm."

"I've had enough of bloody farms."

Not even his physical transformation or the lovely tiled floor and inviting leather sofa diverted her focus. She'd even forgotten to give him a hug.

"Please just give me a lift. It's not far. I'll tell you everything on the way there. OK?"

"You haven't changed," he sighed, lifting a new-looking waterproof coat from its hook by the front door. "But guess what, Delphine Françoise Rougier? I don't want you to."

She smiled.

"Thanks. But I like how *you* have."

"Couldn't go on feeling sorry for myself. Letting things slide. Your mother wouldn't have wanted that."

She just wanted to die.

*

Within minutes, he'd alarmed the house, disabled the central locking system on the white 4X4 monster parked a few metres up the street, and had started its engine. "Not bloody Gauffroi is it?" He said that name with pure hatred in his voice, driving past Saint-Arnoult's mighty church, glazed in a drizzly, other-worldly glow. "Or that other miserable bastard…"

"Longeau? No."

"So, which way now?"

They'd reached a main roundabout, with signs for everywhere, including the Hôpital Marie Curie. Where, as Natalie Lavroche had already stated, and according to the TV news in the student lounge, the four savaged children had been taken.

So much for the black-out.

"Third left towards Pierrefort and Moussac."

Delphine stared at the outskirts of the sprawling *École de la Gendarmerie*, where the dormitory windows nearest the road were mostly in darkness. Unlike her room, set further back, where she hoped Aristide wasn't snooping in her underwear drawer.

"Better not be another wild goose chase," said her father above the engine's noise, slowing down because of two loose sheep in the verge. "I'm getting too old."

"Never too old," she patted his arm. "And anyway, Maman's looking out for us."

A lie, but then hadn't she graduated with honours in that department? As if her unhappy life had been rubbed away like a red wine stain on a table.

48

"So, what's this about?" he quizzed.

"OK. Here goes."

*

Once finished, she realised he'd stopped the car and switched off the engine.

"I might have guessed," he stared straight ahead. "I wish I'd never told you about the bloody wolves."

"Well, you did."

"I'm not going there. Sorry." He turned to her, moisturiser still glistening around his eyes. "Have you any idea just how fanatical these wildlife-lovers are? They tried to foist boars on us in St. Eustache when you were just about to start school. But I tell you what," his once-handsome face etched by anxiety, "they've got friends in very high places. Get me?"

So, Natalie Lavroche hadn't been making things up.

"You said Lefties, so who else do you mean?"

"Bolsheviks who want to sabotage privately-owned land. Think Stalin and Kazhakstan in the early thirties when at least a million people died." He re-started the engine. "It might seem far-fetched to you, but I've heard things I shouldn't. That's why I'm hardly champing at the bit by going down that particular road. And as for you, do you really want to put your new life at risk?"

*

Despite the Shogun's warmth, Delphine felt suddenly cold. Here he was, faltering, with less to lose than her. While she, with a secret aim to eventually join the GIGN (the Gendarmerie de France's élite counter-terrorism operation), was even more determined to investigate.

"OK," she said, unclicking her seat belt. "I know you've got Patrick Gauffroi in your brain, taking up your every waking thought, and that

49

you've got a new life. But I've got mine, and I want to use it my way."

"And Colonel Valon? What about him? He did a lot for you, as I recall."

That hurt.

"You mean, put *his* career on the line?" she countered, opening her door. "Thanks."

Her father gripped her left arm. "Look, Delphine, this could all get pretty nasty, especially since that little kid's died. You mustn't get involved. I'm telling you." His grip tightened. "So, I'll spell it out. You're all I've got and if that's being selfish, well, I'm being selfish."

Silence.

*

Their surroundings were almost too quiet. Too unlit. His big car too claustrophobic. She had her own wheels after all, she reasoned to herself. And tomorrow was the weekend where, after Zanowski's 'post-mortem' session, she could please herself.

"Just drop me off up there," she pointed towards the *École*. "I should never have asked you. Sorry."

He drove without speaking and left her by the walkway into the student car park. "Keep in touch," he said. "And be careful."

Why? She asked herself, as his driver's window slid upwards and he moved away. Where had being careful got anybody? Besides, he'd hardly been cautious up on the Causses eighteen months ago, hunting down the evil Henri and Eva Seghers like a man possessed. And not for the first time did she wonder if another woman hadn't entered his life. Someone re-shaping him into a person she might not recognise.

*

As she ran towards the lit main entrance, having retrieved her pass from the check-in machine, Delphine became faintly aware of a strange noise coming from the fields surrounding the Pont d'Argent. She stopped and listened hard, soon sensing the wet, dark night muffling sounds of frantic barking. But why were dogs roaming around, unless…

Definitely not dogs.

"There may be wolves over the other side of the bridge," she alerted Véronique Morel's male replacement on reception, bent over his computer looking stressed. "Not so far away."

"Damned timesheets," he muttered, without looking up. "I'm not some bloody robot…"

She left him, and within seconds, was opening the door to her room, finding it empty. Worse, both sets of her notes she'd written up had vanished.

8

Not everyone was pleased to be detained after breakfast for yesterday's surveillance post-mortem, least of all Delphine and certainly not Lieutenant Colonel Mikhail Zanowski, whose face was abnormally pink. As for Aristide, whom she'd stupidly trusted to stay in her room, he'd been out for a run when she'd called in on his dormitory. The newly shaven-headed Romain Vileneuf who'd guarded their door had then asked if she preferred black cock to white and if so, why?

Seething and undecided whether or not to report him for sexist behaviour, she sat at the back of the lecture hall with her Samsung phone containing useful photographs, plus a few hastily-composed notes on her lap.

Aristide was, unsurprisingly, ignoring her, but Romain, three rows ahead, kept glancing back. What was his problem? Could *he* have gone into her room as well? She'd not dared ask at the time, but she would. Meanwhile, the hot and bothered course leader was beginning his introduction, glancing her way.

"Quite an eventful session, by all accounts," he began, holding up his list of student contributions. "However, there seem to be two reports missing. From Rougier and Bellefosse." The other female student from Brive, blushed to crimson, making her psoriasis patches worse, as she muttered something about the time of the month. This time, no-one sniggered, because Zanowski was in a bad mood.

"And you?" he addressed Delphine. "Your excuse?"

"My notes are on here, sir." She held up her phone. No way could she

52

admit she'd left her room unlocked, with Aristide Abolego free to roam inside. Or that she'd gone AWOL without permission.

The Parisian glanced her way.

Don't make eye contact...

"Print it off for me within ten minutes," said the colonel, and to the other girl, "I expect a better excuse than that."

"I've got one, colonel. Romain Vileneuf was chasing me through the Zone Industrielle. I spent most of the afternoon getting away from him."

"Really?" Those odd brown eyes fixed on the shaven-headed rebel from Toulouse. "That area wasn't in your remit. So, these are fairy tales, yes?" He waved two dog-eared sheets of paper in the culprit's direction.

Vileneuf bristled, but Zanowski beat him to any response. "In my office. Now!"

The scowling student twisted himself out of his seat and, having given the blushing girl and Delphine a death stare, pushed his way to the back of the hall, slamming the door behind him. In that moment, she knew that his days in Saint-Arnoult could be numbered. Almost as if he wanted to be 'on the outside pissing in' as her father once said. Causing mischief. Getting his own back. Whatever, she'd give him a few minutes to be off the scene, then, having excused herself from the lecture room, begged the guy on reception to print out her three handwritten pages from his computer. Thankfully, he had a rare gap in his paper mountain and was able to oblige.

*

She handed in the real version of what had happened that afternoon, all too aware of Aristide staring at her every move. The colonel gave her a nod, then continued reading from the pile of notes in front of him. However, he kept eyeing hers, keeping it separate from the others.

Then after a few questions dutifully answered, Aristide was told to stand up.

Delphine held her breath. She watched the colonel's lips as the Parisian began to repeat what was her original account of seeing the Lavroche couple by the stream. How they were missing, and their adult daughter had seemed to despise them, suddenly imitating a wolf's howl.

Don't react.

She felt more than sick but kept her composure. The colonel would surely know whose account was genuine. But that wasn't the point.

"You seem, Abolego, to have the uncanny ability to be in two places at once," he observed, setting the sheet of paper to one side. "On the one hand near the quarry, the other… I'll see you afterwards, too. In my office."

Silence.

Aristide sat down and no more was said, while beyond the windows, Delphine saw ominous black clouds had covered the sun.

*

Zanowski didn't read out her printed account until at 09:55hrs. With the lecture hall emptied and a cleaner waiting with her mop and bucket, he lowered his voice.

"I am aware of what's happened. Abolego's a promising student whose swift actions yesterday afternoon may have saved your life. That's no exaggeration. Once the serious matter of plagiarism has been spelled out to him, he'll get another chance."

"But why use my material?"

The cleaner rattled her bucket while Zanowski lowered his head and almost whispered. "If you knew his background, you'd probably understand."

"About his dead brother?"

A nod.

"He wasn't there to protect him. He let him down, and his mother and sister. I can't say more except that he has to prove himself. Something our counsellor will be re-addressing."

"Re-addressing?"

"I shouldn't have said that."

He checked both his expensive watches, then faced her with a look she'd not seen before. His blue eyes larger than ever.

"Rougier, I have to tell you that unlike your other tasks here, which as you know, have been graded from average to good, your surveillance operation yesterday was outstanding. I'm only sorry how it ended. You'll be recommended for a Merit badge, which as you know, is rare for anyone in Compagnie 1."

Delphine felt herself blush. Then came an unexpected question.

"How did Abolego actually get hold of your notes? I'll be asking him too, of course."

She hesitated. That coveted Merit award already slipping away. In fact, everything, leaving her with yet another shitty job to look forward to. Best to come clean, she told herself, and when she'd finished her account of how she'd been impelled to ask her father to take her to the *Air du Vent* farm, was rewarded with a look that surprised her. A tiny pucker between his almost invisible eyebrows. An even tinier smile.

"I confess, Rougier, I was the same when I started here. Never seeing obstacles once the bit was between my teeth, but," he then fixed her with an alarming stare, "we work as a team. Mavericks are dangerous. They cost lives. Is that what you want?"

Delphine composed herself for her reply. She mustn't buckle, not after everything that had happened at *Bellevue* and elsewhere. Still raw. Still hurting.

"Sir, if I'd not met Natalie Lavroche and heard her make that weird imitation of a wolf's howl, then news of their attack on that school wouldn't have affected me so much." She took another deep breath. "I had to do something. Find out where her parents might be, and if she had anything to do with them being missing. Even her partner…"

"Partner?" His eyes flickered.

"Apparently, he belongs to LVS. *La Vie Sauvage.* Have you heard of them, sir?"

At this, the senior gendarme checked his watches again as if suddenly in a hurry to be away.

"May I suggest, Rougier, to help take your mind off things, that you make use of several sporting activities today."

I don't want my mind taken off any of it…

"Sir." She gave him a brief salute and began walking away towards her room until the previous night came to mind. "I've been hearing wolves howling near here," she called after him. "Shouldn't your students be warned? I'm not easily scared, but I was when…"

He stopped. Raised a forefinger ending in a perfectly-shaped nail with its gleaming, half-moon cuticle.

"Judo begins in half an hour. Then it's unisex football or the gym. Take your pick. And should anything happen to your phone, print out a copy of your notes for yourself to keep."

With that, he walked away, leaving her between a rock and an even harder place, yet unable to shift his obvious interest in the word 'partner.'

Having reached her room, Delphine worked out a strategy to move matters on for herself only. If Aristide Abolego approached her, she'd tell him - dead brother or not - to fuck off and leave her alone.

9

Sod judo and the gym, Delphine told herself while securing her two-way radio in her locker, then in her room, choosing the most appropriate gear to wear from her single, overcrowded wardrobe. She didn't want to see anyone or explain anything else. This was *her* weekend, and she'd be spending it following her instincts. Monday morning was another matter, with a re-run of survival techniques plus a three-day practical course on the challenging and desolate Plateau de Millevaches. Hopefully, her experiences on the Causses de Quercy would stand her in good stead.

For now, however, she must focus on yesterday.

*

She drove away from the *École de la Gendarmerie*'s almost empty car park and, though tempted for a moment to call in on her father who'd not so far made contact since last night, continued across the Pont'd'Argent towards the *Air du Vent* farm.

Everything looked the same as yesterday. That air of emptiness, of possible danger, yet the sleek, brown bulls and cows were still in their separate, electrified enclosures. As before, the child's scooter still leant against the bigger barn which could, judging by the extra cables leading to it, be used for milking. Nothing seemed to have been disturbed, but why no car in the yard? Not even the daughter's red Twingo?

Her anxiety grew, and in the silence, her phone trilled out its ring tone. No number visible, but she recognised that brittle, female voice belonged to Natalie Lavroche.

"He's out of danger, thank God, even though I'm not a believer."

Keep her talking…

"You mean Joel?" Just to make sure.

"Who else? But…" she stalled, sounding as if about to cry, "I'm in serious trouble."

"Where are you?"

"Still in the hospital, and not letting him out of my sight. Even though I had to spend the night in a chair by his bed. Can you blame me?"

"I'd have done the same. And your parents? Any news?"

"Nothing. And…"

"Go on," urged Delphine. "Please trust me. I'm on your side." This wasn't entirely true, but she sensed even more was at stake, and things could get worse.

"It's my partner. He's been threatening me…"

"Why? About that attack?"

A pause, during which one of the bulls began mounting another. Normally, she'd have smiled at such a clumsy, comical sight. But not then.

"Natalie?" she prompted. "You still there?"

"You guessed correctly. I'm to say nothing to anyone, especially as it's in the national newspapers. God knows how. He wants it all hushed up."

"I bet he does." Delphine recalled her father's comment about 'friends in high places.' Wondering whose Maurice's might be.

"His surname is…?"

"Christ. Do I have to?"

"I only want to help. Like I said, Natalie, trust me."

"OK. It's Amance. He's insane. I realise that now. As for being concerned about Joel, what a joke. It's his precious wolves that come first. Him and…" Here she stopped.

"Who?"

"No-one."

Delphine let it go, but wouldn't forget.

"Have you seen him recently?" She asked as a huge shadow of starlings swarmed overhead and vanished.

"Just that one call telling me to shut my face."

"Charming. Where's he now?"

A snort.

"Are you trying to get me killed? What planet are you on?"

The line went dead, with no number given for replying. Natalie Lavroche was scared. Torn between a dangerous obsessive and getting justice for her son, those other children and the dead Amélie Massenet.

It was then that the name Amance re-surfaced.

Damn.

Why hadn't she remembered when Natalie had mentioned it? Was she losing her marbles already? Ten years ago she'd gone to Haute-Saône and the Vosges with her convent school where the main agenda was to explore the fine local churches. And where had they been billeted for two weeks? In a hostel in St. Loup-sur-Semouse, the village of Amance just a short drive away. And where else had they gone? Domrémy, the humble birthplace of Jehanne d'Arc, which they'd visited on the second day.

*

Delphine deliberately left her car unlocked, just in case. Having gathered up her leather pouch containing her wallet, phone, ID and driving licence, which fit snugly into her cagoule pocket, she made her way towards an arched, solid wood gate set within a stone wall. It seemed considerably older than the farmhouse and was probably a relic from a larger building long gone.

To her surprise, it was also unlocked. Its padlock hanging loose from the latch as if someone had left in a hurry.

Indeed they had...

She covered her hand with her cagoule's sleeve to avoid leaving prints and lifted the latch, wondering if there might be a guard dog or two tucked away. So far, she'd not seen or heard any, and it was more than odd for a farm to be without such protection. Even the dingy, non-functioning *Bellevue* in St. Eustache had been home to an aggressive Alsatian, then Julie, an almost-human border collie...

Faltering for a moment, she also recalled how massive Pyrenean mountain dogs were equipped with fearsome spiked collars, so why not here, given this latest problem? She pulled up her cagoule's hood and ventured further into a tiled passageway, leading to a spacious storeroom given over to a large boiler, still ticking over. A range of outdoor clothing, fishing rods and further paraphernalia of outdoor lives lined the nearest wall. But what made her pause were three empty dog baskets piled on top of each other. The topmost one smelling of damp, with several coarse brown hairs trapped in its weave. Occupied at some point, but not recently.

Delphine paused again, on even higher alert for the faintest sound, but there was none. Just her breath, quicker than usual. She began searching the clothes' pockets, but with each one, felt increasingly like a trespasser. The place seeming more like a trap. But something impelled her to persevere.

François Rougier's coat pockets had housed everything from parking tickets, to *loto* receipts, and scraped-at scratch cards. Yes, he'd really believed that one day he'd hit the jackpot, with his dream of taking over an established vineyard.

Hang on...

From an inner pocket of what was clearly a woman's full-length waterproof, Delphine pulled out a folded scrap of paper. A numbered receipt dated Thursday 2nd of June. Ets. Fabien Guirros. Franchised manufacturers of the acidic, industrial-strength Viteprop drain-blocker, based near Usssel some thirty kilometres away. Five hundred litres, paid for in cash by Élisabeth Lavroche herself.

She forgot to breathe. Could this hazardous product have been what was poured into the stream? If so, what about children paddling in the water, as they sometimes did? Would their skin peel away? Their organs collapse? It didn't bear thinking about.

Damn.

She paused with the receipt in mid-air. She'd heard a noise which had nothing to do with the boiler whose light still glowed green. No, this was coming from outside and definitely not man-made. She pushed the receipt into her cagoule's pocket and opened the back door a fraction to stand poised in the attack position, the way she and the other students had been shown only on their second day at the *École.*

Mère de Dieu...

Normally, she'd have screamed. In the furthest enclosure, one of the cows who minutes before, had been peacefully grazing, was on her back. Four legs uselessly grinding the air while what appeared to be two large, grey-black dogs repeatedly tore at her gaping, bloodied throat, pulling out her windpipe...

But these weren't dogs. Maybe they were those same creatures she'd heard last night?

Using her car as cover, she crept forwards, hoping there must be some implement or other to use as a weapon inside the smaller barn.

She was right.

Once inside, she unravelled a knot of wire acting as a substitute for a padlock, and in the semi-darkness, spotted a cluster of ancient-looking rifles. She snatched at the least rusty one, which luckily still housed three cartridges.

"Go!" she told herself. And once again outside, had to blink hard as the hidden sun had blindingly, malevolently, burst through the clouds.

*

Squinting into the brightness, she took aim at the wolves and just about to pull back the trigger, when she felt a rush of air and the sudden slice of a huge spade knocking the rifle from her grasp. Its din against the flagstone floor drowned her scream as someone taller, reeking of sweat, shoved her against the barn wall.

"Meddling bitch. Who the fuck are you? Where you from?" His accent gutteral, certainly not from central France. Two fierce, blue eyes encased in a black balaclava were too close to hers. She could kick as she'd been trained, even do a headlock. But his body, thick-set, bulked out by a typical *bleu de travail,* was too strong. Besides, her right arm felt badly jarred, weakened.

"I said, who the fuck are you?"

"Marie Lebrun from Seilhac," she lied, trying to regain her balance. "And Natalie Lavroche is my friend. I've known her for a while. Her son's just been injured by savages like those two over there. Look at them! How can you just stand by? It's disgusting." She could have pulled out her phone as if to call for help, but the risk of having it snatched or broken was too great.

"Liar!" Snarled the hulk, ignoring her plea. "She's got no friends. We know that."

"Shut it!" A shorter, brown-eyed one with a similarly shaped head stamped on his booted feet. "For Christ's sake."

"And why am I here?" Delphine continued as if to herself, trying not to look at what was going on in the enclosure, where the poor cow had died in a pool of blood. "Because if you must know, I'm worried sick about her and her little boy."

"*I'll* make you fucking sick…"

"Not here you won't," hissed the other man, beginning to break up the battered rifle with the spade before kicking its fragments and the three bullets across the yard. "Crétin."

Suddenly, Blue Eyes produced a whistle, puckered his lips around it, and created a high-pitched blast, causing both wolves to look up from their carnage and slither away beneath a section of the fencing's lowest strand. They'd already dug enough of a gap enabling them to enter. Now they fled like shadows in the night, across the flat pasture and away from the bellowing bulls towards the dense grove of chestnut trees.

Having stuffed the whistle in his pocket, the hulk turned to her. "Now beat it. If we see you again, you'll be dead meat too. Got it?"

He kicked the front of her precious car, leaving a dent above the number plate. That was it. Fury's fire was lit. It was as if he'd kicked *her*. As if the past years' trauma had coalesced into that one destructively symbolic act.

As a former farmer's daughter, despite being slightly built with an aching arm, she was fit and strong. She spun round and thwacked his head, sending him falling with nothing to hold on to. While the other thug was momentarily off guard, she dealt with the backs of his knees, and with both cowards squirming on the ground and screaming curses, she reached her car.

Having taken two surreptitious photos on her phone, Delphine revved as hard as she could, apologising to her old, turquoise servant, before willing her to shift as quickly as possible. Little did she realise as she passed that same dense plantation of chestnut trees, how four hidden amber eyes were following her every move, sniffing her scent. That odd word 'meddling' lingered in her mind. Why had that *con* used it if they'd only been interested in rifling through an unprotected property? Preventing her intervention in the slaughter?

At least her leather pouch and the receipt were still safe, and despite her loss of faith, she crossed herself in thanks for small mercies.

10

"Breaking and entering could be the kiss of death to your career, Rougier. Do you understand?"

Delphine nodded. "But the *Air du Vent* farm was already open, sir."

"So, who were these two men? Had you seen them before?"

She stared back at Lieutenant Colonel Zanowski and his sidekick, a younger, brown-haired Lieutenant she'd not met before. His tan suggested he'd been recruited from further south, and his accent proved it.

"Never."

They were in the interview room next to the lecture hall. The smell of coffee wafted in each time the door was opened by someone expecting the room to be empty.

"Sir, I didn't need to tell you anything," she added, feeling dazed but determined, her right arm still throbbing. "But the fact is that Guy Lavroche's farm had been left unsecured, and both these creeps had obviously followed me there to stop me looking around." She then addressed the stranger, who hopefully might have a more engaged attitude. "I'd like to think they had nothing to do with the slaughter going on in that enclosure, but they certainly didn't want me shooting those two wolves."

The Lieutenant simply shrugged. In that moment, it was the most disappointing gesture in the whole world.

"How come their whistling made both wolves leave?" Delphine pressed on. "I wouldn't have known to do that."

Another shrug.

"And I'm guessing now that the two holes beneath the electric fence had been dug beforehand to allow them access."

Zanowski was pressing numbers on his phone.

What was it with both of them? She asked herself. Why on earth was she wasting her time here? Her tone grew more impatient.

"Someone needs to get over there quick, because God knows what they might have helped themselves to by now. And where's Natalie Lavroche? Her son Joel? And her parents who - yes - I'd thought were nuts - but they've been proved right, haven't they?"

"Poisoning a public water supply is a criminal offence, whatever the reason," Zanowski opined, cancelling his call. He glanced at both his watches as if bored already. Or was he?

"They're frightened," said the Lieutenant. "I would be."

"I'm still convinced something bad has happened to them. Maybe to their daughter and grandson too. I'm sure if the police in Saint-Arnoult were told, they'd be over there like a shot." Delphine made sure both gendarmes registered the frustration on her face. Her neck began to redden. "I was tempted to call them straight away. So," she fixed on him. "Why not you, sir?"

The sun suddenly hogged the big skylight window overhead, casting both military men in a surreal glow. Zanowski, whose hair looked white-hot, was frowning - with good reason.

"Because Rougier, you're one of our students, currently destined for a Merit award, and we've an inspection looming at the end of the month. We must remain detached from these unfortunate incidents." He leant sideways to whisper in his companion's ear before straightening. "Should a leak occur, we'll claim that in this case, your curiosity and imagination clearly got the better of you."

The Lieutenant gave the slightest of nods. But a nod, nevertheless.

Anger further reddened her neck.

"Sir," she protested. "With respect, how can you allow defenceless animals to be left at such risk from these vicious predators? I saw what they did to that poor cow, and it isn't some dump of a place. *Air du Vent* is obviously the Lavroches' pride and joy."

She rubbed her sore arm, aware of the look of anxiety on both men's faces. Their priority was to present a well-oiled front to the outside world, and not for the first time did she wonder if all her and Colonel Valon's efforts to secure a place here had been yet another big mistake, compounded by her father having sold up and moved nearby.

"I'll contact Chief Inspector Casson in Saint-Arnoult," Zanowski said finally, without much enthusiasm. "He'll send a team out there and try and locate the owners." He jotted something down in a pad and looked up. "Nothing more from the daughter? Are you sure?"

"Yes." Delphine knew she'd already told him how the young mother's phone was dead. So why was he pushing it? She just wanted to flee, as if *she* was at fault. But Zanowski wasn't finished.

"Two more questions," he said, closing his pad with a click. "When this bigger stranger had hit that rifle from your grasp, did you retaliate? I mean..."

"Hit him?" Filled in the other. "Either of them?"

"No," she lied. "They were too big. Too quick, like rugby players."

However, relief was short-lived.

"Did you give them your name? Or where you were currently staying?"

That's all he was worried about. She warned herself to stay calm. That she'd soon be free.

"No on both counts, sir. I'm not stupid."

She rubbed her arm again. "And I never knew theirs. There wasn't time, what with that terrible attack going on, and me trying to get away."

"The police will soon find out." He gestured towards the door, where the cleaner had given up and gone elsewhere. "And remember, Rougier, that your second visit there stays under wraps. Understood?"

"Yessir." She added the customary salute to both interrogators and turned on her heels. "But just in case, I took two photographs of that poor dead cow, and after I'd left, what must have been the men's grey Ford Transit."

"On your phone?"

"Yes. Is that wrong?"

Big mistake.

A short, spiked laugh followed. "Foolish is a better word," Zanowski held out a pale pink hand in readiness. "I'd like to see them."

Tough.

"That's fine, sir," she lied again. "Except right now I can't seem to find it. I've looked everywhere."

Immediately, the younger Lieutenant came too close. He turned her round and, muttering something about 'necessary protocol,' began frisking her cagoule's pockets.

"Stop!" Snapped Zanowski. "That's not necessary. Rougier is not a security risk. At least, not yet."

He turned to her, indicating the door. "But be advised, that if your missing phone does come to light, I am your first port of call. Understood?"

"Sir." But this time, her salute was limp, half-hearted. But not her stride, taking her out of that too-bright room, with that unnerving threat still murmuring in her ear.

'... dead meat.'

11

12:05 hrs.

She could have slunk back to her room or the lounge set aside for students and their weekend visitors, where invariably the latest *Gala* and other more salacious magazines lay abandoned, but no. Even though her arm was still painful, how could she stick around after what she'd seen? How she'd been treated? She couldn't.

With no-one else in sight, she entered the nearby *toilettes* and once inside a locked cubicle, retrieved her leather pouch from the front of her briefs. Her Samsung and the receipt from Ussel were still safe. However, her incontinent tongue had made this phone of significant interest. But why, if Zanowski had no intention of getting involved?

She swore at herself for having mentioned the photos, but hadn't this been her problem for as long as she could remember? A naïve gullibility? An inbuilt admiration for a uniform, never mind who occupied it? Eagerness to please?

"Get a grip," she muttered, knowing that if she wasn't careful, she could end up like that poor cow in the *Air du Vent* farm, who'd harmed no-one.

*

Having bought a Gruyère cheese sandwich from the newly-replenished dispenser, Delphine made her way to the almost deserted student car park. Not furtively this time, as this was *le weekend* and only those saddos - as Aristide called them, despite being one himself - too unwell or too far from home, would be left behind.

Suddenly, a distinct and familiar whiff of aftershave meant one thing, and a sudden reluctance to see Aristide Abolego made her speed up into a run. If he wanted to say sorry for nicking her story, it was too late. He'd been a sneaky cheat, even though he'd kept Jean-Marie Longeau off her back.

"Yo, bro," he called out, but by then her key was in her car door's lock and she'd climbed in, slamming its tinny door behind her.

"I'm sorry." He pressed his face close to her window. And he actually looked it. "I've had a major bollocking."

"Good."

"I just wanted to make my afternoon look better than The Roman's."

"The Roman?" She lowered her window a fraction. The aftershave overpowering. "Who's that?"

"Vileneuf. He has to upstage me, all the bloody time."

"But it was you who stopped Longeau in his tracks."

He frowned and glanced down at the main campus and its bright green sports fields. She noticed his hair gel glistening on his cropped curls. How he'd made an effort with his appearance. "Do you know what he found yesterday after surveillance? Why he's strutting around with his head the size of a beach ball?"

"Tell me."

"A torched 4X4 off the road to Lauzance. Apparently near a disused railway line."

"What colour?"

"He didn't say."

"And?"

"A man's left boot near its chassis. Its insole under the heel built up for some reason. The whole thing looked suspicious."

Delphine pulled down her visor against a suddenly fierce sun. Hadn't Guy Lavroche, whom she'd seen running upstream with the woman who had to be Élisabeth, his wife, possessed a limp?

"When exactly was this?"

"About 17:30 hours. He'd gone off on his bike to clear his head. He wouldn't say much more."

"I bet he wouldn't." Delphine held his gaze. "So why wasn't it mentioned at the post-mortem this morning? Why make out he'd not seen anything?"

"Guess."

"Get in," she said, and when the Parisian was beside her, his weight having noticeably tilted her car to the right, pulled out her 'missing' phone. The possibility that it could be tapped was swept aside.

"What's his number?"

Hesitation.

"I'm not sure about this."

"I am. And you'd understand why if you knew about the inquisition and threats I've just had."

"Really? From whom?"

"Tell you later." She then softened her voice. It usually worked with her father. "Please, that number."

Once Aristide had obliged, she began plotting how to begin her call, what tone to adopt. She'd been right to worry about the Lavroches, but she also needed information.

"Who is it?" Romain Vileneuf answered, sounding wary. "I don't recognise the number."

"You wouldn't. It's Delphine Rougier. Compagnie 1. Can you spare a minute?"

"What for? Is this some kind of chat line? Sex by phone?"

She glanced in despair at her companion, who was too busy checking his own phone to have heard. "There's a middle-aged couple missing from their farm near here," she persevered, wondering if even this was exciting the exile from Toulouse. "I'd seen them during surveillance pouring what might have been drain unblocker liquid into the Ruiseau d'Argent stream. Then driving over the bridge in a hurry towards Lauzances in a brown 4X4 of some sort." She didn't mention the receipt.

"What's this to do with me?"

Perhaps he'd been warned off, too.

A pause in which Delphine guessed he was in the sports hall, accompanied by the thudding of balls and bursts of shouting. Aristide was now listening intently.

"I think they're in trouble."

"Which farm?"

She glanced at Aristide, who shook his head.

"*Air du Vent*," she ignored him.

"Where's all this leading?" Romain Vileneuf challenged. "Why call me like this, out of the blue?"

Here goes.

"Because I think you like me, and I see you as being reliable and trustworthy."

"Is that all?"

"No. Of course not." She felt pathetic the moment she'd said it. He was making her look ridiculous, and even Aristide was smiling to himself. She was just about to end the abortive call when the Toulousian said, "OK. I did come across a burnt-out 4X4 yesterday afternoon, but…"

"What?"

"It's hot" he whispered. "I've been told to keep stumm."

"By whom?"

A pause, during which the last cloud in the sky drifted away.

"Only if you see me later. How about the Caméo?"

An art-house cinema behind the station. She'd not yet been there but on-trend Cécile had described it as 'intimate.'

So what? Delphine reminded herself she was twenty-two, not fourteen, and if in trouble, could defend herself. Couldn't she?

"You said hot," she quizzed Romain. "Why?"

Pause.

"OK," he relented. "I swear to God there were two adults in it. Male and female. Both still in the boot. Charred to buggery."

Mère Marie…

"That's terrible."

"And don't ask if the car was brown because there was no trace of any paint. But definitely a 4X4. I could tell by the shape of what remained of the chassis and by the size of…"

"Couldn't you have tried bringing them out? Called the police?"

"Have you seen '*The Godfather*'? I'm not dumb, but I also keep wondering whether they'd shut themselves in on purpose and started the fire to make it look like a crime, I don't know. Perhaps no-one ever will. So," he added, "see you at seven. Oh, and by the way…" Here he was interrupted, followed by sounds of more frantic basketball action. "Solo. OK?"

All on his terms, thought Delphine bleakly. Was she really that interested? Yes, very. But a question remained. "I heard a whisper that Lieutenant Colonel Zanowski's in the know, and what interests me is why he never mentioned anything earlier this morning."

Aristide was noisily chewing his cherry-flavoured gum.

"Who whispered? The nigger?" Romain questioned.

Her passenger flinched.

"I hate that word," she said, knowing full well if he uttered it within hearing at the *École*, he'd be out on his ear.

"Sorry." But he didn't sound it.

"Someone else," she managed to reply.

"I'll need to know. So, seven it is. See you then."

Delphine turned to look at her passenger who, like her, didn't look at all happy. For a split-second, she thought of Patrick Gauffroi probably boiling over in his cramped cell some four hundred kilometres away. Was she again leaning too close to someone she shouldn't? Being reckless with her friendship? All in a cause, which, being honest, had nothing to do with her? But she had no choice. Too much had happened. Too many people were missing, including a six-year-old boy. The town's Commissariat de Police was her next port of call.

"And, Romain, please bring that boot with you, or someone else might take it."

No reply.

12

Ominously dark clouds from the east had gradually overcome the sun, adding to the air of despondency in that almost miniature, twelve-year-old car, whose milometer gauge was showing six figures.

"I'll be at the Caméo, too," said Aristide, re-clicking his seatbelt. "In disguise, if necessary."

"Thanks, but I'll be fine."

"I'm not so sure. Besides, I want to make it up to you about nicking your notes," he persevered as they reached the busy town centre and parked in the last remaining space a few metres away from the Commissariat de Police in the Rue des Cygnes.

"Look, I'll only be for half an hour or so, and it could really move things on. If Zanowski and his shitty little sidekick had shown me normal behaviour this morning, I wouldn't even be doing this. I have to find out what I can, and I won't be holding my breath in here either."

"OK. But at least let me pay for parking."

While he fed coins into the metre, Delphine couldn't shift the thought of those two people trapped inside a blazing furnace. Had they even been the car's owners? If only Natalie Lavroche's phone was switched on. If only...

"Let's go," said Aristide, handing her the ticket then pulling up his cagoule's hood against the first drops of rain. "And afterwards, I'll treat you to a Macdo."

He knew which buttons to press. She wasn't too proud to admit she loved McDonald's, especially its 'veggie burger' with *frites*. A new outlet had opened within walking distance, and besides, she was starving.

Before mounting the steps to the commissariat's unimposing entrance, Delphine checked they weren't being observed. Her gaze strayed further along to her left, where the Parc Voltaire looked quite different now in the grey, drizzly afternoon.

"What's up?" Aristide asked. "Anything wrong?"

"Not exactly." She then explained how that same Tabac, with its Loto sign clearly visible, was where she'd seen Jean-Marie Longeau on Friday lunchtime.

"You need to ask about him." He reminded her. "You've every right."

"Aren't you coming in?"

He shook his hooded head. "I'm better off out here. Just in case."

She didn't argue. She rang the bell and waited for the intercom to kick in, feeling suddenly cold and, despite Aristide's unthreatening presence, too vulnerable.

"Name?" Barked a sharp, invisible female.

"Delphine Rougier." Her own voice sounded strained, unusually high-pitched, and she knew why. Wondering if that ruthless, wronged reporter from the Pays de la Loire was still lurking somewhere on the premises.

"Alone or accompanied?"

"Alone."

Aristide duly edged away.

"Address?"

She then gave the *École de la Gendarmerie Nationale's* details. It made not the slightest difference. She could almost hear a sneer.

"Reason for visit?"

"I may have some useful information about yesterday's wolves' attack at the *École Primaire St. Bernard.*"

The intercom crackled in her ear. She winced.

"Information? What exactly? Our Crime Investigation Unit's fully stretched at the moment."

I bet it is. Well, here goes…

"I believe the Lavroche family from the *Air du Vent* farm may be in danger. And, that events surrounding them are being hushed up."

*

Her father would be proud of her. That did the trick, and within a minute, she was in a small office given over to three desks housing a computer each, a communal printer, several filing cabinets, and four grey vinyl chairs with spindly, metal legs, only suitable for the young and mobile.

A middle-aged Detective Ginette Camart, whose prominent black eyebrows almost met across the top of her nose, indicated the nearest chair. Its slippery surface almost deposited Delphine on the floor. Not an auspicious start and, having scoured her ID, listened to how she'd first seen the couple by the stream, to that very morning when the cow had been mutilated and she'd come up against two 'marginaux.'

"Lieutenant Colonel Zanowski from the *École* said he'd be in touch with you." Delphine added. "Has he?"

Camart swivelled round twice to face Delphine with an altogether meaner expression.

"Do you often do this?"

"Do what?" The sky beyond the one, barred window became black.

"Fantasise?"

Shit.

Delphine scraped back her cut-price chair and began to stand. A snack at McDonalds was suddenly a more inviting prospect than battling with a perverse sceptic - or worse - whose agenda was unclear. But why? Why too, had Zanowski and his shadow so blatantly dismissed her and hardly bothered to contact anyone else?

"Are you implying I do drugs?" She countered.

Camart sighed.

"Please sit down. We need to get to the bottom of this. And fast."

"I agree."

Romain Vileneuf's news, if true, was literally explosive. It was maybe time to share it, whatever the consequences. But watch the eyes, Delphine reminded herself. These were the blackest, hardest, most unchanging she'd ever seen.

*

When she'd finished her account, Camart made no further eye contact and said nothing. Instead, she picked up her desk phone.

Almost immediately, a short, bespectacled, pock-faced Inspector Raymond Serra joined them, his two-way radio buzzing into life. Acknowledging Delphine with the briefest of glances, he listened to whoever had called with a deepening frown.

"When?" he snapped into it, walking towards the door, then stopping. Something serious was up. "There must be some mistake... Why? Because..." He eyed Delphine again, lowering his voice. "I can't speak now."

She was aware of Camart staring at her. Then knew that for some big reason, everything had changed.

*

For the second time, Delphine stood up and, ignoring the seated officer, followed the inspector into the corridor outside. Bare walls, plain tiles, dirty strip-lights - nothing to distract her.

"Is it the Lavroches?" she said to his back. "Were they the couple burnt in that car?"

He twisted round, his glasses tilting across the bridge of his fleshy nose, his colour pink as a pig. "Be careful, Mademoiselle Rougier. Keep yourself out of all this, because," he hesitated, "certain things are beyond our control..."

Beyond our control?

What the hell did that mean? Wasn't law and order, the protection of life, paramount to both the police and all gendarmeries?

She'd once seen the whole of *The Godfather* in Pauline Fillol's bedroom and never forgotten it. Gripping yet repellent.

"You mean the Mafia?"

Bad move.

"No." He pushed in the aerial of his radio and placed it back in its holster strapped around his generous waist. "And my advice to you and that *noir* loitering outside is to return to barracks and stay away from matters that have nothing to do with you."

Noir...

Despite the airless warmth, Delphine felt a familiar warning chill return. "I was attacked, remember?" she challenged him. "By two thugs who could have killed me."

"That's not what *we've* heard," he interrupted. His voice like sour cream, making her feel queasy. "And, more to the point, we have your name."

Fuck you.

"Is that a threat?"

His large hand rested on the EXIT button of the outer door, but she wasn't ready to go just yet.

"Yesterday, Lieutenant Colonel Zanowski said Jean-Marie Longeau, a reporter from Cousteaux in the Sarthe, was being kept here overnight. Has

79

he gone, and has the Lieutenant Colonel been in contact about it?"

"For someone with your history, Mademoiselle, you have a remarkable lack of self-preservation."

With your history...

She felt cold all over again.

"Another threat, inspector? Is that all you can do?"

The buzzer sounded and he pulled the door open for her, allowing his underarm odour to reach her. Although rain was falling vertically, with Aristide still waiting, she wasn't finished. Her mother might have died in vain, but not Guy and Élisabeth Lavroche. Nor their young grandson who might well suffer the effects of such an attack for the rest of his life.

"There was a man's left boot found under that car and I want to know who it belonged to. And who'd been burnt to death."

Crétine. You shouldn't have mentioned it...

The padded-out jaw tightened. Eyes narrowing to become mean hyphens. "For a very good reason, Mademoiselle, this matter is not yet the public domain. And now, if you'll excuse me, I have work to do."

The sudden, sharp push between her shoulder blades gave her no time to balance herself before bumping down the two steps towards the sodden, gravel pavement. If Aristide hadn't been there to break her fall, she'd have hit it hard enough to break her already weakened arm, if not her back.

The door slammed shut behind her.

"Shit, man!" Aristide pulled her up, brushing bits of gravel and debris off her cagoule. "You OK?"

"I think so." Delphine felt down her sore arm, wincing as she did so. "What's his problem? And the other one in there?" She turned to him, a dripping mass of dark green. Even his eyelashes bore the weight of water as she repeated her assailant's parting shot.

"It's a cover-up," she added. "They must think I'm thick. But for how long can the lid be kept on the cess-pit?"

Aristide eyed the closed door with a pure, pent-up anger. He then checked his watch. "I'd say five and a half hours?"

"Why?"

"Because that's when you're meeting Romain Vileneuf."

13

"You're joking?" Delphine crashed the 2CV's gears before reversing out of the parking slot. "We'd decided."

"*You'd* decided," Aristide said quietly. "And with good reason. But it's the only way forward. Yes, we can go to the hospital, then try and find wherever that car was along that road to Lauzances…"

"Could be a trap, with Romain Vileneuf as bait." She changed gear badly. Her little car, which smelt of damp clothes, was clearly unhappy with her handling. "Think about it."

"I am, but I'll be there."

"Right."

The silence, even despite the rain punishing her car's fabric roof, was solid, and now wasn't the time for her to break it. Besides, a lot could happen between now and then…

He offered her a fresh chewing gum, which she slipped into her pocket for later, then accessed the Hôpital Marie Curie on his BlackBerry. "Visiting times daily from 13:00 hrs. until 18:00 hrs."

"Natalie may be there with her son."

"Or may not. We could phone first," he suggested. "Save a wasted journey."

"It won't be wasted."

*

The slanting downpour, now from the west, seemed to push the 2CV along the Avenue Voltaire as if actually aiding and abetting their mission. However, the tiny windscreen wipers were frequently overwhelmed, and spray from the road on both sides almost engulfed them.

Aristide was clearly nervous. A city dweller who was used to public transport, not some sardine can whose wheels were not much bigger than on a kid's scooter. And that brought back the picture of Joel's abandoned blue toy leaning against that farm's probable milking shed.

"He called you a *noir*," she then said, almost without thinking.

"Who did?"

"That snotty Inspector Serra, back there."

Her companion's body stiffened. His whole face changed. He was a coiled spring, ready to go.

"I'm sorry. I shouldn't have mentioned..."

"Don't worry. He's not worth it. None of them are, and I tell you what..." He blew out an increasingly large, pink bubble of gum, then popped it with his lips, making her jump. "We'll be out of the loop after Monday morning, so we do what we can till then, yeah?"

"Meaning?"

"Our way." He raised his right hand, palm towards her for a high-five, full of spirit and resolve.

*

While François Rougier was gobbling down a late lunch at home, about to use his untraceable pay-as-you go Nokia to call his Paris contact, Delphine drove past the *École Primaire St. Bernard*, surprised not to see a police cordon around its small playground at the front. In fact, it was deserted. As if such a terrible event had never happened. However, something else had caught Aristide's eye.

"Look!" he pointed further along the railings, unbuckling his stretched seat belt. "Won't be a minute."

The road they needed for the hospital was further along on the right, so

Delphine slowed to a stop, keeping the rattling engine chugging over. True to his word, once he'd sussed out the circular sign, which to her seemed similar to the ubiquitous '*Ne pas stationner*' warning, he was climbing back in, baring his beautiful teeth as Natalie Lavroche had done. Except this was no joke.

"Well?" she said.

"Holy shit," he kept staring out of the windscreen. "It's a head on image of a wolf, ready to attack. '*Je suis roi*,' written underneath. How sick is that?"

"Take a photo, quick," she said, passing him her Samsung. "It may not be around for long after what's been happening."

"There are at least two more," he said.

"Even sicker."

"I could check out local sign makers. Mind you, those could have been imported. You know, China. Taiwan…"

He returned her phone and began scrolling on his grey, metallic BlackBerry. The latest model, as he'd once boasted. Paid for by helping his mother on her stall. "Not getting very far," he admitted, before glancing up to help find the hospital car park. "I'll check again once we've finished here. Oh, and by the way…"

"What?"

"Do the letters LVS mean anything to you?"

*

As they approached the large, white rectangular building, whose front area was filled by ambulances and several top-of-the range vehicles probably belonging to executives and consultants, Delphine saw that snarling wolf's face replicated along the whole length of the new wire fence. She recalled Natalie Lavroche's fear. But had it been real or fake?

"Someone means business," muttered Aristide, taking her camera for yet more shots. "But do you see any CCTV anywhere?"

Delphine had already been looking. "No, but some cameras can be tiny and well-disguised."

"I know that. And there's an overflow car park around the corner."

"We'll try there," she said, switching her wipers to max again to avoid a collision, which would be the icing on the shitty cake. "If not, we'll just have to leg it."

"Not me."

"Why?"

He hesitated.

"That racist inspector, for a start. I'd stand out again, wouldn't I? I mean how many blacks have you seen here?"

He was right.

Delphine studied him for a moment. A young man of her age from a background which would have made most turn to drugs or other stuff. Who'd been doing his best to make it up to her for nicking her surveillance notes, only to have something so deep-seated and ever-present to derail him.

"If you don't go, neither will I," she said. "Even though I'm convinced there's a lot at stake here."

Rain slanted towards the tiny windscreen. She shivered despite him being so close. His body warmth noticeable, and in the distance, came the growl of thunder. Or could it be wolves, hungrier than ever? She was almost relieved to see lightning dancing in the sky.

"OK. Perhaps you're the one to help me cut the crap. Sort myself out." He said.

No pressure...

Then, on the spur of the moment, Delphine recounted the events of November 2003 and what had shaped them. How her depressed mother had been shot for nothing.

Silence save for the hardening rain on glass.

"Like my little brother, Aaron," he said, before she took his hand and squeezed it tight.

"So, are we in this together, or not?"

His reply was to squeeze hers back, and she then drove into the overspill car park where just two spaces remained. She watched as he walked over to the pay and display unit. Although his score was 7 on a scale of 1 to 10 for trustworthiness, the fewer people who knew about those images from the farm in her phone, the better. And no way would Zanowski get his weirdly pale hands on them. Before Monday was out, she'd pass them to her father, then delete them.

14

Before both she and Aristide ventured towards the hospital's main entrance, he produced his BlackBerry and scrolled down its lit screen. "I've found two sign manufacturers," he announced. "One in the Passage des Sonnettes, the other in the Rue Jean Moulin. Not far from the commissariat."

"Hours of opening?"

"Zilch."

"Phone numbers?"

He nodded.

"We'll try them after here. Then LVS."

Delphine also had to find out more about the Viteprop drain un-blocker and if Élisabeth Lavroche had let slip to the firm why she'd needed so much of it.

*

The hospital visit didn't take long. Yes, Natalie Lavroche and Joel had been and gone, so the young, uniformed and heavily bespectacled woman in reception had told them while continually glancing at her computer screen as if they were invisible. Finally, she enquired if they were family or friends.

"Friends," said Delphine. "Worried friends."

"Why worried?" Quizzed the automaton, still avoiding eye contact. "Her son was fine. Just a few scratches and shaken up, that's all. He's been discharged."

"Really? His mother made out he was in a bad way, and now she's not answering her phone. As for her parents…"

Aristide nudged her to stay silent, and immediately, any cordiality evaporated. They were stared at through those thick-lensed glasses as if they were beggars off the street. Delphine knew the end of the road had come and was about to turn away, when Aristide produced his phone.

"Look," he said, showing this gatekeeper the LVS wolf signs in all their alarming glory. "You think these are acceptable? Boasting, almost welcoming these savages back? They're all along your fence out there."

"I'm amazed your cameras and security staff haven't picked up on them," added Delphine. "What sort of place is this?"

But the receptionist, sniffing trouble, was already on her phone, asking for the Maintenance Section's Director. Meanwhile, other visitors had arrived, looking Aristide up and down, like the ignorant peasants they probably were.

"Let's go. I've another idea," Delphine whispered to him. Then, raising her voice above the newcomers, said to the uniformed disappointment, "Don't think for one moment we're leaving this matter alone. In fact, your attitude has made us more determined to find out the truth. Be warned."

*

Leaning into the rain and dodging the biggest puddles, they both reached the 2CV with barely enough room on either side to get in. Once installed, Aristide wiped his face with a duster his mother had given him to keep his room clean.

"Are you thinking the same as me?" he said. "As if there's something really shite going on?"

"We've a few things to do, starting with the sign people."

Having hid his number, he discovered that the sign-making business in the Rue Jean Moulin had, according to its answering service, been closed since April due to illness, and wouldn't be re-opening until the autumn. However, its female receptionist in the Passage des Sonnettes, although wary, at least gave a name once Aristide said he was a cop.

"Amance. Maurice."

Delphine blinked.

"Did he leave an address?"

Silence.

"Madame?"

"Sorry. No. He paid cash up front and waited while the order was processed. He had the template on a CD and only wanted fifty printed."

"He must have given you some contact informa…"

Delphine heard the ominous 'call ended' sound, and Aristide re-dialled without success. "Fucking typical," he sighed. "No wonder hardly any crime gets solved." He turned to her. "You wait. Once I'm out there, I'll be banging a few heads together. It's hardly suprising that people take the law into their own hands. And don't talk to me about serial killing investigations if they happen to involve different departments…"

Delphine nudged him. "Amance is Natalie Lavroche's partner's surname."

"Plot thickens."

"Too right. And did you see Joel's original one scrubbed out in the ledger next to that bitch's computer?"

"Yes. Kouchia. Odd, isn't it? But why is she Lavroche, and not Amance?"

"She told me her partner's a controlling bully."

"That's strange," he mused. "You're hardly her best friend."

"My thoughts exactly."

"I could look up birth certificates from the *préfecture* or the *mairie*."

"I reckon we've enough on at the moment."

*

Instead of turning on to the D10 to Lauzances, Delphine took a chance on a single-track lane that followed the stream along from the Pont d'Argent's northern side. The only sign indicated it ended at a property called *Les Chênes*, and a map on Aristide's BlackBerry showed it to be some eight kilometers away.

"Not sure about this," he said.

"It could give us a different view of the farm and we'd not be so conspicuous."

"Access?"

"Via the stream."

"You mean, wade through it? Not if it's been poisoned." He snapped the BlackBerry shut.

"Chicken."

His half-smile didn't last long, for despite poor visibility, the Lavroche's farm seemed abandoned, not a vehicle in sight. However, appearances could be deceptive, and it was possible those two thugs could still be there, rifling through the place. Even helping themselves to a late lunch. As for that disembowelled cow, was she still stranded in her own blood?

"Wait there," Aristide said, getting out and retrieving his binoculars from his cagoule pocket. "It's too quiet. Something's up." He kept adjusting the focus until Delphine suggested they get a move on. She was stressing about her forthcoming date.

"I'm not seeing Romain Vileneuf tonight," she finally admitted when Aristide returned to the car. "I know you think I should, but I don't quite trust him. And worse than that," she paused, "it could be a trap."

"I've tried to reassure you that I'd be lurking around."

90

"I know, and thanks, but I have to respect my instincts. Talking of which, we should try and get to the farm from the other side. This is a no-no."

"OK, boss."

"Then we try and find that 4X4."

*

The summer afternoon had seemed to fast-forward into autumn, with a blue-black sky reminding her of El Greco's '*Gethsemane.*' A huge reproduction of which had dominated her convent's dining hall, spoiling what should have been a welcome break from grim obeisance.

They negotiated the bridge, then puttered along the familiar, wet, narrow road where there was no-one else in sight. While Delphine drove past the towering chestnut grove to her right, her companion again checked his phone, scrolling back and forth until holding it up for a closer look.

"LVS. Got it. '*La Vie Sauvage*' website. About time someone paid it a visit."

Delphine bristled. She'd hardly been idle since her ordeal that morning and said so.

"I wasn't being personal." Aristide peered at his screen again. "Four men, yes, but where exactly *are* they? Could be anywhere."

Delphine couldn't look - the road was too narrow, and the grass on either side lay embedded in treacherous mud.

"Ah. More pix and titles. 'The grey wolf in its natural habitat,' so this one says," he continued. "'Where adults are trapped using the finest raw beef as bait, then re-located elsewhere, and cubs hand-reared.' *Jésus.* There must be at least fifty of them in this shot, all looking hungry."

They're not always hungry...

"Can you screenshot some images and store them?" she said, avoiding an enormous pothole she'd forgotten. "Especially of those *cons* involved."

"Good thinking. Except they're all in black from head from foot. Balaclavas, too. Youngish and fit."

"Damn."

"What?"

"Nothing. Just keep looking." She'd visualised fir trees. Huge ones. And rocks...

"Will do."

When he'd finished, he offered her a chewing gum - normal mint this time - which she gladly took.

"Can't find any contact details or means of getting in touch." He then glanced at her. "Can you believe it?"

"There must be something. Who designed the site?"

Aristide scrolled again, frowned then shook his head.

"No joy there, either." He tucked his BlackBerry in his jeans' pocket.

"Natalie Lavroche might help, even though she was scared stiff."

"Worth a try."

Delphine stopped the car and punched in the number.

"Dead." She glanced at Aristide before putting her own phone away. "So, what's going on?"

"Fuck knows."

"But we've got some clues. Her car had a Vosges number plate, and her partner's surname is the same as a village in the next department." The word 'Vosges' was like a black moth fluttering in her mind.

"Look. There it is!" said Aristide as the *Air du Vent* farm came into view. She braked, unsure where to park. They were too conspicuous, and the only possibility seemed an ancient ruin of some sort, lying further east, along the Ruiseau d'Argent.

"What are you staring at?" Aristide flipped his BlackBerry into action.

"Over there. See it?"

"Never noticed that from the other side," he muttered, fixed on his screen. "Might have been a religious retreat of some sort."

"Whatever. It'll do as a hiding place."

"Hang on," he said as he angled his smartphone's screen her way. "Look at these."

"I can't. We should reach it as soon as possible."

But her fellow traveller was on a roll, keen to compensate some more for his recent plagiarism. "I've just found more faces. In close up. Six in all."

"Great." Delphine switched her wipers to max, realising that architectural relic, made up of old tumbledown stones, could indeed have held a religious purpose. A twisted, metal cross lay askew of a half-demolished wall. Its ragged profile, bleak against the sky, reminding her of the one her father had erected at *Bellevue*.

Then she focused on the farm.

*

No... No...

Her hands suddenly slid from the steering wheel, causing the car to veer off into a rutted ditch made deeper by the rain.

"Damn!"

"What's going on?" Aristide craned forwards, but they were stuck fast, the engine too small to get them out of trouble. "Didn't you see the gulley?"

No answer.

"We'll just have to push," he said, baling out, while she stayed in her seat, numb with horror.

Is he blind?

What she'd just glimpsed was too vile for words, so that when she finally joined him outside, she actually turned his head towards the two broken enclosures where not a single cow or bull remained alive. Only scattered bones and horns. Half-chewed tails. A head or two. Grass no longer summer green, but smeared as red as a setting sun.

15

"Jesus wept." A trembling Aristide was taking more photos of the horrific scene in front of them. They'd managed to creep along the bank of the stream and both had frozen in shock.

"Hell is empty. All the devils are here." Delphine murmured to herself, glad of his arm around her shoulder.

"Who said that?"

"My mother. Well, Shakespeare's Caliban originally, but it's true."

He nodded, then said, "Why aren't you recording this as well? I mean, what more proof is needed of this total madness?"

"I daren't."

He faced her. "Meaning?"

"Zanowski wants to check the two photos I took earlier."

"That stinks." Aristide withdrew his arm, removed his chewing gum and dropped it down the nearest drain. "You don't have to hand *anything* over. They're yours. We're not in some police state yet."

"Really?" He'd obviously had a smoother ride than she at the *École*. And of course, helped get Jean-Marie Longeau named. "Poor beasts," she said for the third time, aware of a stench of wolf scats filled with bits of bone and skin rising from the ground nearby. "There must have been a whole pack of..."

"Sssh!"

And sure enough, in the damp, humid afternoon air came a horribly familiar sound from the north, where the land sloped upwards behind the *École*'s compound to more sparse grazing studded with rocky outcrops and

95

ridges. Wilder altogether, towards the Plâteau de Millevaches. Monday's destination.

Delphine pulled her cagoule tighter around her body.

"Better shift," Aristide said as he glanced back at her 2CV, its tyres bulked out by mud. "We're not safe."

"Just one thing," she pointed to that same discreet gateway she'd already used. "If you go into the yard that way, there's the smaller barn with electric meters. Can you check if the supply's been cut off, because if it has, someone must have deliberately disabled the fencing."

"But you said that those two wolves squeezing under the electric fence didn't seem to be affected by any current."

She pointed to where a sizeable hole still showed. "See how deep they'd already dug to get in?"

"Cunning bastards."

*

Aristide emerged a long four minutes later, his face notably paler.

"Power all off," he said. "So, what does that say?"

"Enough. Let's go."

"Lauzances? Like you said?"

"I've plenty of petrol."

When they reached the car, hidden by blueberry bushes gone wild, Delphine remembered something. "Did you notice any bits of a rifle strewn on that yard? Or three bullets?"

"No. I thought how clean it all looked. Almost too clean."

"Those two *cons* must have been thorough."

"Who?"

"The *connards* I walloped here this morning. They wore balaclavas too. The coward's gear of choice. And the *bleu de travail*..."

"You're kidding. What exactly happened?"

When she'd told him, he rolled his eyes to the still-gloomy sky. "You're lucky to be alive. My God, Delphine, have you some kind of death wish?"

My mother did…

Suddenly, the sun burst through the dense penumbra overhead. Delphine tore off her cagoule and bundled it under her arm.

"I just want to say again," she began, suppressing a moment's panic and climbing into her car, "whatever we discover next, I won't be seeing Vileneuf tonight. But thank you again for offering to be my chaperone." She waited as Aristide landed beside her, his weight as before, tilting the 2CV to the right. "I've another plan."

She started the engine and engaged first gear. The car inched away from their hiding place and picked up speed.

"Spill." He clicked in his seatbelt, which was stretched to within a centimetre of its life.

"There's someone my father got to know when he first moved here and felt in danger. She listened to him when he needed it. Unlike our Mikhail Zanoswski and 'the brute' who couldn't get rid of me quick enough when I mentioned those wolves I heard last night."

"I'm intrigued."

"A woman in a man's world," Delphine explained, careful not to reveal too much at this stage. "Someone I could trust. She helped arrange our enemy's move to La Santé in Paris. A place she'd vowed he'd never leave."

"She sounds pretty important."

"Too right."

*

The winding D978 road to Lauzances looked pretty enough in the

97

sunshine, but those charcoal-coloured clouds still loomed nearby. The only other traffic moving along not far from the Dordogne River was a horsebox, several mobile homes and a posse of lycra-clad cyclists who, judging by their wrinkles, were obviously retired.

Delphine kept to below the speed limit, giving Aristide the opportunity to look for any signs of a car having left the road, or of scorching. What both noticed however, was that for the first five kilometres, there were no exits into the densely wooded hills. Not even to a house, farm or other enterprise.

"So?" Aristide pulled down his little visor. "What now?"

"There must be some lay-bys. Somewhere for people to stop and have a pee," she said. "We keep going until we see one. This is hardly the Champs Élysées, so a car could be quickly burnt and either hidden or towed away. Yes, I know Vileneuf said he'd seen it with that left boot under the chassis, but he might be full of lies."

"Slow down," Aristide interrupted instead of commenting. "There's a level crossing ahead." Then, in readiness, he extracted his BlackBerry. "Are you thinking what I'm thinking? That a passing train out here would be like rain in the desert."

"Romain was right. It's a disused line. And you've just made my shitty day."

Aristide leant over and planted a hot, little kiss on her right cheek, then apologised.

Delphine laughed, and it sounded all wrong, but if the tricky Vileneuf was to be believed, here, at last, was hope.

*

Not for the first time did she wish her 2CV was either black or at least grey. Here, parked in an unkempt layby just before the tatty red and white level crossing barrier wedged back by nettles, it might just as well have sported a giant-sized Tricolore. But there was nowhere else, and Aristide was already striding along the side of the upwards-sloping single track railway, whose old, wooden sleepers were secured by rusted bolts.

At one point, he knelt down, but soon sprang up, rubbing his knees.

"What is it?" Delphine joined him, at the same time checking the occasional vehicle passing over the crossing below.

"Not sure, but there are signs of disturbance. I mean, see how the aggregate's been shifted. And here - look! Tyre tracks in the weeds."

Delphine guessed what was coming next. With him leading the way, they reached the edge of an almost vertical embankment to their right, and steadied each other while looking down on to a wide area of black, singed grass. Home to an equally blackened carcass of what could only have been a large 4X4, almost toppled from falling off the railway line, its rear wheels hung in mid-air like mechanical roadkill.

"Hey, look at this!"

Aristide stopped to stare beneath what would have been the driver's side, where a slightly singed brown leather boot for an adult's left foot was visible.

"Could be anyone's," she observed, taking care to use a paper towel from her pocket with which to hold it. "Almost everyone farms round here."

"You're right. But look inside at its raised heel."

"*Jésus.*"

"So why did Romain leave this behind? It doesn't make sense."

"Perhaps he'll tell you."

*

The silence surrounding them was choking, as was the lingering smell of death. But where were the bodies? Any other possessions? Impossible to tell, although the 4X4's rear section where Romain claimed there'd been two corpses, seemed empty. Plus, both number plates were missing.

This was no accident, and this realisation made Delphine's almost empty stomach suddenly revolt. There was nothing she could do except lay the boot down, lean over a forest of nearby nettles and let nature take its swift course. Once recovered, she wiped her mouth and apologised before asking Aristide to check for the chassis number.

"You'll be lucky."

Nevertheless, he duly bent this way and that, scouring every degraded portion of steel, until straightening, shaking his head.

"Nothing doing."

Delphine eyed the boot again and examined inside it, where several thick, grey woollen fibres, most probably from the wearer's sock, had adhered to the sole, particularly on that built-up heel where there'd been more pressure.

"What are you looking for?"

She told him how fibres from the wearer's sock might reveal vital DNA.

"Cool. So what next?"

She tried thinking logically, then suggested he take care of it, hide his number and phone her father. "Tell him what we've just found. He'll know what to do."

"OK." But the word 'father' had triggered a frown.

"And he's to let me know me when he's done it," Delphine went on.

He bit his lower lip. "I'm not sure."

"What are you saying?"

"Best coming from you. I mean, he doesn't know me."

"He knows *of* you." Delphine then sighed. "And you might have more clout."

"OK. I'll do it."

"Thanks. Here's his number."

"I've already…"

"What?"

"Nothing." He bit his lip again.

"And tell him about the farm, yes?"

"That too."

As they hurried back to her car, he tapped in François Rougier's number, and the very faintest 'ping' broke the thick, vegetative silence.

16

Until Delphine heard back from her father, there was nothing else to be done. She decided to lie low. But that didn't mean doing nothing, because she'd changed her mind about Romain Vileneuf. She'd become too paranoid. Too cynical. The wine growers' son had told the truth, hadn't he? If she was honest, he'd seemed genuine. Despite her earlier doubts, she'd be seeing him after all.

*

"I'll be in the sports hall chucking a ball around," Aristide said once they'd arrived back at the *École*. "To take my mind off things, at least for an hour or so. If you still need a chaperone for later, let me know."

"I will."

With the Caméo date drawing nearer, she watched him head for his room with that same boot tucked inside his leather jacket, claiming to have found a safe hiding place for it. An intriguing item, which, if part of a crime scene, had either been left by accident or to mislead. On the other hand, if a joint suicide, was it a deliberate or accidental souvenir?

As far as the *École* was concerned, their trip to Lauzances would be kept secret. If she was spotted out again with her helpful friend, it might be noticed. Besides, he'd done enough.

*

Delphine leant against her car, feeling the weight of obstruction and denial press ever harder on her will to pursue what she must. A way forward without jeopardising her hard-won place at the *École* seemed impossible.

All at once, her phone rang out. The perky hit, '*Un Monde Parfait*' all wrong.

Her father sounded tense, as if he was still in *Bellevue*. Not a good sign.

"Where are you?" he began.

"Back at the *École*. Did you get my message about…?"

"Yes," he butted in. "And there's more trouble. Seen the news?"

"No. Go on." A small posse of students from Compagnie 2 jogged by on their way to the running track.

"Local farmers with their tractors are occupying the Place Gambetta outside the *mairie*. Simone's just told me."

Delphine blinked. "Who's she?"

Pause.

"Simone Gallas," he explained. "The mayor. There's been another serious incident over near Seilhac. Fifty Charolais ewes ripped to bits."

Her heart began to burn. So, the lid was off. Suddenly, 19:00 hours snapped into her mind. The farmer's disruption could go on and on, and the Caméo just streets away from it.

"She's called for an emergency meeting with the police Crime Investigation Unit here, as well as the Préfet. He'll be pleased, just two months from retirement."

"You'd told her about the *Air du Vent* farm as well? Those poor, helpless cows; the two bullies, now this carnage?"

"Of course. It's atrocious. She was deeply shocked."

"Good, because there's nothing happening this end."

Delphine stared down between the dining hall and sports hall towards the Pont d'Argent, where the land beyond seemed weirdly normal, without the faintest hint of those two murderous wolves, who'd headed for the chestnut grove probably to touch base.

Fresh drops of rain met her forehead. She pulled up her cagoule hood and asked if he was still there.

"Course I am. Just jotting it all down. By the way, is that Aristide with you?"

"Not now. Why?"

He seemed caught off guard.

"No reason."

"I don't want him getting too involved. It's his big chance here."

"Yours too, remember?"

At least this time, he'd not referred to Aristide as a 'noir.'

"Meaning?"

"Step back, Delphine. Keep out of it. Have you forgotten the last time?"

"Course not."

Then, without warning, pent-up tears sprang into her eyes, mingling with the soft, sly rain.

*

"Just words," she told herself, dabbing her face dry with the end of her sleeve. But her father had known which buttons to press. As for her, she must find Romain before he set off into Saint-Arnoult. Or maybe he was already ensconced in the Caméo's bar, getting drunk. Being a cyclist, who took his mountain bike everywhere on the train, he was able to.

She called Aristide's number, but for some reason his BlackBerry was switched off, while Romain Vileneuf's made no response at all. Nor was his distinctive yellow bike in the cycle rack.

That didn't necessarily mean anything. His phone could have packed up, and he might have taken the bike to reach another part of campus. Then she noticed Émilie Bellefosse leaving the sports hall, red-faced and wet hair clinging to her cheeks.

Delphine ran towards her departing figure, her too-tight tracksuit showing every bump and lump of her wide body.

"Hi," she tapped her on the shoulder. "You don't happen to have seen Vileneuf anywhere?" Surnames were *de rigueur*, and one got used to using them. Anything else could risk giving the wrong impression.

"Don't talk to me about that shit-head. He tried nicking my phone, saying his had gone missing."

"When?" Yet Delphine was putting two and two together, given what he'd claimed to have seen. His phone might have been very useful to someone.

"Is that all you can say?" The disgruntled girl was about to move off, when Delphine blocked her way, risking a third shove of the day.

"Look, it's important."

"No idea. Anyway, try the showers. I saw his arse in there about forty minutes ago, and that was enough. Now, can I go?"

That attitude seemed to sum the place up. Not so much an air of rivalry and competitiveness - although that morning had exposed it in Aristide - but of detachment. This, to Delphine, who'd known friends like Pauline Fillol and fellow escapees from the convent school in Beaumont-sur-Sarthe after the Bac, was foreign. Here, it was everyone for themselves. Male and female. Even the final year contingent barely acknowledged her group of not-so-new recruits, and for a fleeting moment, she wondered how long she'd stick it. Her GIGN dream already fraying round the edges.

*

17:40 hrs.

Delphine smelled the shower gels and heard the laughter even before

105

reaching the shower block's sliding, metal doors. Once they'd opened, she was soon enveloped in thick, almost fetid air. She hesitated, glancing around. With no sports gear, she might be seen as some kind of weirdo.

"What d'you want?" Came a harsh male voice from her left. "You know where the fannies are…"

Fannies…

That did it.

"It's urgent," she snapped back. "Where's Romain Vileneuf? Compagnie 1?"

The voice, belonging to a big man in an orange all-in-one with a MAINTENANCE label on his chest, was caught by surpise. "Gone. Half an hour ago, and good riddance."

"Where?"

The charmer eyed her in the same way as Jean-Marie Longeau had done eighteen months ago when she'd turned up unannounced at his house in Cousteaux. "Fancy him, do you?" he sneered.

Be careful.

The sexist bully wasn't worth it, and despite her fury, she turned away and made for the exit.

*

Almost 18:00 hrs.

As she passed the visitors' lounge, Delphine heard strains of some pop concert on its TV, while various friends and relatives were beginning to leave. She stepped inside its large space, all-too aware of her dishevelled appearance, scanning it for any sign of the twenty-one-year-old. But no.

"Rougier?"

The gruff growl behind her caused several people to stare. She turned to see the brute, this time in body-clinging fatigues and sweat patches beneath each armpit. His padded-out face was even ruddier than before, yet still those miniature eyes lasered hers. She detected more than a whiff of *anisette* on his breath, which came in short, wheezy gasps.

"Sir?"

"Follow me."

"But sir, I'm looking for…"

"I wouldn't argue if I were you, Rougier. Not the way things are going, and your future here in the balance."

Non…

"Why? Lieutenant Colonel Zanoswki told me only this morning I was being recommended for a Merit badge."

The brute's former redness returned. Spittle nestled in each corner of his mouth. She felt sick all over again. "I said, follow me. And any further insubordination, I'll personally see to it that serious punishment will follow."

17

18:05 hrs.

During the convoluted walk to his office on the first floor of the administration block, Delphine, feeling unnerved and angry, kept a look out for Aristide.

Like her former, murdered boss at the *Hôtel les Palmiers*, silence was this bully's weapon, with no reason given as to why she'd been singled out. As they reached a steel, soundproofed door embellished by his name, rank and PRIVÉE, plus an intercom and spy hole, she felt a sudden urge to flee.

The sun had re-appeared with a vengeance, almost blinding her as he held the door open just enough for her to squeeze through, pointing towards his polished slate desk. She was tempted to pull down the delicately thin blinds to give herself some small advantage.

"Sit, Rougier," he grunted, lumbering over to his own black and chrome chair which sighed as he filled it. "This won't take long."

While he opened a drawer and pulled out a red, unnamed file, she noticed other details of this strange setting. To the left stood a glistening black leather sofa, too large for the room and bearing three grey cushions. To the right, a curved, slate-topped bar, home to a group of red wine bottles with expensive labels. Three were already opened, alongside various liqueurs and *apéros*. Crystal glasses too, she noticed, so no expense spared there. As for both framed photographs on his desk, one was an aerial view of the École during its construction, while the other, angled towards her, showed him, rifle in hand, with a black Alsatian dog close by. Aggression in its stance and expression.

'Wolf' came to mind.

Apart from Hitler, most dog lovers weren't bad people, but here was another exception, making no attempt to disguise it.

He opened the file.

"We are a highly-regarded establishment," he began, resting both rigid forefingers beneath his two chins. "For training, Rougier. *Not* operations. Not trespassing and interrogating those in positions of responsibility. Or impertinence and insubordination. Damaging our considerable reputation. Causing riots…"

"What?"

He pointed one of his fingers at her. The wide nail, unlike Zanowski's, bitten to the quick. "Aristide Abolego will also be cautioned. And may I add," he withdrew his finger and glanced down at the open file, "given both your - how shall I say - questionable backgrounds, your need of us is greater than ours of you."

Delphine sat back in her trendy chair, sensing a seismic charge through her whole body, bringing with it a primal sense of survival.

She wasn't going to survive here. Ever. Not with a bully like this chucking his bulk around, and Lieutenant Colonel Zanowski who, despite his earlier words of encouragement, had proved to be another snake in the grass. Unless he was just weak and easily influenced. Whatever, it was her turn to show she was no pushover, and that meant giving this lump of lard nothing else to go on except action.

She recalled her mother in her simple coffin. Covered over, invisible, because of what Patrick Gauffroi had done

"Go," she seemed to be telling her for the very first time since her death. "*Vite.*"

And she did. She climbed out of her chair to stand silent by the brushed steel door. Of course, only he could sanction its opening, and in the tense interim, playing his power games, he could be accused of holding her against her will. Even of making an improper suggestion…

As if by magic, that daunting barrier slid open, then sighed shut, releasing her from the blinding sunlight into the corridor where, to her astonishment, Aristide was waiting.

*

"Émilie Bellefosse saw you being summoned," he said, linking arms and striding in unison together away from that strange room and its threatening incumbent. "Said you looked scared."

Thanks, Émilie.

"Are you OK?" he asked.

"Never better."

He looked at her as if he'd misheard. But by then, they'd reached the administration block's ground floor and headed outside to where her beloved old 2CV glowed like an exotic jewel beneath the sun. At least outdoors didn't have ears.

"What now?" he said.

"You're next for a grilling. Fact." She then gave the attractive-looking building the 'finger.' "Good, *hein*?"

"Bastard. I'll show him. We've only been trying to get…"

"I know," she interrupted. "But don't waste your breath. Just tell him what he wants to hear. As for me…"

"Yes?"

"I'm off. As from now. I'm sorry."

He let go. Took a step back.

"You can't!"

"I can, and I have to. Please don't worry about me. I've somewhere to live and we'll keep in touch, but best hide your phone and get another one.

I mean it. As the late Lyndon Johnson said, 'better to be on the inside pissing out, than on the outside pissing in.' Which'll suit me fine."

His hug was huge and lasted at least a minute. When they separated, Delphine noticed his big, brown eyes were watering. She was profoundly touched, of course. Despite his stupid attempt at one-upmanship yesterday, he was a lovely guy, and deep down she knew that somehow they'd stay connected. However, inside her remained that same resolve that had driven her on during the lethal, dying embers of 2003.

This time, she was motherless. Her father widowed. They'd lost too much for no good reason. So had those poor cattle and other stock. Those who'd cared for them. As for Natalie Lavroche, wherever she was, she might well be an orphan.

"I'll be officially discharging myself," Delphine added. "Which I'm quite entitled to do, and they know that if they mess me about, their bullying will be out in the open."

Aristide wiped his eyes. "Are you totally sure about this?"

"I am, and hopefully - for your ears only - I'll be at Papa's house till I've sorted my next move. But I need to get the *Air du Vent* farm secured and that burnt-out car examined."

"What about that boot?"

Damn.

Her visit to the brute had made her forget.

"I'll wait here. Do you have an ordinary plastic bag you could put it in?" He asked.

A miserable nod.

"Fine." She glanced around to confirm that the operational CCTV cameras were near the entrance and exit, and nearest to the compound itself. "Not a whisper to anyone, OK?"

"What d'you think I am?"

"Amazing, actually." And instead of replying, he bounded away his cagoule flapping behind him and his still-wet hair glistening in the late sun.

*

Delphine waited on the far side of her car to check out the familiar landscape beyond the Pont d'Argent, and immediately felt her heartbeat quicken.

With her old binoculars in place, she saw a black saloon car leading two police cars, followed by an ambulance and finally, a large, slatted-sided animal transporter heading towards the *Air du Vent* farm.

If she'd not been waiting for Aristide, she'd have joined them. But with that specially-adapted left boot being such a potentially vital item, what was a few seconds? However, seconds became minutes. Ten in fact, with several visitors leaving the car park, giving her strange glances. She must look odd, she thought, growing aware that the silent line of vehicles had speeded up.

Come on...

Then she saw him. But where was the carrier bag? Maybe tucked away under his cagoule as before. But why was his head lowered? His run back towards her almost reluctant? He seemed defeated, and as he drew closer, she recognised fear.

*

"It's gone," he muttered. "Fuck whoever it was." He looked at her, and yet despite this reaction, she sensed he knew. "It took me at least a minute to find the right money for my Coke before coming back to you. So, it must have been snatched while..."

"Was it visible?"

Pause.

112

"Yeah. Had to put it down next to my leg."

"Those machines give change," she argued, keeping her tone even. "And their glass fronts reflect who's behind you. Didn't you notice anyone?"

She peered at him, recalling Patrick Gauffroi's duplicity. She couldn't help it, except that Aristide Abolego was surely no betrayer. Surely no killer.

"At least I came back to tell you."

Great.

"So, who was it?"

The Parisian glanced back at the sprawling campus, sparkling in the sun. Except she knew that behind those pristine walls lay nests which mustn't be disturbed. Lies to remain hidden, and this young *étudiant* had probably just signed up to it. Might even have been paid a handsome sum.

What about that burnt-out wreck? No point in making him sweat any more or wasting precious time. Once she was free, she'd make her own way, unencumbered. Aristide loped back the way he'd come, while beyond the unnatural whiteness of his temporary home, Delphine realised with a jolt, that the silent, solemn convoy of vehicles had disappeared from view.

18

18:40 hrs.

As she made her way back to her room to pack her few belongings, Delphine wondered again if Aristide Abolego hadn't become a full-blown turncoat. But with whom?

Just to think of it made her cram her pyjamas and other sale-bought items into her rucksack and small suitcase as quickly as possible. Her favourite hairbrush almost forgotten, as was the little diary kept since day one last September. But not her mother's post-war, tortoisehell comb still harbouring a few of her prematurely grey hairs. All that remained...

The switched-off Samsung went into her briefs, cold against the top of her right thigh. If anyone wanted it, they'd have to assault her first. As for those *ad hoc* weapon security searches which could pick up on it, the longer she stayed there, the bigger the risk.

A soap her father had given her lay almost finished on the tiny washbasin. Mauve and lavender-scented, it had represented a small, feminine luxury in a place where, just after a few months, feeling genderless had become almost natural. Indeed, she'd not so much as enjoyed a proper kiss. Perhaps tonight with Romain might have ended the drought.

Romain?

Could *he* have been the thief? If there'd even been one. But why hadn't he removed the boot from the wreckage in the first place?

She was just about to lock her door and return her key to reception, when a loud buzzer sounded overhead. Its din drowned out any comment that the surly Véronique Morel was about to make.

"All Compagnie 1 recruits are to assemble in the Main Lecture Hall by 19.30 hours prompt. I repeat, 19:30 hours prompt."

Something's up…

"I'll be back before then," Delphine lied. "My father's not very well."

"You don't normally leave your key."

"Always a first time," Delphine smiled, handing it over.

"I smell trouble." Morel glanced up, still holding it. "I've heard rumours."

Delphine took a punt. With nothing to lose, it was worth a try. "About Romain Vileneuf being missing?"

Those hard eyes met hers.

"How did you know?"

"Just a guess. He was supposed to meet up with me for a game of tennis and never showed up."

"When?"

Think…

"An hour ago. Seemed keen, too."

"You're not the only one saying that."

*

Delphine hurried away through the double exit doors, and once finally outside, drew in gulps of air. So, either her 'date' with him at the Caméo really had been a trap, with someone else there to meet her, or he'd waited too long and not made it back. Either way, this was bad news.

The loss of Aristide wasn't something she could brush away either. He might have been under huge pressure. Malevolent pressure, who knew? And who, if he'd not lied, possessed that item now? Zanoswki? Not such a crazy idea. After all, he'd wanted her two photographs. Probably still did. Or the brute? Even more likely. She must escape and contact people who mattered, and keep Colonel Serge Valon in the loop.

There wasn't time to fret over the abandonment of her dream of a well-paid job as a gendarme, or GIGN member, or more immediately, that trip to Millevaches on Monday. She had to run. She must stay in control and true to her sense of justice which, despite the traumas of eighteen months ago, had never left her.

No way could she have tagged on to that convoy to the *Air du Vent* farm. Her best move would be to put her father in the picture and find a room somewhere with an internet connection from which to operate. Involving him wasn't an option. As for any refund for her fees for the remaining month, she could just about reimburse him herself.

With her phone digging into her hip bone as she drove away from the car park, Delphine planned her first words. Yes, he'd be disappointed and would wonder what she'd do to survive. That she'd been as reckless and impulsive as a teenager on crack. But once knowing how the net had been tightening, surely the man who'd risked his own life to save hers, would see sense?

*

To arrive at his house whilst avoiding any other possible blockades, she'd made a detour of the town centre, but needn't have worried. A passer-by told her that most of the tractors and 4X4s had been forcibly moved on. Only mud and hose water remained, filling the drains.

When Delphine eventually arrived at 19:20 hrs, she noticed the white Mitsubishi had gone from its designated parking bay outside her father's house. His downstairs curtains partly drawn. She had a key and knew his alarm code, and before any neighbour could begin an interrogation, she let herself in.

The faint aroma of herbs and roast chicken meant at some point, he'd been cooking. However, she didn't linger on the two plates or wine glasses in the dishwasher even though one bore a distinct line of red lipstick near its rim. Instead, she picked up his landline phone in the hall.

*

If Colonel Valon, about to leave home in Labradelle for a charity event, was shocked by her news of quitting the École, he didn't show it.

"Are you sure this is what you want to do?"

"Yes. And I'm sorry to be letting you down, after all you did."

"I was glad to. You'd gone through enough."

Not for the first time did her eyes begin to sting, and Delphine found herself gripping the receiver as if without it, she'd unravel.

"Are you still there?" he asked.

"I am. And I know what the leaving procedure is, but it doesn't relate to why. Nowhere near…"

She heard his doorbell ring. Someone picking him up, maybe, because his voice quickened.

"You could say the course wasn't what you expected."

Delphine felt her cheeks begin to burn. Glad he couldn't see her.

"But that's not true."

"Sometimes it's the best way. Excuse me for a moment…"

Whoever had rung his doorbell was being invited in. A man called Philippe. She also heard Valon call his wife to welcome him in.

"But sir, I've been threatened," she tried not to raise her voice once the colonel re-focused. "Twice. Also pushed twice. How can I not mention that?"

Silence.

"I'd be grateful if you could find anything about a Lieutenant Colonel Mikhail Zanowski and Commander Alain de Soulibris, known there as 'the brute.'"

A hesitation, with Philippe, whoever he was, telling Valon they'd be late.

"Why?" said the colonel. "But be quick."

She was.

*

Having asked his visitor to wait a moment longer, Valon's tone became serious.

"It's unbelievable. Why their defensiveness? The first reaction to what you'd seen at the farm and near Lauzances should have been to liaise with colleagues in Sainte Arnoult, as well as the public prosecutor."

"Exactly. And now I suspect Aristide may be under pressure to co-operate and withhold possible evidence of a crime. As for Romain Vileneuf, who first discovered the wreck, his phone's been dead, his bike gone, and he's vanished too."

"I'll see what I can do. "

"Thank you." Then she mentioned Maurice Amance and his significance.

"Him as well? OK." Valon then added how farmers near Beaumont-sur-Sarthe, angered by losses to their livestock, had joined forces in shooting any foxes or stray dogs found nearby. "But with wolves, feelings run high. Especially with *La Vie Sauvage* being so determined with their rewilding mission. They're backed by some big players."

High places…

"Who?"

"Rumours, so one must be careful. But fortunately, wolves haven't yet been brought to our area. If they were, well… wars have started for less. And," he continued, "regarding your treatment at the *École*, make sure everything's written down in chronological order and leave a copy with two non-elderly people and a lawyer from outside the area. And a trusted member of your family or a friend."

Delphine frowned. There'd only been Pauline Fillol, whose young life had ended last August following a fall from a Euro Disney ride. "As for family, there's just my father."

Another pause, more loaded and longer than the first.

"What's the matter?" she asked.

"Just a whisper, that's all. Don't worry."

Delphine's hungry stomach tightened. She eyed the front door for any signs of François Rougier's return.

"About whom?"

"Your Papa."

"Is he in trouble? Something from the past? *His* past?"

"If I tell you, you must pretend to him that it's you yourself who are curious. I can't compromise my informant."

Delphine steadied herself on the staircase's slender newel post.

"Informant? What on earth's going on?"

Valon coughed. Paused a third time.

"He's tried to spring Patrick Gauufroi from jail. The man's been in solitary confinement for the past few months and on suicide watch since Fresnes."

Merde...

Although the room wasn't cold, it had just turned arctic.

"But why?"

"I'm sorry, Delphine, I really have to go. But meanwhile, be very vigilant, and I promise I'll be in touch."

19

20:00 hrs.

She peered through the drawn curtains to see dusk had fallen. *Le crépuscule.* A word she'd always loved, and normally a time for unwinding, looking back at the day's events. Even anticipating a nice evening ahead. But not for her, waiting for the idiotic François Rougier to return home. What the hell was he playing at? Did he want to risk both their lives too?

Colonel Valon's last drop of news overshadowed everything else, making her rigid with apprehension. She was numb to her planned check of the *mairie*'s electoral roll, an important call to a retired newspaper editor now an archivist, and the fact that the meeting for Compagnie 1 was in progress without her and she'd be noticed as missing.

Her phone.

Damn.

She'd forgotten it was still hidden in her briefs. It rang four times then cut out. Number withheld, which always left too many unwelcome possibilities. She hoped it hadn't been Aristide, because when she tried his number, he was 'unavailable' with no means of leaving a message. As for Romain Vileneuf, his was still suspiciously dead.

The longer she waited, the more she realised that Colonel Valon, being even more senior in the *Gendarmerie de France*, would hardly be enthusiastic about digging the dirt on two fellow senior officers - especially with a lucrative pension deal on offer when he retired. No, the more she dwelt on his responses, the more they'd merely been polite. However, as far as her father was concerned, she'd surely been entitled to more detail.

*

Delphine stared at the wall-mounted clock facing her. One of the few souvenirs from *Bellevue*. Its minute hand travelling round too fast within a chipped mahogany frame depicting various leaves.

Enough.

Having hidden her father's landline number, she dialled his mobile, only to hear a woman answering.

This could be anybody. A warning bell began to ring.

"Who's speaking?" She asked politely, just in case.

"Simone Gallas. Mayor of Saint-Arnoult. Is it urgent?"

Hello?

"You could say that. Is François Rougier there by any chance? It is important."

"He's driving along a tricky road right now. Can I take a message?" Her voice was more Parisian than local. Smart, efficient.

"Are you with him?"

Pause.

"That's our business, especially since you've so far not yet given me your name."

Our business?

"I'm his daughter, Delphine. I need to speak to him. Urgently."

Beyond the gap in the lounge curtains, a nearby street light flickered into life.

"Ah, Delphine," the mayor's tone immediately lightened. "I've heard quite a bit about you." Then an all-too familiar, gruff voice filled her ear.

"What on earth do you want? We're on a single track in the middle of bloody nowhere…"

We…

"Why so ratty? What's going on?"

If Colonel Valon's rumour was true, she already knew the answer. But no.

"Your friend called me."

"Pauline Fillol? She's dead."

"Don't be ridiculous. Abolego. And we've just seen that car he told us about. A burnt-out Isuzu Trooper. He also told me who's got that left boot. Does that make any sense? He wouldn't say any more."

My God.

"Who?"

"Commander Alain de Soulibris, no less."

Delphine heard Simone Gallas let out a cry of shock.

She felt more than sick. This was unreal. And when on earth could she mention Patrick Gauffroi?

"You still there?" demanded her father.

"Just about." Her mind was on fire. "So, he's the one who stole it?"

"Your friend had to hand it over. Or else."

Jésus...

"The boot could provide proof it belonged to Guy Lavroche. His left leg is shorter than the other, and this one has a specially raised insole above the heel. Did Aristide seem frightened?" Delphine prodded.

"That's an understatement."

"Terrified, more like," added his companion. "He needs protection."

"And I need you, Papa, to tell Lieutenant Colonel Zanowski that I can't go back to the *École*. My blood pressure's up and I'm self-harming. Will that do?"

"Am I hearing things?"

Simone Gallas was suggesting he calm down. Her voice stern; a woman clearly rattled.

"There's no way I can face him and the brute. Not after being bullied... So please..."

"Who is 'the brute'?" Gallas was sharp as a pin.

"The commander. A prize shit. We know that now."

Silence.

"Anything else to be mentioned?" Her father sounded quite different.

"No, François!" snapped the mayor. "That will get us nowhere."

Coming from a senior government official with a reputation for getting things done and apparently still investigating her late husband's death, this seemed odd. But Delphine wasn't finished...

Then came the dreaded click, just as she'd begun her last question. Another silence.

Fuck.

Anger and shame took hold. She'd sounded like a coward, when instead should have bulldozed him straight away about Colonel Valon's frightening rumour.

She pulled both curtains together and, having re-set the alarm, let herself out of the house. Her car was her giveaway, should anyone come looking, and it was only when she'd reached the end of his street that she noticed her space had been filled by a much larger car, black as night, whose dipped headlights swiftly cut out.

Perhaps someone had stopped to check directions or use a phone. Perhaps... There wasn't time to find out. She had to move, but where to? Suddenly, Delphine felt unnervingly alone. Yes, there was Jules Charbon, who'd helped her out in the Causses de Quercy, but Figeac was too far south, and his one favour her ration.

She had ninety euros in cash and a healthy Banque Populaire savings account, thanks to compensation from the Les Palmiers' group of hotels. Enough to support herself for at least another six months. So, the Mercure hotel on the small industrial estate outside Brive would do for the night, especially as its car park was at the rear. There'd also be a free internet connection and TV for the latest news. Then tomorrow, with or without her father and Simone Gallas' help, she'd have to plan her next moves, because if that so-called 'whisper' was true and her father's efforts had succeeded, she could be next on Patrick Gauffroi's list to die.

*

Giving a false name to the young male receptionist would be a short-sighted move which could impede her plans. Hopefully, anyone on her tail wouldn't see his computer screen, and he'd protect her privacy. However, she nonchalantly asked him to phone her room should anyone enquire.

"No problem," he answered in a funny accent, then explained he was from Brisbane on a training scheme with this commercial chain of French hotels. "Always fancied farming, though," he added, "but EU regulations are getting more complicated, and besides, it's a risky business. I mean, look what's happened here. Damned wolves, if you please. Just like the dingos back home. And why's nothing in the local paper?"

She agreed it was odd. "But perhaps the injured children's families aren't keen," and decided to leave it at that.

"By the way, the restaurant shuts at nine-thirty," the Aussie checked his watch. "As you can see, we're hardly chokker. But just wait once the Folk Festival gets under way."

Delphine couldn't imagine anything further removed from what else was happening in the outside world, and indeed, a glance at the trendily-furnished dining room showed only a middle-aged couple eating in the far corner. She guessed it was their grey Citroën Picasso in the car park. The kind of car to make an eighteen-year-old seem elderly.

Having thanked him, she was soon on the second floor - avoiding the lift, just in case - and five minutes later in the welcome shower, letting the past forty-eight hours sluice away from her shoulders. Despite a growing hunger, she had no urge to eat. In fact, the opposite, as a thread of nausea snaked through her body.

When would be the right moment to ask her father what in God's name he was up to? She needed him to get her out of the hole she'd dug herself, and in truth, wasn't she just as impulsive as he? Hadn't her dead mother said so often enough?

Hopefully Simone Gallas would help Aristide reclaim that boot and find Romain, as well as locate the puzzling Lavroche family. Rocking the boat wasn't an option, but perhaps she could manoeuvre around him like she'd done with the late Lieutenant Lise Confrère; killer and betrayer. But here mightn't be so easy.

*

With a half-empty bottle of Orangina in her hand and a towel knotted around her wet hair, she switched on the TV and began channel-hopping for any local news. Just as she was about to give up, an announcement flashed up on TV2 that Maître Gérard Massenet, father of Amélie who'd died during the wolf attack, would be seeking two million euros in damages from the *La Vie Sauvage* for 'our family's unbearable loss.'

Her fingers tightened around her drink as she then listened to how - as a lawyer - he'd found solid 'proof' of their guilt. His face was sharpened by pain. His words were softly spoken, while in the background, inside their comfortable home, his pale, brown-haired wife stared mutely at the camera, comforted by an older, greyer woman, presumably a grandmother.

Their number was still stored on her phone and immediately she tried it.

'No longer in service.' Was the automated reply.

Who could blame them?

*

20:20 hrs.

As Delphine rubbed her hair dry with a fluffy towel, she kept the TV on in case of further developments, because hour by hour this local horror was reaching a wider audience, highlighting a posse of deluded fanatics, two of whom could have killed her. Their close-up hatred scorched on her memory.

Whilst she waited for her Samsung to charge, she plotted a list of what to do next, beginning with Saint-Arnoult's electoral roll. Yes, she could ply the mayor about this tomorrow, but Delphine didn't know her and her allegiances well enough.

Not yet.

But just as she was deciding whether she'd have to visit the *mairie* or the *préfecture*, she found an unofficial link listed on *La France Privée* website. Despite a big red warning, she soon struck lucky.

*

In May 2002, the Pont d'Argent Commune had consisted of eight hearths, including the *Air du Vent* farm occupied by Guy and Élisabeth Lavroche, both then aged fifty-three. Also listed at that address was a Natalie Claire Lavroche, aged twenty-four, and Joel, her four-year-old son whose surname was recorded as Kouchia. So, where was he? Airbrushed off the scene? Obviously, because she'd neither mentioned him, nor had that unusual name survived in the hospital ledger.

Delphine resolved to check, already aware of an underlying xenophobia illustrated by a recent article in *Le Figaro*. A mayor of a small town in the

Charente, who'd allowed five hundred Somalian and Iraqui asylum seekers to be accommodated there, had been under police guard ever since, and suffered an aneurysm.

She also recalled Patrick Gauffroi and the Romanian encampment on his land, razed immediately after his trial. A Jekyll and Hyde character if ever there was, and just supposing...

Stop...

Although her room was warm, a sudden shiver lasted too long, before she jotted that census information in her small notebook, thinking how Natalie Lavroche must have either married Omar Kouchia or been willing to use his surname for Joel. Maybe to annoy her parents, for she'd hardly seemed an overly-loving daughter.

Next, Delphine searched for Maurice Amance, and discovered a twenty-eight-year-old living in that eponymous village. In fact, a small tribe of them, although a closer look also revealed a widowed Genéral Olivier Amance then aged 79, sole occupant of the *Château des Illuminations* further to the north.

Her pulse quickened.

So, had Joel's mother since taken up with Maurice Amance? Someone she was now patently scared of? So driven by the cause, that to risk young lives at a school was acceptable, as was destroying a prosperous farm and maybe even its owners? Yet if she was so scared, why had her Twingo carried an Haute-Saône number plate?

Delphine was about to jot down a few more notes when the sharp sound of a nearby door shutting made her jerk her eyes away from the TV screen. If the hotel was practically empty, then why the noise? It was a pity her room didn't overlook the rear car park so she could check it out.

She muttered to herself, closing down her Samsung and again sliding it down into her briefs. Next, using the room's phone, she dialled reception, and in little more than a whisper, asked the Australian who answered if anyone had checked in on her floor. He'd obviously been drinking.

"No, but a replacement security guard's been doing the rounds." His words slightly slurred. "So, no worries, right?"

"Who, exactly?"

"Sorry, mate. My other phone's ringing."

She couldn't hear it and didn't quite believe him, but with an important errand to run, it was best to check the corridor and see who might be there.

20

With the wind outside the hotel slapping the electric cables against its walls, Delphine sneaked a look along the thinly-carpeted passageway. Something about this place reminded her too much of the *Hôtel les Palmiers* near Le Mans where she'd made that terrible discovery in one of its bathrooms.

As she listened for the slightest clue of a stalker, her resolve grew to make one final journey that evening.

Go...

With her '*ne pas déranger*' sign in place outside her door, she crept away from room 116 and again, took the stairs rather than the claustrophobic lift.

"Just a reminder, the restaurant shuts in fifteen minutes," said the Aussi, surprised to see her. A half-empty glass of beer near his elbow. "If you're peckish, I can get something sorted."

She thanked him, adding, "Out of interest, could that security guard you mentioned have been on my floor ten minutes ago?"

He checked his computer. It seemed to take a century. "Sorry, bit of a mix-up," he said. "Gilles Ducroix's off sick. It was him I'd been thinking of."

"So, no clients up there either?"

Another look. More scrolling, again taking far too long.

"No."

*

The small, partly-lit car park immediately behind the hotel now contained three other cars, not including that Picasso she recognised from earlier. There was also a Honda motorbike. Delphine mentally logged these changes while letting herself into her luminous 2CV. All bore local number plates. As she was manoeuvring out of her parking space, she also noticed how half the hotel's blue, illuminated sign was missing, and how just two lights showed from behind two curtained windows on the first floor. Nothing unusual in that, she reassured herself, but lower down near the row of jumbo-sized *poubelles*, something moved. Then, in the next moment, one of the bins toppled over with a heavy thud. Its lid flapping open as it did so, spewing everything from food remains to general rubbish on to a wide area around it. Her bare hands froze around the flimsy steering wheel, and when she spotted four luminous eyes fixed in her direction, let out a shriek. Definitely not dogs. No way. The two wolves began to run towards her, howling and snarling. Marshalling their lean, furred strength to reach her car in a few springing leaps. Two grey-black ghosts whose pinkly-glistening jaws hung open, showing teeth embedded in red gums like so many pointed knife blades.

Boom… boom…

Their combined weight against the 2CV's rear doors made the little car rock from side to side. But no way was she going to be their next meal and, as she engaged third gear and surged away from the car park, she let out a scream of relief. Normally she'd have checked the car's wafer-thin bodywork for yet more bumps and scratches, but not there. Not then.

*

Where now?

She'd lost her bearings on the Corrèze plateau until spotting the winking lights of Saint-Arnoult to her left. Seeing an open petrol station ahead, she pulled in and called the hotel to warn of the dangerous intruders and the fallen bin which might attract more.

130

"You OK?" came the even more slurred voice of the Brisbane exile. "Must have been a helluva shock."

"It was. But best keep the outer doors and lower windows locked, just in case."

"And the police? Shall I…?"

"You're joking." But what really lay behind that put-down was she couldn't have the *flics* knowing she was booked in there. Selfish? Yes, but who wouldn't be, in her situation? "They're crap. Done nothing far."

"Thanks for letting me know, anyway, and there'll be a free brekkie tomorrow."

Having ended the call, she brought herself a white Toblerone and a chilled bottle of Coke, then told the cashier to watch out for wolves.

"About time my rifle had an airing," he said, appreciative of her warning and closing the till drawer with a bang. He went off to fetch it while she stood in the forecourt listening in the whining wind for the faintest sounds of the lurking enemy.

*

She waited for the cashier's return, needing to check the local telephone directory as to where that bereaved lawyer lived. The guy obliged, propping his rifle behind him as she began her search.

"Anyone I might know?" he queried, but despite his friendliness, he was still a stranger.

"It's OK," she said, soon realising that the distinctive surname was by no means unique. In fact, the Massenet column, all with different initials and addresses was like a vertical forest. She began with the letter A because Gérard might be a middle name and scrolled down to Y before suddenly recalling the newsreader's skim of the address. Not so much the sounds but the meaning. Particularly, *Abri*. Shelter…

There it was, half-way down.

"You look chuffed," observed the cashier, retrieving the directory. "Hope your date goes well."

But her smile never came.

*

She was going to be late. However, better late than never. The wind buffeted her car along the D1089 until the road dropped downwards and Saint-Arnoult's dominant, lit-up church came into view. She'd lost her faith the moment she'd left that Catholic convent school in Beaumont-sur-Sarthe where original sin, plus guilt and repression overload, had ruled her days. But just then, the church's glowing spire was suddenly reassuring. Beacon-like, adding to her sense of purpose. How in an evil world, she was doing something right.

Voilà.

The Avenue Louis X1 sloped upwards behind this incredible symbol of faith in a nation grown more secular. A street of substantial villas, set back in generous-sized plots which she imagined in daylight, would be full of the colours and scents of summer.

Beaulieu was no exception, complete with double, wrought-iron gates barring her way, until she spotted an intercom next to the unnamed post-box.

Serious money, she thought, except who'd want to be in this harrowing situation? Losing a child - especially an only child - must be unbearable. It was bad enough when the deranged Lieutenant Lise Confrère had tied up and run over Julie, the Rougiers' loyal, affectionate border collie.

Delphine wound down her window and pressed the intercom button.

Immediately, a male voice answered. Definitely edgy.

"Who is it?"

"Delphine Rougier. A first-year student at the *École de la Gendarmerie Nationale*. I've some important information. Are you Maître Gérard Massenet who was on TV2 earlier?"

A pause, during which a clutch of black-tongued cypresses vigorously licked the sky. Would this newly-bereaved father be interested enough to allow her in, she wondered, holding her breath.

"I am. And your information?"

"*La Vie Sauvage*, for a start. And what happened before and after your little girl was killed."

All at once, the ornate barriers sighed open, and before her respondent had a chance to change his mind, Delphine drove through and up the steep, gravel drive, probably designed to alert the homeowners to any visitors. Under the glare of three security lights, she parked on the considerable space in front of the pale green-painted villa, whose three Spanish-style arches sheltered a front door with a prominent camera, set between two half-shuttered windows.

As she parked between a black Lexus and a silver Jaguar convertible - both displaying local number plates - she became aware of the front door opening and the same man, still so vivid from his televised interview, walking towards her wearing the same dark suit and black tie. However, this time, a gun was pointing her way. A silver Glock semi-automatic, a weapon she'd been trained to use during the previous term.

Shit...

"Your ID?" he said, knocking on her car window. His well-proportioned face still taut with grief. A day's stubble darkening his chin. "And I'll need to take a photograph of you."

Delphine forced herself to stay calm as with a free hand, he withdrew a BlackBerry - identical to Aristide's - and in that surreally sharp light, snapped her twice. "I have to be very careful, you see," he explained when he'd finished. "We've suffered no end of *voyeurs* and others pestering. I'm sure you understand."

"Of course." Yet she still found that weapon unnerving.

"Good. It's just me and my Maman here now. Sadly, Caroline, my wife, had to be admitted to the St. Sauveur Clinic last night..."

"I'm so sorry."

Delphine locked her car, careful not to say too much at this stage. That news didn't surprise her. She herself had been close to jumping in the flooded River Sarthe after Julie died, but was Saint-Arnoult's only psychiatric clinic really the best place for a bereaved mother?

"So are we all," the lawyer beckoned towards the house. "And the sooner these maniacs are brought to justice, the better."

"What about the school's head teacher? Has he or she been supportive? There's been nothing at all about this incident in the local papers."

His sudden snort took her by surprise.

"We're not celebrities who need the media circus. We need privacy, and as for Jacques Delorient, if he's not careful, I'll be suing him as well as LVS. There wasn't a single staff member on duty yesterday afternoon once the gates had been opened. Last year, a known paedophile almost managed to entice a little boy into his car until a passer-by raised the alarm. No, Delorient couldn't give a damn, despite his smarmy words. It's what lies in the heart that matters."

"Coming from a head teacher, that's beyond odd."

The lawyer turned to her before leading the way up the four steps to the front door. "Really? Perhaps this will explain it. He was an enthusiastic member of FERAL while teaching in a school in Prades in the Pyrenees. And look what's happening there."

Delphine followed him into a gloomy hallway lit by a single table lamp next to an antique telephone, and a pile of papers whose various headings revealed a man on a mission, leaving no stone unturned.

"I can't ask you to stay," he said, "but I appreciate your coming here with whatever information you can share." He glanced at her expectantly, ignoring the figure of an elderly woman in black, hovering in silence further down the corridor. The same as Delphine had seen on TV. Two bunches of wrapped white roses clutched to her chest as she muttered about 'the work of the devil.'

"So, shall we begin?"

*

"You said you have proof that LVS are responsible," Delphine ventured once both accounts of the past two days had been exchanged. "Enough to demand two million euros compensation. But is anybody listening?"

"Somebody will be," he half-smiled while ushering her back towards the front door and handing her his business card. "But it's dangerous territory, even for me with all my connections." His gaze then drifted to a monochrome photograph of his pretty, Italian-looking wife holding hands with their equally pretty young daughter on a white beach. Somewhere exotic, judging by a palm tree's frond in the top left-hand corner. "Even worse for Caroline in hospital, which is why she too must be protected. And as for you, Mademoiselle, young and brave just as Amélie was while defending her school friends, be careful."

*

Ten minutes later, under that same startling glare of lights, with his precious card hidden deep inside her jean's back pocket, Delphine was reversing away from between the two luxury cars and rejoining the road past Saint-Arnoult's church. Her thoughts were tumbling around in her mind like washing in a machine. Gérard Massenet knew everybody. He had an opinion on everybody too, including Simone Gallas, whose late husband had regularly played golf with him.

"I'd trust her with my life," he'd admitted with sudden candour. "She's indomitable."

"And seeing my father," Delphine had added inwardly, with a tangible sense of foreboding. But it was the lawyer's hug, the choked-back tears and gratitude for what she'd delivered that stayed with her as she followed the route back towards Brive and the hotel. All the while watching for signs of those grey shadowy figures for whom darkness was a gift.

Damn.

Her phone suddenly broke her concentration, making her slow down so as to extract it, with some difficulty, from inside her briefs.

Not him. How dumb to think he'd be calling her back so soon.

Dilemma...

She recognised the number, but should she ignore it or respond? If so, was she really ready for what might come next?

21

It wasn't François Rougier calling either, but the concerned mayor herself, asking Delphine how she was, and where she'd planned to spend the night. Simone Gallas must have been ignorant of the outcome to their *École* visit, or if she'd known, was sparing her feelings. As for that stolen boot, Delphine still had to formulate a plan.

"I'm fine, thank you, and I've got a bed, so please tell Papa not to worry. However, I *am* worried about Aristide Abolego and Romain Vileneuf. Never mind the Lavroche family. Do you have any news?"

She could hear what sounded like her father returning to the car from wherever he'd been. Unusually, without saying a word.

"Look, Delphine," said Simone Gallas suddenly in a hurry. "It's getting late and we've so much to discuss. Why not come over to my house tomorrow morning, say ten o'clock? And in case you're wondering, I'm not a churchgoer, much as I ought to be."

Delphine was liking her more and more with each second that ticked away. She could see why the lawyer was part of her fan club.

"It's *La Bergerie*, next to the Parc Voltaire," the official added.

"I'll be there. Thank you again."

"Good. And by the way, please bring your phone and any of those surveillance notes you'd told your father about. I'll make copies, and to reassure you, I do have a bomb-proof safe. But," she laughed, "only the chosen few know that."

The chosen few?

Like the lawyer's reaction to her news, this lifted Delphine's spirits until recalling how flattering Lieutenant Lise Confrére had been. Someone she'd trusted.

Enough...

Surely her father, blessed with the biggest crap detector on the planet, wouldn't be spending time with anyone dodgy? And yet, to think of them together - yes, even in bed - brought a painful pang of loss for Irène Rougier, whose life was snatched away without a chance to fight back.

*

The *Hôtel Mercure's poubelle* had been righted and its scattered contents cleared away. However, Delphine didn't linger, and having parked her 2CV in the nearest space to the gate, ran full tilt towards the entrance, aware of her precious phone about to slip out of her briefs.

Merde...

Tomorrow, she must wear a tighter pair because that would be *chez Samsung* for the foreseeable future until her paranoia had loosened its grip.

In the lobby, she noticed Dan Fisher had been replaced by an even younger woman, whose vivid blonde hair was betrayed by a thin, dark parting almost dividing her head in two. Her muttered '*bonsoir*' whilst reading *Paris Match* once Delphine had flashed her room key in her direction was fine. It meant that there was no need for further conversation. More important was the TV upstairs.

*

When Delphine reached the second floor, she paused to listen for any other sounds, but perhaps not for long enough. Once inside room 116, she immediately pulled her phone free of its precarious position and switched on the TV.

She soon wished she hadn't.

After the metéo, a newsflash began with a close-up photograph of

Romain Vileneuf grinning from ear to ear, resplendent in the Toulouse Rugby team's strip. Younger, yes, but definitely the fellow student she knew.

Or known.

He'd been found yesterday evening at 19:00 hours by a local jogger, fully dressed and face down at the bottom of a small, natural lake near the Lippizaner stud farm just off the road to Pierrefort. There'd been distinct bruising around his throat, while patches of bare scalp also suggested a struggle.

"The body appeared to have been under water for approximately four hours, and so far, his bicycle and mobile phone remain missing."

Then came Commandant Alain de Soulibris, whose unusually tense porcine features seemed to fill the screen. Saliva lay trapped in the corners of his fleshy mouth as he expressed 'deep regret' at what could still prove to have been a tragic accident.

"Romain had been a valued and conscientious member of Compagnie 1," the brute went on, while in the background several other students Delphine recognised slowed down for their half second of fame in front of the camera.

She'd forgotten to breathe, and grabbed her less-than-chilled Coke for a long gulp to steady her nerves. So, what exactly had happened to Romain between his sighting in the showers and maybe setting off to meet her at the Caméo? Had he too heard about tractors blocking the town centre, and tried calling her to cancel? And what about his mobile and his yellow mountain bike. A gift from his father?

What of him or his mother? Not a whisper.

Delphine half-listened to other news-feeds, including more military deaths in Kabul, while she checked her curtains were closed tight and the little chain by her door lock was in place. She wondered if the Vileneufs had been muzzled because their only son had died knowing too many secrets. She also questioned how she'd sleep at all after what the day had brought. Not forgetting her brief meeting with Gérard Massenet, a man whom she knew in her bones, could become a pivotal influence in her new life outside the *École da la Gendarmerie Nationale*.

'It's what lies in the heart that matters,' lingered too long in her mind, replacing all the other conversations she'd had that day. Then she wondered how Aristide was faring. Would he be next?

22

Sunday 12th June. 09:30 hrs.

No breakfast. Delphine was far too pre-occupied, not only with Romain Vileneuf's horrible death and her forthcoming visit to *La Bergerie,* but also Colonel Valon's veiled 'whisper' about her father, to think of much else, including that stolen boot. With her hotel bill paid, she'd said goodbye to the sober Aussie once again at his post and left the building, watching out for those two wolves. Rewinding her memory as to exactly when she'd heard that door closing near her room, she asked herself why François Rougier wasn't answering his phone.

*

As for Simone Gallas, her imposing 19th century home lay at the end of a long, laurel-lined driveway, adjoining the full-blown beeches and oaks of the Parc Voltaire. The laurels' leaves shone a glossy green in the morning sunlight, complementing the house's pink- stuccoed façade. Host to eight tall windows - four to each storey - and topped by a northern-style Mansard roof of dark slate, with two gables jutting from between twin chimneys. To the right, near two discreetly-placed *poubelles,* stood a silver Renault Kangoo sporting a small flag bearing Saint-Arnoult's coat of arms on its roof.

Unlike the Massenet's *Beaulieu,* Delphine so far hadn't seen either an intercom or visible camera. So here was a well-known widow, whom Delphine guessed must be of a certain age, living alone next to a busy, public space as normally as possible.

But where on earth was François Rougier's large, white 4X4? She'd assumed he might have stayed the night here and was enjoying a late breakfast…

She checked her watch. 10:00 hours exactly. Perhaps his car was parked out of sight. But where? The two gaps on either side of *La Bergerie* were barely big enough for a bicycle.

Delphine waited a moment, glancing expectantly in her rear-view mirror, but nothing doing. Then she remembered her host hadn't actually said her father would be there. However, she had to know what, if anything, had transpired at the *École* yesterday evening. Had he even walked through its doors? With her?

All at once, her thoughts were interrupted by a short, slim woman, possibly in her mid-fifties, wearing a summery dress and white pumps, approaching from behind a large, flowering shrub. Secateurs in one hand and a long, straw basket in the other, half-filled with various cuttings of flowers and foliage. Her vivid - possibly dyed - red hair loosely pinned to the top of her head.

"*Bienvenue*," she smiled pretty little teeth while Delphine gathered her bag from her car's passenger seat. "Bang on time, and look," she glanced upwards. "The sun's come out especially."

They shook hands warmly. No varnish on those well-shaped nails, Delphine noticed, but on her wedding finger, an expensive-looking emerald and diamond engagement ring lay under a thick, pale gold band. Good skin, too, with hardly any wrinkles or age spots, save for around her sharp, blue eyes, telling a different story.

Here was someone who'd not only lost her husband in a tragic way, but had a very public, demanding career. Nevertheless, as Delphine had already gathered, she was doing a good job.

"Will my father be here?" She ventured, studying any reaction with interest. There came a flicker of anxiety, a slight tightening of that unpainted mouth.

"*Non*. He left me a message late last night. And perhaps I shouldn't tell you, but he didn't sound like his usual self at all."

*

"Is he in Saint-Arnoult?" Delphine chose her moment to ask in the immaculate, granite-slabbed kitchen, while Simone Gallas busied herself with the luxury-brand coffee machine which emitted a sudden squall of steam.

"What an odd question."

Not if you were me…

"I wish I knew," the mayor conceded, seeing her concern. "He always lets me know his whereabouts. We both do, just in case…"

Always?

That word spoke volumes.

"In case of what?"

The other woman finished clicking this and that switch before turning to face her. "Please sit down." She indicated a long, smoked-glass table surrounded by eight trendy, black leather chairs. At the far end, by the basket of cuttings, lay yet another BlackBerry. The same model as Aristide's and Gérard Massenet's, while closer to, was a copy of the day's *Le Figaro* together with a catalogue for a forthcoming exhibition of landscape paintings to be held at the *mairie*. The artist's name made Delphine start.

ÉLISABETH LAVROCHE.

"We live in tricky times," explained her host. "And of course, François and I are mindful of events involving you both in late 2003." She came over and rested a warm hand on Delphine's shoulder. "I am so sorry about your poor mother. You must be still hurting. I know he is, although he tries

143

hard to keep it hidden."

Delphine watched as she returned to the task of filling two porcelain mugs and adding more brown sugar lumps to a matching bowl. She wondered what was coming next.

"I like to think I'm giving him some stability," she continued. "A reason to keep going, because when I first met him quite by chance in the library last February, he was still in a bad way. A broken man."

"I know. But…"

"What?" Simone passed Delphine one of the hot mugs, the sugar bowl and tongs, then a plate of *petits fours* which normally would have lasted two seconds.

"Just a whisper. Perhaps something *I* shouldn't say…"

"Please, you must!" Her tone had tightened. Those sharp, blue eyes fixed on her expectantly.

"Last October, the man who shot my mother was transferred La Santé in Paris from Fresnes and put on suicide watch, then solitary confinement."

"So?" Simone sat next to her, ignoring her coffee. "Go on."

"My stupid father may be trying to free him."

The mayor immediately paled. Looked quite different. Suddenly older…

"Why, in the name of God?"

"To kill him. In revenge."

*

Immediately, this previously strong woman crumpled. Clasped the sides of her lowered head, moving it from side to side in disbelief.

"I'm sorry, Madame. I shouldn't have told you. It was supposed to be a secret, but to be honest, I was finding it harder and harder to keep hidden."

Simone Gallas finally looked up. Resolve suddenly restored in the way she picked up her mug and took a mouthful of black coffee, banging it down afterwards.

"So, I've picked an imbecile. *Merde*." She reached for her phone and punched in a number, assuring Delphine it was her father's landline. "Who told you?" She quizzed, waiting for a reply. "It would be useful to know."

Delphine hesitated. She couldn't betray any more of Colonel Valon's trust. Never. This was bad enough.

"You'll just have to believe me, Madame."

"Call me Simone, please." The woman then pressed her BlackBerry closer to her delicate ear. "Look, Delphine, I understand. You're loyal and empathic. You have principles. Therefore," she paused, still listening. "We can do business."

Business?

"Damn. There's no reply, and I can't leave a message, either."

"Thank you for trying, but I'm worried he could be a target. And me. Please call the police."

"Wait," she said, trying a different number.

"I saw a big black 4X4 parked in his space late last night," said Delphine. "The more I think about it, the more I'm suspicious. I'd never seen it there before."

Simone Gallas raised a hand. She'd got through to La Santé itself. Delphine was impressed she'd even had its number stored. Having introduced herself, the mayor then enquired if a Patrick Gauffroi was still at the prison. Could his cell be checked immediately, and the appropriate guard located?

The wait was torture. Simone Gallas paced back and forth, her attractive face set like stone. Her knuckles strained white through her skin, while Delphine found that merely looking at those delicate little biscuits arranged in a neat circle made her stomach heave.

Then came the reply.

Too indistinct for Delphine to hear, but just then, all thoughts of wolves and blood and Romain Vileneuf being dumped in that lake, dissolved. Her worst fear had just come true. But that wasn't to be the end of it.

*

"Since when?" barked the red-head to whoever had answered.

Another silence, while a blackbird with a wriggling worm trapped in its beak, settled on the windowsill to swallow it before flying off.

"Friday morning?" she repeated. "Two whole days ago? That's impossible." She eyed Delphine with a look of unnerving vulnerability. Of fear? "This is a killer in solitary confinement serving a full life sentence. I mean, someone like that doesn't just vanish. Do you have any more details?"

Pause.

"Only that the name François Rougier has come up."

No…

"How?"

No reply.

Simone Gallas shook her head, while Delphine clutched at her own churning stomach, wondering when and how her father had sneaked off to Paris. Her spreading pool of dread bore her back to the second floor of the *Hôtel Mercure*. No way had she imagined the sound of that nearby door closing…

Her host was speaking into the phone again. "I'm concerned for the safety of someone who knew Patrick Gauffroi before he went to Fresnes, and for that reason this criminal must not know who was responsible. I expect to be regularly updated. Understood?"

146

Another silence, after which she added her contact details, repeating them as if clearly unimpressed by the security there. Having ended the call, she sat next to Delphine and pulled the day's *Le Figaro* towards them both.

"If what else I've just heard is true, the media will have a feast, just like those dreadful wolves." She covered Delphine's hand with hers. "You must stay here for the duration. That's an order. We have seven bedrooms. You can take your pick."

"We? But I thought…"

The other woman blushed. That same hand like a clamp on hers. "I mean, *I*. You see, my late husband is never far away."

"Thank you, but I've a key to my father's place. My belongings are all there."

"Best not."

Delphine stared at her.

"What are you saying?"

Simone Gallas released her grip and looked away at nothing in particular. "You were right. I mean, about your father. His name came over loud and clear." Delphine kept staring at her while she continued. "He'll need to come clean immediately, which might sway Hervé Latrisant."

"Who is?"

"Don't you know? Our new examining magistrate, appointed by the public prosecutor to investigate the Lavroche case." She turned back to her listener. "Especially given the history and motivation, but," with those blue eyes beginning to moisten. "Where does that leave me?"

And me?

Delphine barely heard the question, thinking only of herself.

"How could I have stayed on at the *École* if he's to blame?"

"It's early days, but have you formally left? I mean, appeared before their Extenuating Circumstances Tribunal, for example? Explained your reasons for leaving and signed yourself out?"

Delphine's eyes widened. "You seem to know a lot about procedures there," she observed, still thinking about her father.

"Naturally. It's one of our major employers. A world-famous institution, envied by many... Look," she picked up a *petit four* then put it back. "I'll deal with your situation in a moment, because it needs serious thought. Meanwhile, as for my future, I'm due to retire in five years' time, and although I've no children and grandchildren to support, my pension will hardly be bountiful."

"But guaranteed until you die, surely?" Delphine was still dwelling on her father, and herself if she didn't find a decent job. Where a reference from the *École* wouldn't be needed. Where she might even have to change her name.

"Certainly," Simone blinked. "However, if I'm replaced for some reason, I'll be unemployable. *Une chômeuse.* After all I've done."

In that charged moment, Delphine realised what an idiotic, foolhardy man her father really was and, if proven guilty, at least three lives could be ruined. His, hers and the widow next to her, burrowing in her dress pocket before pulling out a small photograph of a kindly, dark-eyed man dressed in golfing clothes. His greying hair falling over the left side of his forehead.

"Julien. My soul-mate."

"He looks really nice," Delphine observed truthfully, with a big question hogging her mind.

"He was. But his death was no accident. And if it's the last thing I do, I'll find out what really happened."

"And if Patrick Gauffroi learns it really was my stupid father who set him free?"

Simone Gallas laid a protective hand on her arm. "Don't worry. He won't."

*

After several calls to various allies mired in the French bureaucracy, Simone Gallas then asked Delphine for her surveillance notes and her photos of the *Air du Vent* farm. "Just in case, you understand? One can never be too careful."

Delphine duly opened her bag for them, aware that in the heat, her half-eaten Toblerone had lost its triangularity. She then stood up and turned away to retrieve her phone.

"Did you actually go into the *École* last night?" she ventured, because that oddly abrupt ending of her phone call had left too much unsaid.

The smallest of pauses followed.

"No. But your father did. He'd insisted on going alone, and when he came out, I'd never seen such a temper. Rage, in fact."

Strange too, he'd not mentioned it.

Delphine could visualise the scene, yet also wondered why, with her influence, Simone Gallas hadn't accompanied him.

"Had he told them about me? Did he ask about that boot? Did they try to cover things up?"

A small flush appeared on each of her distinctive cheek bones.

"What do you think? Which is why I'm now on a mission. Apparently, your Lieutenant Colonel Zanowski and his commander ended up calling him an inveterate liar, and worst of all..."

"What?"

"A coward who'd known his wife's dangerous secret too long, who'd betrayed his *patrimoine*."

Delphine felt sick and dizzy. The sunlight was too fierce. The enormity of this injustice too great for her to remain sitting.

"But he didn't know anything about it! This is outrageous."

"Where are you going?" Simone also stood up, wary, undecided as to what to do or say next.

"*I've* got contacts too. And I'm going to use them. Whatever my father's done, he didn't deserve that slur."

"Be careful, now. The black tentacles go deep." The mayor stood by her and placed her arm around her quivering shoulders. "You and me, we have a common enemy, and watch this space, Delphine. Because make no mistake, I'll personally be finding out what happened to Guy and Élisabeth Lavroche." She pointed to the catalogue. "She was an artist whom Julien and I collected for years."

"Was?"

That delicate flush had deepened.

"Is, of course. And I'll find out what exactly happened to poor Romain Vileneuf." She stabbed at the catalogue's cover with a forefinger. "Saint-Arnoult has a dark enough history without these terrible events, especially with the tourist season getting under way. I'll be at the forefront, have no fear."

Her arm slipped from Delphine's shoulders. She'd never liked being touched by females, even on rare visits to the hairdressers. Not that she had a problem with lesbians. There were enough of them at the *École*. That was their business.

"And then there's your *copain*, Aristide," the mayor added, as if for good measure. "Your father said he was referred to as a '*marginal*.'" She waited for a reaction and Delphine obliged.

"That's so disgusting. Just because he comes from a poor *banlieu* in

Paris. He's kind. He's loyal. He saved my life on Friday afternoon. Who are these people? Threatening him like Romain probably was. And me..." Here she stopped.

"Well, like I said, I have friends in very high places. People with clean hands and good hearts, which, believe me, is rare."

High places...

That phrase kept repeating like heartburn.

"Do you happen to know Maître Gérard Massenet whose daughter was killed by those wolves at her school?" Delphine ventured as casually as she could, but detected no visible reaction.

"Top of my list, and should your father need a defence lawyer, he'd be the best. Now then, let's make haste and see what you've brought me."

23

"I'll deal with your situation in a moment, because it needs serious thought..." so the mayor had said, but when would that be? Delphine wondered as eleven o'clock came and went.

She'd accompanied Simone Gallas into her book-lined study overlooking the Parc Voltaire, where more photographs of her husband – framed, this time - and his various certificates from the Sorbonne, shared space with bookshelves of fiction and memoirs from around the world. Of more interest was proof of his achievements in the controversial world of ecology and herbicide use, where his papers, warning of their cancer-causing harm, were not only housed in every major university library, but also aimed at the French government and Brussels.

"He seemed truly passionate about this," Delphine observed.

"A remarkable legacy. I'm so proud. Now then, let's get cracking."

She swiftly transferred Delphine's photographs and notes on to her Apple Mac which took up most of an antique desk, and when all the contents of the Samsung had been printed out in colour, she then suggested for security reasons, they be deleted at the source.

"Phones get stolen," she reasoned. "And hacked."

"No. Never," Delphine objected. "They're back-up."

A flicker of disappointment spoilt Simone Gallas' fine eyes.

"Up to you, but don't say I didn't warn you."

She then bore the print-outs into a smaller, adjoining room where a white safe resembling a fridge lay discreetly beneath a shelf of legal dictionaries and tomes on every aspect of public life.

Shielding Delphine from view, she tapped in what sounded like a long code on a tiny keypad, and once the papers were installed alongside much more grand-looking documents, closed the heavy door and re-locked it.

"*Voilà.* That's step one," she smiled. "Step two – I need to speak to both chiefs of police in Brive and here. We have a good rapport, especially since Julien was killed."

Delphine felt cold, despite the morning sun's warmth filling the panelled space.

She wondered if his contentious line of research had been to blame. After all, when *Bellevue* was a working farm, her parents had been under pressure to spray this and that on their barley fields. And resisted, to their cost.

"It's time they checked out the *École*, leaving no stone unturned," said the older woman, "and before I make contact, please say you'll stay here until you're sorted out."

The latest look in her eyes hinted at a previously hidden loneliness, and Delphine made up her wavering mind. They could certainly achieve more together and might prevent her father lurching into more trouble. Also, and crucially, if Patrick Gauffroi *was* on the loose and heading her way, she wouldn't be on her own.

*

"What exactly did Lieutenant Colonel Zanowski and the brute say about *me*?" Delphine persisted as they headed towards her 2CV. "Did my father repeat anything to you?"

Simone Gallas stalled, frowning. "Remind me. Who is this so-called brute?"

"You know, that fat, smelly Commander Alain de what's-his-name? A prize pig if ever there was, and normally I like pigs."

"I see," Simone Gallas resumed walking, her frown still in place.

"Was their tone still threatening? Did they believe what my father told them? Did they slag me off? I have to know."

"He only saw Zanowski who kept trying to blacken your name, but François was proud of how he'd walked all over him. Said the *École* had been lucky to have had you there. Quite right, too. How the disappearance of vital evidence from a possible crime scene would trigger very serious consequences. Starting immediately."

"Meaning that left boot, of course?"

"I presume so."

"What a farce. Did my father mention how the brute took it off Aristide?"

The mayor's frown hardened. "I have no idea. You know what your father's like. I'm as fond of him as you are, but he has his secrets."

She waited until Delphine was in her car, then, with the driver's window open, added how two things had struck her. "Firstly, Guy Lavroche suffered a bad fall from his tractor last year. He'd fractured his left femur and after his operation, needed built-up insoles on all his left boots and shoes. So Élisabeth told me when she came here to hang her painting. I mean, what are the odds of a missing boot matching that particular one?"

"Huge."

"You're right. Secondly, as for that burnt-out Isuzu Trooper. I knew immediately it was theirs even though the rear seats were down. I've arranged for SAUR to test that stretch of water, and if they'd tried to kill the wolves, you can understand the motive."

"Probably their death sentence."

Simone Gallas flinched. "That's too terrible to contemplate." She then re-focused. "Before you go, how would you describe this Patrick

Gauffroi?"

"You mean physically?"

"And mentally."

"Why?"

"Don't worry now. I did keep a cutting at the time of his trial, but you've seen how crowded my study is. A most interesting case last year, and still unresolved."

"In what way?"

"Never mind." The widow patted the 2CV's hot, sloping bonnet almost affectionately. "Meanwhile, could you try and contact Natalie Lavroche? We need to know she and her son are safe. Worm your way in…"

"I did. Now her phone's dead."

Surprise was the wrong word.

"What has she said?"

Delphine stalled. "I'm sorry, it was private."

"I quite understand." Simone Gallas took a step back. "See you later," she smiled. "And if you fancy an *omelette aux herbes*, Julien's favourite…"

Delphine thanked her, but memory and instinct again warned her to keep a certain distance. Yes, a bed was fine. She was more than grateful for that. But it was also important to have her own space. Especially now, to follow things up her way and unearth those callous individuals behind the recent carnage. Besides, there was François Rougier out there somewhere, playing a seriously dangerous game.

"By the way," she added, setting her funny little gear stick into first. "I've been meaning to ask, why didn't you go with my father into the *École* yesterday evening? It was rather important…"

But Simone Gallas had already turned on her pretty little heels and was hurrying back towards *La Bergerie.*

*

There'd not been time for Delphine to check *Le Figaro* in the mayor's kitchen, and, having left that grand house with oddly mixed feelings, mindful of possibly being followed, she stopped near a kiosk in the busy main square to buy her own copy, as well as *La Campagne.*

Only that one hadn't sold out, and the recent, close-up photographs of Guy and Élisabeth Lavroche on its front page were shocking in their detail. The image of the torched 4X4 was officially identified as a brown Isuzu Trooper registered in January 2001 and purchased in the August by Guy Lavroche from a Brive dealership.

At last...

'The Lavroches had been seen pouring a suspicious-looking liquid into the Pont d'Argent stream, perhaps reacting to a perceived threat of grey wolves. Inspector Raymond Serra of Saint-Arnoult's Crime Investigation Unit feels their motive also relates to their wider family. He's keen to interview Delphine Rougier, aged 22, a witness and student at the *École de la Gendarmerie Nationale*, as well as Omar Kouchia, aged 32, ex-husband of their only daughter Natalie and father of their six-year-old son, Joel. The Harkis Algerian, already cautioned in February in Marseille after a drunken brawl, is believed to have worked locally. However, his current whereabouts are unknown.'

The chief reporter's name, Claude Ridal, and his email address lay beneath this main story which contained too many lies. And why had *La Campagne* waited so long to publish anything on the case? Why nothing about Friday's wolf attack on the primary school children? As for the graceless Inspector Serra who'd pushed her out of the commissariat, he could boil his head.

So, Natalie Lavroche *had* given birth to Joel before meeting Maurice Amance. And as for the word 'perceived,' was Claude Ridal another closet LVS supporter?

On impulse, she phoned *Beaulieu,* and the nameless grandmother who answered said her son was visiting his wife in her clinic, followed by another urgent commitment locally. Delphine wondered what that might be.

"I hope she's receiving good care," was said, with genuine feeling supplanting her disappointment.

"She is. And he was grateful for your information."

"Thank you."

"Have you any other message for him?

"Yes. Why is there no news in the local paper of what happened to Amélie and the others?"

Silence.

"I agree and suggested he contact them. But this loss has felled him."

"I can imagine, and I shouldn't have mentioned it. I'll leave you in peace."

"I doubt there'll be much of that, Mademoiselle. I'm Renée Massenet, by the way. My son often forgets to introduce me to strangers, but he's a good man. And talking of forgetfulness, I should have added with Amélie's post-mortem completed on Tuesday, her funeral is at the Église Saint Luc on Wednesday at 2p.m. I'm sure he'll be in touch before then."

*

More bells. Too loud, too long. Each twelve chimes from the dominant church and several others made Delphine's head spin, almost drowning the sound of her ringing phone.

An unfamiliar number, but not the voice.

Aristide was panting. His sentences urgent. He'd just visited the lake where Romain had been found and despite the police cordon, managed to take photos on his BlackBerry.

"I also noticed blobs of engine oil," he added. "Leading from that road to Pierrefort to the reeds."

"Did you get a sample?"

"Shit, no. But lots had been crushed as if something had been dragged through them to the water."

"My God…"

"I'm sending you that phone," he announced, still panting. "It's not safe here. Where are you staying? I'll post it after three o'clock. Christ, these long lunch breaks are a pain in the arse…"

Should she give *La Bergerie's* address?

Instead, she relayed her father's, then asked why he was so out of breath.

"Since the brute stole that boot, I've been followed, and this phone's been playing up all of a sudden. I told my mother first thing this morning but didn't want to worry her. Being here was my dream…"

Was?

"And?" Too many people were milling around. A convenient screen should Patrick Gauffroi be lurking nearby.

"She said to stick at it. Be an example to my sister and the other kids in that shit hole of a *banlieu* and not be so paranoid. But with Millevaches coming up tomorrow, fuck knows what could happen up there. It's wild as hell…"

Pause.

She'd never known him swear so much. This was bad.

"From where are you sending your phone?"

"Belvère. Just next to…"

"I know it, and will be there in person. People won't recognise us, and we need to catch up properly."

"You said I was amazing, but *you* are, Delphine. You escaped. Yeah, some *cons* are calling you 'chicken' but what the hell…"

Here the line broke up, leaving his sentence dangling, and too much unsaid. Delphine added his new number to her list, wondering if it really was bugged, and what she would say to him that wouldn't make things worse when she and Aristide next met.

With the midday sun at full strength overhead, and fifteen minutes of her parking time left, she had two important calls to make, starting with the Labradelle *gendarmerie*.

24

12:20 hrs.

Delphine refused to hide her number. She wanted Colonel Valon to see it. If he didn't answer and the usual answerphone facility wasn't available, she could assume he'd drawn a veil over her and her problems.

But no.

He picked up after just two rings, as if expecting her.

"You may already have heard," he began, without any formalities, "but I had to get my facts right. To make sure before I got back to you…"

"About my father again, isn't it? And yes, I've been told."

"Who by?"

"The Mayor of Saint-Arnoult, no less. Simone Gallas. She even phoned La Santé prison almost two hours ago."

Silence.

"Colonel Valon? Is everything alright?"

"Sorry, my mind was on slow for a moment. Didn't get home till the early hours…"

But why had the tiniest niggling seed of doubt planted itself in her mind?

"Apparently, Patrick Gauffroi gave his 'saviour' the slip at 09:00 hours this morning and was later spotted near the Gare de l'Est hailing a taxi."

"Who was this so-called 'saviour? Are you allowed to tell me?"

An uneasy pause followed.

"Mixed race. Possibly part-African. Mid-twenties, fit and tooled up."

Something wasn't right. Omar Kouchia had come to mind, but he was thirty-two. And Algerian.

"I'm sure my father doesn't know anyone like that."

160

"Fixers are easy to find. Some advertise on legitimate-looking sites, masquerading as potential partners for business, sex or whatever. They're everywhere, but if Gauffroi hears your father was behind it, he could be in trouble. Not just with the law. Whatever Gauffroi was told, he must know he was sprung to be killed, and can probably guess which enemy. You're François Rougier's only child, don't forget."

*

Delphine felt more than cold, with a numbness in her heart too, as she returned to open her car's windows and make the second phone call. However, when reaching the boot to check her possessions were still intact, she spotted what had been stuck on just below its lock. The shock made her lose her footing on the lumpy gravel.

Merde…

That same image of a snarling wolf's face she'd seen plastered all over the primary school's railings and at the hospital, stared her in the face before she got to her feet.

'Je suis roi…'

She scanned the surrounding square, almost seeing double the number of tourists and black-clad churchgoers mingling with dog walkers and various beggars trying to catch their eye. A gaggle of teenage girls passed by, laughing and joking; epitomising carefree years she'd never had.

Now this.

She glanced upwards but saw no sign of any surveillance camera. So, someone who'd followed her had gone undetected. Then she recalled that mysterious big, black car parked outside her father's house. Could it somehow be connected?

While trying to peel off the wretched sticker, she broke the tops off two fingernails and swore again. Not only had her car been defiled a second time, but that hideous image represented the cowardly enemy.

A half-empty can of anti-freeze loosened some of it, leaving the wolf's rabid, open jaw in a turquoise limbo.

Damn.

With five minutes left on her ticket and her Samsung's charge running low, she was in a foul mood. But so what? With any luck, she'd find out if chief reporter Claude Ridal was at his desk, despite this strange, unholy day of rest.

*

Having located *La Campagne's* phone number, Delphine asked its switchboard in Clermont-Ferrand if their chief reporter was available. If so, she told herself, he must quickly be put in the picture. And anonymously.

"I don't speak to strangers over the phone," began the wary guy. "Nor do I..."

"Not a stranger much longer," she interrupted. "So kindly tell me who's been leaning on you to cook up that crap about Natalie Lavroche's ex, who conveniently happens to be black, or your fabrication will bite you on the *derriére*. I know what I'm talking about, Monsieur Ridal, and secondly..."

The unbroken pause held several possibilities - she'd either be taken seriously, or she'd be seen as a nutter.

The first was correct.

"I'm making a note, hang on..."

"Secondly, why is there no news in *La Campagne* of the wolves' attack at the *école primaire* here in Saint Arnoult where young Amelie Massenet died and others were injured?"

Pause.

"When?"

"Friday."

"Where are you?"

"By the Maison de la Chasse in the Place Gambetta."

A haunting old building whose second floor featured a stone sculpture of a wounded wild boar driving a knife into its own heart. *'Le Suicide.'* Something she'd never noticed.

"Be with you in five minutes. I'm in town anyway, although my car's at Gimel-les-Cascades."

Think…

Don't lose him.

"OK. But I think I'm being followed. How about the Musée des Arts Paysans? It's open all day."

Another curiosity tucked away in the oldest part of the town.

"That's doable."

"How would I recognise you?"

"Think of Tintin. Or do you have a problem with that as well?"

She ignored the quip and gave her name.

"I can see why you're on edge," he said. "I would be too, with my mother killed like that, and a gruelling trial to follow."

He was full of surprises…

"That seems the least of it now," she said.

"I quite agree."

"See you there."

She then paid for an extra hour's parking, just in case.

*

Delphine wasn't sure about the Tintin bit, because Claude Ridal was more than tall and certainly older than the immortal cartoon character. Besides, he sported the full cycling regalia of black and green Lycra, with a giant-sized crash helmet slung over the handlebars of a blue racing bike.

His cropped brown hair bristled and glowed in the sunshine, capping a tanned, not unfriendly face enlivened by a pair of distinctive red ears.

Mid-thirties, thought Delphine, watching him lock up his machine in a free cycle rack, as if it belonged to royalty.

"I'll be taking her trialling on the Plateau de Millevaches next Saturday." He patted the impossibly narrow, lethal-looking saddle. "That should test us both."

She thought of Monday morning.

"My Compagnie from the *École da la Gendarmerie* will be there for a week beginning tomorrow," she said, stifling a pang of regret.

"Let's hope they're properly equipped."

He ushered her into the foyer leading to a large space filled with ancient farming and domestic implements, and gloomy daguerrotypes from the mid-nineteenth century.

"A dangerous place at the best of times," he added, paying for them both at the reception desk. "Especially with bloody wolves roaming around."

Bloody wolves?

"What?" That was a surprise from he who'd made Omar Kouchia an easy scapegoat. "Are you serious?"

Ridal almost crumpled against the nearest wall, peeling open his Lycra top. Her silence was the oxygen he seemed to need.

"Have you *any* idea what pressure I'm under? Have you?" He was so loud that several other visitors turned to stare. "For a start, there's Brigadier Alain de Soulibris from your *École Nationale de la...*"

"You mean 'the brute'?"

"Shit. How come you know that?"

"I've just bunked off from there after almost a year. Long story. I've been bullied too."

He stared at her, as if still composing his list of culprits, still using the wall as a prop.

"What about Zanowski, his sidekick?"

"You mean, pretty boy? Probably doing as he was told. But it's the top brass here and in Brive that want the re-wilding thing down-played. If the farmers hadn't protested yesterday, it would…"

"So, when will that primary school attack be reported?" Delphine interrupted. "Tomorrow? Tuesday? The day of Amélie Massenet's post-mortem, or Wednesday, when she's being buried?"

Ridal straightened.

"Not my fault. The parents don't want any publicity, and we need to maintain our circulation. End of."

Delphine could smell defeat a mile off. Courage came top of her agenda and this guy, with such a responsible job, just didn't cut it.

*

More summer visitors were arriving, snapping the exhibits and quizzing the curator, a grey-haired woman in her sixties. Just then, Delphine also noticed a grainy, monochrome daguerrotype of a familiar-looking farmstead in its still familiar pastoral surroundings.

"Do you recognise that?" she nudged Ridal, who still seemed unsettled. "The *Air du Vent* farm, no less."

He nodded.

"And over there are the Lavroches." She indicated a newer clutch of photographs nearby. Some bearing pin holes in each corner, curled and bleached by time and extremes of climate.

"They look young."

Indeed, they did, and Delphine felt herself pale as if to match those two figures' ghost-like forms, standing by that same archway on what must have been another sunny day. In front of them, a young girl of five or six. Natalie Lavroche, holding a doll in one hand and what seemed a very realistic toy gun in the other.

That detail, and the editor's unease at his predicament, made her take him into her confidence. Not about her father, as news of his recklessness obviously hadn't reached him. But about everything else, beginning with her Friday morning surveillance and ending with Genéral Olivier Amance, his elder son, Maurice and his partner's Haute-Saône registered car.

Twenty minutes later she had one last question.

"What's your opinion of the mayor here?"

The cyclist zipped up his two-tone top and frowned.

"Why?"

"Nothing, really."

She waited.

"Curate's egg, I suppose" he said finally, checking his elaborate watch. "As the Brits say. Look, best be going. News keeps flooding into my office like a neap tide. But," his frown returned. "Her husband's death *was* a huge shock. Shot in the heart by an unseen marksman while visiting a new vineyard near Peyrat."

"Marksman?"

"A word I prefer to use, even though it was the hunting season. Never been traced. She and Julien had been a class act for so long…"

"And?" Delphine wondering about the bad bits of this 'curate's egg.'

"Let's just say her moorings slipped a little after that. Some of her decisions didn't go down too well."

"Such as?"

"Has anyone said you ask too many questions?"

"All the time."

166

"OK." He led the way towards the exit. "Supporting the appointment of Jacques Delorient as head of the *École Primaire St.Bernard* for a start."

Silence.

"You're joking?"

"Ask her. No, better not."

"Do you have a card?" she asked.

He handed one over, containing his official and personal details.

"We'll keep in touch. This Lavroche case is going to be like Topsy. Growing and growing, and *entre nous*, Kouchia may be the witness we should be looking after, not vilifying."

"Stick to your guns, then."

"I can't." He looked like he meant it.

"Thank you for paying," she said, not realising that a gaunt-looking man of around her age wearing new denim gear had just emerged from the WC, keeping her in his sights.

25

'Growing and growing...'

The chief reporter's ominous prediction lodged in Delphine's mind as she checked her map before setting off for Belvère, battling with his hesitation over Simone Gallas and her own need to revisit the car's burnt skeleton to check its boot area again. Why? Because it was possible that Romain Vileneuf had over-egged the pudding by mentioning those two charred bodies he'd seen. Another possible nail in his coffin, especially after Compagnie 1's first lecture nine months ago had emphasised caution following any apparently significant discovery.

Yes, that was Lieutenant Colonel Mikhail Zanowski in his prime, with his eager new group grasping at his every word. Yet hadn't he, like Claude Ridal, given the impression of sitting on his hands? Of being not entirely autonomous, under control?

She glanced at her watch. There was an hour and a half to spare before meeting Aristide and, as a huge, shark-shaped cloud monetarily stole the sun, she resolved to follow her hunch. Meanwhile, the Amance name had also re-floated into her mind.

*

Having made sure she wasn't being ogled, Delphine pulled her phone from her crowded bag and typed the name Genéral Olivier Amance into its limited search engine. Apparently, he was a heavily-decorated veteran of the Algerian Civil War. His sixty-one-year-old wife had pre-deceased him in 2000, and of his three sons, the eldest, Charles, had died from a drug overdose the year before. Further scrolling down the Samsung's small screen delivered two more names that made her blink.

Maurice Amance was now the elder son and Paul the youngest. Co-founders with their father of *La Vie Sauvage,* whose proud aim was for the grey wolf to roam France unfettered.

Merci, Jésus.

Then another surprise. A photograph of the grey-haired genéral, this time accompanied by two youngish, dark-haired men Delphine immediately recognised, posing by an ornate, spurting fountain. All three had a hunting rifle propped against their legs, while each man proudly held up a sheep's carcass. Throats darkly gaping.

Sickos...

But at the same time as the sun re-appeared, so did her father's shocking theory about privately-owned farmland being commandeered for a shady purpose. Perhaps not so far-fetched after all? Again, no contact details were shown, and could that fountain belong to the *Château des Illuminations*? If so, another important clue.

*

In any normal car, she'd be on the speed limit to reach Lauzances, then arrive at Belvère by three. However, just then, her diminutive, third-hand wheels was all she had to rely on. The 2CV rarely let her down but, like everyone else, she had her limitations. However, as Jules Charbon had said before her nightmare in the Causses two winters ago, being rare, she'd doubled in value.

They were bound together through thick and thin. She wouldn't be pushing her to her limits past those same wooded hillsides in full leaf towards where that badly charred relic had lain.

Damn.

No 4X4, nor anything else.

While the mid-June sun bore down on her between lead-bellied clouds, she made sure she'd reached that same defunct level crossing, and if the foliage hadn't been so impenetrable, she'd have fought her way through it. But with what?

She also noticed how the aggregate between each of the old railway sleepers sloping above the former nest had been smoothed over.

Why?

Having slithered down that same scree slope where she and Aristide had first found the wreck, she wondered if they'd been hallucinating. Hardly, for there were plainly two sets of curved, muddy depressions leading towards the incline and hauled upwards. Any giveaway footprints raked over.

She added several photographs to her already stored collection; some in close-up to determine what might have been used to hoist the wreck away. A breakdown truck could certainly have reached the railway line, but what of the Lavroches? If it had indeed been their Isuzu Trooper, where were they? Had they been removed after Romain Vileneuf had first seen them, with that half-burnt boot unnoticed?

Suddenly, a stiff-winged hawk hovered overhead as she re-climbed the slope. It then dropped in height some ten metres away, before disappearing behind a clump of hawthorn. Then came another, beak wide open, and she knew theirs was a return journey. But for what? She dared not imagine.

Non…

*

A once-pregnant vixen, strewn about like some rubbish, lay in the lush, green grass while her unborn cub trailed away from the bloodied hollow of what had been her womb. A black mist of flies still busily feasted as both hawks suddenly and silently rose from the scene, each bearing a lump of red flesh apiece.

There was neither a breeze to shift the stink of death, nor anything else to distract her from the same horror she'd seen on Friday and Saturday. She listened keenly for any sound of nearby wolves, then, hearing nothing, began reciting the Paternoster. It was perfectly recited until reaching 'thy will be done,' when a small noise behind her made her stop and spin round.

"Who's there?"

No reply.

Instead, the unrecognisable figure of a thinly-built man in his late twenties dressed from head to toe in a stone-washed denim, slunk away from the rusted railway lines and into a substantial blackthorn bush. Its once white spring blossom become an ugly brown.

Jean-Marie Longeau?

No. It couldn't be. He'd been returned to Le Mans and was under surveillance.

Who else?

Another name stayed flickering even though she willed it to die.

Patrick Gauffroi? Merde…

Yet, if Colonel Valon was right, he could have reached here from Paris by various means, and this made her legs suddenly feel leaden. Just like that poor vixen, she could see her predators approach.

*

"Who's there?" she yelled again into the sullen heat. "Why are you hiding? Only cowards do that when…"

But before she'd finished, Patrick Gauffroi, almost skeletal, with that same nut-brown hair showing beneath his denim cap, stumbled into the brightness. She took too long to take in the sunken eyes and hollow cheeks. Prominent red weals around his neck. Then wished she hadn't. The once sturdy farmer, like a living ghost, was walking towards her. A killer jailbird on the run, now breathing her air…

"I only want to talk," he said, holding out a bare, scarred hand. Both side pockets of his jeans ominously bulging. Clearly tooled up, so all of a sudden, like her mother, she'd be a sitting duck. "And it's not what you're thinking."

She stepped back, having already plotted her escape.

"I've nothing to say to you," she replied, keeping an iron band on her emotions, ready to punch in 17 on her phone if need be. "Eighteen months ago, I trusted you, and what did you do? So just leave me alone or be banged up again in that stinking hole. Is that what you want, you *marginal*?"

His flecked, hazel eyes which had once showed her kindness and concern now seemed to belong to one of those hungry raptors still busy with their prey. He was half the weight from when she'd last seen him. Half the man altogether.

"I want you, Delphine. I always have…"

No…

She recalled Karolina Adamsky, the attractive Romanian widow who camped with her brave little daughter Roza near his farm. How he'd smelt of her perfume while visiting them both in hospital. How could she believe him now? She couldn't.

"As for your father," he added by way of explanation. "He gave me real hope."

"What the hell do you mean?" A knot of panic tightened in her chest. She picked up a substantial branch lying near her feet. Some defence at least.

"That you were waiting for me. How he'd forgiven me for my crime, and wanted us to enjoy some happiness before prison killed me…"

"What?"

"It's true."

Liar.

"You're making this up. Where is he?"

"No idea." His shrug not in the least flippant. Rather, of sadness. Tough, she told herself, raising her branch. Her nearby car seemingly on another planet. "We do need to talk. Please."

"No, we don't. You've been following me, and don't deny it. Were you by any chance in the *Hôtel Mercure* last night, on my corridor? If so, that was pretty sneaky. And how did you get there? Was yours that Honda motorbike?"

"Delphine, you don't understand… You're in danger. Big danger. I've seen the news."

"It's called stalking," she ignored him. "And I just want to get on with my life, or what you've so kindly left of it. If you prevent me from leaving here, I'll…"

"What?"

"Try me. And by the way…" She was about to boast how her target practice final grade had been 98.5%, when he began moving towards her, his right hand deep in his jeans' pocket.

Run…

She twisted away from him and careered past the recent slaughter until her 2CV came into view. Normally, while out training, she'd conserve her air, not snatch for breath, never having enough.

Damn…

Dizzy and weakening, she dropped the branch and managed to unlock her driver's door. Once inside, she re-locked it and revved away from Patrick Gauffroi's stumbling, yet purposeful form.

"*Merci, merci Dieu,*" she whispered, pushing the little car as fast as it would go, back towards Saint-Arnoult. She was more than furious at her father's duplicity - if indeed Gauffroi had told the truth - all the while aware of a large, familiar black 4X4 monopolising her rear-view mirror.

26

14:20 hrs.

Was it his? If so, how come?

But no time to wonder any more. She simply must escape. However, it was almost impossible to drive and concentrate at the same time, knowing that a killer, for whom she'd once harboured more than affectionate feelings, was on her tail.

She mustn't panic. He surely wasn't so stupid as to create a scene in public, but in her heart, couldn't begin to assess the strength of his rage at having been incarcerated in such a sewer as La Santé, only to be sprung on a no-hope dream. The more she stared at the Toyota's aggressive radiator grille and fish-eyed dipped headlights now switched on, the more she was convinced that very same car had been parked outside her father's house last night. But why? How had he acquired it and where else might he have followed her?

The surrounding wooded hills receded, giving way to pasture and infrequent, granite-built, single-storey dwellings, either abandoned or, in complete contrast, sparkling new. The kind her mother had always coveted, with a plot big enough for a washing line and a few chickens. Just like most of Oradour-sur-Glane had been before its destruction.

She daren't dwell on any of this, otherwise she'd do an emergency stop, bringing the killer into the back of the car. There must be a better way to lose him, so why hadn't she done it already?

Move…

Yet despite her efforts, the gap between them was closing, allowing her to see his expression. Earnest, focused. His denim cap pulled down to his eyebrows.

She had to act, and fast. Despite her car's limitations, at the next large roundabout she signed for places she'd never heard of, kept up her revs and circled it several times before scooting off down a single track road where a fingerpost for *La Jalousie B&B* soon caught her eye.

A risk, but one which a glance in all three mirrors told her had been worth taking. He and his aggressive-looking radiator grille had gone, caught up in the heavier traffic which had pushed its way between them. Delphine sighed relief and with the white-painted guest house beckoning invitingly on her left, she slipped through its open gates and parked facing the exit. Out of sight of the track.

For the next few minutes she tried to calm down, all the while keeping the engine running, just in case. But no. He'd obviously lost her trail and, in that small interlude, she dialled Colonel Serge Valon's number to update him.

"Are you quite sure it was Patrick Gaufffroi?" he asked, obviously munching a late lunch. "Think carefully."

"I am," before adding a description of him and his 4x4, plus its Parisian number plate. She explained how he may even have been hanging around last night in the *Hôtel Mercure* where she'd stayed and survived a wolf attack.

"OK." This was followed by the sound of a drawer slamming shut. Then another's voice interrupting things. "Take my advice, Delphine," he then added. "Are you listening?"

"Yes." As a sudden swarm of wasps hovered over her car bonnet before dispersing.

"Tell no-one else. Understood? Gauffroi's bound to have made the wrong kind of contacts while banged up in both prisons…"

"Not even my father, wherever he is?"

"*Especially* your father. And by the way, he was seen out and about yesterday."

Black tentacles…

Delphine's pulse seemed to stop as she expected that huge Toyota to loom up in front of her.

"When exactly? Where?"

"Early afternoon at the Jardin de Limousin Services outside Limoges. I'll never be officially assigned to this case, and if the public prosecutor there realises I'm interfering from another department, it'll be bad news all round. So, this stays *entre-nous,* OK?"

"OK."

But her first disobedient thought was to tell Simone Gallas. Yes, François Rougier had lied about his own daughter in the most devious, risky way, giving Gauffroi false hopes, only to have him probably killed. But he was still her father.

"If caught, what then?"

Silence.

"He knew what he was doing."

"And your informant? Who's he?"

"A she." He said.

The first name that came to Delphine's mind was pushed aside abruptly. Simone Gallas, a well-connected widow, in the know, was maybe not only her father's companion. This rationale reassured her, but not for long. If she *had* involved Colonel Valon, then why? He was nothing to do with the Corrèze. Perhaps later, having arrived at *La Bergerie* for supper, she could enquire.

She also had to update him about that missing Isuzu Trooper so a proper search could begin, but no way could she admit that Gauffroi had joined her once she'd realised it had gone.

"Useful information," he said straightaway. "And I'll pass it on without mentioning your name. Alright?"

"Thank you, sir."

"There are protocols. Remember what I said about the public prosecutor?"

"I do, but not sure if one's been appointed at this end. Although Simone Gallas did mention a Hervé Latrisant, examining magistrate. But please, colonel, he just might talk to you."

Valon sighed, after which she read out Ets. Fabien Guirros' number, adding how she'd found their card with the product name at the *Air du Vent* farm.

"Good. I'll let you know."

If only he could see her smile as she left the B&B's car park.

*

Still no sign of that black 4X4 as she negotiated a sharp turning and steep drop to the Corrèze River, where close to a generous curve of calm water lay Belvère, with its slender church spire rising above the cluster of pink-brown roofs. A picture of rural tranquillity, yet like Saint-Arnoult and elsewhere, hiding a dangerous menace.

She soon found the small, main square, where various stalls of produce and *vide-grenier* goods lined two sides of it. The smell of freshly-baked croissants and other treats reminded her she'd eaten nothing since breakfast. Beyond the various colourful canopies, she spotted the *Bureau de Poste* and, having parked in the nearest space to it, jogged over the busy street to wait for Aristide two doors down.

Sure enough, as the church bells struck three, she saw him about to step inside the plain-fronted building just as its security grille slid away to one side. He'd said he wouldn't be posting her phone, so why so keen to be the first in there? And he'd hardly looked around to see where she might be.

Delphine was about to follow him into the gloomy space beyond the door, when something solid tugged hard at her cagoule's sleeve, pulling her off the shallow step.

Shit…

"Move! Now," came a man's deep bark. "Look normal and not a single sound, or else."

Before she could protest or even see who it was, a black-gloved hand gripped the back of her neck, squeezing her carotids. His bad breath was laced with spirits, never mind the body odour.

Gauffroi?

No. He'd actually smelt clean.

Defence and survival sessions at the *École* hadn't prepared her for this attack, and all she could do was kick backwards and scream at the top of her voice. But what was the point? Loud music had just blared out from the public address system's tannoy overhead. The *Marche Militaire* blasted from the speakers, as her powerful, grunting assailant pulled her round to face him.

Merde.

The brute.

In all his disgusting, fleshy glory. Red with rage, his overfed body straining against his fatigues, especially in the crotch area. Delphine screamed again, but it was lost to the rowdy march which had reached a crescendo. She kicked again, this time at his groin, but misfired. Now with added impetus, he began dragging her towards a narrow passageway on the right. This time, his fibrous hands around her throat were too strong, her combat training disabled.

"Fight me, sly little cow, and you're dead meat," he snarled more bad breath. "So, let's just get on with it, *hein*?"

Dead meat?

"You won't get away with this. I've got friends," she gargled, before being manhandled into a large, muddy people carrier that smelt of dog, parked at the nearest end of the public car park. The sharp rip of parcel tape sealed her lips together, and a thick wad of material pulled tight around her head made her suddenly blind, but did nothing to soften the blow to the side of her head, bringing a thousand stars orbiting each other in a mad, hellish spin.

27

Where the hell was she? What was the time? Where was anybody?

Like a rock climber suddenly hitting *terra firma*, Delphine found herself on a tiled floor in a small, windowless room with lime-washed walls and not much else, except a throbbing headache and a fear that the brute might make a return trip.

Then, with a plunging despair she noticed her watch missing from her wrist and her precious bag, with everything important in it, was nowhere to be seen.

Bastard.

Think.

She sniffed, and the distinctive fishy smell of *bouillabaisse* ekeing in from somewhere, reminding her not only of *Bellevue* farm, but something else. Wasn't this particular soup the *École*'s regular Sunday evening offering to its hungry students?

Of course...

He'd brought her back to his comfort zone. How original was that?   But more importantly, why? Her muzzy head clawed at a horrible image of Romain Vileneuf begging for mercy. Was his grim fate to be hers too?

Despite feeling wrecked, she pressed a sore ear to the one door set halfway along the nearest wall. Similar to those she'd used while working at the *Hôtel les Palmiers* in a previous life, they separated bedrooms from storage areas, out of bounds to guests. The doors were usually made from MDF rather than solid wood, with a simple lock and key system. Certainly not fire-resistant or tamper- proof, and this gave her the seed of an idea.

Shhh...

Muffled voices suddenly reached her. Male or female, it was impossible to tell. Was the brigadier informing his puppet Zanowski as to the next step? Or something else entirely? Perhaps she'd be left here to rot. Out of sight, out of mind, with just a tiny washbasin and toilet. A crudely cut slab of foam for a bed.

As for her precious possessions, not only did her bag contain too much that connected her with the outside world, but closer to home, her missing father, Colonel Serge Valon and latterly, Claude Ridal. Plus, Gérard Massenet and her incriminating photos of where that burnt carcass of a car had been.

Shit.

Then she thought of Simone Gallas. What would her reaction be if she didn't show up for supper as agreed? Would she assume a change of plan, albeit a discourteous one with no apology? Or would she try and find out why? So many questions, when really this featureless white cube could soon be her last memory.

*

She then explored the pipework and fitments around the basin and WC for a detachable part to scrape with at the cheapskate door. However, first impressions were wrong. Everything in the weird little dump seemed solid. But she persevered and found that by turning off the water supply into the WC, she could then lift up the cistern lid and detach the handle. This, she realised too late, had a seriously sharp edge.

She sucked her bleeding thumb while unscrewing the part, and soon got to work on what separated her from what she suspected was either the brute's own bedroom or his office. Although, when she'd been in there earlier, she hadn't noticed another door. Never mind. This one was what mattered and, bit by bit, after sustained scraping, she reached its hollow interior.

The rest was easy. Another small hole in the opposite section of MDF was enough to see through to a large, walk-in wardrobe hung with men's clothes. All huge, from a morning suit to smoking jackets and various uniforms. Beyond these, it was hard to identify anything that might suggest a bedroom. Meanwhile, that *bouillabaisse* smell had strengthened.

Idiote…

Who *didn't* make that for a meal? Her mother for a start. So, her assumption about having been brought back to the *École* was crap. And in the brute's case, why risk fouling your own nest?

Think some more…

Within seconds, she had guessed a possible answer.

*

Delphine glanced around her windowless prison again. It could be high up or below ground, part of a cellar. Part of anything, in fact, but why the rudimentary WC and basin and that poky little bed? Was the smiley, hospitable Simone Gallas in the habit of holding trouble-makers prisoner in *La Bergerie?* Those who disrupted her enviably well-connected life? And did such connectivity also apply to the brute? If so, had he or the mayor brought her here? Maybe for a large sum of money to keep her out of the way.

A sudden, biting cold stung each nerve ending when she thought of the extraordinary trust she'd placed in the seemingly friendly woman. Letting her print off her phone's photos and the rest. But how close was she really to the brigadier? Hardly sex on legs. And how, if they *were* an item, was she managing him and François Rougier at the same time?

Not only was she in permanent danger from Gauffroi, her stalker, but

Alain de Soulibris, the biggest thug on the planet. And what would Aristide be thinking, having missed her in Belvère? Would he find her empty car and think the worst? If so, hopefully, he'd have raised the alarm.

*

That was her main hunch. The attractive, successful bureaucrat, whom Gérard Massenet had admitted he'd 'trust with my life,' was probably nothing more than a scheming Venus flytrap. Who, for whatever reason, had abused her position.

Bitch...

Delphine sucked again at her sore thumb while scouring every centimetre of wall for any more clues as to where she might be. Then her eyes alighted on the foam bed. Its strange depressions, perhaps where another's elbow or knee had been. However, there was something else...

Three, straight, light brown hairs of the same short length lay trapped where the foam's smooth surface had been corrupted - even bitten - who could say? She clicked her muggy brain into action. These specimens were definitely human, uniformly fine with almost black roots. If from a female, they could have been dyed a darker tone a few weeks before. If male, they suggested an outdoor life in plenty of sun. With the utmost care, she slotted them inside one of her bra cups.

The argument that wild guesswork rarely worked had been drummed into Compagnie 1 since last September, to subversive mutterings about freedom of thought and speech. But hadn't guesswork played a big part in solving the Seghers' crimes during the winter of 2003? And those of almost sixty years before that?

So, was it possible this strange, minimal space could also have been Romain Vileneuf's prison before his final trip to the lake, and that the souvenir of three hairs had been left deliberately? His straight hair had also been fine. Cut to the regulation length.

These thoughts brought another shudder. She had to somehow get out.

Having reached through the hole she'd made, her scraped left hand located the handle. A surprisingly generous affair with, thank Jesus and all His saints, a small key still in place.

How slack was that?

A desperate desire to reclaim her watch and bag with all it contained, drove her to break more skin. Endure the stinging pain of more blood being drawn, even risking a dislocated shoulder to turn that damned key just once.

Voilà.

Having finally pushed open the barrier to possible freedom, she smelt not more of that fishy *bouillabaise*, but something quite different. Dank, sour, slightly meaty.

She sniffed again, then through the gap between an outsize khaki greatcoat and a morning suit, saw two amber-coloured eyes level with her knees. Extra keen, on high alert just like those predators when she'd re-visited that fateful farm. Whatever it was, it stood close enough to cause trouble, but in an instant, she recognised that same black Alsatian from the photograph on the brute's desk, before an ominous growl was accompanied by movement towards her. A pink, wet tongue uncurling.

28

The sudden sound of church bells from somewhere, giving no clue as to the time, made the black Alsatian's ears prick up, distracting it for the few seconds Delphine needed. She seized one of the walking sticks which had a steel spike at the end and prod the creature away.

For a moment, she expected the snarling mass of black, bristling fur to go for her, but instead, the surprised coward slunk away whining.

And she still had the stick.

Having pushed her way through the outsize clothes, she took a rib-swelling breath before getting her bearings. Dog breath still lingered in the closed air of yet another windowless room.

Curiouser and curiouser…

The Alsatian had gone, but where or how she had no idea, until she spotted a double bed draped in a purple silk cover, with not a wrinkle in sight. Next to it, another door partly open.

*

Delphine's heartbeat was like a march, while fear became a taste in her mouth. What if that dog returned, bringing someone with it?

On impulse, she turned back to the wardrobe which she then realised took up most of the wall opposite the bed, reflected in its wide, glass panel. A glimpse of herself looking worse than rough made her start, but so what? She was alive, which was the main thing, and determined to keep her punishment there as brief as possible.

Jackets and trousers had pockets, didn't they? So, she must be quick and thorough. Working from left to right as she'd done at the *Air du Vent* farm, she reached the last of three coat hangers, home to a brushed cotton checked shirt and corduroy trousers. Her fingers touched a small card in their side pocket and withdrew it.

She held her breath. This was an invitation of some sort, and intact enough for her to recognise a small, black replica of that wolf's head she and Aristide has seen outside the primary school and the hospital, as well as what still stubbornly stuck to the boot of her car.

Jésus…

Commander Alain de Soulibris et Mme. Julien Gallas
***Le Château des Illuminations*, St.Loup-sur-Semouse. Haut-Saöne.**
Thursday 16th June 2005. From 19:00 hrs. onwards.
Genéral Olivier Amance, Croix de Guerre, cordially requests the pleasure
of your company to a reception and banquet to celebrate the success of the
first of *La Vie Sauvage* operations in the Corrèze. Evening attire.

RSVP.

She didn't have the time or a clear enough head to read the tiniest of print on the reverse. Instead, she secreted it inside her other bra cup. Whether the brute and Simone Gallas attended or not, what more evidence did she need of their duplicity? That two important figures of trust and responsibility - people she and others had relied upon - were the enemy no longer at the gate?

*

Once she'd recovered from the shock, Delphine found that the half-open door led into a kitchenette which, although small, was nevertheless on-trend with polished granite worktops, an expensive-looking tiled floor and huge wine rack half full of high-end wines and spirits. Just like in his study. However, a glance inside the dishwasher showed it was empty.

Again, all very discreet.

Never mind the luxury. There was a small window to her left, through which, in the dying light, she could make out the tops of sycamore and beech. The very same trees as in the neighbouring Parc Voltaire. This surely proved that this was, in fact, *La Bergerie?*

With her pulse once more in panic mode, the implications loomed large. This accommodation was seriously high up. Was she mad to consider exiting via that window? Had she totally lost it? And what about her belongings? Was she prepared to risk life and limb to get out at all costs without them?

Having inwardly asked her dead mother, who seemed to say *'oui,'* Delphine stared down at what awaited her.

*

She pushed open the wooden-framed window in to the drizzle. No PVC or double-glazing up here, which, although odd, served her purpose. However, the steep slope down the shining mansard roof towards the gutter meant two bad things. She'd be in full view at the front, with a long drop to the ground which would probably kill her or see her in a wheelchair for the rest of her life, like her poor, brave friend, Pauline Fillol.

Nevertheless, her options were limited. No way could she risk entering the rest of the house via the normal route of stairs or even a possible lift. She simply had to trust her fitness and her resolve to get justice not only for the missing Lavroches, but also little Amélie Massenet needlessly killed for a warped zealotry. Also, Romain Vileneuf whose distraught parents were sure to be making their way north.

*

Damn the drizzle.

She'd not banked on this particular obstacle and, forgetting all her convent's rules on blasphemy, swore again at heartless God who'd set it up, and the slate roof tiles issuing their darkly glistening challenge.

In a moment of panic, she eyed that half-open door.

Don't.

Delphine wiped her prints off the useful stick and reluctantly returned it to the wardrobe. It had probably saved her life, but where she was going, it would be a hindrance not a help.

Then, without hesitation, she clambered on to the draining board and out into the wet evening. Clinging to the window frame, she paused to listen, observing before making her next move. The muffled view of other dark rooftops and the church of Saint-Arnoult's looming spire would have been welcome sights to any tourist, but from her precarious position, they reinforced how high up she was.

Frighteningly high up.

Impossible.

Way below, she spotted a black shadow snaking in and out between the trees and bushes which bordered the nearest edge of lawn. That same dog on some scent or other, probably hers from earlier in the day, letting out a succession of barks, occasionally looking upwards.

Non...

It surely wouldn't be long before someone would come looking. The fragrant Simone Gallas, no less. Or her overweight, influential '*copain*' who could even be her lover...

That's enough.

Delphine manoeuvred herself on to all fours, bum in the air as both hands and trainers kept contact with those treacherous tiles. Having reassured herself that the gutter seemed substantial enough to take her weight should she slip, she inched her way down towards the end of it, nearest the park.

It did.

She'd not slid far, but enough for her to cry out at the suddenness of it. That sturdy-looking barrier didn't seem so sturdy after all. However, it took the weight of her left trainer, but when her right one became wedged among the accretion of black, sodden leaves, bird bones and other debris, she felt it judder, then crack.

Fuck...

In those next few seconds, the rest of her life contracted into a blur of air and horror, with all that fine architecture sliding by, ending mercifully on a soft, grassy area in front of a newly-arrived reception party. But not the one she was expecting.

*

Through her dazed disorientation and crippling pain in both her feet, she realised who was there. Her father for a start, calling out, trying to reach her, asking if she was alright. His casual clothes crumpled. The lower part of his face lightened by grey stubble. But these surprises were nothing compared to what made her stare as if at a stranger. He was handcuffed to two police officers, both half his age, immaculate in their navy-blue strip and obviously new haircuts. Behind them, stood a large, black van; its roof lights the only bright thing in the dreary evening light.

There was no sign of the dog. Nor of the mayor and the brute.

"Papa?" She struggled over the gravel drive towards him, only to be held in check by another uniform whom she recognised immediately as Lieutenant Colonel Zanowski. He of the white hair and even pinker complexion leaned in towards her, whispering an apology. Saving his skin, no doubt.

"I have already explained your situation to the GN in Paris," he added, sheepishly. "And the public prosecutor in Brive, so there'll be no repercussions on you."

"How kind." She dismissed him, instead making eye contact with François Rougier, who was still fighting his restraints. "But I *will* be making a complaint about my treatment at the *École*."

"That is absolutely your right."

"And what about your esteemed commander? Has he scuttled off somewhere with Simone Gallas? It wouldn't surprise me." Dizzy and beyond angry, she didn't care what she said or what he thought. It was time to fight back. "I want my bag and my watch. *Now!*"

"You'll have them in a moment. We're doing our best…"

"We?" Delphine challenged, feeling the persistent drizzle invading the collar of her cagoule. "Where are the criminals who stole them? Has Gallas's safe been checked?"

That caught him off guard.

"What safe?"

She let out a groan of frustration.

"Am I hearing things? It's in a small room off her study. She scanned all my pictures off my phone, then photocopied them, the sly cow."

He immediately muttered something into his mobile. The word '*coffre-fort*' being the most audible. "And you must have a safe house," he said afterwards. "Which I will personally organise."

"*You* could have kept me safe, you hypocrite. And what about Romain Vileneuf? Have you been covering up his death too? Just like with the Lavroches?" She stared at him, willing her feet to keep supporting her, suddenly seeing this tall, military man begin to crumble.

Before he could reply, François Rougier shouted out again, while fighting his handlers with even more determination. "Delphine! Come here! Let me check you're not injured."

She hesitated. She'd not yet finished with the Lieutenant Colonel, but the police holding her father were trying to force him back to their van. With a huge effort, she reached him in time. This was no dream. It was an ongoing nightmare.

He looked even more dreadful in close-up, his dry lips quivering as he spoke.

"I have to tell you that when I was in Alain de Saloubris's office I saw him hide a photo of Simone Gallas. I knew then what a double-crosser she was. And him. But how to tell you, given my situation? That was why I became more suspicious. I'm sorry. And, for getting that murdering Gauffroi out with a sick lie."

He stared at her in such a way that, because she couldn't hug him, let alone touch him, she too turned aside to witness that simpering, muzzled black dog being forced into a cage which was carried towards a smaller van half-hidden by bushes.

"Move, Monsieur!" snapped one of her father's cling-ons. "You've had long enough."

But he stood his ground, not finished either. "Those two crooks have been taken to Brive, off their home turf. And there's something else you should know." The way he said it made her face him again, edging closer.

"Private," he snarled back at his keepers. "So, show me some respect." He then leant forwards so she could feel his stale breath on her cheek. "That boot," he began, barely moving his lips. "I've got it."

What?

"From ...?"

A nod, meaning the brigadier's office.

Mère Marie...

"Safe in my bed," he breathed, and that was it, before being hauled away, leaving her mouthing the word 'invitation' behind him.

*

Delphine could only stare after the departing van and, despite fighting exhaustion and fear, at least knew where she'd be spending the night, especially since that *omelette aux herbes* and a normal bed at *La Bergerie* was now off the menu. But what about him? Would he be kept in a cell until morning, or… or…?

Her thoughts were interrupted by seeing Lieutenant Colonel Zanowski being escorted to an unmarked car, just as a plain white van appeared at the gateway and pulled up by the front door. A burly guy in a *bleu de travail* was hurriedly led into the house by a female officer carrying a briefcase.

Delphine wondered if he was a safe-breaker and didn't have to wait long for the answer. Detective Geneviève Patry returned to accompany her back indoors to the kitchen and sat her down in the same chair she'd occupied yesterday morning. Although *Le Figaro* and the Élisabeth Lavroche exhibition catalogue still lay on the table, it was the large *Le Creuset* crock full of cold *bouillabaisse* on the cooker which attracted Delphine's attention. Still emitting a hint of that same smell as before. She'd not imagined it, after all…

However, as the dishwasher's half-open door showed it to be empty, no-one had eaten, unless everything had been washed up by hand.

Patry sniffed the air and checked the crock's lid was on tight, before boiling a kettle and making Delphine a welcome mug of Nescoré.

She then opened her briefcase and extracted the missing bag and watch for her to inspect. "I've tested these for prints," she said. "And if you're agreeable, we'd also like to keep those photocopies Madame Gallas made. They could be useful."

"Fine." But those three hairs and that invitation still tucked away in her bra weren't for sharing. At least, not yet.

Patry seemed nice, normal and above all, efficient. Once Delphine had drunk her chicory-flavoured coffee and signed her own statement, which denied any collusion with her father, she led the way up to the top of the house where that prison had been.

*

"You've been extremely brave," Patry said to her afterwards on their way down, occasionally holding out a helping hand on the narrow stairs. "Are you sure you wouldn't like a police guard for a week or so?"

"I'll be fine, thanks."

"Or a check-up, just in case?"

Delphine shook her head. Suddenly, she felt like one of those sycamore saplings she'd watched grow at *Bellevue* over the years. Spindly, vulnerable specimens at first, defying the wild, scouring winds, to grow and strengthen, providing valuable shade and shelter.

"Call me at any time if you feel uneasy or frightened." Patry then handed her a small, laminated card. "I mean it."

"I will." But after 2003 - especially the deadly Lieutenant Lise Confrère - Delphine knew however 'nice' anyone might seem, she wouldn't be in a hurry to take their word. That sinister invitation to the *Château des Illuminations* and those three hairs would, for the time being, remain her secrets.

29

Monday 13th June. 07:00 hrs.

She'd slipped from the roof of a large house. Seen her only living relative taken away in handcuffs and most of the new world she'd dreamt of for so long, collapse. No wonder she'd barely slept in her father's bed alongside the *Carrefour* carrier bag bulked out by what had to be Guy Lavroche's left boot.

Even the substantial armchair shoved against the bedroom door hadn't added a shred of security; the house's sturdy, granite fabric had seemed no more than paper. Despite her brief, inner resilience before leaving *La Bergerie*, Delphine hadn't dared switch on a light to visit the WC. Even an emergency candle flame could have shown through the curtains, front and back. Unlike *Bellevue* and its isolating hectares, her father's new house was distinctly urban, with a small terrace at the rear, ending in a climbable wall separating it from a public path to the Place Gambetta.

An added insecurity but, having swallowed two UPSAS tablets with some warm, leftover Cola, she carefully extracted Général Olivier Amance's invitation and those three hairs from inside her bra, then folded both separately inside two separate pieces of toilet paper from the en suite bathroom. She laid them temporarily on his bedside table next to a framed sepia photograph of her mother aged five, and a well-thumbed library book on the massacre of Tulle. Its cover was a photo of one of the ninety men hanged by the Gestapo, a young man dangling from a lamp post.

Next, she crammed her moss-stained clothes and trainers from yesterday into the bottom of his wardrobe, then showered and dressed in clean jeans, a grey tee-shirt and new Nikes she'd planned to save for the holidays. With the two small packages in one hand and the supermarket bag in the other, she climbed the stairs to the second floor. Here, in an unused spare bedroom, dawn's pale light from the window overhead enabled her to fully examine what could solve the identity and fate of its owner.

She placed her two small packages on the single bed's bare mattress and sat alongside them to check out the boot in greater detail than she had near Lauzances. On closer inspection, the leather and polymer mix, designed for looks and durability, was mostly singed to black, softened into hollows, making any possible fingerprints unreliable. However, careful to add none of her own, she explored the sole composed of a slightly worn diagonal pattern under the main part of the foot, and a horizontal one beneath the enhanced heel. Those singed grasses she'd seen trapped in some of the grooves, had gone, suggesting someone had cleaned up.

Guess who?

Using her tweezers, Delphine removed a few of those grey, woollen fibres for extra safe-keeping, thankful they'd been missed.

Next, the invitation.

Relieved her original store of images was still intact, she took several close-up photographs of both sides. Perhaps Simone Gallas, the sly thief, hadn't time to destroy everything, what with the brute and his dog showing up, but seeing the italicized *feather blade steak* included in the menu at the back made her pause. What on earth was it? Despite the warm room, she felt a shiver under her clothes. She then re-focused on those three hairs and the boot.

Given her father's already vulnerable situation, she couldn't risk leaving it in his house for too long. Meanwhile, to handle and probe what might be the sole remnant of a desperate man whose livelihood had been attacked felt like another violation. But she had no choice, because that's what

Romain Vileneuf had found by the burnt-out wreck, possibly costing his life too. She owed it to all three to leave no stone unturned.

Once the boot was safely back in the carrier bag, she decided to retrieve her car, then, if possible, visit her father. One step at a time, she reminded herself, before venturing onto even more dangerous terrain, where one false move could be her last.

*

The taxi, driven by a straw-haired woman who, save for picking up messages on her radio phone, stayed silent throughout the trip back to Belvère. She deposited Delphine immediately behind her abandoned 2CV and, having been paid, turned towards her.

"I recognised you from your photo in the paper. I know it's not my business, Mademoiselle Rougier, but please look after yourself. Bad times are coming."

"What paper?"

But the taxi was already moving away. A thick trail of exhaust in its wake caused Delphine to cough as she stepped into the post office, a queue having formed behind someone sending parcels to Australia. Eventually, having reached the front and shown her ID to the clerk behind the grille, she asked if he recalled a young man matching Aristide's description posting anything of significance yesterday at 15.00 hours and if had he seemed tense, wary.

The guy nodded, before calling for a colleague to help reduce the queue behind her. "I remember Mr. Abolego clearly. And yes, he did seem agitated - I almost rang for assistance. But he didn't post anything. Instead, he gave me this." He began rummaging below the counter and held up a small, padded envelope bearing only her name, which he handed over. "He offered to pay me something, but I refused. And in case you're wondering, a letter bomb did come to mind, but I've not been behind this counter for twenty years for nothing."

"Meaning?"

"I could tell he was kosher."

"You're right."

She signed for the package before withdrawing a slightly crumpled brown envelope addressed to Colonel Serge Valon at the Labradelle *gendarmerie* in the Sarthe.

"First class, please."

With the stamp attached and sent on its way by the cashier, she left as discreetly as the sweaty crowd of people behind her allowed. It was only while sitting in her 2CV, ready to call in at *Beaulieu* that she prised open the package's gummed seal and pulled out not only a metallic grey BlackBerry she immediately recognised, but also a message in block capitals on a hastily torn out page of a notebook.

Romain Vileneuf's parents' mobile number.

The Parisian had taken a huge risk leaving this at the post office, but perhaps he'd spotted her beforehand and lost his nerve about meeting up. Maybe he was in some kind of trouble and didn't want her involved.

But she had been. Up to her neck.

Delphine caught sight of dirty marks on her cagoule's sleeves and rips in the fabric she'd not noticed before. She cursed again at both *cons* who'd caused her ordeal and switched on Aristide's BlackBerry only to be warned its battery was very low.

Why on earth hadn't he enclosed its charger? Perhaps he wasn't thinking straight. Just then, despite her annoyance, she suddenly and deeply missed him.

*

198

Still in a daze, with too many unsolved events swilling around in her mind, Delphine drove out of the village towards Saint-Arnoult and its ever-present River Corrèze. The smiling widow, Simone Gallas, would probably charm her questioners from their purpose, and as for the commander of the *École de la Gendarmerie*, he'd surely prove untouchable.

Then she saw it behind her. The same car and number plate. Same everything, especially the haggard-looking driver staring her way.

Patrick Gauffroi.

Non...

She was also running out of fuel, her small tank less than a quarter full. Being stranded with a killer in tow wasn't the plan, and a two-pump garage just outside Mirat came just in time. Instead of following her, as expected, he drove on by, reducing speed as he did so, making her misplace the fuel nozzle and spray her trainers with petrol instead.

Once done, she snatched a copy of *La Campagne* from the rack outside the tiny shop to scan its headline and main news while making her way to the cashier.

ÉCOLE DE LA GENDARMERIE NATIONALE CLOSED FOR A WEEK DURING INVESTIGATIONS OF CORRUPTION.

Then, following several paragraphs detailing the history and achievements of the establishment, came one which stopped her in her tracks.

Brigadier Alain de Soulibris and the Mayor of Saint-Arnoult, Mme. Simone Gallas are also helping police with their enquiries into yesterday's abduction from Belvère, of Delphine Françoise Rougier, a twenty-two-year-old female student at the same establishment. The public prosecutor, examining magistrate and the town's Crime Investigation Unit urge anyone recognising her, that she contact any commissariat. Her evidence is vital.

Delphine's photograph, taken just after enrolling in Compagnie 1, almost made her cry. So keen and happy she had seemed. Beneath this, attributed to chief reporter Claude Ridal, came another paragraph just as disturbing.

A badly burnt Isuzu Trooper 4x4, possibly belonging to the still-missing Guy and Élisabeth Lavroche of the *Air du Vent* farm near Saint-Arnoult, has been found by a hiker at the bottom of La Gorge de l'Abbaye. Police are linking it to a similar wreck previously sighted near Lauzances, and expect it to be retrieved by tomorrow morning.

That gorge was at least ten kilometres away? What was going on?

Delphine paid too much, but didn't care, before running out to check if that black beast who'd been following her had gone. A few moments later, in the fading drizzle, she found Claude Ridal's card and punched in his number. An automated reply kicked in, and she asked herself if her obvious prodding yesterday had forced his hand. Plus, what other information did he know?

Voicemail.

Damn.

What next?

She tried Vileneuf's number, her pulse drumming in her neck.

The line wasn't good, but at least this time, someone picked up. A man, clearly in distress and whose strong Languedoc dialect was hard to understand, confirmed he was Enzo Vileneuf. Romain's father.

"I'm so very sorry," said Delphine, who'd given her name, "but I had to tell you that I knew him. He was in my year here at the *École*..."

"He'd mentioned you several times..." The man stifled a sob. "In fact, we - my wife and I - had the feeling he..."

Delphine gently broke in as to why she was calling. "Monsieur, I want to find out what happened to him."

"Pah! The wine-grower snorted. "You think so? With big players pulling all the strings?"

High places again...

"You really believe that?"

"I *know*. But first we must collect his body from the hospital morgue in Saint-Arnoult..." His voice faltered again. "Now the post-mortem's over, we want to bring him home."

Delphine blinked. No-one had mentioned it. Not even the press. "What was the outcome?" Although she'd already guessed.

"Natural causes, according to the police pathologist. It makes us sick, sick, sick..."

"You must plead for another one. Immediately. That's rubbish."

"Are you sure? We've never challenged officialdom before. Just got on with our lives."

"Absolutely. Where are you now?"

"On the A20 just past Cahors. Traffic's been heavy for most of the way."

"I've something important to tell you in person. And to give you."

Another pause, during which a pair of seagulls, too far inland, investigated the shabby premises' *poubelle* and flew off with half a sandwich each.

She thought of those wolves, equally resourceful and ruthless.

"How can we trust you?" The bereaved father said finally. "We're still in terrible shock."

"Of course, Monsieur. But you must, because I've an item of evidence connected to a possible double murder which your son saw before anyone else. I believe this is a matter of life and..." She almost added 'death,' but stopped herself.

"When could we meet? We're due at the Hôpital Marie Curie in half an hour."

"How about the Parc Voltaire at midday?" She could also then check on any further activity at *La Bergerie*. "There's parking nearby."

"May I ask what you look like? Romain had said you looked like a blackbird. A pretty blackbird…"

Thank you…

However, once Delphine had painted a more truthful image of herself to avoid complications, she thanked him, again expressing her sincere condolences and ended the call. Surely that schedule would give her time to also see her father and collect the boot from his house? But when she noticed Patrick Gauffroi's Toyota blocking the garage's one mean exit to the road, her plan quickly evaporated.

30

At least this dilemma was in public, unlike that railway near Lauzances. Delphine, with her newspaper safe in her bag, strode towards Gauffroi's 4X4, wondering how he was driving such expensive wheels. She was aware too, of the sun emerging from between separating clouds.

She tapped on his tinted window and addressed the man who'd taken her mother from this earth with just one shot to the heart.

"I'll get you followed!" she shouted. "Unless you fuck off and leave me alone. Do you hear? Go back where you belong. Out of my life. What you so kindly left me and my father."

Without warning, his door swung open, almost toppling her over. She gripped the sturdy chrome wing mirror, reflecting his half-open mouth. The whiff of expensive aftershave snaking out into the morning.

"Blame him, the cruel, lying rat." He was newly-shaved, in the same denim gear she'd seen yesterday, except for the cap. A hint of redness above his jacket's collar. "I fucking believed him, that you really fancied me."

Delphine took a deep breath. A big effort after her fall from that roof. "You've five seconds to shove off or I'm making that call. I mean it."

The new sun caught the fleeting fear before defiance returned. His stubble-free jaw clenched and unclenched as if trying to shift an obstruction. Suddenly, with no warning, he leapt from his seat and flung both arms around her, burying his bare head against her neck. His hands were tight around her waist, pulling her even closer towards him.

"I had a madness," he murmured. "For which I'll pay for the rest of my

203

life. A blind rage for *ma patrie*. What France had lost. Each time since I visited you in hospital, I thought of that stricken village. All I could see was your foolish grandmother, sowing seeds of destruction…"

"There's proof she didn't."

His laugh soon faded, then someone behind them blasted their horn and Delphine pulled away, aware of how he'd stiffened against her, desire pulsing in his eyes.

"Can't you see, I've loved you from the moment you turned up at *Le Fin du Monde*? You with your red nose and red eyes after losing Julie?"

The way he'd said 'Julie' was hard to ignore. With her bullshit detector on max, he sounded genuinely sorry. As another impatient motorist slewed away from the gritty forecourt, Patrick Gauffroi stroked her cheek, triggering an almost electrical charge. He then passed her a folded card with a mobile number printed inside. "Special limited edition," he half-smiled. "I know what you went through yesterday. I'm not an idiot. Just so bloody glad you're OK." He backed away towards his car. "Call me if there's any more trouble. I mean it."

"Normally, I'd suggest you see my father, but he's in custody. Up to his neck in it, and he's all I've got…"

"I said, he's a lying rat."

"And I'd no idea what he'd planned. As for the future…"

"What future?" The farmer vaulted back into his seat. "Do tell me. I'll probably get shot in the head before you can say '*bonnes vacances*.' Get real, Delphine. I'm a dead man walking."

She hated that expression which brought an instant chill. But there were two things she had to find out. "What about Karolina and Roza? Do they know you're on the run?"

He didn't even blink.

"No idea. God's truth."

"So, who sprung you from La Santé? A friend or some passing *marginal*? And how come you've bagged a car like this?" She had to hear the answers for herself, but his door had slammed shut. The engine revved, shrouding her in diesel exhaust and spraying grit as it powered away towards Saint-Arnoult.

*

Although she'd just left details of the car's make and number plate on Colonel Valon's private voicemail, Delphine wrote it down in her *Petit Prince* notebook she'd kept since school, adding Gauffroi's folded card. When stressed, her memory sometimes let her down, so doing this was useful. She headed back to her own miniscule wheels, dwelling on how the ex-con, despite his emotional outburst, might actually be plotting to silence her. And should a camera capture her with him, she could be done for perjury.

What a bloody mess...

Normally, she'd also pass this Paris number to the Crime Investigation Unit in Saint-Arnoult. Soon, she told herself. Soon...

Just then, a florist's van parked up alongside her and a fresh-faced woman leaned out to attract Delphine's attention.

"Have you heard about the latest wolf attack?" she began. "It's terrible. Truly terrible. My son's just phoned me."

An elderly cyclist joined them, looking equally concerned.

"No. Where?" said Delphine, thinking of the *Hôtel Mercure*.

"That Lipizzaner stud farm over in Pierrefort. Three of their best stallions were brought down and mauled to death in their paddock by a pack of grey wolves. An hour ago. I tell you, I'm scared to even take my dog out. And to think I was only there yesterday, delivering a birthday bouquet..."

She drove off in the same direction as Gauffroi's Toyota, and the cyclist remounted, shaking his unprotected head. "Bad times," he said. "And if our farmers give up rearing livestock, then where will we be? Reliant on damned imports."

Delphine suppressed her answer which was too awful to think about.

*

With an hour to spare before meeting the Vileneufs, and as the stud farm wasn't far from Saint-Arnoult, she decided to visit this latest scene of carnage. Not only to look, but to introduce herself as someone who'd discovered the *Air du Vent* farm's attack. Someone with useful information.

However, once she'd crossed the Pont d'Argent bridge and travelled past the quarry, almost reaching the village of Pierrefort itself, she soon realised that nothing and no-one was being allowed to pass or stop near the magnificent red-brick mansion house and its adjoining stables. Yellow diversion signs were already in place, and outside its cordoned-off gateway, a booth had been erected, housing two gendarmes from a unit in Argentat who, on seeing her turquoise 2CV, promptly waved her back the way she'd come.

Damn.

But she wasn't so easily deterred and, once over that same bridge, pulled over on to the verge and grabbed her phone. Using Numéro Vert, she soon accessed the stud farm's main number, and began dialling. She'd already decided to play it safe by hiding her own number and name, and speaking through a paper handkerchief. Just in case. When an unnamed woman finally answered, Delphine simply began, "I'm so sorry to hear what's happened to the stallions, but you need to get a Maurice Amance and possibly his brother Paul investigated immediately. They were responsible for the *Air du Vent's* cattle deaths. Maybe even their owners' disappearance as well. I believe Maurice Amance is their daughter Natalie's latest partner."

The other, still anonymous woman was listening.

"Who are you?" she asked eventually. Her voice taut with fear.

"Never mind. But please make the police sit up. That family are still missing, including the daughter and her young son."

"Joel?"

"Yes."

Silence.

"Our granddaughter knows him at school."

"Here's another name. Genéral Olivier Amance. Based near St. Loup-sur-Semouse. A big player…"

"What do you mean?"

"*La Vie Sauvage.* It's growing fast."

Delphine sensed she was writing that down.

"I'm afraid I have to go…"

"Again, I'm sorry."

With that, and the glaringly bright *École de La Gendarmerie National* sprawled in front of her, Delphine drove into the town centre for a meeting with two people also suffering a terrible loss.

*

Another cordon, but this time, no police cubicle outside *La Bergerie's* equally impressive gateway. Perhaps surplus personnel were in short supply, or that three valuable stallions were considered more important than yesterday's sordid business. Perhaps in a way, they were.

She was five minutes' late, chewing hurriedly on the last piece of already stale *brioche*. Its dryness clung to her teeth, becoming hard to swallow.

Then she saw them. Two short, slightly stooped figures dressed in black, wintry clothes. Sombre amongst the flowers, greenery and bright bunting slung between branches. She then remembered how the Australian at the *Hôtel Mercure* had mentioned an imminent folk festival. Just then, the prospect of jaunty music filling the air seemed almost obscene.

They'd spotted her and began walking her way, supporting each other along the narrow gravel path, before the man edged ahead of the woman, as if meeting a stranger first was his duty. Delphine noticed their faces, lined and brown from an outdoor life, were shrunken by grief. Where Romain had been tall, both parents were half his size with none of his lithe ease, as if his death had also affected their muscles.

"Delphine Rougier," she began. "It's good to see you, and again, my deepest sympathy."

"Enzo Vileneuf," the man said, stretching out an equally brown hand which felt skeletal. "And this is Romain's mother."

She nodded before warily scrutinising Delphine, her knobbly wedding finger showing a thin, gold band.

"How did you get my mobile number?" asked her husband.

"Another friend of Romain's gave it to me."

"Who?" Those sun-wizened eyes narrowed.

"Aristide Abolego. He's alright."

The man relaxed a little.

"We had heard."

They weren't alone in suffering a loss of trust, thought Delphine, wanting to give both a hug. Instead, she showed them her ID card, aware that she still didn't know the mother's first name. She probably didn't have her own phone, maybe not even a bank account. Perhaps equality hadn't reached their corner of the world. But just then, what the hell did that matter?

Enzo Vileneuf then eyed her carrier bag. "Is this what you said was for us?"

Delphine nodded, gripping the handles, fighting the urge not to part with it. "A man's left boot, but not any old boot. As I said, I'm convinced it's crucial piece of evidence which may have contributed to..."

"Go on, please."

"Your son's death."

Silence, save for the rippling chatter of birds overhead. So detached, so obscenely sweet.

"Can we please sit down?" Romain's mother asked, pointing to a nearby vacant bench. "We've had quite a journey, with the worst yet to come."

Delphine passed the bag to her husband. "I'm sorry, Madame, but you must get this to a secure place as soon as possible. I'm sure the boot inside belongs to a Guy Lavroche, a local farmer who..."

Immediately, Madame Vileneuf's hand covered her mouth. "Not the one whose cattle were all killed? And their car found in the Gorge de l'Abbaye?"

"Yes."

The Vileneufs looked inside the bag as Delphine also produced the folded copy of *La Campagne* and watched them scour its front page. Their faces rigid until seeing the photograph.

"That's you!"

"Come along, Laure," her husband said finally giving her name. "Or we'll be late."

"Whoever published this could be risking your life," she ignored him. "How stupid and irresponsible."

Delphine found herself shivering. Laure Vileneuf was right. Claude Ridal, in his desire to please, had gone to the other extreme.

"Just a few more things you should know." She'd composed herself enough to relay more details of LVS; the collusion between the mayor and brigadier, never mind the weak Lieutenant Colonel Zanowski.

"You're the only one showing real concern about Romain," his mother added. "And because of you, we will challenge that post-mortem result. Romain was a strong swimmer. A sportsman. He must have been either killed beforehand, or while in the lake. They must think we're idiots."

Her tone had strengthened, and Delphine felt it appropriate to add how so far, the local police had clammed up. How no other official must see that crucial left boot until Commander Alain de Soulbris had been formally charged with her abduction.

"Not even Inspector Serra?"

"Especially not him. And after today, just *entre nous*," Delphine added, lowering her voice. "I won't be around for a few days, but please keep in touch and let's hope I can soon get justice for your son." She paused. "We were due to go on a date last night because he wanted to tell me something. I'm sure of it. How he'd first found the Lavroche's car, but sadly, it wasn't to be."

Laure Vileneuf took her phone number, promising not to mention their meeting and warning her to be vigilant. The couple then joined hands and made their way to the park's nearest exit, their shadows leading the way. On reaching the pavement, Enzo Vileneuf turned and raised a hand in a gesture of hope and, it seemed, gratitude. As they soon disappeared amongst other pedestrians, Delphine hoped they'd stay strong and together, wanting to tell them she'd already posted those three distinctive hairs retrieved from *La Bergerie* to the one official she could trust, some three hundred kilometres away.

31

12:25 hrs.

"Delphine Rougier?"

A half-familiar female voice made her twist round to see Véronique Morel, perennial sour-puss of the *École*'s reception desk, looking like someone she'd never seen before. Her normally neatly tied mouse-brown hair straggled over shapeless shoulders covered by a stained green tee-shirt, which drooped loose over tracksuit botttoms. Her scuffed trainers completed the picture of neglect. But it was her face which made Delphine start. Her lack of any make-up made that pointed nose shine like a beak, while her normally probing eyes were red-rimmed and swollen. In one hand she carried a full plastic bag from *P'tit Prix,* a huge discount store with the biggest packets of frozen *frites* for the cheapest prices.

My God...

"Have you heard the very latest about the *École*'s closure?" said the sous-Lieutenant producing a folded *Le Figaro*.

"Not yet," lied Delphine, wanting to hear maybe more than what *La Campagne* had revealed.

"Well, the place could be closed until the start of October. Some week, *hein*?"

Merde.

Bad news indeed. The *Hôtel les Palmiers* all over again, thought Delphine, but not for long. "I could have died yesterday," she reminded her former adversary, still puzzling as to why the sous-Lieutenant looked so awful.

"Well, I *am* going to die."

What?

"Are you ill? Have you got…?"

"I've three kids, all in school, and what'll happen to them when the job ends and I can't get another? I'll tell you. Into care." She broke off to take a breath. "My ex-husband doesn't pay a *centime* towards their upkeep, so what's the bloody point of me going on?"

A trilling birdsong in that surreally pretty park sounded even more out of place as the woman began to cry. "After all the scandal, they're either re-locating staff or cutting altogether, and I'm one of those. So, thank you, Brigadier fucking Alain de Soulibris." Her wet eyes fixed on the mayor's house, just visible through the trees. "And you, deceitful bitch."

"Surely you have rights?" Delphine was stunned by this previously cool official's raw and honest anger, ashamed of her own earlier, negative preconceptions. "Do you belong to a union?"

Morel wiped her eyes with her fist, took another huge breath and shook her head. "I stopped my membership a few weeks back because my hours had been cut. It was either that, or a proper meal for us all at the weekends."

She then composed herself enough to unfold and open the newspaper to page 4. "You again," she said, "with Romain Vileneuf on a search and rescue trip last spring." Beneath this, lay the heading 'TWO BRAVE STUDENTS' followed by their descriptions and potted biographies.

Then, brief details of her abduction and Romain's grief-stricken parents, unsatisfied with the result of their son's post-mortem. No mention of François Rougier or Patrick Gauffroi, or even any update on Simone Gallas and her unlikely helper, still being questioned in Brive. Claude Ridal again, the chief reporter, obviously putting himself about. Her message had stuck.

However, Delphine wondered who'd supplied the photograph and the rest.

"You *are* brave, mind," Morel was saying. "And I've been following your story. I'm sorry I was never very pleasant to you, but you reminded me of when I was starting out. Before the *con* that I shouldn't have married and..." Her voice juddered to a halt. Her breathing came in short gasps as tears reached her eyes.

Delphine stepped forward to place her arms around the woman's heaving shoulders. "It doesn't matter," she said, and meant it. "You've had a lot to worry about, and a job to hold down as well." She let go so she could look her in the eye. "You mustn't do anything stupid. Promise?"

"I won't. Thank you. And by the by, it's only Lieutenant Colonel Zanowski who's spoken up for me. And for you as well. I think what happened to Romain affected him badly too, as if he was somehow responsible..."

"He saw me briefly there yesterday," said Delphine, gesturing towards *La Bergerie*. "Before the police led him away for questioning. He didn't look too happy then."

"Not surprised." The single mother checked her watch and frowned as if she was late. "But I am worried about him. He was bullied all the time by that fat bastard of a brigadier. But I kept notes, so who knows?"

"That's something. Good."

Delphine then wished her well and, having checked she had her phone number, moved away in the opposite direction with yet another worry pecking at her mind.

*

She glanced briefly to her right to see Véronique Morel take a short cut to another, smaller car park behind a busy café fronted by a duck-filled pond, then glanced at her own watch, wondering whether to contact Claude

213

Ridal yet again, to ask why he kept using photographs of her. But first was François Rougier, before he's accused of perverting the course of justice. Or worse.

She had to tell him - as if he didn't already know - what a dangerous dissembler the widowed Simone Gallas had turned out to be. If necessary, to help save his skin, she'd back up his story. But before all this, she must send a special envelope by express delivery to her loyal archivist friend near Le Mans, then withdraw three hundred euros from her ever-diminishing funds. Its purpose filled her with renewed energy threaded by fear.

In the meantime, where on earth could she locate a phone charger for Aristide's BlackBerry? Ordering via the internet was unfeasible, and there were no specialist outlets in Saint-Arnoult. The nearest superstore was beyond Brive, and she couldn't risk another journey before the big one. Whatever that phone contained, it would have to wait. Patrick Gauffroi was out there somewhere, and after his recent, maniacal embrace, what might he have in mind next?

*

Before visiting her bank, she called Ets. Fabien Guirros in the Vigeois industrial one some twelve kilometres from the town to check if anyone had enquired about invoice number 1XD 39600.

The recorded message simply stated that since closing time on Saturday afternoon, the business had ceased trading, and any suppliers and clients owed money and or refunds should contact the liquidators in Limoges.

32

Just like the post office in Belvère, the Banque Populaire was heaving. Half of Saint-Arnoult were, it seemed, queuing impatiently by the cash machines and the one counter manned by just two female staff. Scattergun opinions on the scandal surrounding the mayor and her brigadier, the wolf attacks and the still-missing Lavroches reached Delphine's ears, but at least despite Claude Ridal's best efforts, no-one so far, had recognised her. Only after a third cashier appeared, could Delphine finally begin her transaction. Having glanced at her for longer than usual, the guy took her credit card, and after the usual processing and acceptance of her PIN number, passed over the money.

While counting it, making sure too that no-one's eyes were on her, a man called out her name. A second later, from further back nearer the entrance, another made a strange, growling noise.

She immediately stuffed the three hundred euros into her bag and butted her way towards the locked, triple-glazed door. Normally, she'd have apologized to those immediately around her, but she'd spotted those same two thugs from the Lavroche's farm. Their now crisp, clean white shirts and once thick, unkempt hair shaved close to their sunburnt heads were no disguise. Surely they were Maurice and Paul Amance?

They were way too close, while that damned door with its flashing red light was keeping her trapped.

A hand clawed at her left arm, hot breath burning her ear.

"Remember that gay from Toulouse, *hein*? You want to join him?"

Gay?

That 'g' word had hit like a hollow bullet, and the door's red light finally changed to green.

"What you deserve too, interfering bitch," said the other one, his French distinctly gutteral as before. Hatred burned in both brown and blue eyes before they pushed their way out first.

Delphine still managed to yell after them. "Call me what you like, you cowardly morons! That won't stop me. Nothing will."

There. She'd spelt it out and felt better. Then she was outside, dazzled by the sudden sun, forgetting in that moment where she'd left her car, but remebered her phone. Within two seconds, she'd taken a shot of them running away, which could help identify them later, if necessary. As for Romain Vileneuf, had he really been gay? If so, neither his fellow students nor his parents had even hinted at it. This made his wanting to see her at the Caméo cinema on Saturday evening doubly intriguing. Had she misread the signs all along?

Delphine then withdrew into the doorway of an insurance company to sort out her cash, tempted to wait in case the bullies returned. But precious seconds were slipping by, with still her father to visit.

*

The main custody suite in Saint Arnoult's commissariat was also full, overlaid by smells of lunch and body odour. But where was François Rougier? Through a semi-opaque glass panel in its custody suite door, guarded by a grizzled, armed officer, she could just about make out the backs of Simone Gallas and the brute, who'd obviously returned from Brive. Perhaps there'd not been enough security there, or Brive had decided their home turf should have the honour of questioning them. Whatever the reason, she wanted to barge in and shriek what despicable bastards they were. How she'd been humiliated, and most importantly, why? To be weakened before the final squeeze of the throat? The bundling up before a trip to the same picturesque lake where Romain had ended up? And where in all this was the apparently remorseful Lieutenant Colonel Zanowski? Who, if Véronique Morel was to be believed, had at least admitted how Delphine deserved another start? Was he somewhere else in this drab, anonymous building, confessing to being the go-between? The unhappy sous-Lieutenant hadn't said.

The guard was just about to ask her to move on, when she felt a tap on her shoulder.

"Mademoiselle Rougier? Excuse me, but your father's asking to see you."

A voice she recognised. And when she turned, Delphine saw that same man she'd met on Saturday. Police Inspector Raymond Serra. This time, showing her rather more respect. "He has a lawyer with him. Just so you know," he added, and after a brief exchange with the other guy, led her down a corridor, those lunch and body smells replaced by cigarette smoke and pee.

"Who?" she pressed.

"Maître Gérard Massenet. A great white shark if ever there was."

Delphine almost stopped. His description seemed grotesque and totally out of order.

"Why say that? His daughter's just been killed in the most awful way."

A pause. Then a surreptitious mutter.

"Not fussed what goes in his mouth."

And with that, the inspector knocked on a plain steel door marked 3 and used his tab to open it.

*

Their eyes met. Massenet's, although still ringed by grief lines, were holding hers with a fierce intensity as they shook hands. His, cool and strong, while her father slumped between two young officers at the far end of the cheerless, concrete-rendered room, stared at her with a rare blank expression.

Where was the fire, the anger she'd seen yesterday at *La Bergerie*? Delphine tried to imagine what her late mother might say, but the lawyer was speaking.

"You've endured a frightening ordeal, Mademoiselle. And naturally, the matter is still *sub judice*, but I'm as shocked as you. Like everyone else in Saint-Arnoult, I never for a moment considered Madame Gallas to be anything other than a remarkable, high-principled woman." He glanced over at his client. "As, I might add, did your father."

"Too damned right!" François Rougier declared, straightened himself, then faced Delphine. "You'd think I'd have had more bloody sense, especially with having my daughter to keep an eye on. Not that you needed me, but…"

I did…

"It's OK," Delphine said instead, then addressed the lawyer. "With respect, Maître Massenet, if and when I'm called as a witness in both cases, I'll be representing myself."

A charged silence followed. Her father's mouth inched into a smile, and the lawyer subtly cleared his throat. "As far as my client is concerned, I'll be pursuing the diminished responsibility line. Especially since he's…"

"Speak up!" shouted her father. "I'm not some invalid at death's door. If you've something to say, then let's all hear. God knows, I'm paying you enough!"

Massenet showed no reaction. Clearly used to being harangued and challenged at every turn. "I was simply saying, Monsieur, that in my

218

professional opinion, you've been in a vulnerable state of mind since your wife's death. That there's a real risk of self-harm or even..."

"Go on. Spit it out!" François Rougier reared up, pushing away both his guards. "You were about to say 'suicide,' weren't you? Well let me tell you, I've every reason to live. I have Delphine who's got more balls than any of you lot here put together. She stood up to the sexist bullies at that *École*. Survived an abduction - hell, I can't believe I'm saying this..." Then he stopped, his lips trembling. His eyes welled up, but were still on her. "I just wanted you to be happy. You know that. Patrick Gauffroi said he loved you from the moment he saw you at *Bellevue* that freezing Monday morning. And I'd forgiven him, I really had. You do realise that?"

He slumped back in his chair. Spent, yes, but he'd pushed her into a corner.

One more burden. One more lie...

Massenet re-focused on her. Of course, he knew. Another father whose own daughter was in a coffin in a funeral parlour. But had he flinched during that speech?

Non.

"Who was this contact of yours?" he enquired of his client, as if asking the time.

Silence, during which one of the guards switched on the overhead fan. Its whirring sounded like a throng of migrating birds, as the lawyer moved towards the three men. Delphine took in his straight back, his long legs moving with ease and confidence. She shamefully imagined him in a completely different setting. Undressed...

Great white shark...

She then listened hard to her father's obstructiveness, his sheer bloody-mindedness. When he'd finished, she made another decision that could change the lives of half of those in that bleak space.

*

After a strained farewell, with Delphine advising him to keep eating and to try and get some sleep, she was escorted out. She felt guilty she'd withheld the reassurance he needed as much as any food and drink, and how she pretended to believe he'd acted in her best interests.

Gérard Massenet passed her in the foyer on his way out to his car.

"You do realise you'll be needed as chief witness if Madame Gallas and Brigadier de Soulibris are sent for trial?"

"If? Surely you mean 'when?'"

A small smile twitched his lips.

"Delphine, in this life one can only be sure of two things. Death and taxes. I'm urging you not to travel too far. The new examining magistrate will shortly be in touch, and as you've stated your wish to represent yourself during any cross-examination, you'll need to be prepared."

"Fine. No problem."

"Good."

Having promised he would also stay connected, Massenet affectionately touched her shoulder, and as he did so, another shameful tremor of desire moved south.

*

This deliberate gesture of his was to light up the rest of the day, beginning with her checking her over-sized Michelin map for the quickest route to France's north-east which thankfully was mostly via autoroutes and dual carriageways.

She parked a few streets away from her father's house, all the while watching out for Patrick Gauffroi and those two *cons* from the bank. She then remembered Thursday's banquet at the *Château des Illuminations*. If

220

Maurice and Paul Amance were attending, they'd surely be on their way, if not there already?

The thought made her press harder than usual on the tiny accelerator. Her destination was hardly around the corner, and her car not the Formula One variety. But because of Amélie Massenet and those other poor kids, she'd be leaving for a place she had not seen since she was twelve. Somewhere which could lead to the heart of the tragedies that had taken place so far.

*

She bundled her clothes from the upstairs wardrobe into the washing machine for its fastest wash, spin and tumble dry cycle. Then, having checked that the items still shared each bra cup with her unspectacular breasts, she packed her rucksack bought last year especially for the *École*. Not exactly a waste of money, rather a reminder of broken dreams.

At 13:30 hours, with the noisy drying cycle finished, she left a short, simple note for her father on the kitchen worktop nearest the kettle. His and her matching mugs stood empty. *For how long?* she wondered, fighting back tears before emptying the machine and arranging her damp clothes on a plastic rack. All traces of that steep roof and its filthy guttering gone from their various fibres, but not the legacy to come.

She then extracted Aristide's phone from her briefs and switched it on. As before, the same message and blank screen appeared.

Damn.

She was about to switch it off, when it stuttered into life with a shaky image of what was surely the River Seine. After MENU she tapped on VOICEMAIL INBOX in case Aristide had left any more clues, either deliberately or not. But above the various noises from the street, she heard a muffled, male voice calling himself *L'Aigle Noir*.

"Job done," he began. "Wish my others were as easy."

Call ended. No sender number, but the time was surely significant. Friday 10th June. 08:45 hrs.

*

Jésus…

The date when Patrick Gauffroi had been freed.

But why hadn't Aristide deleted that bragging message? Had he wanted her to hear it?

Odder and odder.

All too aware of the BlackBerry's death throes, Delphine quickly scrolled through several texts, mostly from his fellow students at the *École*, and one from his mother begging him to keep out of trouble, hoping he'd be back home in Paris for the holidays.

There must be more…

She was right.

On Saturday 11th June at 17:00 hours came another male voice, so fearful, so broken she didn't at first recognise it.

"Help! Help! Where the fuck *is* anybody? Help!"

Then nothing.

She replayed it, all the while watching for predators, human and vulpine. Then, she knew with mounting horror that poor Romain Vileneuf, wherever he'd been at the time, hadn't long to live. Suddenly, that blank screen re-appeared as if a dark star had collided with her already unsettled world, and vanished into space.

33

14:00 hrs.

Having alarmed her father's house, Delphine ran as fast as both aching ankles could carry her to where her car was waiting, unbeknown to her that another stood concealed in a shady driveway, engine purring, prepared.

Still pre-occupied by what she'd heard, she stored her rucksack in the 2CV's tiny boot and settled herself in her hot driver's seat.

The full, glaring sun was giving her a headache, but not so much that she couldn't retrieve Colonel Valon's number and tell him about Romain Vileneuf's desperate voicemail message.

The senior gendarme was on his own at the Labradelle *gendarmerie,* eating lunch at his desk, still chewing, as he replied. "And your friend never reported it?"

"He must have tried to. I know he would have…"

"I can get it checked," Valon added. "As a formality. For Abolego to entrust you with his phone, it does suggest he was frightened too."

"Like me," she said drily, before revealing the other strange voicemail message.

A pause followed.

"*L'Aigle Noir*? The same name as *I* was given on Saturday morning. Took a while to dig, mind you, so finding his real identity and any birth certificate and address could prove difficult, especially since his prison records were lost in a mysterious fire five years ago."

"Prison?"

"La Santé. So, he knows the ropes there. He's also vanished off the face of the earth, and I'm sorry Delphine but '*fait accompli*' or not, plus the identical timings, I'll have to step back. Treading on too many judicial toes could cause problems all round. If what I suspect has happened was on my patch…"

"Of course," she broke in, not really wanting to hear about his bureaucratic limitations. But too much wasn't adding up. Why couldn't this normally dependable cop just cut out the riddles?

"Can I ask who gave you that *nom de plume*? The same informant you said was a she?"

"I can't say. I'm sorry. It was given in confidence."

Silence. He'd stopped munching.

Simone Gallas…

Delphine relayed her conversation with that slippery character yesterday morning in her kitchen. How she'd phoned the prison itself.

"Perhaps to make herself smell sweeter. Show she cared…" he finally volunteered.

"Nothing can make her any sweeter. And why would this *l'Aigle Noir* use Aristide Abolego's phone to say 'job done?' I mean, what's the connection between them except that they're both half-West African?" And that made her pulse quicken. "Is it possible they're related?"

Another loaded silence, before the crackle of writing paper or perhaps another sandwich wrapper. Valon was either really hungry or nervous.

"And who more desperate than your father?" Came out of the blue.

At last.

*

"Could he have contacted Aristide through my knowing him?" Delphine persisted. "By finding his number on my phone?"

"That would seem the obvious answer. Both will have to be questioned, and if your friend *is* involved, he could be in serious trouble. You must tell him."

Delphine shut her eyes against the sun. Even wearing shades didn't help. She suddenly felt hemmed in, overpowered by the thickening tide of deception and double-crossing.

"Just to put you in the loop, Patrick Gauffroi is still following me," she said, offloading some of that pressure on the one person she could trust. "Is it OK for me to tell you?"

He sighed.

"This is different, because his home address is still in the Sarthe. Tell me the next time it happens, understood? I can easily get his car tracked with number plate recognition cameras."

"I know, but…"

Shit…

Someone parked too close in front of her, adding to her claustrophobia.

"What?"

Delphine could hear her hot, frantic heart. "I'm not sure. He'll realise it's me who's spilled."

"Do you have anywhere else to go in Saint-Arnoult?" Valon asked, as if avoiding the 'perjury' word.

"Yes," she breathed out too quickly, and he didn't sound convinced.

"Well do it."

"I will." But that was another slick lie.

"If you were still in this area, you could have had our spare room until things calmed down, but…"

"Thank you."

Delphine squeezed her eyes even more tightly shut. She mustn't cry. Not here. Not now. That surprise speck of kindness had caught her by. She ended the call, crammed Aristide's dead phone deep into her jeans' side pocket and set her little car's quirky gear stick into reverse. So keen was she to escape the confines of that narrow street that she almost hit that wretched car in front.

Whoa...

A warning to cool it, before she really did trigger an accident. And then where would those children, Romain Vileneuf, and the so-far unaccounted for Guy and Élisabeth Lavroche be?

*

At 14:20 hours, Delphine joined the busy A89 *péage* signed for Clermant-Ferrand. Although expensive, she could stop to re-fill her small petrol tank and take the chance to check out newspapers on the way. With luck, she might even make Lyon in one go, before heading north-east to Dijon and beyond on Tuesday.

She'd always loved maps, and never been persuaded to save for a car equipped with a Satnav, even though that Suzuki kindly loaned by Jules Charbon last November had enabled her to find *Les Cigales* in the middle of nowhere. Like her beloved late friend Pauline Fillol, she didn't trust the technology, and even Lieutenant Colonel Zanowski in his introductory lecture on observation and surveillance had hinted their data could be compromised by snoopers, especially once an exercise had been completed.

"They're for wimps and ponces," her father had added to the negativity, so here she was, with her map's page after slightly crumpled page of soft greens and greys, criss-crossed by red and yellow veins and arteries for roads and strands of blue rivers swelling into lakes like small tumours. The wonder of maps lay in what they *didn't* show, leaving much to the imagination, making each kilometre a surprise. As she drove along the inside lane with her canvas roof rolled back, she felt a brief release from events beyond her control. Despite Inspector Serra's startling description of Gérard Massenet, the lawyer was still her father's best bet.

Maybe one day, for her too...

Enough.

"Bad girl. Sinner, destined for the ninth circle of hell," the smooth-skinned Sister Marthe at the convent school had once said, with her dead fish eyes, and smell to match, seeping from beneath her moth-coloured clothes. Delphine wasn't the only pupil to wonder if, beneath those whiffy layers, she actually went commando.

*

She switched on the radio, and after random voices and snatches of music, tuned in to a report on the proposed re-introduction of panthers and wild boars into the Rhône. Above the intermittent crackling and loss of sound exacerbated by passing traffic came a visceral fear of those not only with young families in more rural areas, but *vignerons* with prosperous vineyards and owners of valuable livestock.

The spokeswoman for this organisation, whose name she'd missed, was at pains to disassociate it from LVS, whose zeal, she claimed, had been alienating and irresponsible, and that wolves of whatever colour near urban settlements posed a risk. The name of Saint-Arnoult, its schoolchildren victims and the *Air du Vent* farm came over loud and clear, as did the village of Pierrefort, where those valuable stallions had perished.

Annemarie Colbert, originally from Ontario and based in Thiers, ended by arguing that both man and wild beasts could co-exist, but only after careful planning and consultation. Delphine reminded herself to get in touch to discover what else she might know about LVS.

This item segued into news of a dawn attack on a synagogue in Avignon, and its next announcement almost made Delphine lose control of the steering wheel, sending her vulnerable 'sardine can' over the motorway's single white line, not far from a sneaky grey and yellow camera.

"The body of Lieutenant Colonel Mikhail Zanowski has been found in his locked room at the *École de la Gendarmerie Nationale* in Saint-Arnoult. According to colleagues, he'd not only recently been diagnosed with stage four prostate cancer, but a handwritten note found nearby cites the corrosive culture of bullying at this renowned establishment to have been a factor. The recent, unexplained death of Romain Vileneuf, a valued, first-year student, and the investigation of Brigadier Alain de Soulibris for the abduction of a promising female recruit, may have been the last straws... So says his widowed father, travelling from Warsaw. At this stage, the senior gendarme's death is not being regarded as suspicious, and a post-mortem will be carried out tomorrow morning..."

*

My God...

"No mention of the saintly mayor, then," Delphine said out loud, slowing down, thinking of Zanowski's white hair and delicate, pink skin. His contradictory brown eyes. How unusual he'd looked in that quasi-military role. Had he been married, or had a partner? Even been gay? That wouldn't have surprised her. Whatever, he'd danced to the brute's tune and made herself, Aristide and others fearful. He'd probably known the truth about Romain too, but at least he'd finally spoken well of her to Véronique Morel, which was something.

After this, coincidentally, came breaking news of the arrest of both the brigadier and the town's mayor, Simone Gallas, being held separately in secret locations. Their victim, Delphine Françoise Rougier was urged to make contact with Saint-Arnoult's Crime Investigation Unit as soon as possible. Like those sudden thunderclaps which frequently shook the homesteads in her former hamlet of St. Eustache came the realisation that she might also be needed to give her account of events leading to the Polish officer's suicide.

Of course, she would. But first, and despite Gérard Massenet's advice not to travel too far, those densely-forested hills and wilder mountains of the north-east were beckoning.

34

Tuesday 21ˢᵗ June. 9:00 hrs. Arbresle.

The summer solstice began not with a benign and calm dawn, but with blowing clouds disgorging solid rain, and nothing had changed by the time Delphine left the *Hôtel du Jardin* tucked away in a small business park to the north of Arbresle, not far from Lyon. She'd made extremely good time the evening before and, having been too tired to turn on the TV in her room, watched the news while queuing with her tray for the coffee machine at breakfast.

She'd glimpsed images of a sunny Saint-Arnoult and the almost grotesquely gleaming *École de la Gendarmerie*, with police vehicles stationed at its entrance. The commentary was almost mute, and when Gérard Massenet's mesmerising face and black tie flashed by, she almost knocked over her glass of orange juice.

Not yet, she told herself, mentally fast-forwarding to another less public encounter with him. Definitely not yet…

*

Her hastily arranged meeting with Annemarie Colbert was in half an hour, so she had to get a move on. Yet, while negotiating a huge roundabout, hemmed in by the biggest juggernauts she'd ever seen, that resolve faltered. Something strikingly familiar distracted her enough to stray into the path of a *convoi exceptionel* carrying a mobile home. A massive billboard featuring that same wolf's head and open jaw, big enough to accommodate herself and her car.

LA VIE SAUVAGE.

Je suis roi.

The driver justifiably hooted her back into her lane, and the rest of the journey saw her even more careful to stay alive. There'd been too many needless deaths already.

*

"Maniacs," admitted the smartly-dressed Canadian woman in her distinctive accent, as she and Delphine shared a table in the nearest service tation on the A6 out of Lyon. "And giving us all in Domus a bad name."

"Easily done, when an innocent young life has been lost. Everyone's tarred with the same brush."

Her companion nodded. At thirty-three, she'd just been promoted to regional officer for the Rhône with a remit - as her interview had stated - to organise the conservation and rehabilitation of threatened species of birds and small reptiles. Many lost to hunting, natural predators or vandalism. Not only was she successful, but enviably tanned, with telegenic good looks, including blonde highlights in her shoulder-length hair. Delphine briefly wondered what she must think of her simple crop and chain store clothes. And, though unbidden, what sort of future had she herself got? But Annemarie Colbert was angry nevertheless.

"Unlike us who have to grovel for every last euro from Brussels, LVS seem to have *largesse* a-plenty, and freedom to operate how they like. It defies belief."

Delphine agreed, finishing off her small strawberry tart, yet still hungry.

"But you see, wolves symbolise that freedom. A certain power and nobility, which is sentimental rubbish, because who'll feed them all if there isn't the means?"

"High places," murmured Delphine cryptically. Then, careful not to mention phones, she described the images of the Amance brothers both as adults in the wild somewhere with grey wolves she'd seen on the internet.

231

Alongside their highly-decorated father, Genéral Olivier Amance, she added. "Proudly showing off slaughtered sheep, if you please."

"Ugh." Then a flicker of interest. "Where?"

"I'm guessing outside his *Château des Illuminations*."

"Is that where you're going?" her acquaintance asked, then ordered refills of coffee. "Please say no."

Delphine hesitated. Trusting the wrong people had cost her dear, but so far, all her vibes about Annemarie Colbert had been positive. "Maybe. There's a farming couple from near Saint-Arnoult still missing, plus their daughter and grandson. I have to get to the bottom of it because I'm sure there's also a huge cover-up which…"

"I *do* know," empathised the summery blonde. "It's my job, and the stronger and more manipulative these morons become, the less attention for everyone else."

"Bullying, in other words."

"Precisely."

Annemarie Colbert passed Delphine a fresh cup of coffee, accompanied by two tiny biscuits in the saucer. Their spicy smell reminded her of the same which Charles Rosheim, her great-grandfather, had brought with him from Lorraine for his own *Café de Lilas* in Beaumont-sur-Sarthe.

"Promise me you won't go into that area on your own," she added. Her green eyes showed real concern. "Do you realise this so-called 'national treasure' keeps a specially armed guard on his land and a punishment block for those caught trespassing or trying to curtail his enterprise?"

Delphine shivered, swallowing the second biscuit. "Really?"

"Yes. And because he's such a law unto himself, you could be put out of sight and out of mind, and no-one would know."

*

Beyond the window, Delphine saw normal people doing normal things, putting the stark alternative she'd planned into too sharp a contrast.

"I need to find out what's really happened to Guy and Élisabeth Lavroche," she said, as if to herself, then added, "I think that despite what their daughter Natalie told me, she's in it up to her neck."

The Canadian smiled, which seemed an odd response. "Happy families, huh?"

"Too right, and until this conspiracy - because that's how I see it - is unravelled, then the Lavroches, Amelie Massenet and those other school kids won't be the first to have suffered."

Annemarie patted Delphine's hand, then mentioned a doctor in Plombières-les-Bains whose niece was savaged by a wolf six months ago. "He was told to keep stumm about it, or else. Just imagine…"

"What happened?"

An exaggerated shrug. "Nothing. Are you surprised?"

"No."

"But when I said 'nothing,' I meant that this same doctor vanished on his way home from the surgery. If you're not careful - and sorry to sound like a big sister - we may hear nothing of you." She glanced at her pricey-looking watch. "Is that what your Papa would want? As if he's not in enough *merde* already."

So, she knew…

"I realise you're only trying to help," said Delphine, still puzzled, retrieving her bag from the neighbouring seat. "And I'm grateful, but if you'd seen that burnt-out Isuzu Trooper which just has to belong to that couple, *and* known Romain Vileneuf personally and met his grieving parents, never mind another terrified student…"

"I can imagine," Annemarie interrupted, looking serious. "And we'll keep in touch, *hein*? We girls must stick together." She stood up, straightened her beige, linen jacket and clasped Delphine's shoulder with a strong, firm hand. "Take care now, and call any time."

"Thanks. I might just do that."

The Canadian let go.

"Oh, I meant to add. Three grey wolves have just been shot dead in a street in St. Germain-Laval. Not so far away. That'll put the cat among the pigeons, as *les Anglais* would say."

*

Delphine watched her go before she was lost in the thickening drizzle and other damp pedestrians hurrying to their destinations.

She also had a destination becoming ever more urgent and, after buying Tuesday's copy of *Le Figaro* and an egg sandwich for later, rejoined her car. She checked the map, still thinking of the idealistic environmentalist and when might be the best time to tell Gérard Massenet about the dodgy goings-on at the général's château.

She was just about to push open the café door when, amongst the morning's steady stream of traffic flowing towards Lyon and the autoroute for the north, a large, black 4X4 travelling more slowly than the car in front, came into view, creating a noticeable gap.

Non...

Oui...

Patrick Gauffroi, no less. Kitted out in camouflage clothing and, like a hunter searching for prey, staring fixedly her way.

35

The drizzle from an oppressively dull sky had morphed into rain, and Delphine reached her little car with wet hair and fresh anxiety. Yes, she'd embarked on a possibly dangerous trip, however, despite Annemarie Colbert's warnings, it wasn't these which made her swiftly lock herself in, but the prospect of that distinctive black Toyota keeping her in its sights.

Once clear of Arbresle on the N7, she pulled on to the hard shoulder and switched on her hazard warning lights before dialling Gérard Massenet's number. However, half way through, she stopped. There was too much to tell him and suddenly felt this was premature. He had his only child's post-mortem and funeral to focus on, and her own tricky father.

"Timing is everything," Colonel Valon had once said, and he was right. His the voice to heed, not her own impulses. And it was then she became aware that the friendly, concerned Annemarie Colbert hadn't left her any contact details.

*

The further north she travelled from Lyon's endless suburbs along the A6 through Mâcon towards the Autoroute du Soleil, the more her 2CV suffered. When she eventually stopped for petrol in a dreary little service station near St. Bonnet, set in even more dreary surroundings, she realised she'd been here before.

This was the very place the coach carrying herself and her classmates had re-fuelled ten years ago. Equally hard to forget was their driver leering at them through his over-sized rear-view mirror, and the grim trio of nuns strategically placed, working their rosary beads while eavesdropping on secret conversations.

But just then, on her own, with what seemed like the weight of dark water pressing from behind, Delphine missed the solidarity of her long-ago school friends, all since flown to other parts of the world as if shedding the misery of Christianity that had encrusted their free spirits in that grey-stoned prison set in the Sarthe flatlands. The increasing distance from there and her possibly temporary base in Saint-Arnoult meant more space between her and the police, as well as the new examining magistrate who'd 'shortly be getting in touch.'

"Where you from?" Quizzed the shop's cashier without even looking up from the till. No more than a schoolgirl, thought Delphine watching her credit card being processed. From then on it would be cash only, in case records of her travels might fall into the wrong hands.

"Paris," she lied, returning the card to her purse and taking the receipt.

"You mean the Marais?"

"Why?"

"You look like a Yid, that's all."

Jésus...

"Is that a problem?" Delphine blinked at that horrible slang word, all too aware that she was the sole customer. She then noticed the black swastikas tattooed on the girl's wrists.

"It will be if you don't fuck off, *vite*." She reached for her phone and dialled a number, holding it up for Delphine to hear the recipient's phone ringing.

"I'm a card-carrying Catholic, if you must know. So, get a life."

With that, she let the outer glass door slam behind her and with a pumping heart, ran back into the rain, glad that since her ordeal at *La Bergerie*, her ankles didn't give up on her.

Suddenly, there came a commotion from behind. Raised voices, the thud of fists on glass. Delphine twisted round to see a large, black Toyota with a 75 plate parked bang up against that same outer door.

Patrick Gauffroi?

He leant out of his driver's side window as two skinny teen boys in black stood behind it. Flick knives at the ready.

"What have you just done?" he demanded.

Two shrugs followed. "Nothing. Just piss off right now or else."

"You frightened my girlfriend," Delphine heard him say. "So now it's *your* turn." And with that, before they'd found another way to reach him, he'd pulled out a neat, black gun - possibly a Beretta - and aimed a shot at the ground by their feet. The door's glass vibrated and crackled into iceberg-sized slabs before splintering on the concrete.

Where had that weapon come from?

One of the teens bent down to clutch his booted foot, yelling obscenities, before Delphine spotted the cashier sneaking round from the far side of the small building.

"Watch out!" she shrieked at Gauffroi, and he briefly glanced her way. She needn't have bothered. He'd clearly learnt some tricks while in both prisons. He stuck his right leg out of his car to stop her then snapped her in a headlock, all without leaving his seat. He must have noticed her swastika tattoo because he kept hold until her panda-like eyes were nearly popping out of their sockets. She screamed for mercy.

He finally let her go. When Delphine reached the dual carriageway, he was behind her again, giving a thumbs up sign. And despite his busy windscreen wipers, she saw a victory grin on his face.

*

'Girlfriend?'

This couldn't go on. No way. She'd fought hard to cling to her dream of being in a GIGN team, and part of her, buried deep, still clung to it. The mysterious case of the missing Lavroches was pulling her away from France's soft middle to the bone and gristle of an ancient regional conflict. Its forested hills might seem harmless from the air - unlike Millevaches, whose scoured rocks were laid bare - but they harboured too much residual hatred, too much damage.

She'd have to send Patrick Gauffroi a clear signal. Subtle hints clearly weren't enough. He was a wanted man who could drag her down even further while time was running out. But why, despite plenty of opportunities to shop his precise whereabouts to Colonel Valon, had she kept him off the radar? Why, indeed? Perhaps now was the time. Perhaps not.

She couldn't keep lying to herself, couldn't forget that frisson of pleasure she felt when he'd first put his hand in hers at the *Fin du Monde* farm. And only hours ago, when he'd pulled her close and his lips had brushed her cheek, hadn't that felt even more intensely pleasurable? She couldn't answer. Or rather, she didn't *want* to answer.

It was more than complicated. However, there still remained the problem that she'd just paid for her fuel using a traceable credit card, and following his 'girlfriend' remark, they'd be linked together, giving more credence to her father's reason for springing him from jail. The dirty word 'accessory' again surfaced in her mind.

Keep moving...

The moment her speed nudged sixty-five kph, a gigantic, white-fronted lorry loomed up behind her and her phone began to ring. A glance at the number made her catch her breath. Was he psychic as well? Whatever he was, Gérard Massenet was in a hurry and sounded decidedly excited.

"Some news," he said without preamble. "Are you driving?"

"No," she lied without quite knowing why.

"I've just heard that the Vileneufs were followed from the hospital morgue as far as Labastide-Murat," he began. "About thirty kilometres north of Cahors, till the truck tailing them sped off once a police car appeared."

"When?" But she already knew the answer. She slowly realised, too, that she'd probably been spotted handing over that significant left boot.

"Yesterday afternoon sometime. No sign of the two idiots on board but the police are looking. Doing their job at last."

"Two idiots?" she repeated, slowing to a crawl in the slow lane. "The same ones I saw in the *Air du Vent* farm last Friday, and the bank this morning?"

"Really?" His tone changed imperceptibly.

"Yes. Maurice Amance and another guy who may have been Paul."

A sharp silence followed, save for the rain pattering against her flimsy roof, and a tailgating lorry behind her, flashing its lights.

"How would you know they were Maurice and Paul Amance?"

Delphine relayed both her encounters, the dots joining up with each syllable. "Research," she added. "Which was quite easy. I also think I know why the Vileneuf's were followed."

"Go on."

And while her tiny wipers battled against the strengthening sluice of water hitting the windscreen, Delphine relayed the history of that medically-altered left boot. How she regretted putting those grieving parents at risk and how her earlier meeting with Annemarie Colbert of Domus had proved useful. By sharing all this information, his estimation of her would surely shoot upwards like mercury in a thermometer at the start of a heatwave.

Wrong.

Yet another awkward pause followed.

"The Vileneufs think you're wonderful," Massenet said as if compensating for it. His voice softening. "So do I." He took a breath, sounding weirdly as if he was beside her. "Giving them my number was an inspired idea. Where are you, by the way? Are you alright?"

Yes, if a surge of conflicting emotions was normal.

"I'm fine, thank you. Just a bit busy preparing my case against Simone…"

A short but distinct cough made her stop before the surname.

"Delphine - Mademoiselle Rougier - look. I should have mentioned that if you change your mind about representing yourself, I'll step in. For free."

She gulped, almost losing concentration with that juggernaut still breathing down her neck.

"I mean it. Not a hoax."

"But you've got Amélie's funeral and everything, and your wife…"

"It's life, Delphine. And life goes on."

"And what about your suing of LVS for two million euros?"

The lorry finally overtook, hooting as it did so, burying her car in a wave of oily muck. When she'd finally composed her reply, she realised the lawyer had ended the call and she was speaking to herself.

36

"It's life, Delphine. And life goes on."

That oddly detached phrase perched in Delphine's mind until she pulled into a McDonald's just outside Dijon and ditched her egg sandwich, which had begun to smell sulphurous. The giant-sized TV next to the counter ran a news story about a former army captain who, that afternoon had seen off two wolves terrorising shoppers in a supermarket car park. He'd hurled a trolley, injuring one of them and, because he received threats to his life, was now under police guard.

Yet another nightmare, she thought, aware of a creeping exhaustion tempting her to find somewhere to stop for the rain-soaked night, sooner than she'd planned.

But no. She had to reach the Haute-Saône by midnight and in particular, the A31 to Nancy before the rain became sleet, or even snow, which wasn't uncommon in these areas.

She finished her veggie burger and Coke and, after Dijon, filled up her too-small tank yet again, constantly alert for both Patrick Gauffroi and any sly, lurking wolves.

*

At 22:15 hrs, she reached Lure, a modest, quiet town and a thankfully half-empty *Hotel du Fôret* situated next to a fire station. Having put her phone on its charger in her narrow, but otherwise comfortable room, she brushed her hair, applied a skim of make-up and made her way down to its small bar.

She urgently needed alcohol and information, but apart from an elderly, bespectacled man sitting in the far corner and a barman of about her age, busying himself behind the curved, mahogany counter, she was alone. He seemed to be her best bet and glanced up at her while setting out new beer mats. His movements were swift, purposeful, reminding her painfully of Martin Dobbs, the doomed restaurant manager at the *Hôtel les Palmiers* near Le Mans. His name tag however, showed THIERRY.

Delphine ordered a large Ricard and while it was being prepared, enquired where the nearest gendarmerie was.

"Are you in trouble?" he asked, scooping ice cubes into a carafe of water. She almost said *not yet*, but instead, smiled and pulled her glass containing the *anise* towards her. "No. But being in a new place, you never know."

"You don't," he agreed. "Especially with what happened near here yesterday evening."

The old man in the corner, looked up from his newspaper, his empty beer glass next to him.

"Please don't say wolves," said Delphine, paying for her drink.

"Well, if we don't watch it, the whole of France will become overrun like the damned Rockies. Never mind its farmers trying to earn a decent living." Thierry's face flushed with anger. His movements quickening, causing an empty liqueur glass to topple over.

"So, what happened?" she questioned, picking up the fallen bottle.

"A widow living in a semi-ruined pile outside Mélisey had most of her rare breeds of sheep torn to shreds. And I mean, torn." He handed Delphine her change. "She's just suffered a heart attack and may not survive."

"Poor woman. How shocking."

"It is. One witness was out walking her dog, saw six grey wolves stalking the meadows before the attack. She'd tried to raise the alarm by using her phone but was threatened by some arsehole with a rifle."

"Really?"

A nod.

"Said he'd be back to finish her and her dog off as well, if she so much as breathed a word. My brother now keeps three weapons on his farm near Épinal, and he'd kill the bloody lot of them if he could."

"I know who that *marginal* is," came that same old man's voice, loaded with venom. Obviously possessing excellent hearing, he set aside his newspaper and came over, touching each round table as he did so, as if getting to his feet had been a problem. "Paul Amance, from St. Loup-sur-Semouse." He almost spat out the name. "That lot should have been finished off by the *Boche* years ago. God knows their patriarch Honoré Amance and his wife deserved it, spawning Olivier. Or rather, *Genéral* Olivier..."

Here he seemed to run out of breath and Thierry passed him a glass of water, before moving on to other tasks. "Stay away, I say. If you want to see your next birthdays."

Thierry snorted while Delphine thought back to that sunny Monday afternoon before the observation and surveillance exercise. How long ago it seemed.

Almost a lifetime away.

*

"You look exhausted, if you'll excuse my saying so," the bespectacled man observed before sampling his water. "Are you from Paris?"

"No." She glanced back towards the glazed double doors, as Patrick Gauffroi and his discreet little gun flashed into her mind. "The Corrèze. And yes, you're right. I *am* all in."

"I'll not bother you, then," said her new companion, whose summer suit looked to be expensive, as did his polished, leather shoes. His teeth too, were all intact and well maintained. His skin, apart from a few age spots, was relatively unwrinkled. A man whose appearance was clearly important to him, yet a slither of grief sharpened his pale eyes. "However, my name's Christophe Beauregard. retired professor of politics and economics from Oppenburg University. Now, there's a place…"

Delphine finally carried her Ricard to the nearest table. Half of her wanted to be alone, but what he'd said had intrigued her. She pulled out a chair for him and gave her name, whereupon he stared at her. Part admiration, part anxiety.

"I recognise you now. You remind me of my wife when she was young," he said, sitting down again. "And our granddaughter. But she's safe in Brittany. Studying to be a vet."

Safe…

He'd painted so many pictures in so few words, Delphine could barely keep track.

"So, you've seen the news?" she asked.

"I have." Another drink of water. His Adam's apple bobbing as it passed down his throat. A hand reached out. A map of veins and yes, a few more age spots. "Mademoiselle Rougier, whatever you're doing here, you should return to the Corrèze tomorrow. This is the devil's garden, and I don't use that term lightly. Since my student days, I've made it my business to measure the revival of Marxist fanaticism in its most sinister and perverse forms. Its adherents adopt Hegel's 'dialectic' of freedom and self-determination to give themselves respectability. I'm afraid it's a cancer, still merrily metastasing."

'The work of the devil…'

So Amélie Massenet's old Mamie had said…

Just then, a clock somewhere chimed out eleven doleful notes, adding to

Delphine's sense of impending doom. She took a slug of her Ricard; its icy coldness startling her throat. She soon finished it in a few moments of rare pleasure, at the same time remembering her somewhat shaky *Baccalauréate* history examination in a chilly, stone-walled room, while beyond the one window, the sunflower harvest had been in full swing. Those withered, pendulous heads succumbing to twisting, growling blades.

"I thought the *Boche* had stamped on Walter Benjamin and his like," she said. "And besides, I've never understood atonal music. As for Brecht, give me Madame Bovary any day…"

"Nothing will stamp out these crackpot ideologies," said Beauregard, running that same hand through his thin hair. "Not even if a thousand people die on our streets, in our fields, parks and schools…"

"What are you saying?"

He leant forwards, both pale brown eyes enlarged behind his lenses.

"*La Vie Sauvage* was brought to birth at my very own university. Yes, for the past ten years Gèneral Olivier Amance has, within its walls, bounteously endowed various projects, this one included, from his own funds. The Adorno Fellowship is awarded bi-annually to whoever creates the most effective interpretation of the doctrine of freedom. And last year, the recipient was?" His substantial eyebrows raised in anticipation. "Guess?"

Behind him, Thierry was closing the bar. Its front shutter unfolding to a dull thud against the counter, making her jump.

"Maurice Amance?"

"Not quite. The other one."

Delphine recalled that group photo on Aristide's phone.

"Who?" She had to hear it.

"Paul Olivier Karl. The younger son. Mr Smooth himself…"

She'd felled them both at the *Air de Vent* farm. And they weren't going to forget it.

*

The former professor pushed back his chair and stood up.

"That's why you're here, isn't it? So far from home?"

That last word sounded more than strange. How, after the past week, could Saint-Arnoult ever be her home? Unless the dead Lieutenant Colonel Zanowski still had some clout. More than he'd had in life…

"No," she lied. "I just had to get away from it all. She then mentioned her previous visit to St. Loup-sur-Semouse with the convent school. "Their town too."

"What? As well as Amance?"

"Of course."

He paused. "By the way, I'm based at *les Papillons* in the *Impasse des Pêcheurs*. In case you need to know."

"Thank you."

"May I ask, did you drive here?"

"Yes. Why?"

"Well, Mademoiselle, if you're staying more than a fortnight, I suggest you acquire a local number plate. You need to fit in and not be seen as *une étrangère méfiante.* Understood?"

She did, all too well, and having jotted his phone number into her little notebook, asked if he'd heard of a Natalie Lavroche and her young son Joel.

"Another time, *hein*?" he said before waving goodbye, but she was too pre-occupied to return the gesture.

37

Wednesday 22nd June. 09:00 hrs.

'Une étrangère méfiante...'

After a broken sleep, the academic's words were still lodged in Delphine's mind as she re-packed her rucksack and made the best of her hair. She tidied her eyebrows, which if left unchecked, would soon resemble her father's.

She then pinned a discreet, blue-enamelled brooch to her tee shirt. A poignant souvenir from the *Café des Lilas* which her parents had inherited and run before buying *Bellevue* farm. A modest reminder that today, following yesterday's post-mortem, was young Amélie Massenet's funeral.

*

She skipped breakfast and, with welcome sunshine warming the car after yesterday's wintry chill, left the hotel and joined the D64 signed for Nancy, all the while checking no black Toyota was in sight.

Her priority was still to buy or borrow a charger for Aristide Abolego's BlackBerry, and not for the first time did she curse its manufacturers for not producing a universal one. She simply had to see what his phone contained. He'd not been so agitated for nothing, especially after more recent revelations.

The early sun, instead of casting the surrounding pine forests in a beatific glow, made them glower darkly on all sides like an invading army poised to strike, a disturbing illustration from a Brothers Grimm fairy tale.

'The devil's garden' indeed. Another of that engaging retiree's remarks which seemed so apt. Delphine thought back to the plantation of chestnuts near the Ruiseau d'Argent, where Aristide had offered her that sickly-

247

sweet chewing gum. How harmless it had all seemed before what came next. So, what might this even more sombre, ancient growth be hiding from prying eyes? A land harbouring too many dead from the *Guerre de Quatorze*. Men and beasts. Home to the largest abattoir in the north east.

She wound down her window and smelt death.

Hers.

*

Just as she reached the busy junction with the N57, she noticed two strategically placed signs. The smaller one welcoming travellers to the spectacular Vosges department was dwarfed by a huge and threatening LVS hoarding. Just then, her phone trilled from inside her bag.

Damn.

Roadworks had sealed off the *bande d'urgence* and its useful emergency phone, while both traffic lanes bore some of the biggest vehicles she'd ever seen. Most were animal transporters, whose slatted sides were covered by tarpaulins. She knew where they were headed, and no way would her vulnerable little car be trapped amongst them on the inside lane. So, while her phone kept ringing until its voicemail kicked in, she stepped on the gas to remain in the outside lane until, shortly after exit 36, a sign for Luxeuil-les-Bains appeared, then ST. LOUP-SUR-SEMOUSE.

This was accompanied by two more images of wolves' open jaws welcoming the businessman and holiday-maker alike. Both might taste the same, but not satisfy a hungry beast for long. The grim reaper. The great leveller.

Stalin and Marx must be applauding in their graves, she thought. Plus, when would Saint-Arnoult's Crime Investigation Unit be liaising with their counterparts here and giving her more grief?

"Delphine?" came a muffled voice from inside her bag. "You there?"

Aristide.

He still sounded scared, just like Romain Vileneuf had been.

"What's up?"

"Call me back," he breathed. "Please. There's no-one else I can turn to, and I daren't go to Paris till next week. Holy shit, man. They're… they're…"

His intense fear became lost to the heavy traffic's din, and all Delphine could do was wait until she'd left the mayhem encircling the popular spa town for the quieter road to her destination. A road little changed since her school trip.

She pulled into a layby at its farthest end in case the persistent Patrick Gauffroi should re-appear and block any getaway. Having locked herself in, she used the ring-back function on her phone and closed her eyes in sudden exhaustion as her friend began and finished his incredible story without interruption.

*

"Your *cousin?*" she said in disbelief, when he'd finished, trying to make sense of it. She thought back to Monday's revelatory lunchtime conversation with Colonel Valon.

"It's now in the papers, on the fucking news. Maman's terrified we'll be dragged through the mud, that her business will fail…"

"He'd known his way round La Santé, then?"

"How did you know?"

"Never mind."

"He'd done three years there for robbery. Learned a load of tricks… And how *l'Aigle Noir* can act…"

There. He'd said it…

"But why?"

"Folding dough. Always was, always will be. Well, not if he gets caught again."

"How on earth did my father find him? It's not as if he's ever been to Paris." Yet even as she asked the question, she knew the answer. It brought a lurch to her stomach. A feeling of utter hopelessness.

"I'm so bloody sorry, Delphine," he burbled. "But he's had a shite life. Far worse than mine. I'd always looked out for him, but when I came to the Corrèze…" Here he faded to nothing until she broke in.

"Was he paid up front?"

"I don't fucking know."

Was this true?

"And you as well, for being the go-between?"

"For Christ's sake!" He sounded even more distraught. Perhaps he could act too. Perhaps not. "The plan was to top the perp straight away."

"Not true."

"Sorry?"

"Never mind." But she did. Terribly.

"But this perp overpowered my cousin and broke free. Nicked his new Landcruiser and his Beretta 92FS, then vanished."

He'd used it at that garage....

"The Gendarmerie de France abandoned that make a few years ago," she said. "But Landcruisers are high end cars. At least forty thousand euros new. You claimed he was hard up."

"He lied to me, the shit." Aristide stalled. "I don't want to know."

"I bet you don't." Her blood was heating up. Her skin beginning to burn. François Rougier was another serial dissembler.

"Why call you on Friday morning at 8:45 hours saying '*fait accompli*. Job done. Wish my others were as easy?'"

"Another lie."

Aristide then stalled. "You got my BlackBerry from Belvère post office?"

"I did. Then the battery died. I'm trying to get a charger."

"Should have left mine with it. Sorry. Wasn't thinking straight."

Dead silence, until a filthy road sweeper positioned itself behind her, blocking out the sun. Heavy metal throbbed from its open windows.

"As for how you and Papa got so cosy - in my innocence, I'd mentioned you to him early on," Delphine said, as if explaining it to herself. "Where you'd come from, etcetera. And about your brother. You and me were friends, remember?"

"Were?"

Silence.

"Look, I'll come clean," Aristide continued more slowly. Calmly, as if the worst part of his secret was out. "Your father phoned me in early October, just after the perp had been transferred from Fresnes. Really friendly, he was. Quizzing me some more about our family... I'm sure he used a public call box, by the way. His number was untraceable."

Delphine pushed her free fist against her churning insides. Hadn't she stayed with her father most weekends, and often left her phone lying around if she was cooking him something or taking a shower? And hadn't Aristide's old number been near the top of her contacts list?

The sly old con, and a stupid one, too.

Aristide had also been given her father's number. Proof lay in that strange phone conversation she'd had with him and Simone Gallas on Saturday evening after the Parisian told him where that burnt wreck and the boot was. When the Venus flytrap's tone had soon changed to acid.

"The frigging cops have been leaning not just on me, but my mother *and* my sister," Aristide resumed his sob story. "As if we know where my cousin is. Just think, we could all get done for aiding and abetting. Perverting the course of justice. I had another grilling this morning from a little creep called Serra."

Big deal...

"And *I've* got Patrick bloody Gauffroi on my tail!" Delphine countered. "Good, *hein*? In his nicked fancy car. And yes, guess what sidearm he's got? A Beretta 92FS, too."

"Fuck."

"Correct. You see, I don't know him. Not really. Except he's seriously damaged goods."

Aristide sounded as if he might be crying, then came a mumbled promise to help catch him.

"*I'm* dealing with it, OK?" She said, still furious with her father, and with the whole shitty world. In four hours' time, an innocent little girl was being buried.

*

The road sweeper's driver was getting out of his cab and unzipping his jeans while facing into the hedge. Delphine saw his unusually pink cock send an arc of pee into the air.

Men...

"I also heard Romain's desperate plea on your phone," she added, leaving her reverie. "And told someone whom I'd trust with my own life."

"Colonel Valon?"

"Yes. He's solid."

Delphine could feel the other's relief through the airwaves.

"I knew I could rely on you. I felt so helpless. Still do. Didn't know where the hell he'd got to, and no-one else seemed to know either, or didn't want to tell me."

"Sadly, all too late."

"Poor bastard."

He paused.

"And the video? Have you seen it?"

"Not yet. Like I said, I need a charger. What's it about?"

"Make damned sure you don't delete it," was all he said, but it was enough. "And guard it with your life."

"OK."

"Are you in Saint-Arnoult?" He then asked, barely audible. "I'm at the youth hostel near the library. Can we meet up? Decide on a plan?"

"What plan? And anyway…" she had to think quickly. "I'm heading south. I need a break. Can you blame me?"

"No."

The road sweeper growled its way back on to the road.

"You'll hear about what's just happened to me, sooner or later," she spoke again and, assuming he'd missed the latest news, summarised her ordeal at *La Bergerie*. How it was probable that Romain Vileneuf had been held there too. How she'd sent three of his possible hairs to Colonel Valon and passed the boot on to his parents. Finally, that Lieutenant Colonel Zanowski had killed himself. Another victim of the brute, perhaps?

"I had heard."

A fraught silence followed, during which a black veil of starlings in flight covered the sky. A bad omen, her mother would say. And she should know…

"Look, wherever you are, I'm coming," Aristide said all of a sudden. His voice stronger, different. But seeing those starlings had spooked her. Her mouth seemed suddenly too dry in the devil's garden.

"No! You mustn't. Just stay where you are," came out harsher than intended.

He couldn't answer that, and instead admitted how on Monday, the *École* was like an empty shell. "Really weird, like a deflated balloon without you being there and everyone else fucked off home."

Tough...

Delphine then had an idea. Risky, but what the hell? She lightened her tone. Smiled, even though it hurt.

"Look, if you really want to help me, can you be at Amélie Massenet's funeral at two o'clock today? At the Église de Saint Luc. I'll pay you back for your taxi, so you can arrive looking smart."

"You're joking."

"I'm not. Can you make it?"

"I'll look out of place. You know what I mean."

She did, of course. A black Parisian amongst the white great and good. However, she needed a spy. This would be an important event for many reasons.

"To be honest, Aristide, you owe me."

"I know that."

"You're to look out for anything odd going on. Plus, two big, shaven-headed guys. Maurice Amance and his brother Paul. They could be lurking around, testing the water." She then described them in detail, including their accents and different eye colours. "They were the two yobs I tackled at the *Air du Vent* farm and who'd followed me to the bank in Saint-Arnoult are behind LVS."

"Got it. Anything else?"

"Amélie's mother had a serious breakdown. She's being treated in a specialist clinic."

"St. Sauveur. I heard that too. How Maître Gérard Massenet will be ripping off your father."

That lawyer's name had made her start, as well as how he'd said it. Best leave that for the time being, she reasoned with herself, sensing jealousy on his part. After all, Massenet's successful career path had been smooth, strewn with celebrities and top brass, unlike Aristide and his family.

"Papa will need a decent lawyer," she countered. "*And* your cousin, come to that."

She blinked at his sudden laugh, sensing another creeping shadow encroaching.

"The Black Eagle can look after himself. Trust me."

But, can *I?*

"Did either of you have any idea what frame of mind Patrick Gauffroi might be in after La Santé?" She then challenged him. "Could he be even more dangerous?" She remembered those red weals around his neck. The other scars…

"Because he'd been on suicide watch then solitary?"

"Not only that. He also has a past. A violent father for a start."

"That's why I need to be with you."

"Just be at St. Luc's church. And report back pronto. OK?"

"And you look at that video. Nearly cost me my life."

All about me….

"What's your cousin's real name?" She had to hear him say it, but just then, an ominous crackling sound filled her ear. "And his phone number. You've obviously been in touch with him since Friday morning. Now it's my turn."

"Shit. My new phone's breaking up…"

That was it.

Delphine pressed END and clicked in her seat belt. No good dwelling on what she couldn't control. Her priority was still to find a battery charger to access his BlackBerry's content, should it be needed as evidence. Her next moves after that also needed fine tuning. Time was already short and getting shorter, with too much at stake for her to fail.

38

With Aristide's confession and his inuendo about Gérard Massenet still on her mind, Delphine re-started her 2CV and drove towards St. Loup-sur-Semouse under a sky too blue, too fairy-tale, and knew from a young age how most of those ended.

At least along the straight stretch of road eventually leading west to Chaumont, it was easy to spot any black Toyota 4X4 which might be following. Just then, a camper van came close behind, enough for her to see a happy, smiling couple in the front. Late middle-aged and, it seemed, all worries behind them, unlike her parents. As the historic town's church spire loomed into view, she fretted for the first time how much her father really had paid *L'Aigle Noir* for a failed job, and what Gérard Massenet, with whom she'd fallen a little in love, would be charging for his services.

Why hadn't the 'inheritance' word troubled her before? Because under French law, everything passed first to the surviving spouse if they'd both signed a *donation entre nous*, then to their offspring, unless convicted of murder. Whispers at *Bellevue* hoped this archaic law might be revised, but the *status quo* remained and no mention was made again.

So, could what her father inherited from her mother and from selling their farm and its fifty-two hectares already be considerably diminished? Could the rest be swallowed up in just a week's worth of fees, especially if his case dragged on for months, even years?

Damn.

Was François Rougier really willing to use it all up on his moment of madness? Equally, was Massenet happy to take it?

Great white shark…

Then, as her father's only dependant, she decided to enquire if his bank account could be checked. Indeed, if this had already happened.

*

Now more than ever, she must focus even harder on why she was here, so far to the north-east, away from the productive pastures around the River Corrèze, where François Rougier had moved to be near her at the *École.*

She mustn't forget that. He'd followed her without a murmur, glad for a fresh start, it seemed. But everything had brightened because he'd met Simone Gallas, making the upheaval even more worthwhile.

She couldn't shoulder all the blame, but had recklessly shared her late mother's deadly secret with Patrick Gauffroi the previous year.

Now look…

Her heartbeat quickened as the spire drew ever closer and the River Semouse, in all its fulsome tranquillity, flowed by to her left, dark against the sky. The camper van couple overtook, giving her a cheery wave. Off somewhere pleasant, no doubt, with a comfortable double bed and home cooking to see them through.

In the increasing heat, those various oddments tucked inside her bra began to make themselves known. *Her* little secrets, until needed. There was simply nowhere else as secure, but meanwhile, her priority was to follow a huge *Mammouth* supermarket sign which had just appeared, bringing a surge of anticipation. There, nine kilometres away would surely be a battery charger.

As she drew closer, she saw it bore several all-too familiar posters stuck around its edges.

LA VIE SAUVAGE – JE SUIS ROI with those same wolves' teeth and jaws facing her way. Christophe Beauregard had been right. She really had entered the devil's garden.

*

The huge supermarket's dazzlingly sunlit car park was almost full, with yet more camper vans and caravans taking up two spaces apiece. Pleasure seekers, either leaving or *en route* to exploring the Vosges. Yes, she was exploring too, but not for herself. For the dead, the missing, and those to come.

Aware of her scratchy bra, Delphine hefted her rucksack on to her back, fearful of leaving it in the car, and grabbed the last available trolley. Its boiling hot handle almost took the skin from her palms. She then noticed it was designed for the disabled and glanced around to see if anyone answered that description. No, and besides, wasn't she one too? Handicapped by other people?

She was in luck, having spotted four less busy tills for shoppers with less than ten items, but by the time she'd finished trawling the aisles, hers amounted to nine. Miraculously, a BlackBerry charger, deodorant, Tampax (should her period arrive), two tubs of coleslaw, three bags of dried fruit pieces, a pack of mini *saucisses bergères* and a bar of nougat.

With so many tourists milling around, speaking anything but French, Delphine realised she should first have booked into another hotel. Having asked the pimply youth at the till to suggest one, he merely shrugged, while searching way too long for her Tampax packet's bar code.

Finally, and very publicly, he handed it back to her.

Great.

The thought of having to drive on to Nancy after all the kilometres she'd already inflicted on her little car dented her resolve, but not for long. Once outside, with her perishable shopping hidden under her father's old rug in the boot, she returned to the store with the receipt for the new charger, found a seat near the *toilettes* and plugged it into a wall socket.

How long would this take? She wondered, but in that moment, it didn't matter.

*

There were suddenly too many people queuing for the WC amid smells of sweat and meat being cooked for the lunchtime hordes in the self-service café. Meat most likely from that industrial-sized slaughterhouse. And then, after twenty long minutes, Aristide's BlackBerry came to life with its moving images, which made her lurch away towards the nearest exit.

Once outside, she almost collided with a minibus bringing a group of pensioners for their weekly shop. No wonder Aristide had sounded so distressed at that rural post office. Yes, some of the eight-minute video timed at 18.45 hours on Saturday had been out of focus, but there was no mistaking the animal lust. The revolting weirdness of a naked Simone Gallas and Alain de Soulibris performing cunnilingus on that couch in his office. The whip, the handcuffs. His grunting orgasm embellished with threats against herself, the 'marginale' and Aristide the 'ape' who should have been aborted. Romain Vileneuf was a 'peasant spawn' who'd deserved to die because he'd been too curious. Too gay.

Jésus.

Even the big, black Alsatian sharing the room, had become aroused, sniffing around them, growling, squealing. Rubbing its cock along the floor.

How on earth had Aristide managed to film it all without that dog sniffing him out? She couldn't imagine. Meanwhile, his BlackBerry still burned in her hand. Why not just delete everything and fling it in one of the bins beside the store? To keep it would be like harbouring a disease, but keep it she must. Gérard Massenet had to know.

*

He'd spoken so highly of the tart's late husband - a golfing companion - and even more highly of her. 'An incredible woman. A force of nature.'

It surely was her duty…

She found some shade beneath one of the few ash trees scattered amongst the parking slots, and without hiding her number, dialled his. The words were ready on her lips, but no. Only the robotic answerphone clicked into action, leaving her planned introduction unsaid and hanging in the thick, diesel-fumed air.

39

11:30 hrs.

Delphine smelt wolves. That same rank, muskiness as in the *Hôtel Mercure's* car park seemed to taint the almost unnatural heat as she studied a large street map outside the car park.

It showed Christophe Beauregard's street to be ten minutes away on the other side of town near the river, and while negotiating a roundabout ablaze with pelagoniums, she noticed a sign for Amance to the left. Not just a name any more, unnoticed on her school trip, but then she'd only been twelve, pre-occupied with her mother's depression. How dowdy she was compared to her more colourful, trendy friends.

Wolf country indeed, confirmed by the increasing number of those all-too familiar, threatening posters wrapped around lamp posts, and now even tree trunks. They defaced the most prominent walls and fences, while a huge, larger-than-life billboard simmered in the sun by a river bridge, depicting three of the creatures roaming in an empty meadow.

Her instinct was to stop and tear it down, to leave a symbolic scar, but her morning was almost over with still too much to do and, as she turned into the *Impasse des Pêcheurs*, checked again in her mirrors that she wasn't being followed.

*

She parked to one side in front of the open, elaborate ironwork gate to *Les Papillons*, the ex-professor's bungalow which squatted behind a substantial plot of land bordered in part by a fir hedge. She also noticed the same kind of electric fencing as at the *Air du Vent* farm. New, too, and she could see why.

Goats. The pretty Saanen variety, twelve in all, as white and plump as the meringues her best friend's mother used to make. The irreplaceable Pauline Fillol, whose sudden heart attack a year ago had felled her, aged just twenty-three.

And here, in another world, these delightful creatures lay sprawled in the sunshine. Their distended stomachs showing slight, quivering movements while delicate nostrils took in the sweet air, ears flicking back and fore as if on the edge of bliss. Soon to give birth. Yet, even with the secure fencing, they seemed far too vulnerable, just like those honey-coloured Limousin cattle before they were reduced to a few bloodied remains. And then the darkest of probabilities struck her. Could Christophe Beauregard be deliberately tempting fate? To nail yet another atrocity at the door of LVS? This was too awful to think about. Besides, these creatures might not even be his.

"Bonjour, Mademoiselle."

She looked up to see him approach, hand outstretched and with a welcoming smile.

"I wondered if I'd see you again," he added. "You left quite an impression, you know."

Delphine returned his smile as they shook hands. He still wore that pale, summer suit, but this time with a carefully folded blue handkerchief in its top pocket, and a discreet Oppenburg University badge. Just right for a retired academic, probably about to leave for some function or other.

She was right.

He explained he'd be having lunch in Nancy, then joining an important forum on the future of farming in the region in the light of re-wilding and EU reductions in subsidies. "All very pertinent and urgent," he said, unlocking the bungalow's three Yale locks with different keys, while she spotted three tiny cameras ranged along the front wall just below the guttering. He then showed her into a warm, bright vestibule, beyond which she also noticed several neat outhouses surrounding an immaculate, paved yard. "And if LVS continue their warped programme with more carnage," he added, "the sheep farmers here will be out in force, blocking the roads."

"They protested in Saint-Arnoult," she said.

"I know, and just you wait. They're a different breed here. Whatever you think of their young leader, he has no fear."

Delphine had seen images of Gaspard Poussot at various gatherings, and he'd supported the farmers in Saint-Arnoult whose action in its centre had been swiftly aborted. A graduate who, like Patrick Gauffroi, had taken over his parents' farm in the Charente. Except, unlike Gauffroi, he had the face of a choirboy, and so far hadn't killed anyone.

"In the meantime, as you can see, I'm doing my best with my girls," Beauregard went on. "Their milk is really good for asthmatics and goats' cheese is still popular." He scanned the scene through the vestibule's one window. "Perhaps what future is allowed rests with everyone like me, rearing stock on a small scale, even in their gardens. At least keeping them safe."

"That's capitulation, surely? And I hate to say it, but a new electric fence didn't protect those poor cattle near Saint-Arnoult."

His eyes behind his glasses grew sharper, as well as his tone. "Just let them try here. And if this plot becomes a battleground, so be it. I'm not the only one making a stand. There were yearling wolves in the churchyard yesterday, digging up fresh graves, damn them." He then glanced at the same not-too distant church spire she'd noticed on her way into the town. "If that doesn't tilt public opinion, then nothing will."

"What also puzzled me about the *Air du Vent* farm was the lack of guard dogs. You don't seem to have one either."

"A dog would be the first to suffer and I love them too much." Her host then checked his watch and pointed to the equally bright kitchen beyond the hallway, where two leather briefcases stood propped up against the table. "The coffee's still hot if you'd like a cup."

"Thank you."

Once he'd prepared it and placed a Madeleine cake in her hand, he explained how Georg Wilhem Hegel's philosophy of self-determination had resulted in the lunacy of such groups as the LVS and Domus.

"Domus?" She stared at him.

"Would *you* like a crocodile in your paddling pool, or a boa constrictor in the bedroom?" He was serious.

"My God. I thought they just dealt with small reptiles and birds…"

The laugh was dismissive. "Did you hear their airhead apologist on the radio yesterday? Talk about brain-washed." He passed Delphine a black coffee in a plain white mug, switched off the cafetière and stayed standing, thinking hard.

"No," Delphine lied, aware of how she didn't really know the ringless Christophe Beauregard and whether he was a bachelor or bereaved. So, best keep things simple. "It's mad."

"And ongoing, unless more people stand up and be counted."

From his suit pocket, he produced a folded section of *Le Figaro* and opened it out on the table. Dated a fortnight ago.

JULIEN GALLAS DEATH POSSIBLY LINKED TO WINE-GROWING CARTEL

Delphine stared at the next four short lines about his growing opposition to dangerous pesticides, ending with… 'According to the Chief of Police in Saint-Arnoult, investigations are still ongoing.'

"Seven months after he'd been shot?" Delphine observed. The date at the top written in ballpoint.

"Why so surprised? It's all lies." Beauregard retrieved the piece, tucking it away again. "A cover up."

And Simone Gallas had still been investigating it. Or not…

The clock's ticking was the only sound in that potent pause before her next question.

"Can I ask where you found that cutting? It's hardly a microfiche printout."

"Through the grapevine. No, seriously, I've a useful contact down in the Corrèze. Useful *and* thorough."

"I'm guessing. Claude Ridal of *La Campagne?*"

"Ten out of ten."

His coffee remained untouched, something important was still clearly on his mind. She drank hers, accompanied not by the Madeleine, but by a thought of that energetic cyclist not answering his phone. Another nagging question. "You said 'all lies…'"

Her host pulled the plain green blind down to cover the one window over the sink.

"Because Julien Gallas was *really* writing a book targeting the IUCN - the International Union for the Conservation of Nature, warning them of their support for the breeding and release of a particular species posing a danger to agriculture and human life."

"You mean wolves?"

A nod. "Canis Lupus. Especially after the success of the Yellowstone Park scheme in 1995, the Polish influx and Iberian lynx introduced to the Jura in the 70's which we still enjoy." His sarcasm obvious. "The result? More loss of sheep, until their farmers were advised to graze them at least two hundred metres from the tree line. Unless they're starving, those cowardly predators won't venture into the open."

"And this book's title?"

"*'The Evil That Men Do*,' which is entirely appropriate. Claude Ridal thought so, too."

"Where is it?"

"No idea," he said, perhaps too quickly, she thought. "But I could make enquiries." He eyed his watch again while Delphine debated whether or not to mention the safe in Simone Gallas's study. She could, in fact, ask that locksmith who'd opened it and the sympathetic Lieutenant Patry if they might have spotted it whilst retrieving her belongings. However, her companion hadn't mentioned her ordeal there, so best let it lie.

"Thank you," she said instead, getting up and taking her mug to the sink. "I realise you have to go, but perhaps we can keep in touch?"

"We will." He replied, gathering up his briefcases and leading the way back to his front door, whose textured glass panels sparkled in the sunshine. Again, he unlocked it three times before half-turning to give her a grandfatherly look of concern and placing his plain card into her hand. "By the way, I do know what happened to you at *La Bergerie*. All the more reason for you to return and keep an eye on your father. At least you'd be safe."

She thought of the invitation to the château, chafing against her skin.

"That word should be made obsolete."

"I'm tempted to agree," and when she'd almost reached the gate, he called out after her, "Paul Olivier Karl Amance lives in *La Bastide* at the end of the Rue des Pins, just along there." He pointed north-east where a black forest of firs rose up against the summer sky, stock still in the midday heat. "And as for that charmer, Maurice, he's just bagged himself a big apartment at the family pile. Nice work, *hein*? All very cosy."

One or two goats who'd raised their pretty little heads in curiosity soon succumbed again to sleep, while Delphine, who'd forgotten to ask about Natalie Lavroche and young Joel, was out of luck again. The busy retiree was already disabling his car's alarm and, having locked the heavily padlocked gate behind himself, re-entered that world which so troubled him.

Having said goodbye to his small flock, willing them and their unborn kids to stay unharmed, Delphine drove towards those dominating trees as if drawn by a magnet, all too aware that some four hundred kilometres away, little Amélie Massenet was soon to be forever hidden from sight.

*

Before venturing any further down the oddly quiet Rue des Pins, Delphine cleaned her sunglasses with a used tissue - the only one left in the box - and looked for somewhere to park out of sight of the target's house.

You're no longer a student...

Nevertheless, she'd not survived an attempt on her life and been snared by her father's deceitful agenda for nothing.

Sod it.

Let the low life in *La Bastide* see her vivid, turquoise car. Aristide had once said it was part of who she was, so with clean shades and a melting dash of '*Rose Douce*' lip gloss, she edged forwards to where the smart, detached villas on either side became further apart. Some boasted stables, others offered gîtes, reflecting the increasing tourism of this historic but previously troubled area.

With the high sun directly in front, Delphine adjusted her sunglasses, pulled both her car's visors right down and found a small, overgrown layby next to a field of grazing ponies. She completed a four-point turn to park in it facing the way out. Just in case. She'd also be better able to see if Patrick

Gauffroi was still on the scene.

She sat for a few moments psyching herself up for what was the start of her data-gathering agenda, and once outside her car, listened hard for the slightest sound. Apart from whinnying from some distant field and the 'pew-pew' of a hunting sparrow hawk, there was nothing to suggest this was wolf territory. All of a sudden, a particular smell met her nose.

With the 2CV locked and her bag safe inside her rucksack, she crept towards *La Bastide*, trying to ignore her bra's crucial contents rubbing even more against her skin.

40

13:00 hrs.

La Bastide matched exactly Christophe Beauregard's description. Money writ large, with those same snarling wolf posters hogging every available surface. A multitude of menace, making Delphine swear out loud.

"Ssh!" She warned herself. Everything had ears, and the silence enveloping this scene was too fraught with unwelcome possibilities. With no near neighbours and the menacing, motionless black forest perched on the hill behind, anything could happen. Just as when she and Aristide had come across the Lavroche couple by the Ruiseau d'Argent. Except that here so far, there were no people.

She'd been trained how to approach a target without being seen. To blend into a hostile environment, which this surely was. She could sense it in the windless, static air, like an open grave.

No people, but…

She picked up that distinctive smell again, plus the faintest of sounds resembling coughing. Or a bark, perhaps? But as she sidled along behind a boundary wall to her right, which marked the hilly pastures from the property's manicured grounds, came the unmistakeable noise of a car engine. Its distinctive *phut… phut* rhythm she recognised from somewhere before.

Think…

And just as the realisation hit her, a red Renault Twingo emerged from behind the sprawling house, heading towards a rustic-looking five barred gate which silently began to open automatically. One glimpse at the driver and the local number plate told her who it was.

Natalie Lavroche, buffed up to the nines, determinedly steely, even with her large shades in place as she drove by. An empty child's seat next to her. Delphine tucked herself out of sight and managed to take a photo on her phone, then wondered, because of no school on Wednesdays, if the young mother might be collecting Joel from somewhere else. However, she wouldn't be staying to find out.

She had to follow, and fast.

Despite a sudden, nagging weakness in both her ankles, she managed to reach her car while the Twingo was held up at the T junction by a slow-moving tractor laden with late-cut silage. Sounds of angry hooting hung in the hot, grass-filled air, followed by shouts. Natalie Lavroche was definitely in a bad mood and in a hurry. But for what?

Delphine kept a discreet distance as the Twingo followed the low-lying River Semouse back into town, before turning right at a building whose tall, narrow shape was instantly recognisable.

La Belvédère, the former hostel where in 1993 she and her fellow convent school pupils had stayed, but this time, in all its restored glory.

She almost lost concentration as she took in the bright, new exterior and white PVC window frames. A far cry from the drab greyness of years gone by, and as far as she could tell, one of the few buildings without a wolf sticker.

Damn...

A transporter bearing a load of sawn tree trunks was tailgating her so closely she could even see the driver's mouth cursing her for having slowed down.

"Come on, let's show him," Delphine muttered to her straining little car, before drawing clear and patting her thanks on its dashboard.

*

Soon, in the land of fir and pine, with no dwelling or a living soul as far as the eye could see, she focused on the two cars that now lay between her and her Twingo target. The first, an ordinary family saloon with a blue sports bike perched on its roof. A strangely familiar image. Behind this, a small, white van with a local number plate. Both had sneaked in front of her on that earlier roundabout and both kept up with the Twingo in front, making no effort to overtake it on the straight, otherwise empty road. Were all three off somewhere together? Or was paranoia now her middle name?

Suddenly, a thin, almost invisible sign on the right caught her eye. Half embedded in a dark hedgerow, LE CHÂTEAU DES ILLUMINATIONS was nevertheless causing all three vehicles ahead to brake and, with no signal, swing left onto a track smothered by overgrown evergreens.

So *that's* where it was. Merely imagining what lay beyond sent a wintry chill straight to her marrow. No way would she risk following them into the unknown. Nor was there anywhere to wait until they showed up again.

Thankfully, a mini roundabout let her lose the giant-sized pest behind her and head back to St. Loup-sur-Semouse. Her errand at *La Bastide* had been interrupted, but more than usefully, especially for tomorrow. Whatever the weather, whatever she might be feeling, Thursday could prove one of the most important days of her life.

Yet the maggot in the apple took the form of a question. With her mother and enough others, including Lieutenant Colonel Zanowski, dead, who was there to impress?

"Pathetic," she admonished herself out loud before the distinguished face of another straight-backed man swam into her mind, bringing with it yet another guilty tremor of desire.

While re-tracing her route to *La Bastide*, with the sun more fierce than before and that same hostel glowing invitingly, Delphine imagined the bereft Gérard Massenet and his mother probably already at the Église de St. Luc. His wife, too, from wherever she was, but her thoughts in that direction were shamefully shallow and fleeting.

'You deserve to fail,' came the ghostly voice of Sister Marthe from her convent school. And this time, Delphine knew she was right.

*

With the contents of her bra still aggravating her skin, she turned once again into the road for *La Bastide*, preparing to park where she had before, when she spotted two men dressed in all black with matching balaclavas, moving up the hillside behind the splendid homestead. She pulled her grandfather's reliable binoculars from her glove box to see that each man carried a large, steel cage apiece, containing what were most definitely not dogs.

Jésus...

Both men were almost certainly those she'd encountered at the Lavroches' farm.

With a rapidly drying throat, she took several photos, as one by one these cages were opened to allow four, fully-grown grey wolves to creep out; their powerful haunches lowered and quivering until, like four shadows, they slunk away upwards to that brooding colony of pines which Christophe Beauregard could see so clearly from his property.

She knew the Office for the Dead liturgy by heart and murmured it to herself while imagining Amélie Massenet's broken body resting in its small white coffin in front of a huge congregation. Imagining her father facing a void without his only child and a wife incarcerated elsewhere. She hoped too, Aristide was at Amélie's funeral, on alert.

Look...

Both men then exchanged triumphant high-fives with each other before dragging their empty cages back towards the rear of the house. And why not? They had a cause to believe in. A reason to get up in the morning. She visualised Christophe Beauregard's pregnant goats not so far away, how they might just be more than a hobby.

Non.

But the 'bait' word lingered in the overheated air. Was their apparently concerned owner really so callous? Anything was possible in this weirdly hot, claustrophobic place. As she was about to put her binoculars away, she caught sight of something quite different.

A young, dark-skinned boy riding a new-looking purple bike had appeared from behind the house. He was dressed in a yellow tee shirt, navy shorts and flip-flops, both his cheeks and legs showed several visible scratches. Could this be Joel Kouchia?

Delphine also took several photographs of him wobbling towards the gate, wanting his Maman, no doubt, until the taller man ran up to him, yelling instructions to get indoors or else. Heavy-jawed and shaven-headed save for an odd black crop of hair dividing his scalp, he'd also featured in Aristide's photo of Général Amance by that fountain.

Surely this was Maurice Amance, and although at that distance, she couldn't see his eye colour or hear any giveaway northern accent, the family likeness was obvious.

However, it was young, scared Joel whose bike was being snatched from under him, who impelled her to take one last photograph before slipping her car into reverse and edging away from thse oppressive, overhanging trees.

"Poor little kid," she muttered, rejoining the road into town. What had his feckless mother been doing at that château with those other cars? Her late best friend Pauline Fillol often said people should apply for a special licence before breeding, but it was also the fate of her own parents which drove Delphine into planning tomorrow's agenda in more detail, until her phone began to ring and Gérard Massenet's number flashed up.

41

To answer his call, she drove into a convenient layby, avoiding an overflowing litter bin and its swarm of wasps. She then snatched up her phone.

"Delphine?" came the voice she'd secretly been wanting to hear which, given the lawyer's unhappy situation, seemed remarkably composed. "You've been on my mind since yesterday morning. Are you alright?"

"Good, thank you. And you?"

A pause, during which came the unmistakeable sounds of traffic. A car's horn. The rumble of a truck. Odd, she thought, because the Église de Saint Luc and its graveyard were situated in a quiet street, and surely the funeral service wouldn't yet be over…

"So-so. Seeing Amélie being covered with earth has been bad enough, and now my wife's on so much medication, she's bedridden. It'll be tough for a while."

She could feel his pain.

"I'm really sorry."

"So, where are you?" He asked, back to business. "Hervé Latrisant's been trying to get in touch. He came to pay his respects earlier this morning and reassure me he's gathering more information on your abduction and the La Santé episode."

That last name brought a ripple of fear. That young judge, previously mentioned in only general terms, was also in the chase.

"Surely he's got my phone number from my father? Even you…"

"There are specific protocols," Massenet replied, almost too quickly.

"Especially with the public prosecutor breathing down his neck."

"What protocols? You mean the police will be tracking me down?"

"In a nutshell, yes. But now, not *will* be. You surely must have studied the basics of French criminal law at your *École*?"

She had, but much of it was too complex.

"The magistrate for detention and release of suspects will have to consider extensions of custody unless key witnesses are in place. That costs money and causes untold tensions."

"That's next year's focus," Delphine argued, almost adding she wouldn't be there anyway, and the longer this conversation struggled along, the more uncertain she became about her plans.

Through her rear-view mirror, she noticed a small, dark blue car pull in at the far end of the layby, behind her. A Citroën, with a black-haired female driver, checking her make-up.

"So, it's best you give me your whereabouts so I can guarantee you a softer landing, if you'd excuse that expression."

She couldn't. In both cases, *she* was the victim. Then the thought sneaked into her mind that this wealthy, ambitious lawyer might have been pissed off at her wanting to represent herself. Perhaps because she'd be out to skin Simone Gallas alive. A woman who, according to Aristide's phone video, had also been enthusiastically fellating the brute to a roaring orgasm.

Just to think of it made her feel queasy all over again. But those lurid few minutes were crucial evidence she'd need.

"I'll wait to hear from him myself, if that's OK," she said. "Because I'm actually trying to scatter my best friend's ashes this afternoon, and tomorrow I'll be…"

"Pauline Fillol?"

What?

Delphine shut her eyes, hoping this might help her out of the hole she was digging for herself. How on earth did Gérard Massenet know about Pauline? Had he been digging around into her own background? Her contacts? And that begged the question, what else had he found?

"Are you still there? Delphine...?"

His tone was imperceptibly sharper, but wherever he was, she let him dangle; dead daughter or not. She had enough to do, beginning with booking herself in at that tempting-looking hostel before any *'complet'* sign went up.

"Your father's worried about you, too," he added in the rumbling interlude. But she wasn't convinced. François Rougier surely had enough on his plate to fret about her after just twenty-four hours. "And the fact that you'll soon learn he paid fifteen thousand euros to someone called *L'Aigle Noir* to release Patrick Gauffroi from la Santé."

His tone had picked up. He was enjoying himself.

Fifteen thousand?

So, Aristide had lied. Big time.

"Happy with that? Especially since it went wrong."

She knew what was coming next. Tried not to listen.

"And guess who this creep's related to?"

Silence.

"Your close friend from the *École*. You know who I mean, Delphine. Aristide Abolego. All the more reason for you to return to Saint-Arnoult to be put fully in the picture."

Return?

Panic reached her heart.

"And meanwhile, to reassure you, in case of any - how-shall-I-say -

awkward phone calls, your Samsung SPHA900 is temporarily being monitored."

She stared at it, as if frozen.

How had he known its model number?

"Who by?"

"For your own safety."

"You?"

No reply.

Delphine repeated that serious sum of money again. Being selfish, it could have bought her a studio flat. Nevertheless, that wasn't what gripped her mind as she drove badly back to St. Loup-sur-Semouse, but the growing sense of a keep-net tightening around her, cutting into her skin. Her insides. Her very life.

*

Although the hostel's exterior had changed out of all recognition, its interior layout remained almost the same, with those large reproductions of mountain scenes on the Donon Massif in which huntsmen crouched with their rifles amongst the gloomy forestry and the River Semouse darkly coursing south.

But when Delphine saw who was allocating rooms to a mixed group of Japanese students, she felt a huge sense of relief. For its owner, Pascale Dulay hadn't changed at all. Still that round, red-cheeked face framed by a matching bandeau, keeping her thick, shoulder-length hair in place. Yes, now grey in places, but that smile still the same, while handing out keys.

When she recognised Delphine, however, that smile evaporated, replaced by a frown.

"Oh Lord," she reached out a hand then moved from behind her glassed-in counter. "Your poor mother, and poor you." Pascale's frank gaze moved from her visitor's messy hair to her scuffed Nike trainers. "Where was *He*, *hein*?"

"Who?" Delphine tried to stem tears, before being encased in those soft but sturdy arms.

"Him up there, of course. Waste of space, I know that now." Pascale paused to pass her a tissue from her tunic's pocket. "And how could I forget those ugly nuns pushing you young girls about with one hand round your necks, the other on their rosaries. And after that dreadful news about your mother, I kept every cutting I could."

"Why?" Delphine beware of more visitors arriving. Belgian, Dutch and English, impatient to be checked in.

"Because you'd struck me as being different from the others. A bit special. Alert, curious." Pascale Dulay eyed her some more, making those new arrivals wait. "So, what's brought you back? Pleasure or trouble?" Her neat eyebrows raised in genuine interest. "Please don't say trouble."

"I'll tell you later," aware of a tall man standing too close behind her. "Is room 8 available?"

"It is, and you'll see the difference. Oh, and by the way, in case you're wondering why we're not covered in LVS stickers, it's because I refused. The whole enterprise is cruel. Wolves should be in the wild, not on the streets. The world's gone mad."

Delphine agreed, then gave her bank card details and took the key. A blur of emotions and imagery accompanied her as she reached the first floor. From stern Sister Marthe watching her undress, to young Joel's scratched, frightened face, and that inscrutable lawyer, Gérard Massenet.

Without another mobile, she'd have to use public call boxes.

Shit…

Surely phone-tapping a private individual not accused of anything was illegal? And how the hell had he known her Samsung's exact model?

*

Amid the clatter of wheeled luggage on the hostel's tiled floors, Delphine opened the door to room 8 and immediately locked it behind her.

Pascale Dulay was right. What a difference…

There'd once been four single beds, two tiny washbasins with a communal toilet at the end of the corridor. Now, in its new, air-conditioned brightness, she stripped off her clinging clothes and laid the precious contents of her bra together on the narrow, teak table under the slatted window. Two items she mustn't let out of her sight.

The *en suite* bathroom was perfect and, while the cool water in its shower coursed over her body, she plotted out the rest of the day, beginning with buying certain clothes she'd never normally wear, including flat, black pumps, a pair of glasses with the lowest corrective lenses and finally, blonde hair dye which she could have bought at *Mammouth* for half the price had she not been so fixed on finding a battery charger.

With a towel tied around her damp waist, Delphine then focused on those two beds. What if the hostel should fill up so that each one was needed? Pascale hadn't said. She'd pay extra, if necessary, to keep it for herself. Even de-camp elsewhere if her privacy couldn't be guaranteed.

So much had happened since she'd last stood here with her three classmates, staring out of that same window at a party of boys arriving by coach from Lille for a week of adventure. How she, Claudine Cresson and Mariette Dujardin had picked those they'd liked best, but because of different timetables, had never seen again. She wondered where they were, especially the slightly stocky character with short, light brown hair and a nice smile, who suddenly reminded her of Patrick Gauffroi.

281

While drying herself, she also wondered, as a dark blue Citroën Saxo circled the nearby roundabout and sped away towards the town, where he might be. Without that distinctively large black Toyota, her persistent follower could be driving anything, unless he was using public transport or hitching lifts.

42

17:00 hrs.

With her shopping contained in a carrier bag, Delphine made her way back through the Rue des Marchands lined with small, half-timbered houses, towards the Church of St. Martin and its car park, home to yet more images of that snarling wolf's face. As for a new phone, there weren't any in the town itself, and *Mammouth* was closed following a fire alert.

The hostel's car park had filled up since she'd left it and, out of habit, cast her shaded eyes over the other vehicles in case that black Toyota had re-appeared. But no, and on impulse, before opening up her broiling car, she decided to pay Christophe Beauregard a call. His pregnant goats still on her mind.

She'd just opened her driver's door and felt the blast of heat on her face, when her phone rang.

Damn…

Colonel Valon.

END.

The carrier bag slipped from her sweaty hand, allowing a black pencil skirt and white blouse to slide from it to the dusty ground. Having retrieved them, she noticed an empty call box over the road. A miracle, even though it was like an oven smelling of pee. Nevertheless, having paid, she dialled the colonel's number.

"Sir, my phone's kaput." she lied. "A call comes in, and that's it. Boom. Why I'm in a call box."

His voice crackled into her ear.

"Can you hear me?"

"Just about."

"Some news. I was in the Gorge de l'Abbaye yesterday morning…"

He'd not wasted much time.

"Is that wreck still there?"

"Was. All hush-hush. I've already said that invading other pitches isn't a good career move, especially with a public prosecutor and judge now in place. I need to be quick. Ready?"

"I am."

"The remains of this wreck were being cut up with arc welders. All highly organised. Four men. Dark-haired, but hard to tell their ages. Late twenties to mid-thirties, I'd say."

Good God…

"I took some film and got their truck's plate. Seventy. Haute-Saône. A step in the right direction."

"A grey Ford Transit?"

"Correct. Also, on Monday afternoon, the Vileneufs were followed on their way back from Saint-Arnoult to Cahors."

"I've heard that too. Are they OK? Have they still got that boot?"

"I assume so. But who told you?"

"Maître Gérard Massenet, yesterday morning."

Pause.

"Really? What's that to do with your father's case?"

"Good question."

"Who's representing him?"

"He is. Why?"

Another pause.

"He won't come cheap."

"Exactly what I've been thinking."

A massive, glistening camper van hovered in front of her 2CV, searching for a vacant space. When the driver realised she wasn't preparing to move, he trundled away to try elsewhere.

"Look, I know someone good who's not got a mansion in Barbados, so just let me know if your father changes his mind."

"Thanks. I will." Yet a further, unexpected facet of this lawyer's life anchored itself like a barnacle in her mind.

And just then, her straining heart seemed to open. This man who'd stood by her in the worst of times had to know...

"I'm actually in St. Loup-sur-Semouse, and that's very hush-hush too. I have to find out what Genéral Olivier Amance is up to." She then recounted how she'd tailed Natalie Lavroche and two other cars to his château.

"And?"

"I also saw her little boy Joel at *La Bastide*, Paul Amance's pile. He was scared. I tell you, colonel, this is where it's at."

"What exactly?"

"Grey wolves. The whole shebang. Big time. They're bred here - maybe elsewhere too, in this region. I saw four of them being released from *La Bastide...*"

Silence.

A sleek VW was reversing into the empty space next to hers. Another young couple with eyes only for each other. The beautiful people, she thought uncharitably, something she'd never be, and yet...

"Delphine?"

"Yes?"

"Get away from there. Leave it alone. Remember last year? The winter before…"

"I know, sir. But in a strange way, I feel Maman's keeping me focused. Her family came from not so far away and she'd be shocked at what's happening. Ruthless killers deliberately freed to roam amongst ordinary people going about their daily lives. Risking death, just by being here. But I'm not scared. Nor was Julien Gallas."

"Hello?" The line became clearer, and Delphine explained about the controversial book he was supposed to have completed, all the while careful to keep the ex-professor out of the frame. At least, for the time being.

"I'm writing this down," said the colonel. "Confidentially, of course. His death was a mystery."

"Thank you. His widow has a big safe at *La Bergerie* where she kept my stuff. It could be in there. Mind you, after Lieutenant Perron opened it, who knows?"

"I've a few friends in the Corrèze. I'll do some digging. And by the way, should a certain Hervé Latrisant gets in touch, tread carefully. He's just out of a very nasty divorce. His judgement may be compromised."

"I trust you," she said. And meant it.

"And I you. But you need to come back as soon as possible. I don't want a…"

…*dead Delphine*…What that sly, corrupt Lieutenant Lise Confrère had said not so long ago…

"I will. Don't worry."

A strange laugh followed. "'Don't *worry*', she says. That's a pretty big ask."

"The answers do lie here," Delphine repeated more emphatically, contradicting her promise. "And I'll be back in Saint-Arnoult before you can say my father's name."

A pause, in which she noticed those same beautiful people eating each other's faces.

"The main reason I'm urging you to return is because of a note found on Lieutenant Colonel Zanowski's body. He'd shot himself in the head."

"No."

Delphine shuddered just to imagine it.

"He demanded you be allowed to continue your course at the *École*. How you'd been an exceptional student in Compagnie 1. Are you listening?"

Shit...

"I am." For the second time that day, hot, salt tears reached her tired eyes. So Véronique Morel hadn't lied.

"Please hang on to that, and whatever your father's fate, he'll know you're getting on with your life. And speaking of him..."

Delphine waited as the neighbouring lovers pulled apart and seemed to be hunting for cigarettes.

"Big news," Valon added decisively. "Then I've a big farm theft to deal with. Are you ready?" And before Delphine could reply, he told her that those three hairs from *La Bergerie* which she'd sent him were a 100% match with those on Romain Vileneuf's head.

*

She closed her eyes.

"I've informed the public prosecutor and Judge Hervé Latrisant. I had to. Another reason for you not to linger there. Things could begin moving pretty quickly."

"Not while the Lavroches are still missing."

"Look, I'm giving you my private number. Meanwhile, please remember the name of this lawyer I know. David Welbeck. He's English and has been practising in Le Mans for twenty years, but also has offices in Poitiers and Brive. I'll alert him you might be getting in touch. Just in case."

"Thank you."

"Now listen. This is important."

Delphine held her breath.

"That black Toyota Landcruiser you told me about has been traced at lunchtime to guess where?"

"I can't." Her lips seemed numb.

"Dijon station car park of all places. Empty and cleaned to perfection. And I'm wondering why."

Me too...

"And I'm wondering how you knew."

Pause.

"Please."

"An anonymous call from a pay-as-you-go phone. It's been checked."

Suspicion, like a black moth, fluttered in her mind.

"Male? Well-spoken?"

"Hardly."

"But still male?"

"Yes."

Just then, without warning, before any chance to admit her Samsung was also being tapped, his line went dead. Perhaps a signal failure. Perhaps he'd said everything. Whatever. She was more than unsettled, not least because Patrick Gauffroi could be still within spitting distance, but also a certain someone with a talent for disguising his voice.

*

Delphine returned to the *La Belvédère* hostel so preoccupied by what she'd heard and imagined, she didn't notice that just three cars along from her 2CV stood a dark blue Citroën Saxo with its female driver, whom she half-recognised from earlier, preening herself in its rear-view mirror.

Thankfully, the dining room was still open and the various cooking smells reminded her she was starving. "No-one ever won a battle on an empty stomach," her mother had said. And she was right. For tomorrow to be a success, she had to be fully prepared in every way, and this propelled her onwards towards the reception desk, where Pascale Dulay was busy taking a call and uncharacteristically frowning as she did so.

43

The call didn't last long, and when Pascale finally glanced up at Delphine, her frown was still in place.

"That was odd. Someone was asking if you were here, without giving their name or saying why."

"A man?" This was becoming a habit.

"Not sure. What with all the racket going on in the background."

"And the number?"

"I'll check."

Don't bother, thought Delphine bleakly, seeing the helpful woman shake her head. The sooner the better she got another phone sorted and shut herself away.

"Zilch. I'm sorry," Pascale said finally, and looked as though she meant it.

"That's the second time it's happened," said Delphine pulling out her Samsung. "And *this* is now being tapped. Good, eh? My father's lawyer. For my own protection, he said…"

Pascale lowered her voice.

"I've heard a whisper about your Papa, and this guy representing him for what he did. And your ordeal last Sunday." She leaned forwards with that earlier concern on her friendly, generous face. "Legally, given the seriousness of what's happened, perhaps he can. Perhaps he should." She then stood up and joined Delphine in front of her office to give her another hug. A squeeze of encouragement. "You've not had much fun, have you?"

Please, don't cry again….

"I really do need to borrow a mobile, if you have a spare one," Delphine reverted to the main problem. "Please say yes. Even if it's old…"

Pascale pulled away. She wasn't stupid. "It may be best if I don't. Not if someone possibly dangerous feels they can contact you."

"You mean, Patrick Gauffroi?"

A nod. "And any other weirdo who might be turned on by the case. I'm being honest."

The three most over-used words.

"There is, however, a public phone further along the first landing."

Delphine thanked her, gathering up her things. "I'll see you tomorrow."

"Take care now."

She would if she could.

*

Having chewed her way through a slice of hard pizza accompanied by a wilting salad, Delphine left the hostel's clamorous dining room with a bottle of chilled Pinot Grigio and a wine glass in hand. The BOISSONS INTERDIT AUX CHAMBRES order from ten years ago had gone, and a guilty rush of pleasure at the prospect of enjoying the wine on her own propelled her onwards.

Once in room 8, she considered searching Julien Gallas' name on her Samsung until realising even that might not be secure.

Fuck it.

She found the hostel's guide, and on page 3, spotted two useful items. With her room locked, she ventured towards the back of the building where, next to the mini-phone booth, a former bedroom had been converted into a study area. Here, four computers on long tables took up two walls. None were occupied.

Here goes…

The only entry she found for the ecologist was a brief account of his accidental death near Peyrat on 8th November 2004. Nothing about any book, published or unpublished. She then tried his name on Amazon Books and the Bibliotèque National. Same result. So, either it still languished in obscurity, or had been deliberately removed.

Delphine let out a loaded sigh. Checking every French publisher and university press could take all night. That wasn't an option, so she left the room and tried calling Christophe Beauregard for more information on '*The Evil That Men Do*,' but no-one answered.

Merde...

She deliberated before dialling Colonel Valon's number, relieved to be able to leave a brief message thanking him for his valuable information and the truly exciting news of those hairs. The end of message click stopped her from adding how she hoped to be in Saint-Arnoult by Friday midday if not before. And then she remembered the funeral.

Back in her room, she tried the main news on TV1 in case it had drawn media attention, but no. Obviously Gérard Massenet had kept things private after the last intrusion into his family's loss. Or was there was a different explanation altogether?

*

After three and a half glasses of wine and with Canal + rolling out an old episode of *Châteauvallon*, Delphine began to doze off on one of the vinyl chairs by the table. Not for weeks had she let alcohol erase the tension in her head and elsewhere, and if noisy trippers in the corridor hadn't woken her up, she'd have probably stayed in that chair all night. Still wearing her jeans and bra shielding those two much-guarded items, she stumbled over to the single bed nearest the window, and flung herself on to its cool, cotton cover.

Bliss…

Despite the first rumble of thunder stirring the heavy air outside, she felt sleep soon return. But not for long.

*

A distinctive smell stirred her from semi-consciousness. Pine and something metallic, which Delphine recognised first, before seeing a black-haired female standing sentry-like at her bedside, staring down at her, half-lit by the car park's powerful sodium lights between the slatted blinds.

My God…

Was this the same stranger she'd seen earlier in that lay-by? Had she been given a duplicate key by mistake? Perhaps she had not been told that room 8 was already occupied, or Pascale, with so many arrivals to accommodate, had panicked? But the other's body language soon made her realise none of these scenarios applied, and fear made her sit up.

"Who the hell are you? And why are you in here?"

Still sleepy-eyed, she was ready to swing her feet to the floor. She prepared to claim her space, defend herself as she'd been taught, but the thin figure, in a loose, patterned summer dress, was too quick. She placed both strong hands on her shoulders.

"For Christ's sake, Delphine. It's me. Don't dare make a sound or we'll be stuffed…"

A man.

Then she knew.

Patrick Gauffroi let go of her, tore off his wig and pulled his dress up over his head, revealing not only those same red marks around his neck, but much more, causing that familiar mix of smells to fill the warm room. Before Delphine could use her close combat skills to deter him, he was alongside her on the bed, locking her in his bare-boned arms. His hot mouth against her ear murmured his own tortured confession of love and longing as she tried to keep her head to one side, fighting a swelling tide of desire laced by loathing.

Fifteen thousand euros…

"I love you more than life itself," he nuzzled her throat, grazing on her skin as he bypassed her bra on his way down her body. "And if your devious, fucking father hadn't said you loved me too, would I have even set foot outside my cell? Risked everything to be with you? No, but if I die tomorrow, darling Delphine, I'd have found Heaven…"

44

Thursday 23rd June. 04:00 hrs.

Afterwards, hot, sticky, confused and alone, Delphine listened to the stormy dawn beyond the half-drawn blinds. The faint crackle of lightning in between sounds of various coaches preparing to leave with their more subdued cargoes.

That shaming moment of alcohol-driven madness accompanied her while padding towards the *en suite* bathroom. Her mind a mixed blur of Sister Marthe's mute disapproval and his fierce rhythm ending with the promise that he'd die for her. That life was meaningless without her…

What in hell's name had she done? She was certainly no virgin since the summer after her *Bac,* when everyone at the convent had let their hair down in celebration of freedom. She'd hardly fought him off either, had she? The man who'd killed her mother. Hardly grappled for her dodgy phone to call reception or threatened him with the police. Why?

Easier than answering these questions was to remove her bra, checking its contents were still intact. Those woollen fibres and the invitation were crumpled and damp with perspiration, just then the least of her problems.

You bloody clown…

*

Accompanied by sounds of happy students heading for breakfast, she removed her tee shirt and the little blue brooch that had clung to it all yesterday, retrieved her briefs, torn below their elastic, and stumbled into the shower.

The water was neither hot nor strong enough to make her feel clean, and afterwards, she almost scrubbed herself dry with a less than fluffy towel.

Dressed in the same clothes as yesterday, she must pretend the sex hadn't happened, and his passionate feelings for her, his life and death promises were all a sick dream. If she couldn't manage that, she might as well return to Saint-Arnoult with nothing resolved or achieved.

On automatic pilot, she packed her remaining things, tidied the bed and opened the blinds. As a well-trained chambermaid in the *Hôtel les Palmiers*, she'd have penned a little card for the next guest, hoping they found the room to their liking and wishing them a *bon voyage*.

Not now. Not ever…

Gauffroi had been the one to leave something, just like her mother's hollow bullet hole in her slowing heart.

*

From her window, Delphine noticed that after the breakfast rush, the car park was only half full. She scoured the scene for that small, dark blue Citroën she now knew had been his. Obviously, a replacement for the stolen Toyota.

Gone.

He'd done what he'd wanted, leaving her with a burgeoning dirty secret, and beneath it all, the knowledge that she'd let him do it. Yes, she had opened her legs while his eager lips had clamped on hers. She had aided and abetted a *coup de foudre*. She had been a willing player.

Sinner…

You will fail.

*

08:45 hrs.

The moment Delphine spotted Pascale Dulay at her desk, her instinct was to challenge her as to how and why someone so obviously dressed in drag had been able to enter and share her room without her knowledge, even possibly without a key. But Gauffroi was a wanted man who'd learnt more than a few tricks while in prison. That would all come into the open soon enough, thanks to her father. Best leave it, she decided. In the meantime, there was a timetable to keep.

"I hope the storm didn't wake you up," said the friendly proprietor before answering her phone. "There've been power cuts everywhere. At least we have our own generator..."

"Good idea."

Pascale covered the receiver and looked up.

"Are you alright? You seem - I don't know - different."

"I'm fine, thank you. Looking forward to some fresh air."

Delphine waited until the call ended and bought a walkers' map of the area which included the northernmost part of the Haute-Saône department and the whole of the Vosges. With a forced smile on her face, she settled the bill and, having pulled her cagoul hood over her still-damp head, lied again how she'd had a great night's sleep and hoped to be passing this way again.

"You're always welcome," Pascale reached out to clasp her hand. "Safe trip."

"Thanks."

Delphine stood in the shelter of the hostel's porch for a few moments, then slapped her left wrist then her right, her cheeks, her chest, her whole body. The pain felt good, necessary. Something Sister Marthe might have done to her had she stolen a donation from her convent's chapel Tronc box or sold her uneaten supper biscuits. As she headed towards her 2CV, all she could think of was how, with Gauffroi's exploring hand between her thighs, those emotions stored and bottled since her mother's murder had melted shamefully into an involuntary and tumultuous collusion.

Having left the hostel's car park and joined the D10 towards Amance, Delphine spotted an *Auchan* poster advertising a sale of baby and toddler clothes at their store in Vesoul. She immediately slowed down to stare at it. The two babies featured in the foreground looked huge, as if made out of pink cheese. How voracious and cunning they seemed.

Fuck.

A hollow feeling took hold. A sudden, cold reality hit, as she mentally logged the date nine months hence.

*

Despite the sorry remnants of last night's storm, the small town seemed to be one of the prettiest settlements Delphine had seen on her journey to the north-east. It was also unnervingly clean. Not a scrap of litter or dog dirt besmirched its neat pavements, and the red-roofed, equally immaculate houses reminded her of a building kit she'd played with as a child. No moss or signs of decrepitude in this little backwater, where everything sparkled against the morose, darkening sky.

However, as testimony to the previous night's storm, several power cables had come adrift from various buildings, including a small supermarket and chemist. Plus, the tiniest library she'd ever seen. All were being repaired as she drew up alongside the kerb in the main street, stopping outside the *Café des Bêtes,* whose few chairs and tables stood in disarray outside. Not only did she need a decent cup of coffee, but also hopefully, useful information.

*

She'd come to the right place. Every centimetre of its porch area and doorway was smothered in wolf stickers, while two large posters of the same image hung slightly crinkled inside the front window.

This wasn't going to take too long because, in answer to her question, the young man – a skinhead - whom she guessed was in his late teens or early twenties, told her exactly and almost proudly where Maurice Amance and other relatives lived.

"The Rue de la Révolution's the main one," he said, smiling extremely white, pointed teeth. "Perfect, that, don't you think?"

She nodded, then placed her order.

"I really admire what they're doing," she dissembled as he constructed her cappuccino from various noisy, steaming machines. "Us humans think we're bloody it. If I had my way, I'd open up all the safari parks, all the zoos and let the poor animals free."

"That's cool." He passed her the coffee and a wrapped Bourbon biscuit, plus two sugar lumps. A small tattoo of a stalking wolf was noticeable on his pale left wrist. Yet Delphine had to keep up the pretence of being sympathetic to the cause. As a supporter of both Domus and LVS, she was a firm believer in puncturing the complacent bourgeois lives of those dependant on others for their comforts.

"I'd like to meet this Maurice guy sometime," she added, collecting her change. "He must be charismatic."

"Well, you can, and he is. He's doing a show at the Stadium in St. Loup tomorrow morning at ten, in fact. I've a couple of spare tickets."

"Thanks."

Delphine took one and, having disguised her shock at seeing a full colour mug shot of that same thug she'd already seen in close up twice before, chose a table by the window. From there, she could watch out not only for Patrick Gauffroi, but that noxious trio who seemed to wield so much power. How come they were free to roam after what she'd told the police and Gérard Massenet? She wondered, taking the first welcome sip of her coffee. It didn't make sense.

But soon, like the barely-lit firework that suddenly ignites, it did.

*

Over the other side of the street, one of those same workmen in hi-vis gear had finished re-connecting a thick, black cable, and was being lowered to the ground.

"So, what's your name?" The café guy came over to her with a freebie pack of mini Prince biscuits and waited expectantly.

"Jeanne Corisot. Why?" One of her mother's few friends who'd died just weeks before her.

His black eyes narrowed.

"You seemed familiar, that's all."

"Really?"

A spasm of tension had reached her heart. He was peering at her more closely as she gathered up her bag and rucksack and began to stand.

"*I* know," his tone and expression had completely changed. "You're that fucking bitch who…"

Delphine didn't stay to hear the rest. At least Lieutenant Colonel Zanowski had shown Compagnie 1 how to duck and dive their way out of trouble, and after the final assessment, she'd gained the second highest score.

Damn.

He was following her, fitter than she after Sunday's drop from *La Bergerie's* roof, and the guilt-fuelled sex last night.

Her nameless pursuer was catching up. She could even feel his breath on the back of her neck. There was nowhere to go. She couldn't risk trying one of the houses or the odd shop in case no-one was in, or if so, took too long to answer.

Stay silent.

She'd learnt how a human scream can light up the amygdala - a primitive region in the human brain - and trigger an opponent's swift response. But right then, in a village where everyone's nest was connected, the less attention the better.

"Stop!" he called in such a way that she wondered if he had a weapon. "Or I'll treat you to my uncle."

Uncle? Who was that?

The spur she needed, and soon, as if by a miracle, found a bank that was open. God bless *Crédit Agricole*, and not a damned wolf sticker in sight. She was lucky. An early client was exiting, cast in the front door's green light.

Delphine squeezed through just before it closed, leaving her pursuer with his nose squashed up against the glass. His eyes, like his teeth, glaring like those of a wolf near its prey.

Quick...

"Keep him out, please!" she screamed at the one cashier, a young woman who'd already had the wit to keep the door on red alert while summoning the manager. Delphine knew that most bank robberies involved some kind of scam, and she herself could be suspected. But when the portly man whose badge read ROBERT SUSSMAN appeared, he soon grasped the situation and led her into his office, locking its door behind her.

Panic reached her bladder. She suddenly had the urge to pee, but told herself to calm down. She pretended she was on another exercise at the *École de la Gendarmerie*, with all eyes on her. He was only trying to help.

"One of the Amance clan," muttered Sussman, wiping his damp forehead with a handkerchief when he returned to his office. "Not long out of the Young Offenders' Institution near Vauvillers where…"

Sounds of a scuffle cut him short. Two of the bank's own guards were on her pursuer with the outer door open on to the street. Passers-by were being ordered to leave immediately because the man she'd been told was Antoine Amance, was armed. Her crazy idea of pitching up at his café had misfired, and this violent, damaged creature now knew who she was.

*

After a welcome glass of ice-cold Perrier water and a tomato sandwich saved for later, Delphine explained she'd simply been re-visiting old haunts from ten years ago. She wanted to have a few days to herself after the problems at the *École de la Gendarmerie* in Saint-Arnoult.

"Don't stay here," the manager said, looking his age - probably late fifties. "Things are turning pretty nasty. Those who object to LVS are being victimized in ways myself and my staff find unbelievable in the 21st century."

"*Le Corbeau?*" She meant the anonymous poison pen writer, a tradition dating from the Middle Ages, often resulting in its recipient's suicide.

"Worse."

Delphine glanced from the manager to the nearest of his two security guards.

"They disappear. Into thin air."

She finished her refreshing drink, aware of new clients waiting to enter. A sudden clap of thunder overhead made her flinch, but not for long.

"You must be wondering why I didn't call the police and get Antoine Amance taken into custody for intimidating you, but…"

"Impossible," butted in that same female cashier that Delphine had first encountered. "Especially after getting death threats for the past six months because you refused to put LVS stickers and posters all over the place. Plus," she eyed him as if unsure whether to continue, "the Amances

302

withdrew their accounts. *Tout à coup.* Even the Genéral. We're talking millions, aren't we, Monsieur?"

Her boss nodded, still pre-occupied.

"What exactly was Antoine Amance's crime?" Delphine queried.

The manager hesitated.

"He'd threatened Odette Beauregard while she was putting out the washing behind her bungalow in St. Loup. Then he broke in and locked her out, so she couldn't raise the alarm. As a result, she suffered a massive and fatal stroke that same night."

"*Les Papillons?*"

A nod.

My God...

Delphine shivered, recalling that property's three Yale locks. The noticeable lack of a woman's influence.

"When?"

"Last November. But it feels like yesterday. Amance was eventually convicted of causing her death. Aged only seventeen at the time, and you'd think he's have learnt a lesson. But no. He pitches up here again without shame or conscience to run the *Café des Bêtes*, funded by his father, of course."

"Who is?" Delphine was thinking how Christophe Beauregard hadn't mentioned it at all.

"Maurice. Sly as a slug. No wonder his wife went off to Spain."

"And Natalie Lavroche?"

Robert Sussman let out a sour laugh.

"Just taken up with his younger brother, Paul, so I heard. I believe she met them both when they settled near Saint-Arnoult in March 2004 to spread their *malaise*. It's the little boy I feel sorry for. Dangerous people."

"Paul? Are you sure?"

Another nod.

Delphine forgot her own troubles, and as for poor Odette Beauregard, her experience must have been terrifying. For her husband, too. A defeatist tremor touched her heart. These fanatics were beyond evil. Did she really want to stick around and dig even deeper into what was hourly becoming more risky? No wonder her widower had advised a local number plate for her 2CV.

"So why do that to Odette? Because her husband so hated the organisation?"

"How did you know?"

"I met him by chance at the *Hôtel la Forêt* on Tuesday night, and called at his home yesterday morning."

"I'd blame a book."

Delphine blinked.

"Really?"

"Apparently a hugely damaging treatise on re-wilding. How much public money has been creamed off to fund it, how it's based on Stalin's Bolshevik principles of what's yours is ours... Have you heard of the forgotten famine in Samsy, Kazakhstan in the early 1930's?"

"A little." Her father had mentioned it, but no way could she include him.

"A holocaust no less, with farmers and peasants perishing from hunger because of one man's demented ideology. When you have time, read about it."

"I thought this book was about the dangers of vineyard pesticides."

Sussman paused.

"He'd revealed too many names."

"Julien Gallas?"

"Indeed. The *late* Julien Gallas. Dead too soon."

Just then, the air in that small foyer area had become almost too heavy to breathe. Delphine had to be outside or her lungs would surely burst and, having thanked Monsieur Sussman and the clerk called Rose, gave him a spontaneous *double-bis*, and was soon outside in the even more gloomy morning.

It wasn't until she found herself in the next alleyway, that she realised her important question about Natalie Lavroche and her young son had gone unasked.

*

Antoine Amance hadn't seen her return to her car, but, nevertheless, she drove past the *Café des Bêtes* wearing sunglasses and her visor down, just in case. A *fermé* sign dominated the wolf-stickered door. No way was she tempted to explore the rest of that delightful family's village, nor stay on until tomorrow's stadium event, although that might have been useful to see who'd show up.

She was known and recognisable, at least until her disguise was in place.

As her thoughts spun round in her mind, lightning appeared behind her to the north, followed by the inevitable growl of thunder. Where she was going could be far worse, but continue she must.

It was only by accident when she reached the Place du Général de Gaulle and was about to turn right past the impressive *mairie*, that she noticed a good-looking, dark-skinned guy in combat fatigues step from its double front door and, for a split second, glance her way.

45

11:10 hrs.

Delphine stared at this stranger through her wing mirror before turning on to another road signed for the D434 for Épinal. This should again take her to the *Château des Illuminations*, but not its main entrance. She had to be smarter than that and, noticing a large placard announcing *'Frites/Boissons. Ouvert 24 hrs',* she pulled into its busy, dirt-covered enclosure where a queue had formed by the one kiosk. Having found the least obvious parking space, she ate her tomato sandwich then unfolded her new map.

Just as she'd located the château's name, printed in the tiniest of fonts and easily missed amongst the green patches representing forestry, her phone began to ring.

Maître Massenet sounded rather less cool than usual.

Tapped, remember?

"Delphine?" he began, weirdly clear, as if sitting next to her. "Are you able to talk?"

Normally, she'd have felt a frisson of expectancy, but not anymore. Last night had made things too complicated…

"Am I? *You* tell me."

The slightest ping.

"There. Your phone's now clear. I confess I overstepped the mark regarding your security. I'm very sorry. Please put it down to my grief."

"Is that why you've phoned?"

"It's about your father. He was put on a defibrillator two hours ago, and…"

Jésus.

"But his heart's always been his strongest feature. I don't understand. Is he still at the gendarmerie?"

"Yes, but custody's been extended while investigations continue. He suggested I make contact, because…"

"So, he's OK?" she interjected, knowing what was coming next.

"We both want to see you, Delphine. I mean…" Here he broke off. The inevitable question on its way. "Where are you?"

"Why?"

"Because Judge Hervé Latrisant also needs to know, as there's the Gallas/de Soulibris case to kick-start as well."

"For which I'm representing myself, remember?"

The distant lightning was moving closer, and a thunder-filled interlude caused several tourists to desert the kiosk and run back towards their various vehicles. Had Massenet's disappointed sigh morphed into "fucking bitch" under his breath? Delphine couldn't be sure, but if so, it was more than shocking. Perhaps, like he'd said, he was stressed after his daughter's burial and his wife's sad predicament. Perhaps…

"Actually, I'm sorting my head out," she added. "With an old school friend near where I used to live. I need some space. Me-time, as they say. I'll be back in Saint-Arnoult tomorrow."

She'd not even convinced herself, but no way was he controlling her. There'd been enough of that at the convent school and growing up in St. Eustache. Besides, she'd a schedule to keep to.

"I was thinking of you yesterday," she said in a more conciliatory tone, noticing a familiar, dark blue Citroën Saxo entering the compound then circling back towards the road. "I hope things weren't too…"

"They were fine, thank you," his tone sharpened even more, "I'm sorry you don't seem to trust me enough to give your whereabouts."

Delphine could have challenged this but didn't. The weather was already worsening, and besides, she'd a call to make. With thunder shaking her skimpy little car, she gave Maître Massenet a polite '*au revoir*', then dialled Hervé Latrisant's office in Brive's Avenue Genéral de Gaulle, deliberately not hiding her number.

*

Not having met the examining magistrate personally, the conflicting opinions she'd heard of him, including Valon's 'tread carefully' warning, made her introduction somewhat uneasy.

Although clearly in a hurry, he was relieved she'd phoned, but nevertheless concerned there'd been no medical check after her ordeal at *La Bergerie* on Sunday.

"I was fine. Really."

"You must see me tomorrow afternoon," he added. "Things are moving on apace, and..." he then paused as if interrupted by something. "Gérard Massenet has informed me you wish to represent yourself when the Gallas/de Soulibris case comes to trial. Is that so?"

He's not wasted much time, she thought.

"It is," she said, then added why. When finished, she agreed to meet him at four o'clock, then asked if he knew her father had suffered heart problems. His answer brought an immediate sense of danger. Of wolves, not only in their natural state, but in sheep's clothing.

The only thing affecting François Rougier was anger at his own stupidity. As if his only child didn't have enough on her mind after her bad experience at the *École de la Gendarmerie Nationale*.

So why had the lawyer lied?

"Shame has kept him from contacting you, but I'm sure a phone call would be appreciated," the judge added and, for a second, Delphine was tempted to confide in this stranger whose firm but gentle voice must have elicited more guilty confessions than by bullying.

"I will."

"Excellent. And incidentally, some very useful evidence has come to light courtesy of the police forensic pathologist in Saint-Arnoult. So, all the more reason to be with us tomorrow."

The Vileneufs and Colonel Valon flashed into her mind.

"Can't you please tell me now?"

"We're currently experiencing intercept problems, so that'll have to wait. As for your part, if you have any, how-shall-I-say, useful photographs to show me, that would be a bonus."

"Of what exactly?"

"Anything that helps me see justice done."

"Of course." But must she seek Aristide's permission first?

Delphine's gaze strayed to her map. All soft creases with swathes of green choking its grids, especially where Haute-Saône slyly segued into the Vosges.

Almost midday and time was slipping by, but why was Hervé Latrisant, who'd been in so much of a hurry, hanging on? Expecting her to end the call, maybe?

No.

He finally cleared his throat.

"Considering that Gérard Massenet will be representing your father, you ought to know that his wife has just passed away at the St. Sauveur clinic where she was being treated. I can't give any details now, but it's a double tragedy, so soon after young Amélie's death."

*

Delphine watched new customers at the kiosk sharing their snacks and bottles of Coke, laughing as if without a care in the world, while the late Colonel Mikhail Zanowski and the word 'suicide' came to mind.

"It's caught everyone by surprise, as physically she wasn't ill. So, if her death *was* self-inflicted, then that makes two in as many days," added Hervé Latrisant, as if reading her mind. "A post-mortem will be carried out within the next hour."

She expressed her genuine sorrow, aware that the poor woman's husband hadn't even alluded to it. So, what was going on there?

The wolves have caused all this, she was about to add, then stopped herself. No more clues, and yet one person knew exactly where she was. A man who, fifteen hours ago, had pushed himself inside her in a hot, urgent possession.

"I've just one query," she then ventured. "Can *anyone* put a tap on my phone?"

"Commissariats and gendarmeries, but only after permission from either myself or the public prosecutor. Why?"

"No reason."

Having again reminded her to contact her father, Hervé Latrisant hung up, leaving Delphine to navigate her way through the labyrinth of doubt and guilt, and how to reach the huge *Forêt de Diane* which adjoined the *Château des Illuminations'* north-eastern boundary. A plantation of some two hundred hectares, not only dedicated to a huntress, but also the subject of a small, framed print she'd spotted in Christophe Beauregard's sunlit lobby. A contrast if ever there was, but clearly significant.

She should have asked him about it at the time, along with Romain Vileneuf's three hairs, but she had to accept not every opportunity could be seized upon.

"All good thing come to those who wait," Sister Marthe had replied when asked yet another question. However, the mysterious *Forêt de Diane* could hardly be called 'a good thing.' Originating in prehistoric times, it had also sheltered a group of resistance fighters before they'd vanished from the face of the earth.

Face of the earth...

That expression always unsettled her, especially when recalling her former home in St. Eustache marooned in endless, untilled soil. Its most miserable feature.

*

Drops of rain began smearing the 2CV's windscreen as she moved the map over to the passenger seat, noticing a dusty, grey Suzuki 4X4 nosing its way on to the *Frites/Boissons'* cinders, before the driver - surely that same guy she'd seen leaving the *mairie* in Amance - parked some three cars down from her.

Delphine locked herself in and waited, sealed in the freakish summer heat, but knowing that on that occasion that prim, controlling Sister Marthe might just be right.

46

Omar Kouchia shook Delphine's hand through her half-open window then showed his ID card, before introducing himself quite formally in a voice that was part Provençal, part Algerian. Certainly not the thuggish 'marginal' she'd once imagined. Clean-shaven with the same short, black curly hair as the young lad she'd seen yesterday.

His deep brown eyes, whose pleasure at meeting her also bore pain, were fringed by the longest lashes she'd ever seen. No wonder Natalie Lavroche had been smitten. He said he'd seen Delphine's photo on the internet, how she'd been responsible for reporting Guy and Élisabeth Lavroche's disappearances, and escaped from *La Bergerie*...

"You reminded me of St. Joan," he added, then eyed his watch, the same type some of her tutors had worn at the *École*. "Someone who stuck to her guns."

"And died a terrible death."

"That's why I'm here, and not at *La Bastide* rescuing Joel."

"What d'you mean? Why you're here?"

"To stop you dying, too. Because that's what'll happen if you tackle these fanatical bastards on your own."

Delphine felt a blush beginning. It was way too soon for compliments, and was this stranger for real?

"Have you been stalking me?" She asked instead.

He nodded, patting the left pocket of his combat fatigues. "You bet. And I've still got the Luger from when I served in the Foreign Legion. She's hungry, I'm telling you, like those bloody wolves. So, do you want a ride or shall I accompany you? I've also got other gear that might come in useful."

She experienced a momentary dizziness, with too many questions still to be answered. His reputation was hardly encouraging, and suddenly she felt like the only person on the planet desperate to make the right decision. While a normal-looking family trekked by, picking at their *frites*, Delphine pointed at his car. Her 2CV was way too conspicuous and, once she'd locked hers up, brought over a bulky black bin liner, her rucksack and bag containing Aristide's BlackBerry, then followed him to his Suzuki. Its number plate 19. Corrèze.

*

"I tried to stay close to Joel," Omar explained once they were back on the road to St. Loup-sur Semouse, under a moody sky still sprinkling drops of rain. "Bad move, because his mother put Maurice Amance and some thicko side-kick on to me. They tried burgling my caravan, letting down its tyres, and yesterday was more of the same. This time with an animal called Antoine. A nephew, I believe."

"I've just met him. Who's his father?"

"Two guesses." Anxiety flickered in Omar's eyes. "The lovely Maurice. Get what I mean?"

"I do."

"And when, as Joel's father, I dared visit his new school here, I was shown the door. I was told that *pied noirs* weren't welcome. The same as in Saint-Arnoult. If I didn't back off, I'd be done for aggression. Like that trumped-up charge in Marseille."

Delphine offered him a *Gauloises* and lit it for him.

"So, I counted for nothing." He took the cigarette, inhaling it just as deeply as she'd once drained the communion goblet at the convent. As if

313

that little extra would give the courage she needed to overcome her worries, her lack of hope.

"That headmaster's bent as hell," she said. "He's also in the LVS."

"What?" The steering wheel almost slid through his free hand and he fought to bring the 4X4 back into position.

"It's true. So's the fact I saw Joel yesterday afternoon."

"Where?" Omar's jaw had tightened, his frown more intense.

"*La Bastide.* I also saw four guys releasing four grey wolves into the field behind it."

"The shits. What did Joel look like? I've not seen him for two years."

"Like you, and on his bike, calling for his mother as she drove away. She still has her red Twingo."

"Prize bitch." He turned to Delphine. "Did you notice any wounds on him?"

She paused.

"A couple of marks on his face and calves," and then, not wanting to worry him, added, "but they seemed to be healing. Look." She extracted her Samsung and soon found the two photos she'd taken. At the first one of Joel, Omar's tense face relaxed into a smile as he peered at the small screen. But not when seeing Natalie Lavroche in her car.

"I also saw her turn into the drive to the *Château des Illuminations*," Delphine added. "You know…"

"Of course I bloody know." He was speeding over the limit. "Sorry," he said.

"It's OK. Two other cars followed her in." She then described them, without mentioning that noticeable blue, racing bike. "The général's hosting a big banquet there tonight."

"Bastards, the lot of them."

314

Delphine stopped short of mentioning the part she hoped to play in it. How the invitation for Simone Gallas and the brute was on her very person, still in her bra. She didn't yet know him *that* well…

Omar Kouchia exhaled so hard it reduced his cigarette to the length of his fingernail and he was about to fling it from his window when she stopped him.

"No. Someone might pick it up. I'm thinking DNA."

He glanced across at her in awe, then irritability, before handing it over. She next explained what was in her black bin liner - items which her father, for sentimental reasons, had transferred to Saint-Arnoult from *Bellevue*. A spare spade, two unused plastic feed bags, a saw and smaller items to help in the search for his missing ex-in-laws. The artist and her farming husband of thirty years with a distinct limp.

"Excellent. You've obviously been trained in forward thinking. I've got a few things which might be useful."

By then, they'd reached the outskirts of St. Loup-sur-Semouse, and Delphine was able to direct him to where his son had been taken. The shaded opening to the Rue des Pins and its affluent little settlement, ending in a cul-de-sac dominated by silence. Not another car in sight.

*

"*Attends*. Wait a minute."

He'd parked much closer to *La Bastide* than she'd previously dared to and, despite his jungle-booted legs, had leapt over its closed gates and vanished from sight. Apart from the car keys, he'd left precise instructions. The first, to turn the Suzuki round to face the main road at the other end. The second, to leave all doors unlocked, especially the boot.

All the while, Delphine wondered how on earth he'd ward off possibly four angry men and an equally angry Natalie Lavroche, who not so long ago had duped her with fabricated fear, her loathing of LVS. She also wondered about the pretty goats in *Les Papillons*, and if those recently released wolves were already stalking them and nearby homes.

Suddenly, as if having pre-empted things by thought, came a low, persistent growl, that distinctive musky smell. Before she could close her window, she felt the 4X4 lurch to the right as a snarling force of nature landed on the bonnet before straining its snarling muzzle through the gap.

Non...

A pair of black and amber eyes bored it seemed, into her very life.

SECTION 6B - The first rule of discovery...

Remain in control.

Do not scream.

Co-operate while mentally exploring possibilities for escape.

Rubbish...

Was she supposed to co-operate with a possibly rabid wolf? Instead, with its hot saliva-flecks pricking the backs of her hands, she pulled her mother's tortoiseshell comb from her bag and forced its length sideways between those vicious jaws.

With a strangled yelp of surprise, the creature slid off the car and loped towards the verge, frantically trying to dislodge the obstacle, vomiting yellow slime as it did so, before vanishing into the undergrowth.

*

Come on, Omar...

Delphine was shaking, frightened that more vulpine friends and family would smell her fear, but she kept her eyes on all mirrors for any sign of movement. Apart from a fading thunderclap, there was nothing, until the sudden upwards shift of a beige blind in *La Bastide's* nearest window on the first floor.

Beneath it, a familiar, dark-skinned boy with that same fear in his eyes. Delphine waved. She saw him turn as if someone was following, then to her enormous relief, he waved back. She wondered who else had been with him. One of the Amance clan? His mother? Was a trap being set, and if so, where on earth was his father?

He'd left his latest model Samsung on top of the dashboard. But why there, and switched off? What use was that in an emergency? Perhaps it was a spare, and he'd taken another one with him. Either way, she reached for its warm casing, curious as to what it might reveal about the man still barely an acquaintance. In a potentially lethal situation, she'd no choice. As if that crazed wolf hadn't been enough.

As she switched it on and waited, she thought of Julien Gallas, Odette Beauregard, and others who'd either perished or were still undiscovered.

Joel was Omar's son, not hers, she then reasoned, checking for any texts or stored photographs and found that everything had been deleted. Perhaps she should never have mentioned seeing the boy here or his duplicitous mother. At 13.00 hours, the time set aside for her real mission was slipping away. Besides, if he *were* to abduct him in this car, she'd be party to that. As if her plate of crap wasn't already overloaded, not least with the remnants of Patrick Gauffroi's hot lust lodged inside her body.

You will fail…

Guilt was already the winner.

*

A long five minutes later, Omar Kouchia was standing below that same window in *La Bastide*, now open, his arms outstretched. After this, everything fast-forwarded to another athletic leap back over the gate, with Joel in a yellow tee shirt and navy shorts clinging like a mini jockey to his back. But as they drew closer, Delphine noticed blood pulsing from a wound in Omar's left cheek. By the time they'd reached her, she had a wad of paper napkins from the hostel at the ready.

"Drive!" he ordered her, pressing them against his cheek, having told Joel to lie flat on his tummy on the floor at the back. "They're fucking armed!"

So they were. But, there was no sign of Natalie Lavroche as the posse of rage and hatred raised their rifles and fired first at the Suzuki's tyres and missed. They then targered its rear window, whose glass crackled around a large, jagged hole. The bullet, having spent its power, lodged in the back of Omar's chair.

"*Non*! *Non*!" Omar shrieked, having nearly been hit, then apologised.

Omar could only lean over to comfort him and tell him how brave he'd been. At this, his son took a deep breath and sat up to relay how Maurice Amance had wanted Delphine dead since he'd first caught sight of her at that farm near Saint-Arnoult, how bedtime meant taking it in turns with 'Uncle' Paul to share his mother's bed. Two men who scared him every day, making him wet himself at night. How Maurice had hit Omar's cheek with a screw driver, calling him 'pig shit.'

Delphine knew there was much, much more. But just then, she had to drive away as if their three lives depended on it, and as they neared the welcome sign for *Frites/Boissons* site, where her car had probably melted in the thunderous heat, her phone began to ring.

Aristide Abolego's name and number flashed up.

47

"Yes?" Delphine confirmed her name then listened hard above the rumble of wheels beneath her on the road's rough tarmac. Aware too, that the rifle bullet in the back of Omar's seat should be retrieved for safe-keeping, as well as proof.

"News. You know…"

"Keep it short, and your voice down."

Omar looked at her, and she was sure Joel was listening as well. When Aristide had finished, she wished she'd eaten breakfast, giving her empty stomach something to work on.

"You OK?" asked Omar, registering her shock. "Is it something you want to share?"

"I'll be alright, thanks." She didn't sound very convincing as she re-buried the phone in her bag, leaving it switched on, just in case.

"You can trust me," he said.

"I do. And as soon as I can, I'll check out your cheek. You may need antiseptic cream and a proper dressing."

"Can't risk that. Not till we're safe."

"It mustn't turn septic."

"Listen to Delphine, Papa."

She glanced at Joel through her rear-view mirror, and in those few seconds knew they really liked each other. "Can I get you something nice from that kiosk?" she asked him. "You've probably not had much to eat."

Joel grinned, then reached up to stroke the back of her head. "And do you mind me saying since that phone call, you still look a bit funny. You can tell Papa why. He won't betray you, not like Uncle Maurice and Uncle Paul.

"I know."

Finally, as they reached the cinder-strewn compound where just a few of the earlier vehicles remained, she recounted the wolf attack outside *La Bastide*. Her mother's old comb had probably saved her life.

"See how brave she is?" Omar remarked before changing places so Delphine could remove the bullet and store it in a tissue in her bag.

"Like Amélie," Joel added. "She was my friend, but she's up with the angels now, isn't she?"

And her mother…

"Yes," Omar agreed, revving up, obviously not wanting to stay a moment longer in such a conspicuous place.

"Mamie Élisabeth bought me a book about them," Joel elaborated. "One of her paintings was in it, but Maman burnt it."

Delphine fastened her seat belt, aware of his young voice faltering. What a world, she thought, wondering if he knew all the cattle there had been killed. Never mind the Vosges. Everywhere, it seemed, was the devil's garden.

*

"Élisabeth was a good woman and a gifted artist," Omar added with real feeling as he drove out on to the main road north. "No-one made me more welcome at the *Air du Vent* farm in the early days. Guy too. They never could understand why their daughter…"

"You're using the past tense," Delphine tested him, aware that kids of Joel's age didn't need to be burdened with everything. "Is that significant?"

"Damn."

320

Another silence, during which yet more distant thunder delivered the overpowering sense that from then on, nothing would ever be the same. Delphine found an opened pack of softened Haribo sweets at the bottom of her bag and passed it back to Joel, and a mini bottle of Coke which felt warm in her hand.

"Are we going to look for them?" He was soon chewing away like a pony.

She looked at Omar, as if to gauge his answer.

"Yes. It's the least we can do."

*

"Before Amélie Massenet's death, had you heard of her father, Gérard?" Delphine ventured once the D10 traffic had thinned, the wolf-stickered sign that they'd entered the Vosges came and went. "He's a lawyer."

"Who hasn't?" Omar said bitterly. "When Natalie kicked me out of the farm, she told the *maire* my ID was forged and that I was a potential terrorist. My life in Marseille was made hell, and she loved every minute of it. As did Massenet, slapping an exclusion order on me never to contact her or Joel again,"

So, the lawyer *had* been close to Simone Gallas…

Delphine saw real pain in Omar's fine eyes. The start of tears.

"That's why I sneaked back to Saint-Arnoult so I could at least see my boy on rare occasions coming out of school. I even found a caravan to rent and a job in a local garage, but always dreaded my phone ringing, or a knock on the door."

More lightning over nearby hills brought a mighty, thunderous roar, making Joel cry out, blocking his ears and dropping his sweets. It was then Delphine noticed old bruising under his upper arms as if he'd either been lifted or dragged roughly by someone bigger and stronger.

Cruel bastards…

"We'll talk more later," she said. "For now, we need to watch our backs and make sure no-one's following, because I don't know about you, but we must reach the *Forêt de Diane* before the weather beats us. Before…"

"I know there!" piped up Joel, retrieving his sweets, then leaning forwards to grip Delphine's headrest. His eyes were alight at the thought of adventure. "Uncle Maurice talked about it the other day when I'd answered him back."

"He threatened you?" Omar eyed him through his mirror.

"Yes, because I'd said I wanted my real Papa, not him or Uncle Paul. That's when he grabbed me and shook me, calling you a black turd. Said I'd end up in the lake there like…"

Delphine's empty stomach seemed to turn over beneath her seat belt. "Like?"

"Nothing."

"You must say."

"Leave it," whispered Omar, avoiding a spillage of straw in the road. "He'll tell us when he's ready."

"Nice people," Delphine muttered. "And what about Maman? Did she ever take your side? Protect you?"

Joel let out a strange, hollow laugh before slumping back in his seat, while the spades and other gear rattled behind him as Omar hit a pothole.

"Her? She liked seeing me get hit. I was *'le petit noir'* wasn't I? The one who had to let the wolves lick my hands to get a taste for humans…"

"Stop!" warned his father. "Or I'll turn right round and shoot the fucking lot of them."

"I wouldn't blame you," Delphine reached back to stroke Joel's hair.

"We're being followed," Omar suddenly announced as the sky grew sombre. "A dark blue Saxo."

Damn...

"Ring any bells?"

"No," she said rather too quickly. Deception on her mind - not only Natalie Lavroche's clever lies, but a tall, black-suited man who, according to Aristide's description, had spent some time with a young, blonde-haired woman before leaving with her just before his daughter's burial.

*

15:00 hrs.

Having devoured his sweets and the Coke, Joel dozed on the Suzuki's back seat, while Delphine and Omar discussed the best way into the *Forêt de Diane*, attracting the minimum attention, especially from police chasing an abduction.

Their destination was private land, not some Forêt Nationale or part of any *Route Randonée*, so having a six-year-old in tow could prove tricky. However, although their choices were limited, they had to try. As Delphine listened to Omar's latest theory as to where the Lavroches might be, she couldn't help thinking how when you're born, most of your time will be spent fending people off or managing their needs and neuroses. Their agendas...

The priority of finding Guy and Élisabeth Lavroche was in danger of being amended to keeping Joel safe, and rightly so. With Omar, he was in good hands. She could see that, but he'd snatched him from his mother, with herself as a visible accomplice, putting all her plans and what future she might have at risk.

While he once again scoured his map of the forest, ringing the possibilities with a red ballpoint, she updated Colonel Valon on his private phone.

"Nothing about us being here, please," Omar hissed, looking worried. "Thank you."

"Right."

Although this went against her sharing nature, especially as a child was involved, she relayed instead how the reassuring image of Maître Gérard Massenet had, like the sky overhead, become darker. How he'd left his daughter's funeral before the burial, accompanied by a younger, blonde woman. How he'd also kindly removed his illegal tap on her Samsung.

"Stay safe." Was all he said.

Omar glanced at her.

"Is there any news of his wife's post-mortem?" Delphine persevered.

"I said, stay safe."

*

When the Suzuki reached the same inconspicuous sign for the track to the *Château des Illuminations*, Omar slowed down, enabling both to see the rear end of a white sports car disappearing around its far bend.

Delphine's pulse quickened.

Hadn't that blonde Annemarie Colbert from Clermont Ferrand mentioned to her in passing how she owned a white Mazda MR5? Hardly the most convenient of cars for someone involved with wildlife. How she might have to sell it...

She took the map from Omar's lap and put her orientation skills into practice, knowing how mere marks on paper could be deceiving.

"Keep going," she encouraged him, trying not to wake a still-dozing Joel. "In another eight kilometres there'll be a second right-hand turning. This leads to a lake approximately one thousand metres long and four hundred wide." She then paused. "Apparently, according to this map, its depth can't be measured. It's bottomless."

They glanced at each other. That last word had brought a shiver beneath her clothes. Neither needed to speak, but as if to change the subject Omar said, "and judging by all those dark green areas in the forest, there'd be enough cover for us for a week."

Damn...

She'd better come clean. And quick.

"I'm sorry, but I have to go back tonight, after..."

"What? Our trout barbecue?"

"The banquet. I told you about it. At the château."

"Shit."

He braked without bothering to use the gears. They came to a stop half on, half off the verge. She couldn't afford to lose him. Not there, not then.

"Look," she said. "Just turn away for a moment," and once he'd obliged, she dug beneath her tee-shirt and inside her bra's left cup.

"Take a look." She held up the even softer, damper oblong of white card, feeling another spasm of betrayal at seeing Simone Gallas' name alongside that of Alain de Saloubris. Omar whistled between his teeth.

"Sssh, Joel might wake up!"

"Never met them."

"The mayor of Saint-Arnoult and her super-size, ugly lover," Delphine explained. "I'll tell you more one day."

"You must."

"Gérard Massenet's her biggest fan."

He snorted contempt.

"Like two rotten apples in the same basket."

Then he scrutinised the tiny, ornate print on both sides. "Featherblade steak. You seen that? On the menu?"

She nodded.

"Do you know what that is?"

"No idea. Meat's not really my bag." She'd also had other matters on her mind. Notably, staying alive.

"I know," came a sleepy, young voice from behind them. "Because out of all the beef's carcass, they contain the most nerve endings. That's what Maman said, which is why I could never eat mine when it was put on the table."

Delphine felt more than cold under that morose, leaden sky full of unleashed disturbance.

"Go on," encouraged his father.

"At *La Bastide* and up on the Donon Massif, I have to feed the wolf cubs morsels of featherblade steak."

Omar glanced round. Shock on his face.

"Why you?" Delphine asked, again thinking of those dead cattle and that inhospitable, mountainous area where unwary hikers and bikers regularly went missing. Joel himself might even be considered expendable.

"Only my hands fit between their cage bars."

"Damn them," snarled Omar. "How dare they! Especially after what happened to you in St-Arnoult. You must have been scared. What did Maman say?"

"Nothing. I had to do it because the male wolves in the pack wouldn't always cough up what they'd eaten, so me feeding the cubs meant they wouldn't starve. But there's something else…"

"What?"

Silence.

"I'll tell you later. OK?"

Omar handed back her card and half-turned to Joel.

"Where exactly on the Donon Massif? Can you remember?"

"*La Caverne d'Hiver.*"

Delphine's sudden chill became a prolonged shiver.

"Had Maman recently mentioned a banquet?"

"What's that?"

"A feast. Like a big dinner with lots of people. It's tonight at Papie Amance's château."

Joel thought for a moment, then said, "maybe that's why she bought a new dress from Épinal yesterday. Maurice started a row for spending too much money. *His* money, he said. It's red, like blood. I didn't like it."

"Try and get some more sleep," Omar suggested, frowning. But by then, the lad looked more alert than ever as his father re-started the car. "It's been a long day and not over yet."

Then came another sign, this time almost covered by those wolf-jawed stickers.

LA FORÊT DE DIANE.

Delphine swiftly scoured the road in front and behind, relieved to see no sign of that dark blue Citroën. However, given its colour and the surreal amount of dense foliage, it could be anywhere.

"Here we go." Omar visibly tensed up as a nocturnal darkness of massive firs consumed them like the brushes of a car wash. A very secret place, barely passable for even modest vehicles. The perfect hideaway, except for that distinct smell of wet fur, scats and the distant, menacing growls of wolves themselves. Delphine found herself wondering about the friendly, retired professor and his tragic, secret life. She couldn't help it. There's been something about him which had drawn her into his world.

"Joel," she began as casually as possible. "Did Uncle Maurice and Uncle Paul or your Maman ever mention the name Christophe Beauregard?"

She waited for the six-year-old to re-summon his memory, and when it came, realised then the danger that he and they were in.

48

"Big mouth will be next," Maurice Amance had apparently let slip after four beers in *La Bastide's* kitchen yesterday evening. "Make no mistake."

At Delphine's prompting, Joel had repeated that thug's ominous threat.

"What did he mean?" the youngster then asked.

"Never mind now," Delphine stepped in. "Just tell us what else you know about Christoph Beauregard's wife, Odette."

Joel paused, fighting his distress, trying to remember.

"I overheard them say how she'd been locked outside their house," he continued, as Omar transferred larger items from the boot to the camouflaged car. They were newer than her equipment from *Bellevue*, but so what? The main thing was they'd work, and despite his earlier, modest reply about what he'd brought, all eventualities had been covered, including rubber waders and storage boxes.

"By Antoine Amance?"

"Yes. And Uncle Paul just said how she'd taken too long to die without telling him where the book was."

The Evil That Men Do…

Delphine felt the dark afternoon closing in around them and was grateful that the Suzuki wasn't as obvious as her car would have been.

"What book?" She needed confirmation. Even from a youngster.

"Don't know."

"But it seemed important?"

"Oh yes, because Paul said Antoine searched everywhere for it."

"One more question. Did Maurice and Paul know you'd heard them?"

"No. I was hiding in the storeroom with some biscuits I'd taken."

As he spoke, Delphine's dot-joining firmed up, then Omar was tapping on her window and Joel opened his door.

"What's the plan?" he said, hopping out and pulling on an oversized cagoule which Omar had also thoughtfully provided. Yes, probably one of his, but its dark green colour was a better camouflage than the bright yellow tee-shirt.

"For a start, we need a look-out rota and a recognisable warning signal," said Delphine, recalling a tough exercise near Donzenac last February. "Also, a decent torch, because visibility will soon be non-existent."

Omar patted her on the back, while Joel admitted that most of all, he liked being invisible, which Delphine thought was strange and slightly sad.

"This is a big area," she added, stating the obvious. "But given what happened to my fellow student Romain Vileneuf in Saint-Arnoult, this big lake has to be our first port of call." She kept her voice low for fear of upsetting Joel any more than he already was. He'd clearly loved his grandparents, but he was a kid full of surprises.

"I once saw a Scooby Doo film when I was at Papie's farm," he began, rolling up the cagoule's sleeves to his elbows, those same scratches on show. "Human body parts had been left in an eagle's nest to feed them. No-one noticed the bones that were left, only Scooby. You should have seen his tongue hanging out."

This mix of humour and the grotesque made Omar stare first at Joel, then her. "No harm in taking a look," he suggested. "It's on our way." And with his son perched on his shoulders and a large waterproof bag containing his gear and two loaded rifles, they led to where the track almost disappeared. Delphine turned to see how his damaged silver car had become merely a blur amongst nature's incontinence.

With each step, the rucksack grew even heavier on her back, making her neck ache. She knew last night was to blame. Patrick Gauffroi's strength and determination had taken most of hers. Yet she'd hardly kicked him away or injured him, which she should have done, having studied and practised self-defence in the event of a sexual attack.

She could hide the rucksack somewhere, but that was too soon. As for Aristide's BlackBerry, bulking out her briefs next to her left hip, its metallic grey form contained too much evidence to be kept anywhere else.

"Look!" Joel, who'd slid down from Omar's shoulders, pulled at her sleeve. "See that huge nest up there? Anything could be in it now the baby birds have flown."

"Indeed," said Delphine, adding what an impressive imagination he had.

"One of my teachers said that!" He shouted back to her while suddenly running towards the towering, ancient spruce whose rough bark was almost black.

She and Omar jogged after him, both encumbered for every contingency. Both too slow, but as she drew closer, Delphine noticed how that same fir's dark 'skin' bore two sets of crudely carved letters.

She blinked and stared at them just to make sure. But they were horribly, frighteningly clear.

GL   EL

Non...

'Sick joke' came to mind. But what if they really did represent the Lavroche couple' names? What if both been taken elsewhere, already dead, and this sign was created to give their searchers false hope? Or had they done it perhaps while on the run? And might there be more? Before she could share her discovery, Delphine heard Omar call out to his son, already halfway up the tree trunk.

"Come down now, Joel! What if you fell?"

As the lad's wiry, scarred little legs were carrying him ever upwards, branch by branch, further out of earshot, Delphine showed his father those initials and saw his expression morph from anger to hope. He gripped her arm. "Shit. They could have been made by someone in a hurry. In a panic, but at least alive."

"Anything's possible," she said as she took two close-up photographs on her phone, then scoured the surrounding cone-strewn ground for any hint of footprints other than their own.

Nothing.

And what implement had been used? Most likely a penknife's blade, judging by some stray, pointed marks. No time to search, because Joel was almost out of sight, too high up. In awe and fear, she watched with his father, imagining hospitals, another funeral. After he'd called out again, there came the unmistakeable smell of damp, wild fur accompanied by warning growls; the shuffling of foliage becoming more obvious.

"Stay where you are!" Omar yelled up at the young rebel who'd obviously been kept under close control since moving to *La Bastide*. "Don't move, OK?"

"Why?"

"Wolves."

Delphine saw the boy glare down at them, clinging to the spruce's narrowing trunk.

"Fucking shoot them all!" he yelled, as she and Omar prepared for war. "I hate them."

*

However, not a shot was fired. The six grey males, still wet from having cooled off somewhere nearby, had seen the rifles turned on them, and slunk into the nearest cover. But not before Delphine had noticed their leader's jaws shining with fresh blood.

"Come on, Joel!" she urged the lad way above her head who'd stayed silent throughout. "They won't hurt us now."

But the six-year-old wasn't so sure. Instead, he reached up and, having called "watch out!" with a carefully aimed shove, dislodged the abnormally large nest above him. As it fell, he crouched against his perch, a trickle of hot pee reaching his socks and trainers.

Merde!

Delphine ducked out of the way as the nest thudded to her feet, displacing not only a spray of small, brown feathers but the remains of prey left for summer's heat to dessicate.

Here a fledgling's wing-bone; there its tiny skull picked clean. A shrivelled claw...Home to buzzards, she thought, recalling her long-ago biology lessons. Near *Bellevue*, it was sparrow hawks and falcons who'd reigned unrivalled for years, outnumbering prey.

"Joel, you were right about all this," acknowledged Omar, breaking her mental flow. "And Scooby. Who'd have guessed?" He hugged his boy, then sniffed how he'd wet himself.

"I'm sorry, Papa. I couldn't help it, up in that tree."

"It doesn't matter," said Delphine, passing him tissues while Omar picked pine needles from his hair. "But we still need to get to that lake as quickly as possible. I've just checked and there's been no rain here for a month, and yet those wolves were drenched."

"I've just remembered something else," said Joel, still cleaning himself up. Fear had replaced embarrassment. "What's this lake called?"

"Gehenna." Delphine hated the sound of it. "An old word meaning hell."

Joel snatched at Omar's arm. "She said Mamie and Papie would go to hell. Yes, that's it…"

Delphine shivered.

"Who did?"

"My Maman."

Silence.

*

She and Omar exchanged a glance, pressed the used tissues deep into her own cagoule's side pocket, and put her arm around Joel's trembling shoulders.

"Are you quite sure? Sometimes we imagine things."

"I don't imagine things like that!" He was suddenly defiant, and in that moment, Delphine was aware of an unexpected breeze and the stirring of upper foliage against the penumbral sky. From her years in the flatlands near the River Sarthe, she knew the signs. The lightning and thunder might have moved further south, but a serious storm was in the offing.

"Follow me," Omar whispered, gathering up his bag of equipment and hefting it over his left shoulder. With Joel in the middle of their little procession and Delphine keeping a look out at the rear, they fought their way in a more northerly direction along the meanest of wildlife tracks once used by other invaders some sixty years ago, towards the bottomless depths of hell.

*

At 16:10 hours, with fat pats of warm rain already hitting their exposed skin, the trio arrived at what must have been the most attractive hell ever. Unlike the accidental water where Romain Vileneuf had been dumped, this feature had been designed for pleasure.

Apart from several well-maintained wooden pontoons spaced around its expansive shore, varied species of trees, shrubs and exotic grasses had been planted for maximum effect. Some specimens in full flower with reds, pinks and yellows contrasting with their dark backdrop of evergreens.

Joel whistled, as if aping the Amance menfolk, until Omar told him to keep as quiet as a mouse and to stay well away from the edge of the grassy bank.

"Obviously, no expense spared," he then whispered to Delphine, sniffing the faintly puzzling smell which seemed to emanate from the lake itself. A lake with seemingly no wildlife. Not even a solitary duck.

She agreed, noting two well maintained rowing boats moored to the nearest pontoon, jostling together on the subtle current. The water's mysteriously sombre surface was peppered by this first rain.

"Can we go in that one?" Joel pointed to the nearest craft. "I've never gone rowing."

Delphine noticed pride but also wariness in his father's expressive eyes when he looked at her.

"I think it's best if I go first in one boat, and you stay in the other one to help Delphine."

"Why?"

"Because who knows what we might find?"

49

16:30 hrs.

Joel had never been in a boat before, let alone handled an oar, whereas Delphine, as part of Compagnie 1, had rowed solo only last month in a heavy downpour along ten kilometres of the River Corrèze. Its flowing, south-easterly current had made returning to the *École* almost impossible. However, she'd arrived back first in good time. A record, in fact, which should have made this prospect a more welcome challenge.

But no.

Not only was this lake's immeasurable depth something she'd rather not dwell on, but her responsibility for an active little lad who, by now, was surely the subject of a search. And what of the outcome? After all, his mother had also removed him from his other parent, but she was white, with no caution or conviction. At least, so far...

As the soft raindrops became harder and more frequent, Omar passed her a long length of rope with a sizeable, new-looking hook welded to a steel band at its far end, plus two large cool-bags. He'd clearly not wasted his time at the garage in Saint-Arnoult. But when he proffered one of the rifles, she hesitated.

"If we have to use them, they'll make too much noise."

"They won't. I'll show you." Joel took it, then mimed the actions. "Bang, bang!" He cried.

"Sshh!" Delphine placed the rifle by her feet and pointed at the bench behind her. "Just sit there, and please be very quiet. We need you to keep a careful look-out for anything under the water and anyone on the bank. Got it?"

"OK."

She didn't add that swimming remained her Achilles heel ever since Mariette Dujardin had held her under water for too long in the flowing River Semouse during that unforgettable convent trip. All the more reason for her boat to be steady, as her search began by dropping the rope down with her left hand, rowing with her right.

*

Above them, the menacing blue-black sky seemed to have lost height, looming closer so that the few gaps left by separating clouds were shot through by a blinding light. Not blue, but something devilish. Hellish the better word.

Omar, just metres in front, held up his hand. That meant 'listen', and she did. She heard the sound of cracking branches above the pit-pat of rain on the lake. He gestured to Joel to lie down.

"Why?"

"I think someone's prowling around. You could be shot."

That did the trick, and minutes later, once the perceived danger seemed to have passed, the fishing trip continued under the fixed stare of another man, this time wearing a long, dark green waterproof protecting his camouflage uniform, lying on a much harder bed than the one he'd shared the previous night. The observer watched the young woman's every movement, imagining her underneath him again, clasping him the way she was clasping her oar, plunging him into a measureless abyss of desire.

*

Fifteen long minutes had passed, and Delphine could tell from Omar's slumped shoulders that this was a task better suited to Sisyphus than two acquaintances with too few clues and too much watery ground to cover...

"Fuck! Look!" Joel breathed, pointing to his right. Delphine, who'd immediately spun round, could see at least four pale, gaping lips plucking at the lake's surface then flitting away.

"You're right."

Delphine then raised her binoculars to see a frenzy of pale, swishing movement even closer to her boat. The activity was short-lived, as the predators drifted downwards into the lake's darker depths.

She signalled to Omar, who rowed over to join them where Joel was leaning over the boat's side.

"Get back now!" he hissed at him, securing both crafts together then dropping both his rope and hers over the very spot. "And don't risk falling in again."

"I won't."

"Carp," she said, still focused on their ghostly, flickering tails. "They're huge. Bloated, in fact. I wonder what's attracted them."

"We'll soon find out."

"Cool," said Joel.

"You spotted them," said Delphine. "Well done." The smile on his little face was the reward to keep persevering. Meanwhile, Omar teased each rope in slightly different directions until all of a sudden, the left line held fast, almost pulling him overboard.

"Careful!" Delphine stared at that sudden, ominous tautness, aware of that same odd smell rising. Sour-sweet, not unpleasant, but not normal either. "Look away, again, you two. Just for a few seconds,"

They did, and without another word, she peeled off her cagoule and placed Aristide's precious BlackBerry in its pocket. Next, she took off her jeans, then her bra and its contents from under her tee shirt, before she donned goggles and a snorkel. Having executed a neat dive into the watery void, a trail of bubbles rose up in her wake.

338

Mère Marie…

Even as she approached the charred, partly-eaten human corpse, the greedy carp ignored her, burrowing inside the remains of what, as far as she could make out, had been a middle-aged female.

Shock made Delphine's hands shake as they tested that the rope's hook was still securely embedded into the victim's nest of grey hair. It was, but all the while, she avoided staring at the charcoal-coloured face whose mouth, or what remained of it, resembled a puckered cave with just a few teeth left in place. As for the body's shell, not only had those carp been hard at work, but something else had opportunistically, finished the gruesome task.

Wolves, perhaps? Before the poor victim had been dumped in the water, or afterwards? That might explain the group's earlier wetness. And if this *was* Élisabeth Lavroche, where on earth was her husband?

*

Delphine felt suddenly ill and began to thrash her way to the lake's surface, where Joel, without a murmur, helped pull her back into their boat, before her churning stomach could hold out no longer.

"What's down there?" he whispered.

"A woman. Élisabeth Lavroche, I'm sure of it," she managed to say as Omar held both ropes in one hand to throw her a blanket. "But what a grotesque punishment. No-one deserves that…"

Omar simply stared at her, while Joel suppressed cries of anguish.

"I shouldn't say this in front of you," she added between shivers. "But she'd definitely been burnt first, so that would tie in with the state of their Isuzu Trooper. Then," she lowered her voice. "I'm guessing wolves."

Omar's hands were still attached to the ropes, but his eyes brimmed with tears. Hers, despite the goggles, stung so badly she had to douse them with the remains of a bottle of Vittel.

"My hook's embedded in her hair," she said as the stinging sensation lessened. "And there's not much of her, so if we both pull on the rope, we might just be able to…" But Joel had leapt up to bury his head against her wet neck and cling to her shoulder.

"Oh, poor Mamie!" he wailed. "Dear Mamie…"

"She's at peace now," Omar tried his best. "With the angels."

"I'm so sorry," Delphine struggled with words, partly because she felt sick again. "But please try not to touch me till I've had a chance to clean myself up. That water seems pretty polluted."

"I'm still going in," announced Omar, already trying to pass her the taut rope. "And don't stop me."

"No!" she almost screamed. "Your Joel's Papa! What if you get into trouble? Let's try pulling the rope together first."

He paid attention. "OK."

"But what about Guy Lavroche?" Delphine ventured. "It could take days to find him, even months, assuming he's here at all. Whoever did this may have had other plans for him."

"She's enough for now, and when we've recovered her - I mean, *if* we recover her - we say a prayer for her soul, take some photos and…" Here Omar stalled. Although they'd brought the right equipment, they'd hardly banked on actually finding anyone.

"Take her to the police." Joel finished his father's sentence, still sobbing.

However, Delphine and Omar knew they had the evening to get through. Timing was everything. Another two or three hours wouldn't forensically make much difference.

*

Delphine was dressed again, but her breasts were not properly dry inside her bra and its two stored items. Omar gripped the still-taut rope, using all his iron strength, while she ensured it wouldn't slip from his grasp. Joel too, with fierce concentration, clung to its very end.

"For fuck's sake, don't let go," he muttered at her, forgetting his language yet again. Just then, it didn't matter.

"I've got her moving," Omar announced. "At last."

Meanwhile, the summer rain had grown more determined, and a stick of lightning bounced over where Delphine guessed the so-far invisible *Château des Illuminations* to be. Then came serious thunder, like a collective roar of all the wild wolves in the world. A terrible warning. A reminder of a different Gehenna to come when the betrayed and their betrayers would be breathing the same champagne-soaked air.

"Pull!" Omar yelled, forgetting their vow of silence. "She's coming."

Joel, red-cheeked, red eyed, breathed, "Come on, Mamie… Come on…"

*

It took less than a minute for their shocking catch to appear, centimetre by awful centimetre. One gaping wound after another, the dead artist, wife, mother and grandmother breached the surface.

No wonder she was so light. All internal organs and muscle had gone, leaving flaps of dimpled, blackened skin and charred bone wherein lay pockets of sodden detritus, including several lifeless minnows.

An incomplete cremation…

From somewhere, came the almost unholy sound of church bells, nevertheless, both Delphine and Omar crossed themselves. They whispered the *Pater Noster* together before finally hauling her up and over into Omar's boat.

"Look away now, please," she addressed Joel and he obeyed, spared the sight of the grandmother he loved, propped up against the stern end's seat. Once Delphine had taken three photographs with a shaking hand, she covered her with that same damp blanket.

The reek of decay made all three cover their mouths and noses with whatever was to hand. Delphine, again fighting nausea, noticed that the only part of the corpse unburnt and uneaten were the blanched toes; each toenail still bearing bright red varnish. Plus, the black bone of her wedding finger was still home to a simple gold ring.

*

"I'm no expert," murmured Delphine, helping Omar carry the blanketed corpse towards the Suzuki. "But she can't have been underwater more than a day. Which means whoever wanted to get rid, must have brought her here yesterday morning. And I can't help thinking…"

"What?" Joel wiped his eyes with his fist, still curious, still wanting to know who could have done such a terrible thing to someone. "You mean those initials on that tree?"

"No." She lied, but there wasn't time to explain. The longer they lingered, the greater chance of being seen and interrupted.

Omar opened his Suzuki's boot and, with care and reverence, wrapped their grim discovery in an industrial-sized black bin-liner and positioned it as flat as space would allow. Then, having removed the recent bullethole's loosest pieces of rear window glass, he completed a rigid, almost invisible repair over the damage. His skill was impressive, and Delphine said so, still thinking of yesterday midday when Natalie Lavroche had seemed in such a hurry to leave *La Bastide*.

*

The small, solemn party eventually left that fateful place of death, but instead of returning to the *Frites/Boissons* compound where Delphine's

2CV still waited, Omar drove some three hundred metres in the direction of the château. On the other side of the road, an overgrown and derelict plantation of deciduous trees rose up from huge brambles, various rampant bushes and unharvested crops of this and that. The vast, semi-rotted sweetcorn foliage would also provide perfect cover for the next few hours.

At 17:25 hrs, Delphine phoned Colonel Valon's mobile and left an emotional message about what the lake had yielded up, then dialled Christophe Beauregard's home number, disappointed that there was still no reply.

50

17:30 hrs.

With Joel mercifully asleep on the Suzuki's back seat, oblivious to the pungent smell coming from immediately behind him, Delphine spent the next silent half hour completely changing her appearance within the car's confines and outside it. Omar had merely added an oil-stained *bleu de travail* to his other clothes, a relic of his garage days. The cut on his cheek had at least stopped bleeding, but it still looked sore. Any kind of covering on it would make him too noticeable.

Finally, his son began to stir, and his first questions to Delphine upon waking were, "why are you in fancy dress? And why's your hair that funny yellow colour, and what's with the glasses? You were much prettier before."

"He's right," Omar agreed, still pre-occupied and tense, checking his phone was functioning. Just in case.

"Thanks," she smiled, but smiling was the last thing she felt like doing, because where on earth could be safe enough for Joel while she and his father proceeded with their plan? Omar hadn't suggested any other possibilities. How could he? Snatching his son and becoming mired in her mission had taken all his concentration, but at least he'd left the *mairie* in Amance with a detailed plan of the *Château des Illuminations* from the days before all the LVS activity, when the historic pile dating from before the French Revolution had been open to the public.

*

In the eerily quiet dampness, invisible to even the most curious passer-by, the trio stood by the Suzuki, now a hearse, to better study this guide for possible access avoiding the chateau's main entrance. They observed how the many ground floor rooms - mostly huge - connected to one another.

"Linen room," observed Joel, pointing at an oblong shape next to a *buanderie* - laundry - adjacent to the kitchen. "That would be OK for me. I'm good at hiding."

"I know you are," said his father, "but it's too close to activity. Someone might open its door by mistake, especially if drunk. Or perhaps for a change of tablecloth."

"There *are* cellars," Delphine noted. "Including one for wine, but if they're anything like ours in *Bellevue*, they could get flooded and there's a mother of a storm coming."

"See this!" Omar's scarred forefinger fell on another oblong labelled STAFF QUARTERS, divided into ten equal sections. However, his tone soon changed to one of disappointment. "I bet they're still in use."

"We could take a look," said Delphine, a blonde, bespectacled waitress, something she'd never done. "There's no way Joel can be left here or…"

"I could guard Mamie," he suggested, and Delphine realised he really needed to change his pants and shorts, but how? He had no clean clothes.

"A lovely thought," she said, taking his hot little hand in hers. "But let's go explore, *hein?*"

Then out loud, she remembered the two rifles.

"Impossible," Omar sighed, keeping watch. "They'll hinder not help us. Besides," he patted his overalls' right-hand pocket, "I've got her." Meaning his Luger.

"Where are they?"

"Never mind. Let's go."

"He chucked them away while you were busy changing your hair," Joel said.

"Thanks," said Omar sarcastically.

What could she say? One would have been useful. Perhaps they'd been stolen goods. Something she couldn't ask as they finally ventured across the deserted road.

"Has your lady got a silencer?" she said instead.

A small smile. A shake of his head.

"Show me one who has."

*

Delphine feared the vivid whiteness of her blouse and Omar's blueness were suddenly too conspicuous under the gunmetal sky. So was her hair, which had taken just ten minutes to alter with a tube of *Lite'n'Brite*, manufactured in the UK and make her dark eyebrows, which she'd not dared alter, look alien.

So what? At the château, all being well, she'd be too busy scuttling from table to kitchen and back again for anyone to query her appearance.

"Rain again," observed Joel as they reached the far verge. Omar went first, then herself shielding Joel, her shoulder bag containing her phone and her purse, while Aristide's BlackBerry was safely back in her new, dry briefs. As for her rucksack, stored under a black mat behind the driver's seat, it might have to be expendable. The few clothes inside it, not important. As for *Bellevue's* tools, she'd have to wait and see what transpired. But she'd kept her mother's little blue brooch.

"Fuck it! Look!"

Joel was right. Sharp little bullets of rain indeed, clever of Omar to have brought his son that big cagoule. He had one too, and hers at least had a hood. There was also a new Meccano set and a book on aeroplanes, still under wraps in case he saw Joel again. You never knew, he'd confided in Delphine. He'd never given up hope of having him back for good. But how long would this hope remain?

*

Once they'd reached a discreet, unkempt track that both she and Omar had agreed would take them to the rear of the château, Delphine switched off her phone and, as before, sniffed what she recognised as the odour of wet wolves. The same ones, or maybe their relatives? She gripped Joel's hand more tightly, at the same time feeling dread leach into her very marrow as it had up on the Causses de Quercy eighteen months ago.

"They're here again," she whispered to the back of Omar's head above the rain's noise on her hood.

"Shit," said Joel, using yet another dodgy word. "But I know what the fuckers *don't* like."

"Go on." Again letting that 'f' word go.

"Humans standing with their legs and arms apart, with no expression on their faces. They made me try it out."

"What?" Omar spun round, eyes ablaze. "You're lying."

"I'm bloody not. I'll fucking show you." The short but bad influence of *La Bastide* was worsening, but Joel had already released Delphine's hand to execute a chillingly static pose.

It was impressive.

"So why not suggest I used that earlier?" His father still frowning.

"Sorry, Papa. I forgot."

Well, he was only six, thought Delphine, whose admiration for his pluck was growing by the minute. "But who made you do it?" Was the question she had to ask.

He looked from one to the other.

"Maman. To show Uncle Maurice and Uncle Paul I wasn't a sissy. Otherwise, they wouldn't have been interested in her."

The trio walked on in silence. Delphine and Omar were speechless with contempt for such a callous, selfish piece of work. Although her new, flat shoes had already let in water and made a squelching sound with each step, nothing mattered except, against increasing odds, to get this brave little boy to some kind of safety.

*

The centuries-old, overblown château certainly lived up to its name, and lights from inside and out cast it like some giant-sized confection amongst its surroundings of black trees as far as the eye could see. Sounds of a furious fountain reached Delphine's ears, reminding her of that grisly group photo still stored on her phone.

"Dammit."

She feared finding any concealed shadow in the strobing glare of newly-arrived Mercedes, Audis and similar luxury cars, and so crouched down with Joel as they followed Omar, who'd obviously done his homework and found a hidden route behind a substantial block of locked garages at the rear.

Thank God.

However, the unforgettable whiff of wolves had become something quite different. Meat was definitely being grilled. She sniffed again. Beef, possibly, which had the opposite effect of making her feel hungry. Were these the featherblade steaks being prepared in advance somewhere nearby for guests? Hard to tell, as they approached a large brick-built outbuilding attached to the château's less well decorated rear wall, where one mean chimney was releasing not only a veil of smoke, but suddenly a much less beefy odour. Pork, maybe?

*

That earlier nausea crept up again from her stomach. Only by swallowing several times could she keep it down. This wasn't where Omar's plan had shown the kitchen to be, so could this be the punishment block that Annemarie Colbert had mentioned? Delphine then wondered how had she known about that? Hearsay or experience?

Father and son were also sniffing as they crept forwards, while she remembered how her late mother had attempted most recipes with varied kinds of produce. But unless her own memory was faulty, nothing ever like this. Joel held his nose as unexpected lightning lit up the firs beyond that horrible lake, far too close.

"That smell," said Joel suddenly. "It's made me remember about feeding the wolf cubs."

Omar nudged Delphine.

"We're listening."

"I didn't always feed them beef. Sometimes, it was…" He stopped, as if waiting for the inevitable thunder.

"Please," Delphine urged him. "We need to know."

"Prisoners, I heard Uncle Paul say. People no-one missed."

Jésus…

"From where?"

"Poland mostly."

Silence, save for the distant sounds of car doors slamming and voices raised in greeting.

"It's beyond barbaric, giving those cubs a taste for humans. I wonder where they're kept."

Any reply was lost to a thunderclap which seemed to shake the very ground beneath their feet. Joel let out a scream and Delphine swiftly covered his mouth with her hand.

"We'll be alright," she whispered, "if we just keep going." Yet hadn't lying to herself become a fine art?

Omar stopped and cocked his head. "Listen. Can you hear something?"

Above the sound of rain came the rustle of footsteps on dead leaves coming noticeably closer as Delphine recalled that Canadian woman's disturbing remark.

"Do you realise this 'national treasure' keeps a specially armed guard on his land?" she repeated.

"Who says?" Omar still jumpy.

"Someone I met on my travels."

Then came the familiar *Lynx* smell overlaying what was surely burning flesh. Omar's right hand was already in his blue pocket.

"Don't shoot!" she hissed to him. "I think I know who it is."

And no sooner than she'd spoken, an all-too familiar figure - male this time, not a black-wigged female, morphed through the wet gloom. His newly-shaven face widening, creasing, in more than relief. In what could only be described as joy.

*

Patrick Gauffroi couldn't take his still strangely hollowed eyes off her, while Omar and Joel also stared at the haggard stranger kitted out in that same camouflage gear Delphine had noticed him wearing on the A6 and at the service station near St. Bonnet. The Beretta strapped to the outside of his right thigh. He could almost pass for a member of a GIGN squad, she thought. Or a hunter...

"Omar Kouchia and his son Joel." Delphine disguised her shock by introducing her companions. She needed to focus on what mattered and reassure them both this stranger was no risk. Inwardly, however, she was asking her dead mother to forgive her.

The one-time farmer ruffled Joel's hair, and held out a hand to Omar, which he tentatively took.

"Sorry if I surprised you all," he began in a whisper. "But Delphine, you had to know you weren't alone. I was chatting to some guys at a bar in St. Loup who said they'd heard a rumour that Genéral Olivier Amance would soon be culling his traitors. That's what he'd called them, and heads would roll. They wouldn't say any more." He held her gaze. "You're too important to me to see you in danger."

"Who are you?" Joel impatient to know. "Her boyfriend?"

A dripping silence followed. Embarrassment was the wrong word.

"You're not here to take me back?" Joel mercifully persisted.

"Back where?"

The youngster seemed to relax, while Delphine gave the stranger's name, suggesting he show his ID. Omar noticed it bore the name of La Santé prison at the top, and immediately reached for his gun.

"No need for that," said Gauffroi. "I'm here to defend you. Make amends. And you'd better believe it."

"Amends?" Joel repeated, looking from one adult to another. That was a new word.

"Delphine knows what I mean," said Gauffroi. "And she might want to tell you at some point how I've wrecked her life." Then, after a pause, "Let alone mine."

And my father?

She choked back her gut response. To blurt out what he'd done. That he was still a wanted man, the killer of an innocent woman. Her unique, unfathomable mother. But then wasn't the time, and Omar clearly hadn't prioritised that particular story from the media. Instead, she had a question.

"Was it you we heard by that lake about an hour ago?"

"Yes. And I saw everything too. No need to talk about it now, but after you'd left, there were others."

"Others?"

"A young woman wearing a black hat, so I couldn't see her hair colour. And sunglasses, which was strange, and a slightly older man. Both in dark waterproofs, taking one of those same boats out. Yelling at each other, so I couldn't quite catch what about. Maybe you know…"

Natalie Lavroche?

Joel reached for her hand as if he too had guessed the same, and suddenly the looming, thunderous evening had cast the past two years in a haze, where the one word 'survival' lingered. Whatever else, Patrick Gauffroi knew how to shoot. To kill. The banquet was due to begin at seven with guests constantly arriving, and time was running out. With a bemused Omar still leading the way, his free hand on his Luger and her switched-off phone resembling a dead limb, the foursome followed each other further along the rear of the chateau in their search to find Joel's place of safety until their risky infiltration was over.

51

18:23 hrs.

"Here," whispered Omar once they'd left behind a more open area of various huge, deciduous trees in full, soaking leaf. "This looks promising."

They were just out of range of the security lights placed along the château's less ornate, undecorated rear wall. The new darkness suddenly startling. Genéral Amance was another man of appearances, thought Delphine, hoping Joel couldn't sense her mounting unease. Aware too, that if she was to start integrating with the other waitresses, seconds were ticking away.

"Servants' quarters," added Omar. "At last."

"I'll hide your cagoules for you," hissed Gauffroi, whose hand accidentally touched hers, igniting a small, electric charge. "Over there." He indicated a stack of pallets next to a concrete road-salting store. "That's where I've already left my mac."

"OK."

Omar then directed his torch's beam at a plain, hardwood external door marked PRIVÉ. It stood half-open, with a dark-haired man, possibly in his twenties, dressed in a badly-cut, black suit sheltered beneath its porch, drawing deeply on a half-length *Gitanes*. Several discarded dimps lay scattered around his polished black shoes, while his badge bore a mini version of that snarling wolf's head and the name MIGUEL SALVEZ. STAFF.

That particular tobacco smoke made Delphine yearn for a cigarette of her own. But now wasn't the time. Here was a chance she must take. Without a word, she released Joel's hand, swung her shoulder bag behind her body and sprinted over to leap upon the unwary stranger. Caught unaware, he was swiftly brought down and, despite the constraints of her black skirt, she managed to pull his hands behind him and squat on his back.

"Check the pockets," she said to the others, keeping his head to one side as Patrick Gauffroi and Omar duly found a wallet, a Nokia phone, a crumpled ID card and at last, what was possibly a room key, whose metal fob bore the number 5. "Lie still," she told him, aware that half her thighs were on full show. "No tricks. We need your help. We have to trust you. Got it?"

"There *are* ways of asking. And who the fuck are you?" he burbled.

"I said, got it?"

"Yes."

"So, what do you do here?" Gauffroi held up the key.

"Waiter. Full time."

Delphine then saw her victim was little more than a teenager with a prematurely old face. His stubbled jaw clenching and unclenching. This was probably the only job he could get, apart from the abattoir, and she knew all about being in that situation. She gestured to Omar and Gauffroi to help Salvez to his feet, praying he wouldn't press for their IDs.

Her prayer was answered.

"You live in, *hein*?" she asked him.

A puzzled nod.

"I have a room. And, Monsieur," he reminded Gauffroi, "I paid twenty euros for that key."

"Here's fifty." Gauffroi extracted a note and pressed it between the guy's clenched fingers. Delphine stared, but let it go.

"Brush yourself down, Miguel," she said, "then we'll explain. You want to keep your job?"

Another nod. More nervous this time.

"So, listen. No interruptions."

*

Afterwards, in a sullen silence, the young stranger led the way along a narrow, semi-lit passageway to the windowless room, whose number 5 matched his key fob.

"There's some Fanta in my cool box," he addressed Joel, having quickly grasped the urgency of the situation. "And cheese crackers. Help yourself. There's also a toilet and wash basin behind that curtain."

"I like cheese crackers," Joel managed a smile as Delphine and Omar settled him on a camp bed with a threadbare cover. They told him to stay silent and that six knocks on the door would mean it was them returning to get him.

Delphine could see how he tried to be brave as he'd been all along, and was again aware he really needed clean underwear and shorts. But that was a minor detail, and he was far better off here than outside.

"Say thank you to Miguel," she said, and he did.

"My pleasure," replied the waiter backing away. "Do you think I've enjoyed it here for the past year? The Amances are a law unto themselves and Sancta Maria help you if you dare speak out…"

"We had heard," she said.

"Is that why you're here? To make trouble? What'll happen to my job?"

"We're just observing, so no eye contact from now on. Pretend we don't exist. OK?"

"Fine."

"I'm sorry I had to waylay you like that. I really am."

"I've got used to it. By the way, there's a loose slab to the left of the outside door as you leave. Please place my key under there when you've finished."

"Will do."

And with that, she locked the six-year-old in, and passed the key to Omar who had more pockets, aware of Patrick Gauffroi following her every move.

"Just one thing," she stalled their benefactor, still brushing off his trousers. "What was that really odd smell coming from the big outhouse back there?"

He paused, looked around, then lowered his head. "I'll go the same way if I tell you."

The same way?

"You must. We'll protect you."

Omar agreed, while Gauffroi could only stare uncomprehendingly.

"Just leave it, OK?" snapped the waiter.

But in her racing heart Delphine guessed the terrible answer. Almost as if it had been pre-ordained. Or was she going mad?

'J'attendrai' all over again…

She clung to the door frame for support. Mute, almost defeated, but not quite, as Miguel Salvez turned on his heels.

"Keep him!" hissed Gauffroi watching his departing figure.

"We can't." Having excused herself for a few minutes, Delphine ran giddily back towards the rain where she pulled her phone from her bag.

*

Colonel Serge Valon answered with an apology for not returning her earlier, frantic call. Having listened to her latest horror story, he reassured her he'd immediately brief the public prosecutor in Saint-Arnoult and Judge Hervé Latrisant, then liaise with Dijon and Épinal to begin searching for Christophe Beauregard and Guy Lavroche. "There'll be a police presence, so keep a low profile. Don't visibly connect with us if you spot us. We'll find you when we're ready. Think of your future, Delphine..."

"I am. And thank you doesn't sound much, does it?" She then added, "I'm convinced more than ever that Natalie Lavroche is involved, with her latest partner and his younger brother. And a nephew." Once she'd added their names, Valon warned that as she was on her own, the risk of being harmed or worse was growing by the minute.

Pause.

"You *are* alone, aren't you?" he queried.

"Honestly, sir, would I lie?"

She spotted Omar, Gauffroi and Joel staring her way. Three semi-silhouetted figures whom she had to protect.

"All I know is that you're determined enough. But what I will say is just watch and listen. Leave the rest to…"

"Of course, sir, and thank you again." She then described her disguise as a waitress and how she'd better get going.

"Remember my warning, and by the way, has that pest Gauffroi re-surfaced along the way?"

Damn.

"No, thank goodness," she lied, but hardly sounded convincing, and in another pause, the rain's overflow tumbled from nearby guttering. She saw those two unmentionable men anxiously beckon her in as she reminded Colonel Valon he was one of the few people she could trust.

"I'm flattered, of course. But as I've said, I'm more concerned you stay safe."

*

With the call ended, leaving guilt savaging her conscience, Delphine switched off her phone, hid it in the usual place, and rejoined her fellow fancy dressers. Frequent lightning and thunder rolls brought a solid downpour, dissipating the strobing headlights of more arriving cars at the chateau's entrance.

"Who did you call?" Gauffroi and Omar challenged her, whispering almost in unison, well past Joel's room. "Not the cops?"

Delphine looked them both in the eye, her yellow hair a mess. Her clothes damp, uncomfortably clinging. "As if."

"Chill," said Omar, passing her a handkerchief. Once she'd dried her face and the worst of her lurid fringe, they finalised their logistics, shook hands and went their separate ways.

They had twenty minutes in which to make a difference. No more, no less.

*

Delphine glanced back at the apocalyptical sky, dark enough for stars, but delivering only doom. While hurrying towards the kitchen to meld with all the other staff to-ing and fro-ing from its extra-terrestrial brightness, she wondered again who or what had been inside that smoking outhouse.

"Check the flower arrangements are in order on the tables," instructed the ugliest woman she'd ever seen through dry, cracked lips the moment she spotted her. "And while you're at it, remove any debris." The plastic bags she handed over resembled the *sacs sanitaires* in the *Hôtel les Palmiers* where Delphine had once worked. Only then did the hag peer at her new recruit through tiny, black eyes, "You're Élise, aren't you? From Faverney?"

"*Oui.*"

"You need an apron. Here. Catch."

Delphine used its large size to conveniently cover her shoulder bag, glad it hadn't been noticed. Plus, her makeshift uniform had seemingly otherwise passed muster. She nodded instead of speaking her replies, as her non-local accent would have been be too much of a giveaway. Then, complete with her ÉLISE CHAUVIER badge on her chest, she left the heaving, steaming industrial-sized food factory, where all the male chefs all seemed pre-pubescent, where no steaks were yet visible, and headed towards the banqueting hall. She just hoped that in the meantime, Joel was OK and Omar Kouchia was successfully managing to be another maintenance guy and not attracting the wrong kind of attention.

52

The devil's garden?

Was this what Christophe Beauregard had specifically meant? Maybe even the last thing he'd seen?

Stop it...

Delphine felt more than cold as her eyes followed the banqueting hall's white, Doric-style pillars upwards to a vast, domed ceiling resembling what she'd seen in her convent school's illustrated books of the Sistine Chapel. Except there was nothing saintly or angelic about the crudely painted scenes of carnage stretching from wall to wall. Here were vulpine marauders with bloodied fangs tearing smaller victims from limb to limb. A defenceless human with a child on his shoulders, felled and feasted on by those very same creatures whom lucky Joel had soon been trained at *La Bastide* and *La Caverne d'Hiver* to raise by hand.

There was music, too, but nothing *France Musique* would air, or any self-respecting orchestra would play. Subliminal terror was the only way to describe the sounds creeping from the discreetly-placed speakers as one by one, guests arrived from the hall, champagne glasses in hand, most already almost empty.

With her four plastic bags full of various rubbish, Delphine followed Sybille, a local girl with thick, white legs, back to the kitchen, relieved to have seen Omar, impressively dispensing champagne re-fills. He also proffered trays of shrimp canapés releasing the same whiff of pee as Joel's shorts.

He'd agreed earlier to resemble a handyman, so where on earth had he found that outfit which made him look terribly smart? Why couldn't men be more reliable? Yet the risky gamble seemed to be paying off. He'd even been given a name badge, which was too far away to read. He must have invented a new ID, which, in the general commotion, hadn't been noticed.

*

That hag seemed to have gone, so Delphine gathered some heavy linen napkins from a pile in the kitchen, plus extra menus, just in case, noting how each bore a small colour photograph of a lush meadow or similar idyllic scene. True to the invitation, featherblade steak was indeed their menu's main feature. She then returned to the splendour where guests would soon be gnawing on their meat, but first...

Non...

She suppressed a squeal of horror and almost dropped her tray.

Those early arrivals had suddenly become unrecognisable. She blinked twice to make sure she wasn't hallucinating, but no. Their horrible masks were real.

Jésus...

She was staring at a mass of grey wolves. Or at least, their faces. Full frontal views of muzzles wide open for the kill. Teeth and glistening gums agape with greed, their eyes not their own. Unlike the painted versions on the ceiling, these masks were as lifelike as anything she'd seen so far. Every hair, every whisker and glossy black nose enlarged for maximum effect.

"Well, well, well," came a nearby voice that trebled her heartbeat. Male, definitely, before another ominous growl rose above the background 'music.' "If it's not the unforgettable Delphine Rougier. Fancy seeing you here, so far from your usual stamping ground. But then, I'm hardly surprised."

361

"Excuse me?"

She turned to see that same hideous mask close-up, which failed to disguise two hard, pale eyes belonging to the straight-backed, lean form of a father who'd apparently left his daughter's funeral early. The widower whose dead wife was still warm.

Gérard Massenet.

But that wasn't all.

Slightly behind him stood an equally tall, slender young woman also sporting a wolf mask. Her one-shouldered gold sheath dress glimmered under the chandeliers, matching her earrings, while her smooth, completely blonde hair strayed to her upturned breasts.

Hélas!

*

"Ah, we meet again." Annemarie Colbert smiled, yet her green eyes seemed as hard as glass. She held out a gloved hand but, after Massenet's warning nudge, withdrew it.

"You must be mistaken." Delphine corrected both in her best north-eastern French. "I'm Élise Chauvier." She tapped her badge with a free hand, wondering how long it would be before she was really was checked and found to be a fraud. "Now, as you can see, I'm really busy."

Another hand then fastened on her left shoulder. Heavy as a rock and cold as ice.

"Being blonde and wearing glasses really doesn't suit you," snarled the lawyer, suddenly tearing her badge from her blouse, leaving a noticeable gap in its cheap fabric. "My souvenir."

"How dare you!" She glared at them both. "That's assault, and you'll be paying for it."

"You too," he murmured under his breath.

362

"Meaning?"

"Come," he said to Colbert, beginning to withdraw, taking her with him to greet others. The perfect couple. Probably perfect killers too, thought Delphine, realising her role must continue for at least half an hour to glean yet more from the evening.

Cunning bitch.

As for him, she'd been an ignorant, pathetic fool. She must let her father and Colonel Valon know as soon as possible. She then spotted Miguel Salvez who, on seeing her, broke their recent agreement by waving.

Idiot!

She shook her head, but he waved again, even more obviously. Was he simply being friendly or was he not to be trusted? Had handing over his key been too easy? And what had her father's lawyer and his 'squeeze' been doing there wearing wolf masks, if not to show LVS loyal support?

*

The huge room was soon almost full of yet more beautiful people in their revolting disguises, behind which they drank and nibbled their way through the all the canapés.

Mingling perfumes and aftershave soon replaced the smell of the sea.

Delphine focused briefly on each one while attending to the tables as far away as possible from Gérard Massenet and his enthralled arm candy. Earlier feelings of awe and attraction had melted like the ice in those silver buckets. How insane to have imagined anything other than a legal relationship connected to her father. Another matter to deal with. Her phone was still in her bag, concealed by her apron. She'd soon be using it.

Suddenly, an invisible and deafening gong was struck, ending the other sound effects, bringing a sudden, thick silence, broken only by the odd burp and remains of small talk.

Where on earth was Omar?

No time to wonder, for a drum roll heralded the entrance of a man of ordinary height, whose close-cropped grey hair cradled a typically Gallic-shaped skull. He'd lost weight since whenever Aristide's photo was taken. His unmasked face showed deeper jowl lines and eyes embedded in creases behind rimless glasses. For an eighty-year-old, he was in pretty good shape, able to hop up the three steps to a fake grass-covered dais where he stood, booted legs apart, before picking up a full flute of champagne from the nearby lectern.

He waited while three, also unmasked but younger men joined him, all in uniforms Delphine didn't recognise. Grey, with silver accoutrements and of course, the wolf insignia on each chest. Boots again, and a holstered pistol strapped above their right knees.

Maurice, Paul and Antoine Amance stood in age order. Dark-haired and dark-hearted. Thank God for her own awful thatch and glasses, because both brothers and their equally criminal nephew knew what she really looked like.

While no eye lingered on her, she was safe, except for 'Maître' Massenet and Annemarie Colbert, who could covertly communicate with that parasitic trio keenly looking towards their founder and future benefactor.

*

While handing out the last of the menus, Delphine wondered where the rest of the clan was, planning how to defend herself if need be, when the old general, who'd been studying his audience through almost invisible glasses, raised a champagne flute to his lips.

"Attention!"

His right hand shook enough for a few drops to slop over its side. Perhaps he'd been drinking beforehand or had a medical condition that would get progressively worse. She fervently hoped so.

"Welcome all our trusted friends. Unlike those dedicated wolf-killers of seventeenth century England and Scotland, where the last noble creature fell in 1680, *you* are our army who has saved Canis Lupus for future generations. I must, at this juncture, also refer to the eighteenth-century Comte de Buffon's ignorant utterance that 'wolves are disagreeable in all ways, with a perverse nature and ferocious habits.' How the creature is 'odious and harmful alive, and useless dead.'" He paused. "However, as you all know, Buffon was an influential fool."

Murmurings of assent followed before the général returned to his script. "This momentous occasion is dedicated to the hard work of my elder cub Maurice, and younger cub Paul. Also, to Maurice's cub, Antoine, who has helped establish *La Caverne d'Hiver* as the beating heart of our enterprise. Although tonight is the second anniversary of the release of our beautiful, vulpine battalions into *la Patrie*, it has been five long years since our plans were first drawn up, and important contacts made, particularly in Poland. While my three officers here still draw breath, *La Vie Sauvage* remains in the best of hands for the foreseeable future. Returning land to its natural owners."

He raised his glass "To them and their future!"

"*Je suis roi!*" came the roared reply, but the général wasn't finished. He pointed to a table directly ahead of him. Raised his glass again. "Also, my trusted lawyer and confidante, Gérard Massenet who, despite recent personal ordeals, is here to celebrate with us and the lovely Annemarie. Heroes who, just hours ago, relieved a deluded old liberal of his copy of *The Evil that Men Do*. A libellous and mercifully so-far unpublished work by Julien Gallas. Another traitor now in the ninth circle of hell." After a third gulp of champagne he raised his glass again. "Heil Hegel!"

"Heil Hegel!"

Gérard Massenet and his glamorous companion kissed then hugged each other, while everyone's smirks and nudgings made Delphine feel sick. She thought of the former professor and his dead wife. Of Joel hiding all alone in that strange room 5 down the corridor. As for Omar and Patrick Gauffroi, they seemed to have vanished.

*

"*Vive les loups!*" Screamed Maurice Amance with that same, almost German accent, as Paul thumped his back in a show of solidarity. "*Viva Canis Lupus!*"

Another solid cheer rose up and, as it subsided, Delphine, still in shock, glanced around for Joel's treacherous mother in her blood red dress. Instead, she noticed Miguel Salvez connect with the younger Amance in an unexpected way. His exaggerated wink followed by a six-teeth smile made Delphine realise that despite Joel's observations, both men might be more than close.

There was also someone else she recognised as his wolf mask had slipped to reveal distinctive red ears and spiky, brown gelled hair. A young man heartily celebrating, sitting near one of the columns with a full glass in his hand.

Tintin.

The proud owner of that bluc racing bike…

*

Thankfully, Claude Ridal hadn't recognised her, nor the sly-looking guy next to him whose seating label read:

JACQUES DELORIENT

No wonder news of the wolf attack on his primary school had been hushed up for so long. Nevertheless, in that overheated, buzzing space, Delphine

366

abandoned her empty tray on the nearest table and sneaked out of the exit for the kitchen the way she'd come in.

To yet more tipsy cheers, the général threw a hail of wolf badges into his adoring throng and the background music roared back into menacing life. From the kitchen door, Delphine smelt then saw thick featherblade steaks being sealed over greedy flames. Their fat, muscle and nerve-endings charring, leaving the centres pink and soft to the knife…

Pure beef…

She also glimpsed that same witch-like woman urging the rest of her flushed team of waitresses to deliver the entrées at top speed. Chicken liver cubes sliding in a yellow *jus*, plus bread baskets of seeded rolls.

For a split second, their eyes met, but Delphine twisted away and ran as if the devil himself was on her tail, breathing pungent smoke and death down her neck.

53

She kept running from the kitchen despite a tiled floor made treacherous by various spillages trickling down the slight slope towards the staff quarters. However, with that earlier brightness faded, another vicious blast of thunder suddenly caused all lights to flicker then die. The unlit *Château des Illuminations* had become the first circle of hell.

In the alarming darkness, she not only had to survive, but reach young Joel before any of their enemies. This kept her slithering on, while her pulse hammered in her head until she reached what was surely that same block of small rooms. Having almost tumbled down an unremembered step, she stopped to listen.

Silence.

She'd already registered his room number would be the third door on her left and with rising fear, felt her way towards it. Her suddenly cold fingers traced each raised number until she reached 5 amidst more thunder and panicked voices. Then, above the primordial clamour, the général's voice boomed out through what must have been a battery-operated megaphone.

"My beloved army, I guarantee you all that power will be restored as soon as possible. Meanwhile, be warned. We have at least four intruders in our midst, all saboteurs. So be on your guard. These are the real beasts who would destroy everything we have strived for since the millennium dawn. Delphine Rougier, dark-haired, skinny as a sparrow, was last seen wearing her usual denim. Omar Kouchia, our very own jungle bunny, in what he considers smart casual. They're who we know so far. There's also an unknown male wearing army fatigues, and Joel Kouchia, a minor, abducted from *La Bastide* this afternoon by that filth calling himself his father."

Delphine barely breathed while the bigot ranted on until the voices faded. Only then could she check if that room 5 door was still locked. It was. She tapped on it six times and called to Joel to tell her he was OK.

Come on...

Nothing.

Damn!

Hadn't Miguel Salvez heard her instruction about the six-knock code? Sure, but she'd been a careless fool. He could have already used it.

She tried knocking again, louder this time, but still Joel didn't answer.

Damn...

Omar had kept the key.

Panic.

"Joel? Answer me! It's Delphine. We need to collect you. You're not safe! Do you hear? Not safe!"

In her throbbing heart, she knew he wasn't there, but managed to reach that loose slab outside the rear door and ease it up. Her hands scoured the damp soil beneath it.

Nothing.

She ran back to room 5 and, with all her strength, banged on its door.

"Joel? For God's sake. Open up!"

She was far too loud, and with no time to retract, felt a rush of air behind her, then the sinister rustle of silk before a solid blow to the back of her knees brought her down on the stone flags with no chance to break her fall. All her victim assault reactions forgotten, her fingers coated in black, wet soil.

"You sly bitch!" came a female voice accompanied by the reek of *'poison.'* "Thought you'd worm your way in here and cause trouble. And what happens to worms, *hein?*"

Delphine glimpsed a curve of blood-red satin. The pointed tip of a matching red shoe before it began stabbing at her shoulder blades.

"Where's my boy? What the fuck have you done with him?"

Natalie Lavroche was neither alone, nor the frightened character who'd pretended to be so scared.

A fleeting memory of that old photo of her holding a doll in one hand and toy gun in the other jerked into Delphine's mind as Miguel Salvez joined in, kneeling on her upper back, squashing the air from her lungs. Her cries for help strangled in her dust-dry throat.

"Tell her, or else!" Came his threat. "Why? Because you made me hand over my room key, remember? Now it's my turn," he sneered, increasing the pressure.

*

Help me, God...Maman...

She'd been close to death before, high on the freezing Causses de Quercy, but at least she'd faced her potential killer. Looked him in the eye.

"Where is he?" Screamed the mother.

"Ask him," Delphine managed to croak under Salvez's weight. "Anyway, you lied to me through your back teeth, so why should I care?"

She could imagine their mean, hard faces. Natalie Lavroche gearing up to strike her again. Salvez saving his own skin. And, in what might prove to be her last breath, said to him, "We trusted you to give him safety. The key's gone from under that stone."

"I'll break down that fucking door if I have to!" Lavroche shrieked again, an octave higher.

"Leave it alone." He moved off Delphine and stood up.

"And you keep off my Paul. You pervert."

My Paul…

*

The screamed accusations continued - thanks to Salvez's collusion, her son, soon to become Amance, had been spirited away by Omar Kouchia, a sex-addict waster who'd forced his way into her life.

"At least I've not killed anyone," he countered.

"What the fuck do you mean by that?" Natalie Lavroche was kicking him with those lethal heels until he groaned and toppled next to Delphine, clinging to her like a giant-sized barnacle, keeping her down for the second time.

"Your parents." he countered. "And don't deny it! I overheard you and Maurice Amance planning to shove both into the lake yesterday afternoon."

Both…

"That's *it*, you liar! You're dead, too! And for rimming Paul, you little shit. He's mine! Mine!"

But before their attacker could finish the job in that terrible darkness, Delphine sensed another movement. The thwack of bone on flesh. A curdling yell. That red satin shape slumping to the ground. The unmistakeable smell of *Lynx*.

*

All at once came the tearing sound of duct tape being unwound. Delphine heard the click of a trigger, the drag of sharp heels against stone accompanied by death threats if she resisted. Patrick Gauffroi had come prepared, and once the violent, cursing Natalie Lavroche was out of action, his torch beamed on to Delphine's own half-closed eyes before focusing on a cringing Miguel Salvez.

"I think he knows the truth," she struggled to say, her heartbeat returning

371

to normal. "He'll talk…"

"Good. Something for later."

"Ask him where Joel is. Did *he* let him out?"

"No! Never!" came Salvez's strangled reply, as if he, too, was being bound and gagged and hauled outside. Meanwhile, Delphine managed to push her way to the wall alongside room 5 and sit up against it.

"Look at me," Gauffroi said to her when he returned, and their eyes met. "You'll be fine. Now, up you come."

"Where are Joel and Omar?"

"Christ knows. How could you ever have trusted him? A double-crossing *musulman*. Say no more."

I don't want to know…

"And those other two?" Meaning Natalie Lavroche and Miguel Salvez.

"Hidden, till needed."

His arms were around her, safe and strong. But still the arms of a killer, gripping her body with a force more intense than she'd ever known. Even more powerful than her father once paramedics had borne her dead mother away from *Bellevue*.

*

With one swift effort, Patrick Gauffroi had lifted her up to lie across his wide, bony shoulders. She was conscious of other swaying arcs of different torchlight against the walls ahead of them, and Aristide's phone slipping to the back of her briefs

"They both won't be found for a while, so let's go," he whispered.

"Where?"

"You'll see."

She heard shouts, then the muffled thud of a bullet connecting with the granite floor behind them, running footsteps becoming louder.

Gauffroi's body tensed before breaking into a jog.

"There's no way out." Came another man's glacial voice. "Stop!"

"Try me."

Gauffroi veered to the right before stepping into a much smaller space that jabbed at Delphine's head and feet as, whatever it was, began to descend into a deep chill that made her catch her breath and curse.

A lift which bumped to a halt.

"Where are we?" she mumbled, trying to free herself, wanting to feel solid ground beneath her feet again, to have options...

"The wine cellar. And please stop wriggling."

"I can't believe what you said about Omar and Joel."

"Why?"

"You were too quick. I *have* done interview mock-ups, you know. And the suspects who answer too..."

"OK. I'll tell you straight." He interrupted, shining his torch on to the biggest wine barrels she'd ever seen. Oak monoliths bound in steel, almost reaching the ceiling. A vast space which smelt of sweet death. "Both were legging it outside as I came in to find you. I couldn't stop them, I'm sorry. They were too far ahead."

Delphine let go of his shoulders and slithered to the tiled floor, smooth and clean as a morgue. Dizziness still keeping her captive, slowing her voice, her everything.

"Which direction?" she persisted. "The way we'd come in?"

"No." He handed her the rest of the duct tape, just in case. "South."

So, they'd not returned to the Suzuki with Élisabeth Lavroche's remains still bundled up in its boot. Delphine swore again under her breath, alarmed that Omar Kouchia could risk so much after everything else. He'd kept that room key all along...

When will you stop trusting people?

A small noise interrupted her thinking next about Joel. The brush of cloth, an intake of breath...

"Someone's behind us," she hissed, suddenly more alert. And before Gauffroi could pull open a wide steel door to their right, an unseen force pushed her hard up against the unforgiving belly of the nearest wine barrel.

*

Gérard Massenet in all his predatory glory. His rabid wolf mask slipped below his chin, covering his shirt's dulled whiteness. His pale grey eyes flickered danger, while behind him, Delphine recognised a masked Annemarie Colbert's golden gown with a steak knife in her hand. A smear of purple blood near the tip of its glinting blade.

"You kill her, or shall I?" she asked, eyeing his silver semi-automatic poised in his hand, the same weapon Delphine had seen on Saturday at his house. A lifetime away.

"You. My macerators make too much mess. Disproportionate to the value of the kill. So, over to you, *cherie*."

"Nosy slapper," she snarled, all trace of that Canadian accent gone. She lunged at her with the knife but Delphine dived away just in time, while Gauffroi head-butted Massenet off balance and snatched his gun.

Colbert's knife blade was lodged in tough, thick oak. "Who the hell do you think you are?" she taunted. "I'll tell you. A piece of shit, with a traitor's blood in your veins."

Bad move.

Delphine pulled the knife clear of the wood and threw it into the farthest corner, where it skittered out of sight beneath another wine barrel. Remembering lesson 6 on disabling an active opponent, she grabbed her enemy's hair, twisted her head around to knock it hard against another

374

barrel's bolted steel band. A trickle of something nasty left her pert nose.

"A piece of shit, am I?" she mocked into an ear missing its earring. "At least I've never betrayed anyone."

Meanwhile, Gérard Massenet had slumped to the floor, clutching his forehead, while Gauffroi adroitly secured Colbert's hands with duct tape.

"Domus, my arse," Delphine taunted, while the lawyer still cradled his head in his hands. He was no longer the imposing figure who'd held her in thrall, the memorable presence on TV and elsewhere. "As for you, great white shark, are you still suing LVS for two million?"

"*Arriviste...*" sneered Massenet, lacking the courage to look her in the eye.

The last straw.

"Just keep your greedy jaws off my father!" she shrieked at him. "And why not admit where Christophe Beauregard is? We've a damned good idea, but best hear it from you, Mister Wolf in Yves St. Laurent clothing. So, you relieved him of Julien Gallas's truthful book. Why, I wonder?"

Those Arctic eyes finally skewered into her.

"I'm invoking my right to remain silent. And by the way, failures should be careful with slander."

Failures?

Bastard.

"I'll get you for tapping my phone as well..."

But before the lawyer could repeat his threat, that same steel door suddenly swung inwards, bringing a burly Lieutenant Colonel Beuys, together with a pair of younger Lieutenants and two muscled-up SWAT officers from Épinal. Having taken in the scene in front of them, they immediately frisked and cuffed a compliant Patrick Gauffroi, before placing both Massenet's guns in separate forensics bags while reminding him of his rights.

"If the bullet recovered yesterday from *Le Bonnet* garage proves a match, you'll be in even more trouble." Beuys stated, addressing Gauffroi.

"Sir, he was only trying to protect me," Delphine tried her best, but she might as well have been invisible. Meanwhile, the Lieutenants replaced the duct tape around the couple's wrists with handcuffs, and with their feet soon freed, were led away in silence. When they reached the door, Massenet turned towards Beuys, his expression the same as if something nasty had stuck to his expensive shoe. "Lieutenant Colonel, it would be a civilised gesture from you and your team, to allow me time to grieve yet again. Is that too much to ask?"

No reply, and Delphine recalled his distraught mother, last seen gripping those two bunches of white roses. That photo of his fragile wife…

Although the reassuring wave of blue, flashing lights swept over the darkness outside, the pair's hate-filled death stares had reached her heart and stayed there while another, more familiar figure appeared unseen through the intermittent darkness.

54

"You're here. Thank God."

Delphine spun round to recognise a man she'd not seen for a whole year, whose dark blue cape still dripped water. His hair and eyebrows in the back glow from his torch were a little greyer, while alert, brown eyes went straight from her to Patrick Gauffroi. He didn't need to say anything, because she'd lied...

His right hand slid inside his cape. Just in case.

Gauffroi also noticed, showing no reaction, playing the few cards he had close to his chest. There'd be many more days, months, years in prison to dwell on things, unless... Unless...

Colonel Serge Valon then introduced himself to Lieutenant Colonel Beuys and, where fine wines were secretly undergoing their own miraculous transformations, they lowered their voices, updating what had happened so far. Delphine struggled to listen, but not Gauffroi, because when they'd finished, he asked if he could speak. Beuys nodded, checking his watch, keen to get away.

"If you want Natalie Lavroche and Miguel Salvez, they're by those three oak trees," he said. "Someone had to sort them out or Delphine here wouldn't have a pulse."

"Meaning you?"

A nod.

Beuys made a quick exit and returned two minutes later with the news that both had been removed for questioning. He then instructed the two SWAT guys still guarding Gauffroi that he was also ready to go.

It was as if time had suddenly stood still. Delphine wanted him to stay. Then she didn't... Then she did...

Mère de Dieu...

Valon turned towards her, still getting used to her crazy disguise and sustained economy with the truth. But he *had* shown genuine relief she was alive.

"Thank you for coming all this way, sir. And I know what you're going to say."

"Joel and his father have been picked up," he offered instead of replying. "And yes, despite your loyalty, you should have mentioned them. Especially as Omar Kouchia was armed."

"I couldn't. I'm sorry. I was scared my phone might have been intercepted again. Are they alright? Please say yes."

A slight nod.

"They'd been running alongside the D10 towards Amance and could have been hit. It's a fast road..."

She could imagine it. What was Omar playing at? But then, she wasn't trying to keep hold of a child she loved and might never see again...

Good God.

All at once, electricity was restored, and six spotlights embedded in the ceiling overhead juddered into action, making her blink, revealing Valon's new wrinkles. Stubble, too. And exhaustion.

"They'll soon be safe in Épinal, under guard," he added. "Apparently, Kouchia revealed where his Suzuki was hidden, and handed over its keys, so the deceased female concealed in it will be examined there too. Hopefully soon identified."

Delphine briefly thought of her own belongings still left inside that car. The spade used to dig her dog Julie's grave. The multi-pocketed rucksack

378

bought specially for the *École*... But that poor woman who'd suffered the utmost cruelty deserved urgent justice, then be laid to rest.

"If she *is* definitely Élisabeth Lavroche, what about her husband?"

"Let's hope their delightful daughter and Maurice Amance will see sense and co-operate. Meanwhile, the whole lake's being dredged. You will, of course, be kept informed." He gave the kind of smile she remembered, before reaching out to touch her arm. "On both public prosecutors' final orders - here and in Saint-Arnoult - I have to step aside, but your dogged determination has made a big difference to the investigation."

Lieutenant Colonel Beuys nodded while re-checking his watch.

"God knows what would have happened if you'd not got here," she said.

"Delphine's right," said Gauffroi, before being led away. "Please look after her. That's all I want."

All I want...

"You saved my life," Delphine explained again, feeling a blush hit her neck. "I thought I was going to die when Natalie Lavroche and Miguel Salvez attacked me."

Gauffroi looked back at her in such a way that made her heart seem to contract. She held his gaze until he'd passed through the steel doors.

"Your father's deeply ashamed of himself," Valon addressed her. Still formal, being careful. "He's been waiting for news of you and just wants to give you a hug. However, he may not recognise you looking like this."

"Tell him I forgive him!" Gauffroi suddenly shouted from beyond that steel door. "At least I saw Delphine again."

Then silence.

She reached for Colonel Valon's arm, words redundant, as her hot tears warmed her cold, alien face. She cried for the dead, for the living and whatever life was to come.

They walked in silence to his car, with too many events of the past six days to be rewound. But her one question pushed aside all others.

"Has anyone checked inside that outhouse round the back yet?"

"Why?"

When she'd explained what they'd smelt earlier and what both Joel and later Gérard Massenet had said at the banquet, he snatched his two-way radio from his cape pocket and to whoever answered, requested an immediate search.

"Thank you," she said when he'd finished, trying to block out what might be found. They reached his maroon Mégane, parked discreetly further along from the door where she'd first seen Miguel Salvez. Having turned away to extract Aristide's BlackBerry from its unusual place of safety, she handed it over. Also, from her bra, that incriminating invitation, the bullet which had recently hit the Suzuki, also those grey woollen fibres from the left boot she'd given the grieving Vileneufs.

He placed everything in a sealable plastic bag inside his obviously new briefcase.

"You'll find what's on that phone's video more than useful," she added. "So should the judge."

"Any clues?"

"Sorry, sir, it's too shocking. There's more on my phone, too, which I'll give him tomorrow."

"Good. Keep it safe."

"I will. By the way, Hervé Latrisant has asked to see us at his headquarters tomorrow at 16:00 hours. He at least, despite his personal life, seems a reasonable human being."

"He never mentioned any meeting to me."

"I meant to tell you, but…"

"It's OK."

"Incidentally, he's spoken to the coroner involved with Amélie Massenet's inquest."

"When's that?"

"Next month sometime. Confidentially, he's sure the verdict will be unlawful killing. That'll set the cat among the pigeons."

*

He disabled the car's alarm and opened the passenger door. Warm, dry air met her face as she stepped inside and checked her battered shoulder bag was still intact.

"I can also add that Aristide's already received a caution," Valon flung his wet cape on to the rear seat before starting the engine. "And that his cousin was caught at Dijon station a few hours ago, trying to repair his Toyota's tyres. Émile Abolego is his real name. Someone must have tipped him off that Patrick Gauffroi had left it there before hiring the Saxo you saw."

"Tyres? Why?"

"Gauffroi had obviously slashed them, so it couldn't go anywhere fast." He glanced sideways at her as if to gauge her reaction. "A botched job, remember? Involving big money. Until he's caught it won't go away."

Until…

"Something else. That truck I saw at the Gorge de l'Abbaye - guess where that's just been found? Trapped by weeds beneath the far end of Gehenna."

"The Ford Transit?"

A nod.

"My God."

"As for the Isuzu Trooper probably heading to the bottom of the world, just like Romain Vileneuf's missing bike and phone, the police should have removed it immediately from the Gorge de l'Abbaye after I'd reported it. I's a miracle you and Omar Kouchia found Élisabeth's body in time."

Silence.

"So, it *was* her?"

"Some of her hair was still in that truck. A one-hundred percent match."

Valon turned on the ignition.

Delphine closed her eyes. The engine's purr would normally have been comforting, but not then.

"And her husband?"

"Early days. Maybe more news tomorrow. At the moment it looks as if both badly charred corpses were removed just after Romain Vileneuf had spotted them. Still warm."

"He'd said it was hot," she muttered. "Literally."

"Quite. As for the Ruiseau d'Argent, SAUR confirmed this morning that traces of the Viteprop drain unblocker containing sulphuric acid are almost negligible, and the River Corrèze is unaffected."

Delphine wasn't sure what to say. That the Lavroches had done it for nothing and died for it? On the other hand, a whole town had been spared contamination.

"Had Simone Gallas alerted them like she promised?"

"I did, and it was Maurice and Paul Amance whose death threats caused Fabien Guirros - the local franchise - to pull out."

"What a liar she was. I wonder if she didn't link up with my father just to keep tabs on me."

"My thoughts exactly. Be interesting to hear what she has to say."

"I'm puzzled why Romain's body was left in such shallow water, so near to the *École*. Why not somewhere like Gehenna where he might never have been found?"

"Panic, perhaps. After all, a phone and bike are much easier to shift, and the Amances had enough on their plates."

She recalled those grotesque steaks. Did he *have* to use that expression?

"Speaking of the dead," Valon added, lowering his voice while fastening his seat belt. "Caroline Massenet's post-mortem showed she was given a lethal dose of barbiturates in a cup of coffee at 11:00 hours today at the St. Sauveur Clinic. Her husband had been with her in her room for an hour beforehand."

Delphine drew her cagoule tight around herself, as if that flimsy fabric might keep out yet more evil. Not a chance…

"So *that's* why he left the funeral early with that lover of his, before Amélie's burial."

Valon turned to her in surprise.

"What?"

"I'd told Aristide to be there and observe it all. He owed me that."

"Good Heavens." Surprise became admiration.

"So that vicious female with him in the wine cellar who refused to give her name is his lover?"

"And a fake. Annemarie Colbert."

Delphine explained about being conned, and what ever else she'd seen and heard later in the château, especially about Julien Gallas's contentious book. Valon swiftly made three more phone calls. Suspicion gathered like a storm cloud over the suave and wealthy smart-suited deceiver who'd mingled with the highest and mightiest. Who'd briefly, shamefully, reeled her in.

Delphine too, fastened her seat belt, glad she'd soon be reunited with her own little car, but heading back to what? The world had become a much darker place. The snake pit still alive and well. But return she must, because tomorrow afternoon might hopefully provide more answers.

"Hold tight," Valon said, turning the Mégane's steering wheel almost full circle and revving the throttle. "We need to get you out of here."

Moments later, while circling away from the fully-lit château, once more living up to its name, Delphine blinked as a phalanx of more police vehicles surged towards them before heading towards that still-smoking outhouse. Their sirens' screams lingered in the loaded evening air.

EPILOGUE

Friday 24th June. 16:30 hours.

In the pink-stuccoed *'Villa Hibiscus'* at the end of Brive's Avenue des Voyageurs, the newly-single examining magistrate Hervé Latrisant had laid on a buffet of tapas and crudités, which his elderly housekeeper kept replenishing with brisk discretion. He'd decided against using his official headquarters, and instead had welcomed Delphine - still crudely blonde - and a solemn, black-clad Enzo and Laure Vileneuf to share his dining room with Inspector Raymond Serra and sous-Lieutenant Véronique Morel, wearing a grey two-piece suit and necklace of chunky turquoise beads. Also, by special dispensation from the public prosecutor, a subdued François Rougier, who to Delphine, seemed to have aged considerably.

Despite the floral hand-embroidered linen, the tinkling of crystal glasses, and the Sèvres porcelain crockery and cutlery, the atmosphere was subdued and conversations murmured.

Beyond six, elegant, arched windows, the afternoon was as perfect as it could be. Ancient ash trees which lined the edge of an immaculate lawn complete with croquet hoops, stirred in an invisible breeze. Camille Pisarro, thought Delphine distractedly, then without appetite, eyed the food, then the door.

Colonel Valon.

He'd slipped in unnoticed and glanced her way, giving her a warm smile. He then chatted to Morel while helping himself to a small portion of green olives. Relief at seeing him let some of her exhaustion after arriving back in the early hours to slip away. She'd hardly slept in her father's empty house. How could she, knowing that Omar and Joel, who'd fled the gendarmerie van while at a service station near Xertigny, could be anywhere? In even greater danger?

Memories too, of Gérard Massenet were still too raw, and of the mistress who'd shared his bed for three years. A man who, according to Maurice Amance - perhaps shifting blame from his and Natalie Lavroche's shoulders - had urged Christophe Beauregard be abducted. His seared flesh had been used to nourish the latest wolf cub litters in *La Bastide*.

However, it had been Natalie Lavroche's steak knife with which she'd cynically carved her parents' initials in the *Forêt de Diane*. That devil in a blood red dress…

"Callous freak," Delphine muttered to herself, not for the first time. "And now your poor little boy could be anywhere."

She felt a solid hand on her shoulder and instinctively flinched.

"Talking to yourself, *hein*?" Her father's forced *bonhomie* adding to her grief. "That's the first sign…"

"How can you even think of making a joke after the mess you've caused?"

"Sorry."

"Not good enough, Papa. Letting Gauffroi believe I was besotted, and losing all that money for nothing."

He stared at her, then shook his dishevelled head.

"What money? You've got it all wrong. The judge here had both my bank accounts checked this morning. The hot-head I hired had first of all to top Gauffroi. That was the deal, *then* show me hard evidence before I dipped in my pocket."

Outside, the lovely afternoon seemed to lose its summer glow, becoming as grey as winter.

"He'll want expenses at least?"

"I don't owe him bloody anything." François Rougier shrugged, removing his hand. "As far as I'm concerned, he can whistle."

Idiot.

"Well, maybe fifty euros," he relented, seeing her exasperation. "If he plays his cards right."

Delphine felt her neck begin to burn. After everything she'd endured, he just couldn't see it. He still hadn't addressed her first grievance.

"Great. And what about me?

His hand again. Same place, this time like a dead weight

"Look, Delphine, I've never been so proud of you." His suddenly louder voice caused silence before he continued. "You deserve an honour for helping to expose five murders resulting from a warped depravity which otherwise - and this is true – would have gone unchecked to cause more deaths and injuries."

A murmur of approval rippled upwards as he faced those assembled around the buffet. She noticed his watery eyes, whose depth had vanished the day he'd lost his wife. "Romain Vileneuf also deserves our recognition for alerting her about the Lavroche's burnt car in the first place, and what turned out to be Guy Lavroche's left boot. A crucial piece of evidence."

"Which you retrieved from…"

"Not now," he broke in, squeezing top of her right arm too tight. "This isn't about me."

But it will be…

Meanwhile, Delphine had noticed how Romain's parents, both in mourning clothes, stood closer together, lips quivering. Yesterday's second post-mortem had revealed further evidence of torture to hidden parts of their son's body before the brute had dragged him to the water from the back of his new Land Rover. The bully and coward had only that morning confessed his crime, but how he'd helped his lover, the disgraced mayor, imprison student Rougier at *La Bergerie* with the intention of strangling her and taking her body to *La Bastide* or *La Caverne d'Hiver* as a special treat for the wolves.

Jésus...

Delphine tasted bile. She held on to her father while Hervé Latrisant added how this chilling boast had been uttered without a trace of remorse. He also revealed how four corpses of so-far unidentified, white Caucasian men had been found inside a freezer in the *Château des Illumination's* outhouse.

A carriage clock on the white marble mantlepiece struck the half hour. François Rougier paused before continuing.

"Appalling news, your Honour, and for my part, I deeply regret involving the cousin of my wonderful daughter's friend in what was a..."

"Monsieur! Attention."

The examining magistrate was soon at his side. A warning forefinger pressed over his lips, perspiration shining his unlined forehead as he continued. "Remember, matters are still *sub judice,* and you remain in extended custody while I gather further evidence of your activities. However, Colonel Serge Valon has located a well-respected criminal lawyer, Monsieur David Welbeck - a fluent French speaker - should your case come to trial."

Should?

Delphine stared up at this judge's tallness, having realised he'd let something so legally unprofessional slip from his lips could cost him his job. However, with a trembling, ringless left hand he set down his half-full glass of St.Émilion on the nearest side table, and continued.

"In comparison to what was meted out to Romain Vileneuf, Élisabeth and Guy Lavroche, whose head, as I speak, hasn't yet been recovered from the lake, his was an impulsive act forged from love. Yes, love. For his late wife Irène and Delphine, his daughter here…"

Head? Jésus…

The big room again fell as silent as a tomb, and Delphine watched with increasing concern as he made for the nearest armchair and subsided into it, staring blankly at the floor.

Valon hastened to confer with the concerned-looking housekeeper and Véronique Morel before helping Hervé Latrisant to his feet and leading him from the room.

*

When the colonel returned, his serious expression and air of authority created the necessary calm for him to speak.

"I must explain that Maître Latrisant continues to feel bereft following his recent divorce, of which most of you are probably aware."

"Indeed," added Raymond Serra like a kid pipped to the ice cream van. "But the prosecutor Fournisse is standing by him. And will continue to do so."

"Good."

There followed more sympathetic noises which lasted until an impatient Véronique Morel raised her full glass of sparkling Blanquette de Limoux.

"To Delphine Rougier, who dared shine a light into a world of darkness in which Christophe Beauregard and his beloved wife also perished. As did Julien Gallas and Lieutenant Colonel Mikhail Zanowski, whose untimely deaths are being re-investigated."

Delphine blinked.

Maybe not suicide after all…

"To Delphine." Repeated the Vileneufs in sad unison before glasses were duly raised. "Who'd entrusted that boot to us," continued Enzo. "And if we'd not left it at Cahors gendarmerie after being followed, Guy Lavroche's DNA from the woollen fibres she'd kept from inside it wouldn't have been matched up this morning with that on his toothbrush at the *Air du Vent* farm."

Delphine's earlier dizziness returned. Her father, now gripping her around the waist with one hand and with the other, held up a full glass of red before downing it in one draught. Colonel Serge Valon, without his wedding ring, she noticed, had been joined by Inspector Serra, and came to stand nearby. He'd finished chewing on a green olive and was taking a breath, but she beat him to it with eight simple words.

"Colonel Valon has been my rock. Thank you."

He nodded, momentarily embarrassed, and then resumed what he'd planned to say.

"Because of this courageous young woman wrongfully forced from Saint-Arnoult's *École de la Gendarmerie, La Vie Sauvage* is finished. All re-wilded adult wolves and any cubs will be captured, innoculated against rabies and re-settled near Quebec. LVS's main players are in custody in Épinal facing extremely serious charges, with potentially damaging inquest verdicts still to come. As for Julien Gallas' so-called accidental shooting last year, there *is* a lead suspect who should be very, very afraid. I must be cautious here, even though I've heard that the latest evidence is overwhelming. Someone with yet more to lose since his wife and daughter's untimely passing."

Delphine knew he meant that ecologist's fellow golfer who would always be known as a betrayer, a killer.

Inspector Raymond Serra shifted from polished boot to the other, sidelined again, but sticking to protocol as representative of the local police's Crime Investigation Unit. His glass held fizzy water, his eyes undisguised resentment. He coughed to interrupt the noticeable murmurings.

"We cannot pre-empt anything, and as for Mademoiselle Rougier here, I will personally intervene to ensure that when the *École de la Gendarmerie Nationale* re-opens, she'll be there."

Colonel Serge Valon was the first to clap, his fine, brown eyes beginning to glisten.

Just then, Delphine noticed Véronique Morel pick up an oblong parcel wrapped in green tissue paper and secured by a matching green ribbon.

"Julien Gallas and Christophe Beauregard would have wanted you to read this," she began. "And - like Inspector Serra and everyone here - for you to pursue your dream of becoming a gendarme. Lieutenant Colonel Beuys from Épinal's Crime Investigation Unit found it hidden under the dais in the château's banqueting hall. Claude Ridal, chief reporter of *La Campagne,* who, incidentally, is friends with Jean-Marie Longeau, formerly of *Le Maine Express,* admitted sending it to Professor Beauregard last October. He then told Maître Gérard Massenet who, with Annemarie Colbert, dragged the poor man from his car outside his home yesterday afternoon. This book had been inside his coat as if he'd meant to give it to someone. Maybe you, Delphine. Who knows? His beloved goats had already been ravaged by two specially delivered wolves. So," she paused to regain her composure. "Here it is."

"Thank you."

But was this a poisoned chalice?

Just then, she wanted to run far, far away. But where? Those black tentacles would reach her anywhere...

Véronique Morel squeezed her hand, adding "There's also a copy of

Lieutenant Colonel Zanowski's final letter inside. It should give you hope."

Delphine fought back tears of genuine sorrow then cleared her throat.

"Thank you, and to everyone here. But you have to know that from the outset, I wasn't on my own in all this." Despite her best efforts, her eyes soon misted up, so she didn't see the fleeting form of a bearded, hooded mixed-race young male who'd been crouching outside the nearest arched window.

*

When Aristide Abolego finally entered the dining room, smart in a dark, pinstriped suit and almost shaved head, Delphine hardly recognised him. Her father's arm left her side, and for a moment both men, young and old, faced each other, motionless yet charged as if by the same electric current. She was sure they were about to speak, until François Rougier flung his arms around the newcomer's shoulders, his empty wine glass resting behind her friend's left ear. His genuine remorse was painful to witness.

"It'll be OK," she said to them both, moments later. "You'll see."

Aristide's luminously damp eyes met hers. He'd missed her too, and would make up for his bad judgement, but they'd go on together, putting an imperfect world to rights. Of course they would.

Published by DEATH WATCH BOOKS

.

Printed in Great
Britain
by Amazon

32126175R00239